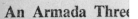
An Armada Three

Three great
Hardy Boys Mysteries

This Armada book belongs to:

_____

_____

_____

This Armada *Hardy Boys Three-in-One* was
first published in the U.K. in 1981 by
Fontana Paperbacks,
14 St. James's Place, London SW1A 1PS.

Published pursuant to agreement with Grosset
& Dunlap Inc., New York, N.Y., U.S.A.

Printed in Great Britain by
Love & Malcomson Ltd., Brighton Road,
Redhill, Surrey.

The Hardy Boys in

The Arctic Patrol Mystery
The Twisted Claw
The Secret of Pirates' Hill

Franklin W. Dixon

1
The Arctic
Patrol Mystery

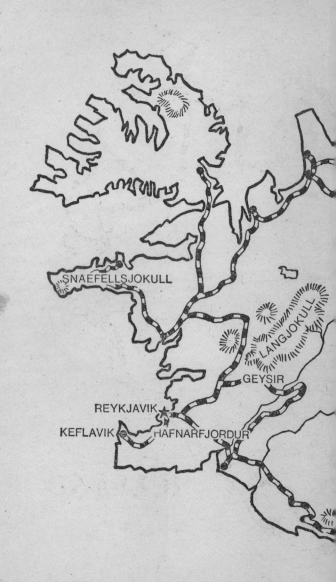

AKUREYRI

HOFS
JOKULL

VATNAJOKULL

HOFN

ICELAND

VIK

Icelandic Secret

"How would you boys like to fly to Iceland?" Mr Hardy asked his sons.

Frank and Joe, seated in their father's study on the second floor of the Hardy home in Bayport, looked stunned.

"Iceland? Up near the Arctic Circle?" asked blond-haired, seventeen-year-old Joe.

Frank, dark-haired and a year older, had the same incredulous look as his brother, but he realized that his famous detective father was not joking. "Of course, Dad! What's the pitch? Another mystery?"

Fenton Hardy rocked slightly in his high-backed swivel chair. "I would call it a mild mystery compared with some others you've handled. But it could develop into the most dangerous one yet, provided . . ." Frowning, he paused for a moment.

Joe asked excitedly, "Provided what, Dad?"

"That depends on another assignment I'm not at liberty to reveal. It's top secret—for the moment at least. Your job is to find a man named Rex Hallbjornsson. An insurance company wants to pay him fifty thousand dollars."

Frank smiled. "That's not hard to take. Who left him that tidy little fortune?"

"A person whose life he saved at sea."

"Then this Hallb—what's his name—is a sailor?" Joe asked.

"Right. Probably one reason why Hallbjornsson hasn't been found. And I have a hunch his long Scandinavian name might have something to do with it, too."

Mr Hardy quickly outlined the important facts. The missing man's last known address was a London steamship company. That was before his ship was sunk by a drifting mine off the coast of France. European detectives tracked him to a family on the coast of Brittany, but Hallbjornsson had long since gone from there. He did leave a clue—a scrap of paper which bore the word 'Island'.

"Island is the Icelandic word for Iceland," Mr Hardy explained. "Hallbjornsson would be in his sixties by now. My guess is that he returned to his native land. Your mission—track him down. There's a direct flight from New York to Reykjavik, the capital of Iceland."

"What about Chet?" Joe asked. "Can he come with us?"

Chet Morton was the Hardys' best friend. He was a stout boy, great as a player on the Bayport High football team, but less than enthusiastic as a sleuth. Chet would side-step danger, if possible. However, when the chips were down, he always proved to be a true friend. He was fond of food and hobbies, the latter changing as often as the weather.

Mr Hardy pondered the question about Chet in silence for a few moments. "Yes," he said finally, "Chet might be of assistance as well as good company. But you must warn him to be silent. Premature disclosure of our plans could prove disastrous."

Frank and Joe made careful note of their father's warning, because Fenton Hardy was an expert in detective work and security. He had been a crack member of the New York Police Department, and his superiors had been disappointed to lose him when he left to start his own agency. Now he was world-famous and his sons were following in his footsteps.

"Great, Dad!" Frank said, jumping to his feet. "With spring holidays coming up we won't miss any time at school!"

"Are your passports up to date?" his father asked.

"Sure, we always keep them that way."

A telephone call brought Chet Morton and his old jalopy backfiring to a halt in front of the Hardy house in Elm Street. Chet lived on a farm several miles out of town. He had a sister, Iola, who was Joe's girl friend.

Frank's special date was Callie Shaw. But girls were far from the minds of the young detectives as they ran out to greet their friend.

Chet hopped out of the car, his round face beaming. "Hi, fellows. Another mystery? By the way, how's your Aunt Gertrude fixed for cakes?"

"Come in. We'll find out."

Laura Hardy, the boys' mother, had gone shopping leaving Aunt Gertrude in sole charge of the kitchen. Miss Hardy, their father's sister, was tall, spare and decisive.

She often looked askance at the mysteries in which her nephews became involved. Nonetheless, Frank and Joe were very special to her as was Chet Morton, chief connoisseur of her excellent culinary abilities.

11

"Well! You sound like a bunch of elephants tramping in here!" Aunt Gertrude said.

"Chet's hungry again," Frank declared with a wink.

"What else?" Joe joked. "That's a permanent condition with him."

"Aw, cut it out, fellows," said Chet, pulling out a kitchen chair and sliding his ample frame into it. "What's your latest in cakes, Aunt Gertrude?"

Miss Hardy pursed her lips in a mock look of annoyance, yet she was secretly pleased with her reputation as a baker.

"Rhubarb tart, Chester. It's in the refrigerator."

A sly smile spread over Chet Morton's face. He leaned forward, elbows on the table. "My favourite! You must have known I was coming!"

"Cut out the baloney, Chet," said Joe. "You'd eat anything."

Chet's hurt look vanished when a large wedge of tart was placed before him, along with a tall glass of milk.

"Thank you, thank you," he said as Aunt Gertrude left to take care of other household chores. Then he turned to his friends. "Now, what's this latest proposition?"

"We're going to Iceland," Frank said seriously, "and would like to take you with us."

Chet grinned broadly. "Good idea!"

"But you must keep this absolutely mum," Joe warned. "Not a word of it to anyone."

"You can trust me to be quiet," Chet stated between mouthfuls.

"And we mean *quiet!*" Frank added emphatically.

"Okay, okay, I'm with you." Chet savoured a long

12

swig of milk. "And what are we going to do there?"

Briefly the Hardys told of their mission, and Chet seemed delighted with the idea. "Finding somebody doesn't seem too dangerous," he said. "Besides, I'd like to see some real Eskimos."

As he finished speaking, Chet banged the side of his hand on the kitchen table, making the plate jump.

"What are you trying to do?" Joe demanded.

"Just practising my karate chop."

"Your latest hobby?" Frank asked.

"Sure. The art of self-defence. Got to get the old hands toughened up. Never can tell when you might need it."

"You're a nut," Joe said, grinning, as the boys stood up and walked to the front door.

"Thanks for the tart," Chet said to Gertrude Hardy whom they met in the hall. "It'll give me lots of strength for our next case."

"Quiet!" Joe said. "You're spilling the beans already."

Aunt Gertrude sniffed, as if scenting danger, and her eyebrows rose above the rim of her glasses. "Another case?" she asked, looking from Frank to Joe. "What is it?"

"Something simple," Frank assured her. "An easy investigation. Don't worry."

"Humph! I worry all the time about you."

"We're only going to Iceland," said Joe.

"Iceland?" Aunt Gertrude made a face as if the entire country were run by wild, long-haired Vikings. "You'll freeze to death up there, if you're not eaten by a polar bear!"

"Or lost on the stormy seas," Joe added.

"Don't get smart, young man," his aunt replied, and marched into the kitchen, where she put the remaining tart and the milk back into the refrigerator.

Frank remembered studying Iceland in school and knew that the weather should be mild in April, although there were occasional storms in the area at that time of year. "Bring some heavy clothes just in case," he told his friend.

"How about skis and snowshoes?"

"Forget it, Chet. I didn't say the North Pole!"

"What about the rest of the gang? Shall I tell them?" asked Chet.

Frank hesitated. "Dad cautioned us not to say anything to anybody."

"Well, Tony and Biff will know the next day that we're gone," Joe put in. "Suppose we tell them we're going away on a secret mission without saying where."

"Okay," Frank agreed. "Maybe we can have a get-together before we leave."

"Good idea." Chet said goodbye and chugged off. He made a stop at the Bayport Hardware Store for some farm supplies before heading for home.

As Chet hoisted a bale of peat moss to his shoulder and carried it to his jalopy, he nearly bumped into Fred Marney, newsreader on the local Bayport TV channel. Marney was well acquainted with the exploits of the Hardys and their friends.

"Hi, Chet. Getting the garden ready?" he greeted the boy.

"Not me. This is for my mother's roses. No time for gardening."

"What? With spring holidays coming up?"

"Oh, I'll be busy," said Chet and moved towards the car.

"Busy with what?" Marney persisted. "Another Hardy boys' case?"

Chet tossed the bale into the back of the car and turned to frown at the newsreader.

"So I hit the nail on the head, eh?" the newsman persisted.

"I didn't say *anything!*" Chet said, sliding behind the wheel. "The trip to Iceland is nobody's business except—"

Chet could have bitten off his tongue as Marney smirked and turned away. He had broken his promise! What would the Hardys say now? Well, maybe it was of so little importance that Fred Marney would forget it.

That evening, just before the TV broadcast, Chet had a phone call from Tony Prito. "Listen, Chet, big doings at our place tonight. My mother's giving a pizza feast. The whole bunch will be here. I've told Iola already. Come with your appetite."

"Then you know about the trip?" Chet asked.

"Biff and I do, but that's all. Frank and Joe want to keep it a secret."

"Yeah, I know about that," Chet said limply. "I'll be there, but I don't know about my appetite."

Tony Prito laughed as he hung up, and Chet tuned in the evening report. His eyes were glued to the TV screen. National news came first, then other reports of statewide importance, and finally an item about the Bayport city council. Chet breathed a sign of relief. His secret had not been revealed!

In the Hardy house Frank, Joe, and Mr Hardy were

watching the same programme while the boys' mother and Aunt Gertrude were preparing supper. After the council report Fred Marney smiled at his viewers and said, "And now a little juicy titbit for fans of the famous Hardy boys." Frank and Joe froze and Mr Hardy frowned deeply.

The reporter went on, "This time it's a trip to Iceland for Frank and Joe and, of course, their pal Chet Morton, too. Since this is not a junket for fun in the sun, we wonder what the detectives are up to now."

"Holy crow!" Joe exclaimed and switched off the set. "How did he find out about that?"

"I'm afraid this means trouble," Mr Hardy said, thumping a fist into the palm of his hand. "Well, what's done is done!"

"Do you suppose it was Chet?" asked Frank.

The answer came with the ringing of the telephone. Joe grabbed it. The voice on the other end was so low that he could hardly hear it. "What? . . . Oh, it's you, Chet. . . . Yes, we heard." There was a long silence while Chet explained.

Then Joe went on, "No, I don't think it'll wipe out the trip, but Dad's very upset. See you later."

Joe told the others what had happened, which was not of much comfort to his father. After supper Mr Hardy announced that he was leaving for an important secret meeting.

Frank and Joe washed and dressed for the party at the Pritos' house. Chet was bringing his sister Iola, and Frank was to pick up Callie Shaw at her home. Just as the boys started out to their car, they heard the phone ringing.

Aunt Gertrude answered. After listening for a few moments, she said, "You shouldn't play pranks like this, Callie Shaw! What is it you—?" Then she turned to the boys with an astonished expression on her face. "Goodness, she hung up on me!"

"That couldn't have been Callie," Frank said. "She wouldn't do a thing like that!"

"What did the caller say?" Joe asked.

"She claimed it was the White House calling Fenton Hardy."

The boys climbed into their convertible, uneasy about the strange call. Had it been a joke?

"We'd better not mention this to anyone," Frank said. Joe agreed.

A few minutes later they pulled up at the Shaws' house, and Frank hurried to pick up his pretty blonde girlfriend.

When they arrived at Tony Prito's house, Frank parked in front, and the three entered. Chet and his vivacious, dark-haired sister were already there. They all trooped down to the basement room, where brawny Biff Hooper and good-looking Tony were playing a game of ping-pong.

Their dates were shouting encouragement to the two, when Tony sent a sizzling backhand shot which nicked the end of the table.

"You win!" Biff said and put down his bat.

"Hi, Frank, Joe! The news is all over town!"

When Frank remained silent, Tony said, "Hey, you guys, where's your bounce tonight?"

"The news shouldn't have leaked out," Joe explained. "Well, let's forget about the whole thing and have some fun."

The boys grabbed billiard cues and went to the large table which occupied one end of the basement. Callie, meanwhile, put on some dance records, and as the evening progressed the fun increased until Mrs Prito appeared carrying a large tray of red-hot pizza.

Frank touched Callie's arm. "I'd like to get out for a little fresh air before we tackle the goodies."

"Me, too," Callie replied. "It's stuffy in here."

The couple stepped out into the star-studded evening. As they walked towards the front of the house, Frank noticed a car parked five feet from the kerb, almost directly behind his convertible. All its doors were open.

Three men approached Frank as he walked forward. Callie lingered behind. When the man in the lead had almost reached Frank, he suddenly commanded, "Come with us!"

Callie stifled a scream and ran back into the house!

· 2 ·

Thug for Hire

FRANK sized up the situation in a split second. The doors of the car stood open, and its motor was running. All prepared, Frank thought, to receive the kidnap victim.

The young detective dodged the man in front of him, raced through the clutching hands of the other two, and dived into the car. In a twinkling he had it in gear and pressed the accelerator.

Shoosh! Tyres screeched as the car bolted ahead. It zigzagged wildly, its doors flying, until Frank gained control and spun round the corner. Now to get back to the thugs as quickly as possible!

Frank circled the block and returned to the Prito house, where everyone was standing on the front lawn.

Only one thug was in evidence, flat on his back, with Tony kneeling on his chest. Moments later two police cars, lights flashing, raced up. Police Chief Collig jumped out, followed by his driver. Patrolman Riley leaped from the other car.

"What's going on?" Collig asked crisply. He was a portly, middle-aged man, a close confidant of the Hardys.

"A kidnap attempt," Frank said.

"Here's the one we caught!" Tony said. "The other

two got away." He pulled the man to his feet. He was thin and of medium height with sunken cheeks and bulging eyes. Tony's hand twisted the thug's shirt front, until the man winced.

"Who are you?" Tony demanded.

"And your pals?" Joe added.

But the captive would not talk.

"We probably have a file on him," Chief Collig said. He handcuffed the prisoner and turned him over to Riley. Then he went to his car and radioed headquarters. Returning, the police chief said, "We'll search for the other two men, don't worry."

"Thanks," Frank said, and the young people went back to their party.

After refreshments, Frank and Joe dropped Callie off, then drove home. Mr Hardy was not back yet, and Frank told their mother what had happened.

He had just finished when the lights of the detective's car swept the front windows as it pulled into the drive. Mr Hardy entered through the back door, looking serious.

When he heard about the kidnapping attempt, he shook his head. "I'm sorry I got you involved in this whole nasty business."

"Don't worry, Dad," Joe said. "We can take care of ourselves."

Mr Hardy seemed lost in thought for a moment, then asked, "Anyone telephone while I was gone?"

"No, dear," his wife replied, but added quickly, "Oh, yes, someone did call. Gertrude thought it was a joke."

Mr Hardy glanced at her in alarm. "Where was the call from?"

"The White House—at least that's what the girl said."

The detective gave a low whistle and shook his head again.

"What's wrong, Dad?" Frank asked sympathetically. He had never seen his father so dejected.

The detective managed a smile and looked at his sons. "I can't tell you now," he said. "Later, perhaps." He gave each boy a pat on the back, then climbed the stairs to his study.

Frank and Joe went to bed, wondering what it was all about. A little later they heard their father go to his bedroom and then make a telephone call on the upstairs extension. He spoke in low tones and they could not hear what he was saying.

In the middle of the night, both boys were wakened by Mr Hardy's footsteps going downstairs. Joe leaped up and opened the door a crack. He heard his father greet two men in whispered tones. Then he led them upstairs to his study.

"Holy crow!" Frank whispered. "This is regular cloak-and-dagger stuff, Joe!"

"You can say that again!"

They returned to bed and slept fitfully until morning. At breakfast no mention was made of the mysterious callers.

Finally Mr Hardy said, "Boys, I'm going on a special mission to Texas. There's something I want to give you to take to Iceland."

Frank and Joe followed him to his study. He unlocked one of the drawers of his desk and pulled out what looked like a small transistor radio.

"What's that?" Joe asked.

21

"It's the latest in decoders," Mr Hardy replied, "and it works on the decibel principle."

He explained that the high peaks of sound in any conversation were the keys to the code. "Once you have established these," he said, "the message can be decoded by using this special book."

He reached down again and handed Frank a small black codebook and a miniature tape recorder. "The recorder can be attached to a telephone or radio," he concluded.

Father and sons went over the principles of the decibel machine. When they had finished, the detective said, "Boys, you must guard this machine and the codebook carefully. These may be much more important on the second case I'm investigating."

"Is it connected with Iceland?" Joe asked.

"Very possible. I want you to leave on tonight's Loftleidir flight to Reykjavik."

Frank made reservations immediately. After their father had left, Joe telephoned Chet.

"We're leaving for Kennedy International Airport at six," he said. "So bring your gear over to the house at five o'clock."

By four all was ready at the Hardy home. As the boys were locking their suitcases, a call came from police headquarters. Frank talked to the chief, and when he had finished, relayed the information to his brother. The prisoner had been identified. He was from New York City, a thug for hire, and seemed fearful about mentioning his employer.

"The other two made a getaway," Frank said. "They're probably in New York. Police there have been alerted."

Half an hour later Frank and Joe were amazed to see Chet's car pull up in front quietly and without backfiring. "Oh, oh, there's the reason," Joe said with a big grin. Frank looked out of the window to see Iola at the wheel with Callie Shaw sitting beside her.

The Hardys ran out to greet them. Chet occupied the back seat along with his suitcase, a flight bag, an extra heavy overcoat, and a small camera and a radio slung around his neck.

"I thought I'd better drive," Iola said with a dimpled smile, "because we wanted Chet to start his trip in good health."

"I just came along to say goodbye," said Callie, looping her arm through Frank's.

"Chet, bring the stuff over here," Joe suggested. "We'll put it all in our car. Iola can drive it back and pick up the jalopy here."

Perspiring under the load of all his equipment, Chet deposited his baggage beside the Hardys' car.

When goodbyes had been said to Mrs Hardy and Aunt Gertrude, he reached down to pick up a black box. "Here, Iola, take this home. I won't need it. Frank and Joe have their short-wave radio."

Iola put the instrument aside, and the three boys loaded their belongings into the convertible.

"Got everything?" Joe asked.

"Yes," Frank replied.

The girls drove them to Bayport Airport in a matter of minutes. There they boarded a plane that arrived at Kennedy International Airport in ample time to check in for the Icelandic trip.

After they had checked in with Loftleidir, Chet asked

the ticket clerk, "Do you serve dinner on this flight?"

"Yes, sir. About an hour after you're airborne."

Chet rolled his eyes with a pleased expression. They headed for Gate 18, where a sleek jet plane was taking on passengers. The boys entered through the front and walked towards the rear. There were three seats on either side of the aisle. Joe sat next to the window, while Chet slipped into the aisle seat, leaving Frank the place in the middle.

Then the plane's door was shut and it taxied to a runway. Buzzing like a bottled bumble-bee, the huge craft lifted off and headed out across the sea towards the north.

Soon seat belts were removed and the boys tilted their seats back to enjoy the flight. By this time darkness had settled over the ocean beneath them.

The attractive stewardesses began bringing trays of food. Frank and Joe, being on the inside, were served first.

"What, no more food left?" Chet asked with a worried expression.

The stewardess smiled down at him. "I'll be right back," she said.

When she returned, Chet started a conversation. "We're going to Iceland to see the Eskimos."

"Oh, really?" The dark-haired girl repressed a laugh. "But there aren't any Eskimos in Iceland."

"What?" Chet was perplexed.

Touching her fingers one at a time, the stewardess explained, "There are no Eskimos, no frogs and no snakes in Iceland."

Joe grinned. "Then what *is* there in Iceland, Miss——?"

"Just call me Steina. You wouldn't remember my last name, it's too long."

The girl went on to say that there were glaciers and hidden people and night trolls—and, of course, ghosts. Then, before the boys could ask any other questions, she moved off to serve their fellow passengers.

"Hey, this is going to be an interesting trip!" Chet remarked, slicing through a juicy piece of steak.

"We'll have to learn more about those ghosts and night trolls," Frank said with a chuckle.

Steina returned later to remove their trays, but could not tarry to chat.

"She sure is good-looking," Chet whispered to Frank.

But Frank's mind was on the special equipment his father had supplied. He reached down into his flight bag tucked under the seat. The tape recorder was there in place. So was the codebook, slipped in tightly beside it. For no special reason, Frank pulled out the decibel counter. Suddenly a curious expression crossed his face.

"Holy crow, Joe, what's this?"

His brother's head was buried in a magazine. Now he turned to look at the object in Frank's hand. "It's the decible counter Dad gave us to—" He stopped short and his eyes grew wide. "Wait a minute—it's a radio!"

"Sure, it's mine," Chet put in. "I wonder how it got into your bag. Just before we left I gave it to Iola!"

·3·

An Ancient Custom

THE brothers stared at the radio they had brought by mistake. Without the decibel counter, the codebook was of no use! If Mr Hardy had an urgent secret message, they could not receive it!

Frank shook his head. "Whew! This Icelandic case is starting off like a disaster! First the attempted kidnapping and now this!"

"I'm to blame for the whole thing," Chet muttered, crestfallen.

"No you're not," Joe said. He tried to console his friend. "It could have happened to anybody. The two cases look very much alike."

Frank realized that they had to get a message back home as soon as possible. He beckoned to the stewardess who hastened up the aisle and bent over the seat.

"Steina," Frank said, "we have an emergency on our hands. We must get a radio message back home."

"Emergency?"

"Yes," Joe added. "This is serious."

"All right. Come with me. We'll go to the captain."

Frank followed the pretty stewardess down the long aisle. When they reached the door of the crew's cabin, Steina knocked lightly and they entered. In the dim glow Frank saw four men who seemed to blend into the console of dials and instruments, which reached straight to the roof of the pilot's cabin.

The captain turned his eyes from the windshield and spoke to Steina in Icelandic. Then he switched to English and addressed Frank. "So you have an emergency, young man? . . . Yes, I can send a message by radio. What is it?"

The co-pilot handed Frank a pad and pencil. Quickly he printed the message to be delivered to his home in Bayport. He asked his parents to collect the black box from Iola Morton and send it to them at Keflavik Airport on the same flight next day.

Then Frank thanked the captain and the stewardess and returned to his seat. Soon the cabin's main lights were switched off and the passengers settled back for a short nap before the early dawn which would come at about two o'clock.

The boys dozed fitfully until the lights came on again and stewardesses busily went up and down the aisles serving breakfast. Frank looked out of the window and gasped in amazement.

"Joe, Chet! Look at that!"

There below them, rising out of the sea like a strange white world, loomed the snow-covered mountains of Greenland.

"Wow! That gives you the chills, doesn't it?" said Chet.

As the view of the great peaks slipped by the wing tip, the boys talked about the huge island of Greenland, which seemed to spell adventure. Frank knew it was owned by Denmark, populated by Eskimos, and that there were several air bases on its shores.

"There's a Danish one called Narssarssuaq," he

stated. He pulled a map from the seat pocket in front of him and opened it. "Here it is, look!"

"Boy, I'm glad I'm not an Eskimo," said Chet. "I could never spell a word like that!"

Their banter was interrupted by Steina who brought them breakfast. Not long after they had eaten, the captain's voice crackled over the loud-speaker.

"We are on our descent to Keflavik. Please fasten your seat belts."

As the plane glided lower, the boys craned their necks for a look at the country below. It had been born of volcanoes, and much of its surface was covered with lava and volcanic ash. Steaming hot springs lay next to its glaciers, and geysers spouted steam high into the air.

When the huge aircraft touched down, Frank swallowed hard to release the pressure in his ears.

"Exit through the front," Steina said. "Goodbye, and have a good time in Iceland."

"We're on business," Chet said importantly. "But we'll try to have fun."

Lugging their hand baggage, Frank, Joe and Chet climbed down the steps, breathing in deeply the crisp fresh air. Snow covered the airfield.

"Pretty bleak," Joe remarked as they hastened into a long, low building to be checked through customs.

An official stamped their passports and directed them to the back of the building, where a bus and taxis were waiting.

Frank talked to the driver standing beside the bus, and learned that Reykjavik was approximately thirty miles away. The bus would leave in twenty minutes.

The trio put their bags by the side of the building,

then looked about the unusual landscape. A wide, black, barren valley swept off into the distance before rising abruptly to a bald, snow-clad mountain ridge.

"That's probably all made of lava," Joe declared, moving off a few paces to get a better look. Not far away an open jeep was parked at the side of the road, its bonnet lifted. A boy about their own age was tinkering with the engine.

Frank, Joe and Chet casually walked over to him. "Find the trouble?" Frank asked.

The youth smiled at them. With a slight accent he replied, "Something's wrong with the carburettor."

"Let's take a look," Joe said. "Maybe we can help."

"Sure, be my guest."

The American colloquialism surprised the Hardys. "Oh, you've been in the States?" asked Frank.

"Yes, just got back a couple of days ago. My name is Gudmundur Bergsson." The boy wiped his hands on a piece of cloth and shook hands with the three. "Just call me Gummi." He told them that he was a student at a flying school in Tulsa, Oklahoma, and was learning to be a mechanic. "Now I'm home for spring holidays," he concluded.

Before Frank and Joe could examine the stalled motor, the loudspeaker blared: "Calling Frank and Joe Hardy!"

The boys looked up in surprise.

"Calling Frank and Joe Hardy," the announcer said again.

Joe started for the building, but Frank restrained him. "Not so fast, Joe. Nobody was to meet us here. Maybe it's another kidnapping attempt!"

"That's right," Chet chimed in. "We can't be too careful."

Gummi looked on, bewildered by the unusual conversation. "Somebody is trying to catch you guys?" he asked.

Frank nodded and said to Chet, "Just stroll inside and see who's paging us."

Chet left, returning a few minutes later. "A short, heavy-set guy with long blond hair and a moustache. Look, here he comes now!"

A square-looking man, his hair flowing, walked from the building. Frank and Joe ducked behind the jeep. The fellow looked right and left before climbing into a small foreign car. Then he drove off.

Frank glanced round for a taxi, but they had all gone. "I wish we could have followed him," he said disappointedly.

Gummi looked at the boys dubiously. "Hey, what's all this? Are you a couple of spies or something?"

Frank grinned. "We're detectives."

" No kidding."

"Look, it's a long story. We'll tell you later."

Gummi returned to his tool kit without asking further questions, and before long he and Frank had dismantled the carburettor.

"There's your trouble," Frank said, and wiped a piece of sludge from the intake.

Gummi laughed. "I can get you a mechanic's job in Reykjavik any time you want," he said and started the engine. "Where are you fellows staying?"

"The Saga Hotel in Reykjavik," Joe replied.

"Want a ride into town?"

"Great!"

The boys got their bags and climbed into the jeep. On the way, they told Gummi about their search for Rex Hallbjornsson.

"Seems like looking for a needle in a haystack," the Icelandic boy commented. "There are two hundred thousand people on this island."

"How big is it?" Frank wanted to know.

"East to west about three hundred miles. Larger than Ireland, but we have not nearly as many inhabitants."

"What do the people do for a living here?" Joe asked.

"Most of our income is derived from fishing," Gummi explained as he drove along a curving road hugging the rugged coastline. Not a tree was in sight Only black lava formations.

Frank pointed to small piles of stone along the road. "What are these for?"

"They guided winter travellers in the olden days," Gummi replied. "And that village over there to the left is Hafnarfjordur."

As they entered the outskirts of Reykjavik, Gummi said, "When the first settlers came to this harbour, called a 'vik', they saw steam coming from the ground in the distance. Thinking it was smoke, or 'reykja', they called the place Reykjavik."

Gummi drove along a wide street lined with buildings which were faced with corrugated iron. The roofs were gaily painted in apple green, white, blue or yellow.

"Quite a colourful place," Chet commented as he banged the side of the car with his right hand.

"Are you practising karate, too?" Gummi asked. "It's the craze in our school just now. But Icelanders like wrestling better."

Finally they reached the centre of town, where a small square was decorated with red, white and blue bunting and American flags.

Joe grinned. "Boy, they must have known we were coming!"

"If I didn't know better, I'd believe it." Gummi chuckled. "This is in honour of three U.S. astronauts who came here to study our lava surface which is very similar to the terrain on the moon." He rounded a corner and pulled up in front of a modern white hotel located at the hub of three radiating roads. "Here you are."

The boys jumped out, unloaded their baggage and thanked Gummi. He gave them his address and phone number. "Call me any time if you need help," he said. "I'll take you round in my jeep."

Frank and Joe occupied one room, and Chet an adjoining one. After unpacking, they took the lift to the eighth-floor restaurant for lunch.

"Well, masterminds," Chet asked between mouthfuls of broiled trout, "how are you going to find your boy Rex?"

"As soon as we're finished, let's look in the telephone book," Frank suggested.

When they consulted the directory, however, they stared at each other in confusion. "I can't make head or tail of this," Joe stated. "It looks as if everything with 'son' at the end is a first name!"

"We'll give Gummi a call. Maybe he can explain," said Frank, and dialled their new friend's number. "Hey, what's all this crazy name business in Iceland?" he asked Gummi. "We can't find anybody by the name of Halbjornsson under H."

Gummi laughed loudly. "People are listed by their first names in the telephone book," he said, and explained that the last name changed with every generation.

"Take me, for example," he said. "My father's name is Bergs Anderson. That makes my last name Bergsson. If I have a son, he'd be called Gudmundurson, and my daughter Gudmundurdottir. It's a hangover from the ancient Scandinavians. We still use it here."

"So we have to look under Rex, it that it?"

"Right. Good luck."

The boys thumbed through the directory. No Rex was listed.

"It looks as if we'll have to scan each page in search of Hallbjornsson," Joe said. "Rex might be a nickname."

About half an hour later Frank said, "Look! Here's an Ingrid Hallbjornsdottir. Maybe she's his sister."

They called Gummi again, who picked them up ten minutes later and drove them to the address. It turned out that the woman had no brothers and had never heard of Rex Hallbjornsson.

"Back to the phone book," Joe grumbled.

"Tell you what," Gummi said. "I'll help you look, and if we come up with any more leads, I'll phone them from your hotel. This way we might save ourselves a few trips."

"Great idea, Gummi," Frank agreed. "You can question those people in Icelandic."

The boys drove back to the hotel and divided the work by getting three telephone directories. Each boy checked a different section. When they finished they had found two more Hallbjornsdottirs and one Hallbjornsson. Gummi phoned him. The man knew nobody by the name of Rex. Calls to the two women proved to be equally futile.

Since it was getting late, the Hardys said good night to Gummi. "Would you take us to the airport tomorrow morning?" Frank asked. "We have to pick up a package arriving on the early flight."

"Sure thing. I'll be here on time."

Next morning after breakfast the boys went to the lobby. Gummi was just coming through the revolving door. "How's this package coming? By air express?" he asked.

Frank said he did not know. They would inquire after the plane had landed.

At the airport the boys went to the waiting room and watched the passengers stream in to claim their baggage.

Suddenly Joe grabbed Frank's arm and turned him towards the door. "Look who's here!"

"Can it be?" Chet exclaimed.

"Sure it is," Frank said excitedly. "Hey, Biff Hooper!"

·4·

Astronauts' Salute

GRINNING broadly, Biff Hooper greeted the Hardys and Chet, then handed Frank a little black box which he carried under his arm.

"Oh boy, am I glad to see this!" Frank said. "Thanks, Biff."

"Your dad phoned me," Biff said. "He didn't want to send it by air express," Then he squared his broad shoulders. "Besides, he thought you might need me!"

"That sounds ominous," Joe stated. "Does Dad think there'll be any trouble?"

"Couldn't say," Biff replied, glancing about the airport building.

Frank beckoned to Gummi who had been standing in the background. After introductions were made, Biff claimed his baggage and the five went out to the jeep. On the ride back to Reykjavik, Frank asked Biff if he had noticed anyone following him.

"No, I didn't see anybody."

Back at the hotel, Biff moved into Chet's room. After he had freshened up, Gummi suggested lunch at the Hotel Borg. "It is in the centre of town, in the square," he said, "and if you like seafood—"

"That's for me!" Chet said quickly.

"Okay, let's go."

They were in the square in no time at all, and after Gummi parked the car, they entered the ground-floor restaurant which looked old-fashioned by American standards. The waiters were young, no older than the Hardys and they moved about with ease and aplomb. Gummi ordered a seafood tray and mentioned something else to the waiter in Icelandic.

"*Yow, yow!*" the waiter replied, grinning.

"What's *yow, yow?*" Chet wanted to know.

"It means yes, yes, spelled *ja,*" Gummi told him.

"I knew I'd learn Icelandic eventually—*yow, yow, yow!*"

"And don't forget, no is *nei.*"

The waiter brought a small plate of yellowish dried fish, cut into small bits.

"It's *hardfisk,*" Gummi explained, "and a speciality of Iceland. You put butter on it and eat it like this."

Chet put a piece in his mouth and started to chew. "Tastes like wood splinters," he complained.

"Keep chewing," Gummi advised.

"Hm! Now it tastes good—it melts in your mouth."

When everyone had tried the *hardfisk,* the waiter arrived with a platter of ten different kinds of seafood; sild herring, small shrimps, caviar and other delicacies.

"Iceland is not a bad place for a detective case," Joe remarked. Just then they heard the sound of horns. The boys looked out of the window.

"I think the astronauts are driving by," Gummi said.

Half rising from the seats of their booth, they looked out on to the street. A car passed, with two small American flags fluttering on the front bumpers.

"They're our astronauts, all right," Frank said. "I recognize them."

Three men were sitting in the back seat. The one in the middle held his head low, with his cap well down over his eyes.

"That one must be Major Kenneth McGeorge," Frank said. "They're probably on their way back to Keflavik for their trip home, now that they know what the moon looks like."

"Next trip for them the moon," Joe said.

"I know they'll make it," Gummi said. "They're great guys."

Chet Morton, as usual, ate more than anyone else. When he had finished the last morsel of shrimp, Gummi Bergsson said, "In regard to your insurance case, I have a suggestion. You should see Anders Sigurdsson at the Foreign Office. Tell him your problem. He might be able to help."

The Foreign Office was located on a small hill near the centre of town. The two-storey building looked like an oversized bungalow. Gummi waited outside with Chet and Biff while the Hardy boys entered. They were ushered to an office on the first floor, where a short, smiling, grey-haired man greeted them. The boys told him their problem.

"So you're looking for Rex Hallbjornsson," the man mused. "I have never heard of him, but that's not unusual. I would suggest that you put an advertisement in our five daily newspapers."

"Five newspapers in a city of seventy-five thousand?" Frank asked in amazement.

"That's right. Icelanders like to read. In fact, there is no illiteracy in our country. Also, these papers are sent to other towns on the island."

'We'll follow your suggestion, Mr Sigurdsson," Frank said. "Thank you very much."

"Not at all. Come back if I can be of more help."

Frank and Joe left the building, stopping at the front door to survey the small city which lay before them. Traffic kept to the right side of the road, as in America, and the narrow streets were filled mostly with European-made cars.

Frank scanned the view from left to right, where the road led down to the waterfront. Suddenly he backed into the doorway. "Joe, duck!"

A German-made Taunus car drove slowly towards the front of the building. Its driver had long blond hair and a flowing moustache! The man pulled to the side of the road and scanned Gummi's jeep.

"That's the fellow who had us paged at the airport!" Frank whispered.

"He must have found out what hotel we're staying at and is following us," Joe said.

The man's eyes went up the long path to the door of the Foreign Office, but he could not see the Hardys.

"Something's fishy," Frank stated. "Maybe he has something to do with the guys who were trying to kidnap me."

"Never can tell," Joe replied. "We'd better be careful until we find out who he really is."

As they watched, the Taunus moved off slowly, turned the corner into Austur Straeti, and disappeared.

The Hardys hurried to the jeep.

"Did you see that guy?" Joe asked Gummi.

"Sure did. Come on. We'll follow him."

Traffic was heavy, and soon the Taunus was out of

sight. "He might have driven down to the harbour area," Gummi said. "Let's try that." He made a few turns but could not pick up the man's trail.

"He gave us the slip," Gummi said. "Where do you want to go now?"

"I saw a newspaper office at the top of Austur Straeti," Frank replied. "Let's go back. I want to place an ad in all the local newspapers."

"Okay, I'll take you to each one of them. Hey, this detective stuff is great!"

It took the rest of the afternoon to place the ads in the five dailies. Frank kept it short. *Will Rex Hallbjornsson please contact the Hardy boys at the Saga Hotel and collect insurance money due him.* Gummi translated it into Icelandic.

"Do you think it's wise to mention money?" Biff Hooper asked.

Frank shrugged. "It might be the only way to get him to reply."

"Sure, what have we got to lose?" Joe said.

On the way back to the hotel, Biff pointed to a cluster of huge tanks sitting on the hill in the centre of Reykjavik. "What a place to put gas tanks!"

Gummi laughed. "Gas tanks? Those are filled with hot water."

"What for?"

Gummi explained that the tanks were located over boiling springs of water, which surged up from the depths of the earth. "The hot water is stored and piped into every home in Reykjavik," he said. "We don't have any heating problems here."

"Quite a system!" Biff remarked.

"And you're always in hot water!" Chet quipped.

"Throw him out!" said Biff.

"Careful of me," Chet replied, and banged his seat with a karate chop.

"What a clown!" Biff said, laughing.

Gummi had some chores to do for his father and left the boys at the hotel. That evening after dinner the Hardys set up their radio, because they expected a message from their father.

"Don't forget there's a four-hour difference in time," Frank said. "I have a hunch Dad won't transmit until night, when the atmosphere is clear."

The boys fiddled with the set, tuning in various stations. They were rewarded at midnight when they received a coded broadcast from Mr Hardy. Frank quickly attached the decibel unit to the radio and started the conversation.

Mr Hardy talked about the opening baseball game in the major leagues. "The Yankees scored three in the ninth to win their game," he said. "With good pitching they should have a great season."

It sounded casual enough. The boys had decided not to reveal their suspicions concerning the blond stranger. They would wait until they had some constructive evidence.

When Mr. Hardy signed off a few minutes later, Frank went to work on the decibel counter. The peaks, visibly recorded on the tape of the machine, were translated into letters.

Then Joe took out the codebook. "Here, give me a pencil, Frank!"

Frank pulled one out of his pocket, and his brother began to decode the message word by word. At the end of the first sentence, Frank and Joe gasped in amazement. One of the U.S. astronauts missing! It couldn't be true. But there were the words: *Ken McGeorge has been lost in Iceland!*

· 5 ·

The Boiling Pit

THE news of Ken McGeorge's disappearance hit the boys like an avalanche. Their hearts beat wildly as they continued to decode Mr Hardy's message:

Keep your eyes open for any clues to McGeorge. Chet and Biff must be sworn to complete secrecy. Space programme at stake.

Mr Hardy added that he had obtained clearance from Washington for his sons and their friends to help.

Chet had been standing with his mouth open. Now he blurted, "But—but—we just saw the three astronauts on their way to Keflavik!"

Frank snapped his fingers. "Remember the fellow in the middle? He had his hat pulled down low over his face. I'll bet he was a stand-in for McGeorge!"

"That's right," said Joe. "Obviously the government doesn't want the news to leak out. It might jeopardize the whole NASA programme."

"What a mystery you got yourselves into this time!" Biff Hooper exclaimed.

"Now the pieces fall into place," Frank said. "Dad must have been working on this case before we left. Remember, Joe, the mysterious call from the White House?"

"Right. And those two men who visited him in the

middle of the night were probably government officials!"
Joe briefly told Biff and Chet about the occurences in the
Hardy home.

"He went to Texas just before we flew to Iceland,"
Frank concluded. "Probably checking on McGeorge's
co-workers and friends."

"If we're going to find the major in Iceland," Joe
said, "we'd better work fast. If he was kidnapped, they
might force information from him."

"Now we're all going to take a pledge of secrecy,"
Frank said. He slapped his hand on the table, Chet
came forward with his, then Joe and finally Biff.

"Not a word to anybody, through thick and thin,"
Frank said.

"Gosh, who knows what'll happen to us!" Chet said
worriedly.

"Whatever does," Biff stated grimly, "nobody will
ever learn anything from us!"

Suddenly the radio crackled again, and another
message came from Mr Hardy, saying that the astronaut had disappeared on the lava plain near Reykjavik.

"We'll go there tomorrow," Frank said. "Maybe
we'll find a clue."

The four companions were up early the next morning, and Frank phoned Gummi. He tried to conceal his
excitement. "How would you like to take us around
today, Gummi?"

"Sure. Where to?"

"The tour the astronauts made on the lava plain
near here sounds interesting."

"Okay. I'll check the newspapers to find the exact
route. It was well publicized."

An hour later he arrived outside the hotel, beeped

his horn, and the Americans climbed into the jeep.

A smooth highway led south out of town, but soon the Icelandic youth turned on to a rugged road leading into a valley of breath-taking desolation. Gaunt, snow-capped mountains rose on either side, and the valley was black with oddly shaped chunks of lava.

"Did the astronauts get out and walk around here?" asked Frank as the jeep bounced along.

"That's what they came for," Gummi replied. "This place is said to resemble the moon's surface."

"I can just see moon people hiding out there now," Biff quipped.

"We have our own hidden people in Iceland," Gummi replied.

"Hidden people?" Biff asked.

Frank recalled Steina's remark on the plane. "Not to mention ghosts?"

Gummi turned in surprise. "You know about the ghosts?"

"Not much," Frank admitted.

"I've got my special ghost," Gummi declared. "He travels with me all the time."

"Who's he?" Joe asked.

"My grandfather."

"What superstition!" Chet said, and Gummi did not look pleased.

"It's a fact!"

"No offence," Chet muttered.

The road meandered to avoid large black masses of lava. Gummi fought the wheel to keep the jeep on course over the rugged terrain.

"This looks as if it leads to nowhere," Frank commented.

Suddenly Joe stepped into a crevice

"What about these hidden people?" Joe asked.

Gummi explained the Icelandic belief. "They live in little green hillocks, and if you look carefully you might see them peering out at you. They wear bright-coloured clothes, and their faces are pale and peaceful."

Chet shuddered a little bit and looked about the eerie valley. Suddenly he leaned forward and gripped Gummi's shoulder.

"Hey-y-y! I just saw one!"

"Saw what?" asked Frank.

"Something moved behind one of those rocks!"

Gummi hit the brakes, and the boys jumped down on to the road.

"Chet, you're letting your imagination run away with you," Joe said with a grin.

"I'm not kidding!" the stout boy replied. "I really saw someone."

Frank and Joe exchanged glances. Maybe there was something in Chet's story! They could not afford to take chances, knowing that the blond man had been following them.

"Okay. Let's see where the ghost appeared," Frank suggested.

The boys followed Chet over the rough surface towards a large chunk of lava which looked rather like a troll bent over.

Gingerly Chet stepped around it. Nobody was there!

"Maybe he went over that way!" Chet said, pointing to the next hiding place behind another rock fragment.

The boys continued their search, circling half a dozen lava rocks. Suddenly Joe cried out as he stepped into a crevice. Wincing, he pulled his right leg out and danced around in pain.

"Wow! I scraped my shin!"

"You must be careful climbing around here," Gummi warned.

"All right, Chet, are you satisfied now?" Joe asked, annoyed by the accident.

"Okay, but I really—"

"Baloney!" Joe replied, hobbling back to the jeep.

Gummi smiled to himself as he started off again. As the road wound higher along the mountain, it grew soggier because of the recently melted snow. Soon they passed a broad lake which lay grey and forbidding in a small pass

"This whole place gives me the creeps," Biff said. "I wish I could see some trees!"

"That's what I like about Oklahoma—the trees," Gummi declared. "There were trees in Iceland centuries ago, but the early settlers cut them down."

"Well, here we are," he said finally as he pulled off the road on to a small trail with several inches of snow.

"Somebody's been here before," Joe observed, pointing to tyre tracks which led in and out.

Soon they came to the place where the other vehicle had stopped. Footprints led from the spot over the brow of a small rise, but they did not come back!

Beyond the rise a jet of steam, hissing like a gigantic snake, rose high into the air.

"That's coming from the sulphur pit over there," Gummi explained, "and the steam hole, too."

Joe leaped out first and ran up over the brow of the hill.

"Careful!" Gummi warned. "You don't want to be cooked in sulphur!"

Frank jumped down from the jeep and surveyed the

terrain. He lingered behind the others so he could look for clues without being questioned.

Several thoughts ran through his mind. How could one astronaut have disappeared? No doubt the three were accompanied by government officials. Major McGeorge must have separated from the rest and been waylaid. But how could he have been carried off without anyone noticing it, and by whom and where to?

Finding no clues, Frank trailed after the other four. When he reached the rise, he looked down at the pit. It was about six feet across, bubbling and boiling from deep in the earth.

The atmosphere was filled with the smell of sulphur, some of which came from the steam shooting out of a huge pipe with an earsplitting roar.

Frank suddenly noticed that only Gummi, Biff and Chet were in sight. He raced towards the trio, standing beside the pit. No use shouting, nobody could hear. Frank glanced about wildly. A black leather glove lay close to the edge of the bubbling sulphur. Footprints were nearby.

A chill ran down Frank's spine as he looked from the glove to his friends. Gummi suddenly caught on. His face took on a look of terror. He gestured at Frank and the other boys, and all had the same thought. Where was Joe? Had he fallen into the pit?

· 6 ·

Tricked in the Sky

FRANTICALLY the boys searched for Joe. Each shouted at the top of his lungs, but the thundering steam bursting out of the pipe like a hundred roaring jet engines drowned every other sound.

Frank suddenly gesticulated towards the stand-pipe, with an expression of utter relief on his face. Joe Hardy emerged from behind it. He hastened over to them as Chet picked up the glove from the snow, and they all moved off to a distance where they could hear each other.

"Holy crow!" Frank sighed. "Joe, you had us scared to death. We thought you'd fallen into the pit."

"Sorry about that," Joe replied. He had bent down to examine the rusted bolts at the foot of the pipe. "The sulphur in that steam is corroding everything," he said. "Someday the whole pipe is going to blow right up into the air."

"I wonder whom the glove belongs to," Gummi mused.

The Hardys and their two friends were thinking the same thought, but did not speak out in front of the Icelander. Did Ken McGeorge drop it while being kidnapped?

The brothers lagged behind to talk in private, while

the others returned to look at the sulphur pit. Frank said, "It stands to reason, Joe, that this place has been searched thoroughly by the authorities."

"That's right. They would have found the glove long before we did."

"The only answer," Frank went on, "is that the glove was dropped recently."

"By Major McGeorge?" Joe asked.

"It's a puzzler," Frank admitted. He walked over to Gummi and asked when it had snowed last.

"Early yesterday morning," Gummi replied.

The split-second glance that Frank exchanged with his brother was significant. If it were the astronaut's glove, he must have returned to the pit the night before But why?

The boys stayed a few minutes longer to look at the sulphur pit and the steam blowhole.

Gummi explained that there were many such phenomena over the entire island. "Iceland probably popped out of the sea just like Surtsey," he said, referring to the underwater volcano which boiled up out of the sea a few years ago, causing the formation of a small island off the south coast.

Frank took the leather glove from Chet and put it in his pocket. It was a clue that might prove significant, but they could not give it to the police without showing their hand.

First thing to do now, Frank thought, was to check the lone set of footprints, which did not return to the spot where they had started. He and Joe followed them for a way, and realized that they were double prints, leading in a roundabout way to the road about two hundred yards distant. Apparently two men had approached the sulphur pit, one behind the other, the second one stepping in the first one's footprints.

"This is fantastic," Joe remarked. "Maybe we should tell the police about this right away."

"No," Frank replied. "Let's first examine this glove and find out if it's government issue.

"And how are we going to do that?"

"We'll have to get another one from the U.S. base in Keflavik. Then we can compare the leather under a microscope."

The Hardys trudged back to the jeep, where the others were already waiting. As they drove back over the bumpy road towards the highway south of Reykjavik, fear gnawed at Frank. Had the astronaut's captors disposed of him in the sulphur pit?

Gummi dropped them at their hotel and left for home. At lunch the Hardys talked about their plans with Chet and Biff.

"Listen, fellows," Frank said. "You two stay here and watch out for any suspicious characters, while Joe and I take a taxi to Keflavik. We'd like to let Gummi in on this, but we'd better not."

After explaining that they would try to find a glove of similar manufacture, Frank and Joe left.

Arriving at Keflavik, they obtained permission to enter the base. Frank spoke to a captain in charge of general issue and asked if he might borrow a leather glove used by officers. The captain was amazed at the request, but after the Hardys identified themselves as American detectives working on an insurance case, the officer gave them a glove.

"We'll return it," Frank promised.

"That's all right. You can keep it."

"Thanks, Captain."

Back at the hotel, Frank asked the desk clerk if he could direct them to a medical laboratory.

"Anybody sick?" the man asked in surprise.

"No," Joe replied. "We have another reason."

The clerk looked at them curiously, riffled through a sheaf of addresses, and came up with one.

Although it was late in the afternoon, Frank and Joe took a chance. They called the lab and found that it was still open. "We would like to borrow a microscope," Frank explained. He was told that no instruments could be taken from the premises, but was invited to come over and use one.

"We close at six," the man said in perfect English.

"We'll be right there," Frank replied.

The Hardys took a taxi to the laboratory which was located at the centre of town, not far from the Foreign Office. A courteous technician greeted them and directed the boys to a small room. A microscope stood on a table to the left. The man asked if they would be examining germ cultures.

"Oh no," Joe said with a smile. "We're just comparing two pieces of leather."

"Go ahead." said the technician and left.

The research did not take long. First they examined the outside leather. Each glove proved to be made of the same general quality. The stitching was made by similar machines, and the woollen linings were identical.

"That does it," Frank said. "This was lost by a military man."

"Should we tell the police now?" Joe asked.

But Frank was adamant about following their father's instructions. "Not yet, Joe. Not yet."

The Hardys thanked the lab technician and left. Returning to the hotel, they found Biff and Chet eagerly waiting for them in the lobby. Biff waved a letter in his hand.

"Frank, Joe, you got an answer to your ad!"

Frank took the envelope and tore it open. It was from Reykjavik's leading newspaper, and inside was another letter. He read the message. It had come from Akureyri, a town on the north coast.

A man signing his name Rex Hallbjornsson wrote that he was the one they were looking for. He requested that the boys come to see him.

"That was easy," Chet commented.

"Too easy," Joe replied.

"I think you're right," his brother said. "We've got to be careful about this."

Chet scratched his head. "Always suspicious."

"Just cautious," Joe said.

Biff agreed with the Hardys. "After all, it's kind of fishy that the guy won't come here. If somebody offered *me* money, I wouldn't mind picking it up myself!"

It was agreed that Frank and Joe would fly to Akureyri the next day, leaving Chet and Biff at the hotel to guard their radio and decoding equipment.

"I'm going to Flugfelag Islands," Frank announced after breakfast the next morning.

"What?" asked Chet.

Frank handed him a travel folder which he had picked up at the desk.

"Flugfelag Islands," Chet read. "I wonder where they are."

"Listen dummy," Biff Hooper said, giving Chet a mock punch to the ribs which his chum parried with a karate chop. "Flugfelag Islands means Iceland Airlines."

"Attaboy, Biff!" Joe grinned. "You're learning the language."

The Hardys recalled seeing a Flugfelag office in the hotel lobby. Joe had noticed a dark-haired woman behind the desk the day before, but when the Hardys went to the office, it was empty. A few seconds later a man came in and sat down.

Frank approached him. "We'd like to take a plane to Akureyri," he said. "Today."

"Sorry," the man replied with a slight accent. "There are no scheduled flights to Akureyri until tomorrow. I would suggest that if you want to go today, you take a small private plane—it is cheaper, too."

"Will you make the arrangements?" Joe asked.

"Of course. What are your names?"

When the boys had given him all the information, the man said, "Be at the Flugfelag terminal at twelve noon. It is quite near the hotel, you know."

"Okay," Frank said. "Please charge it to our room." He gave the man the number. Then the boys hastened to the lift and went back upstairs.

Chet was sprawled on Frank's bed, while Biff sat looking out of the window. "I'd like to see Akureyri, too," he grumbled. "Can't we just leave Chet here to guard the equipment?"

"What's the big idea?" the stout boy said, rising. "I can tackle two, perhaps three guys, but no more. And they might send half a dozen here, you know!" He cleaved the air with a couple of karate strokes.

"All right, I'll stay," said Biff. "But get back soon!"

"Sure." Frank grinned. "And just so your job won't

be too demanding, I'll put this in the safe!" He took the codebook and went down to the lobby.

At eleven-thirty Frank and Joe stood in front of the Saga, where a taxi drove up to get them. Ten minutes later they reached the airfield. As they stepped inside the terminal building, they were met by the agent.

"I thought I would be here to help," he said. "Follow me." He led them out on to the field, where they saw a small twin-engined plane warming up.

"The pilot does not speak very good English," the agent explained, pulling open the cabin door against the propeller's slipstream. "But he will take you to Akureyri in less than an hour."

Frank and Joe climbed in, fastened their seat belts, and glanced towards the pilot's cabin. The door was shut. Outside, the agent waved to them, then the plane taxied for take-off. Soon they were airborne, and the boys looked down on the bright-coloured roofs of Reykjavik.

"Well, let's find out where Akureyri is, exactly," said Frank after a while and pulled a map of Iceland from his pocket. Both studied it, then sat back to watch the mountainous terrain unfolding before them.

Frank, who was sitting next to the window on the starboard side, glanced up at the sun.

"Hey, Joe, this is funny. We're supposed to be heading north, aren't we?"

"Sure," Joe replied. "That's where Akureyri is."

"But look! We're going east. See the position of the sun?"

According to the boy's reckoning, they were flying in the wrong direction. Frank's fears were confirmed when he glanced down and saw the jagged south coast of Iceland far beneath them.

"What's going on with that pilot?" Joe asked, annoyed.

"We'd better find out."

The boys slipped from their seats and approached the cabin. Joe opened the door and cried out in alarm. The pilot was their blond enemy!

"Where are you taking us?" Joe demanded.

The man motioned the boys away. "No speak!"

"Of course you speak English!" Frank said angrily, realizing that every pilot had to be versed in that language.

Joe pulled his brother out of the cabin so they could speak without being overheard.

"Frank, what are we going to do about this guy? You know what's happening—we're being kidnapped."

"We'll have to take over," Frank replied tersely.

Both boys were skilful pilots. Although they did most of their flying in single-engined planes, they felt sure they could handle the twin-engine job.

"Where'll we land?" Joe asked.

"Once we have control of the plane, we can radio Reykjavik for instructions," Frank stated, glancing out of the window. Below, a huge glacier came into view. The boys had studied the map carefully and realized that they were over Vatnajokull, the largest and most forbidding glacier in all of Iceland.

'We'll go in and I'll drag him from behind the wheel," Frank said. "You grab the joy-stick on the co-pilot's side. Okay?"

"Let's go!"

They approached the pilot. Frank reached forward

to get a headlock on him, but the man swung round and clipped him on the chin. As Frank staggered back, the port-side engine began to splutter. Seconds later the starboard engine died out. And all at once the pilot spoke perfect English!

"Let me handle this!" he said. "We'll have to land on the glacier!"

·7·

A Harrowing Blizzard

STILL groggy from the blow on the chin, Frank dropped into the co-pilot's seat. He grasped the wheel as Joe, his eyes flashing anger over the brazen kidnapping, swung a hard right at the pilot. The fist caught the man at the side of the jaw, and he slumped unconscious in his seat.

Wind whistled eerily over the wings as the plane glided towards the gigantic sheet of white ice beneath them.

Closer and closer it angled down towards Vatnajkull. Now the boys saw that much of the glacier was serrated with jagged knife-edged ridges. Small hills of ice and crevasses came into sharp focus.

"Frank, we'll never make it!" Joe cried out.

His brother sat grim and silent. Skilfully he guided the descent so as not to lose flying speed. His feet firmly on the rudder bar, Frank banked the plane and headed for what appeared to be a smoother spot in the sloping glacier about half a mile away.

Landing on the slope would be tricky enough for the most skilled pilot. With the wheels now inches above what proved to be bumpy ice, Frank pulled back on the joy-stick.

The whiteness rushed up to meet them! Their plane

bounced with a terrifying crunch, lifted into the air and settled again with tyres squealing.

The aircraft slid back a few feet before finally coming to a halt. Joe felt limp. "Thanks, Frank," was all he could say. "That was the greatest!"

Both boys felt lucky to come out of the crash-landing alive, but were furiously angry with the man responsible for their dire predicament.

The pilot was now conscious. He lifted his head and looked about dazedly.

"Okay now," Joe said, shaking him by the shoulder. "Who are you? And what's your racket?"

"Help—we need help," was the weak reply.

"You know the ropes!" Frank said impatiently. "Get on the radio and call for aid!" He climbed out of the co-pilot's seat and looked about the plane.

Meanwhile, the man picked up the microphone and slowly transmitted their position. There was silence for a minute or two, then he signed off.

"Someone will come for us," he reported.

"Okay—but that doesn't explain who you are!" Frank resumed their interrogation. But the man remained mute, shaking his head as if still in a stupor.

The Hardys were both aggravated and frightened. "Here we are, wrecked on top of the world," Joe muttered, "and this dummy won't tell us anything!"

He pulled the man from his seat and pushed him to the plane's door. Frank searched the pilot to make sure he had no weapons.

The icy air blanketing the glacier hit them like a bucketful of cold water as they stepped on to the slippery surface. They looked the plane over. Both propellers were bent, and even if the engines could have been repaired, a take-off looked impossible.

Despite continued questioning by the Hardys the pilot remained silent. As they were about to give up, they suddenly heard the distant sound of a helicopter.

"Wow! That chopper came pretty fast!" Joe said, shielding his eyes to watch the craft hover over the glacier.

"Good grief!" Frank exclaimed. "It's only a two-seater job!"

"Well, you know who goes out first—in hand-cuffs. Old blondie here is getting a ride to jail!"

Frank looked at their sullen kidnapper, whose shifty eyes glanced up at the rescue craft. "You'll talk when the Reykjavik police get hold of you," he said. "They'll find out what's behind all this hocus-pocus."

The helicopter landed close to the aeroplane, and a man of medium height hopped down. He had black hair, rugged features and a long nose, and he looked anything but Scandinavian. He began speaking immediately in a foreign tongue.

"Can you speak English, sir?" Frank interrupted.

"A little."

"This joker tried to kidnap us, but the engines failed. You don't happen to have a pair of hand-cuffs, do you?"

"No. But I have some rope."

The man reached into the seat of the helicopter and produced a length of stout twine. Frank bound the wrists of their captive.

"We'll press charges when we get to Reykjavik ourselves," Frank went on. "Please turn this man over to the police and come back for us as soon as you can."

With a smart salute, the chopper pilot pushed the prisoner into the helicopter, then climbed into his seat and took off.

"Am I glad to get rid of blondie!" Joe said. "That guy gave me the creeps."

"Pretty evil-looking character," his brother agreed, then added, "Just to double-check, I'm calling Reykjavik on the radio to tell them the helicopter's coming back."

The boys climbed back into the plane, closing the door to keep out the freezing air.

Then Frank tried to activate the radio. No luck! "Hey, Joe, look at this!"

"What's the matter?" his brother asked, coming forward along the sloping cabin.

"The radio's conked out!"

All at once a chill of realization surged over the Hardys. The pilot had sabotaged the set! Frank quickly examined it. The frequency crystal was missing.

"I don't believe he sent a rescue message at all," Frank stated. "We've really been had, Joe!"

"You mean the helicopter was following us all the time?"

"I'm afraid so. Now we're in a real pickle!"

Perspiration stood out on Joe's forehead. "What'll we do, Frank?"

"Look for the part. Our blond Viking might have dropped it on to the ice when we weren't looking."

The boys hopped out of the plane again and searched the icy surface, but in vain! Dark clouds sped in from the south, drooping lower and lower.

"Now we're in for it!" Joe muttered. He looked up to see snowflakes land on the disabled plane.

"Looks as if it might be a bad storm," Frank said, and the boys climbed back inside the cabin.

Before long, the snow fell so thickly that they could not see three feet ahead. The wind rose, and by nightfall the Hardys were caught in a howling glacial blizzard. At the same time, the temperature dropped sharply.

"We didn't come dressed for anything like this," Frank said, shivering. He glanced about for some extra clothing. Joe found a repair locker. In it were some tools and a greasy overall.

"You put that on," Frank said.

"What about you?"

"Don't worry. We'll have to start a fire to keep us warm."

"And burn the plane up?"

"We'll have to take that chance."

Although the remaining fuel in the tank might have provided the much-needed heat, Frank and Joe decided against using the highly volatile petrol. Instead, they opened the door a crack for ventilation, then tore off bits of interior woodwork with which they built a small fire on the floor of the aircraft.

The resultant warmth proved to be adequate. "At least we won't *freeze* to death now," Joe said with a wry grin.

"We'll take turns tending this fire all night," Frank suggested, glancing out of the window. Nothing could be seen but the thick covering of snow and the crack in the door revealed only the blackness of the storm's fury.

The boys agreed to sit up in shifts, feeding the fire with whatever material they could find to burn.

Near dawn, the howling winds abated, and Joe tore one of the passenger's seats apart for fuel. Suddenly he let out a cry of delight.

"Frank, I've found it!"

· 8 ·

Something Fishy

ROUSED from a fitful sleep, Frank sat up groggily and rubbed his eyes. "What did you say, Joe? You found something?"

"Sure, look at this!" Joe held up a square-shaped metal piece about the size of a coin. "The frequency crystal for the radio. It was thrown behind one of the seats!"

The news electrified Frank into action. Stepping over the glowing embers of their fire, he hastened to the front of the plane. After he had replaced the part, the radio was in perfect condition. Within seconds, Frank made contact with the radio tower at Reykjavik.

After he had told his story, the dispatcher said that an Icelandic coastguard helicopter would come to their aid.

Frank sent another message to be relayed to Chet and Biff at the Saga Hotel, saying everything was okay.

Despite the cold, the boys jumped from the plane into the deep snow. They trudged about, packing down a place for the helicopter to land. An hour later it came zooming low over the glacier.

The Hardys waved furiously to attract the pilot's attention. In minutes he had the craft on the glacier and stepped out to meet them.

"Are you hurt?" he asked.

"No, we're all right," Frank said.

"Pretty nasty accident. You were lucky to come out alive. Did you hire your plane in Reykjavik?"

Briefly Frank related what had happened, and how their kidnapper had got away.

"That was not one of our rescue copters," the airman stated.

"We decided that," Joe replied.

The pilot got into the copter, with the Hardys following.

"Can we ask you a favour?" Frank said when the craft was airborne.

"What is it?"

"Could you take us directly to Akureyri?"

The man frowned. "Why Akureyri?"

Joe explained that they were American detectives on the trail of a Rex Hallbjornsson who had answered their ad with a letter postmarked Akureyri.

The pilot grinned. "I suppose our government can do a favour for American detectives." With that, he wheeled the craft northwards.

Soon the glacier gave way to rolling meadows, with patches of green showing through the light covering of snow.

"Look sharp," the pilot said, "and let me know if you see any polar bears."

"Polar bears?" Frank asked. "I didn't know there were any in Iceland."

"Usually not," the man replied. He explained that the winter had been severe, causing a huge tongue of ice to extend from Greenland round the north coast of Iceland. It curved down along the eastern shore of the country.

"Several polar bears were carried down on the ice and they climbed on to our island. One has been caught, but some are still roaming around, as far as the west coast. They have killed sheep, and one farmer had to flee for his life."

Frank and Joe kept looking for bears, but all they saw were several small settlements with simple huts and flocks of sheep grazing on the green pastures.

Every now and then the boys spotted small ponies. When they questioned the pilot, he said, "Ponies used to be our chief means of transportation. We still use them a lot here. Icelandic ponies are strong and hardy."

The north coast came into view and the airman pointed to a bay that cut deep inland. "There's Akureyri!"

Shortly afterwards, he landed the craft in a field not far from the centre of town, and the boys got out.

"Good luck to you," the pilot said, waving goodbye. "I'll make a report to the coast guard in Reykjavik."

Frank and Joe soon found a small hotel, where they registered, cleaned up and had breakfast in their room.

Tired out from their harrowing experience, they decided to sleep for a couple of hours. But when they awakened, it was already growing dark.

Frank was annoyed with himself. "We should have told the clerk to wake us earlier," he said.

"Well," Joe replied, stretching luxuriously, "Rex Hallbjornsson probably works, and wouldn't have been home anyway."

The boys ate dinner in the hotel dining room, then set out to find the elusive Icelander. His address was a small house made of ageing brick and plaster, with a steep corrugated roof. It was located on a side street, across from a fish factory.

As they approached, Frank held his nose. "Phew!" he said. "They must be making fertilizer in there!"

Joe knocked and the door was opened by a middle aged woman, who spoke fairly good English. Yes, Hallbjornsson lived there, she said, adding that another American had been looking for him, too.

"Another?" Frank asked, preplexed.

"Yes, come this way," the landlady said, disregarding his query, and ushered the boys down the hall into a small room. Seated in a well-worn easy chair beside a small bed was a man, completely bald. His blue eyes blinked as he stared at the callers.

"We're Frank and Joe Hardy," Frank said. "Are you Rex Hallbjornsson?"

"*Ja.*" In halting English, Hallbjornsson said he was both excited and glad to see the boys. He motioned to them to sit on his bed, then excused himself to make a quick phone call.

When he returned, Frank said, "We understand you're a seaman."

"You were shipwrecked, too," Joe added. "Pretty lucky man to be alive."

Hallbjornsson nodded and proceeded to tell them a long story about his travels to Europe. None of the details agreed with the information their father had given them. And the man did not have the weather-beaten face of a sailor.

"I was shipwrecked in Spain," he went on, "and hit my head on the gunwale of the rescue boat. Then I had—what do you say?—amnesia. For five years I wandered, until one day in Turkey—"

"That was when you worked for the Greek shipping company," Joe put in, embroidering the man's false tale.

"*Ja.* You know about that?"

Frank nodded and pursued Joe's tack. "Then you went to Syria, and finally back to Iceland, right?"

"Good. I am glad you know the details," Hallbjornsson said. "That will make it easier for me to collect. How much money do I get?"

"Fifty thousand dollars," Frank replied.

The man's eyes bulged greedily. "Do you have it with you?"

"No, we don't have any money with us," Frank replied. "Naturally, we'll have to make a report to the insurance company first. But if you're the right man, you'll get what you're entitled to receive."

"*Ja, ja,*" the man murmured. "Make it soon. You see how I am living here in this cheap room. And I am getting old."

The boys said goodbye, stepped out into the hall, and made their way to the front of the house. They tried to find the landlady to question her about the other American, but she was nowhere in sight.

It was pitch dark when they stepped out into the street. Then there was an explosion of light, and darkness again, as Frank and Joe crumpled under blows to their heads!

They awakened to the pungent smell of fish. How much time had passed neither boy knew. Joe looked up, glassy-eyed, into the face of Biff Hooper who was bending over them.

"Take it easy," Biff said. "Just a bad bump on the noggin—both of you!"

Joe raised himself on one elbow and winced. He had a splitting headache. Then he looked about. Both he and Frank were on a conveyor belt.

"Where—where are we?" asked Frank.

"In a fish factory. Don't you smell it?" Biff replied. "Right across the street from Rex Hallbjornsson's."

"That faker!" Joe muttered. He swung into a sitting position and slid off the conveyor belt, rubbing his head gingerly.

Frank followed suit. "For Pete's sake," he said, "tell us what happened, Biff! How did we get here, and where did you come from?"

"Let's get out of here first, and I'll give you the whole story," Biff suggested. Walking with the Hardys to their hotel, he explained that he had become worried about their trip to Akureyri. "I had a feeling you might be ambushed there. So I got a regular flight this morning and followed you."

"You must have left before our message arrived," Frank said. "When you didn't find us here, then what?"

Biff had gone to Hallbjornsson's address, but he was not in. "The landlady told me the guy had come there only recently," he explained, "and she thought he was a foreigner."

Biff said he had wandered around town, watching the fishing boats and talking to American tourists. Then he had returned to Hallbjornsson's in the evening.

"I guess we arrived before you," Joe put in.

"Right. When I got here, I saw two men lurking in front of the house. I decided to play it by ear and stepped into an alley to see what would happen. A few minutes later you came out, and these fellows jumped you."

Frank gave a low whistle. "Now I know why

Hallbjornsson got on the phone as soon as we came in!"

"Then," Biff continued, "a siren sounded, and you should have seen those fellows go to work. They dragged you into the fish factory. I was hoping it would be the police, but it was only an ambulance going past."

"So you followed the guys?" Joe asked.

Biff said that when the men did not come out of the building, he stole in to find the Hardys on the conveyor belt. "They must have scrammed out a side door," he concluded. "Now tell me, what happened to you?"

Frank gave him a brief report, and soon they reached the hotel. Frank and Joe got ice packs to apply to the lumps on their heads, and ordered a bed to be put in their room for Biff.

Next morning after breakfast the trio caught a plane back to Reykjavik. When their taxi arrived at the Saga Hotel, a strange sight greeted them. Chet was in front of the hotel, wandering about aimlessly.

"Hey, Chet!" Frank called out. The stout boy turned slowly and stood still. "Hi," he said listlessly.

"He sure looks funny," Frank stated. He said to Chet, "Come here!"

Chet obeyed, childlike.

Biff looked closely at him. "He isn't right. Look, Frank, his eyes are dilated."

Chet's head lolled as if he was in a stupor.

"I'll bet he's been drugged!" Joe cried out. "Holy toledo! Maybe somebody's upstairs fooling around with our radio and decoder!"

"Biff, take Chet to the front desk and get a doctor for him," Frank said quickly. "Joe and I will go upstairs."

The Hardys hastened into the hotel, dashed to a lift, and let themselves out on their floor. Tiptoeing down the carpeted corridor, they came to their room.

Someone was inside, moving about!

Frank silently inserted the key in the lock, turned it, and swung the door open.

Two men, taken by surprise, whirled round—the blond pilot and his phoney rescuer!

Man of the Sea

CAUGHT red-handed, the two men glared hatefully at the Hardys before diving for the door. Frank and Joe were bowled over and a furious mêlée ensued. Punching and cursing, the intruders forced their way past the two boys.

Joe made a plunge for the blond man and got a firm grip of his wavy hair. But suddenly he was holding a wig in his hand! The thug was utterly bald!

Rex Hallbjornsson!

"Get him, Frank!"

The Hardys dashed along the corridor, but the intruders reached the lift ahead of them.

"Down the stairs, Joe!"

The boys leaped three steps at a time in an effort to beat the lift to the lobby. On the first floor the lift doors opened. Out rushed the two men and raced down an adjacent corridor into a huge ballroom filled with tables and chairs.

Grabbing chairs as they ran, the thugs flung them into the path of their pursuers.

Frank hit one and fell flat. Joe stumbled over his brother. By the time they picked themselves up, the men had vanished down a back staircase and out of the building!

Disappointed, the Hardys limped upstairs. In Biff's

room a doctor was examining Chet, a stethoscope to his ears.

"You say you had a cup of coffee with two strangers?" he asked as Frank and Joe walked in.

"That's right, Doc," replied Chet, who seemed much improved.

The Hardys introduced themselves, and the physician said, "Your friend will get over it all right. He was drugged. Do you have enemies?"

"Perhaps." Frank did not want to reveal their mission.

"Well, be careful. I am sorry such a thing had to happen to you in Iceland."

"Thanks for coming over so soon, Doc," said Biff. "What do we owe you?"

The doctor waved them off with a smile. "Nothing. Glad to help visitors." He put away his stethoscope and picked up his bag. "I would advise some exercise for you, young man. How about a swim in one of our warm water pools?"

"That'd be great!" Chet said, a big smile returning to his round face. "Where?"

"I suggest Sundholl. It is indoors, and not far from here."

The boys thanked the doctor again, and he left. Frank picked up the codebook from the safe, and they all went to the Hardys' room.

"Looks as if a cyclone hit it," Biff stated. "Are you sure one of them was Hallbjornsson?"

"No doubt about it," Joe replied. "First he looked for us at Keflavik Airport, then he followed us around the centre of town and finally kidnapped us in that plane."

The tumbling chairs barred the boys' way

75

"I feel kind of silly," Frank replied. "The blond wig and moustache disguise had us completely fooled."

The young detectives were relieved to find that the radio had not been damaged, nor had the intruders had time to locate the black box hidden in a corner of the wardrobe.

As Frank smoothed out two crumpled shirts the telephone rang.

"Okay," he said. "Quiet, fellows. I have a hunch that these are our phoney friends." Quickly he attached the recording device to the telephone and picked up the receiver. "Hello?" The boy made a wry face as he said, "Yes, sir. Thank you," and hung up.

"What was it?"

"The hotel manager. Asked us to cut down on the noise. Somebody complained."

They all laughed, and Chet quipped, "Sure, we'll be quiet, if the crooks promise, too."

The phone rang again, and this time Joe scooped it up. The voice on the other end was harsh. "Hardys, get out of Iceland!" This was followed by heavy breathing into the mouthpiece, then the caller hung up.

"Why—those dirty rats!" Joe said hotly. "They're trying to scare us out of this country!"

"Fat chance!" Chet said bravely.

"Did you recognize the voice?" asked Biff.

"The phoney Hallbjornsson! Who else?"

With the room set to rights again, the four boys had lunch, then sprawled on the beds and the two chairs, trying to find a logical answer to all that had happened.

Why did the phoney Hallbjornsson want to kidnap Frank and Joe? Obviously he had impersonated

Hallbjornsson only for that purpose. Who was he really?

Finally Chet Morton stood up and stretched. "Well, Frank and Joe, you're the brains department. Try to figure it out while Biff and I go for a warm water swim!"

"I'm for it!" said Biff.

"You can get the address at the desk," Joe advised. "Call a taxi, but be careful about drinking coffee with strangers!"

A few minutes later there was a light tap on the Hardys' door. Frank opened it. Gummi stood outside.

"Come on in," Frank invited. "What's new?"

"Plenty!" Gummi took a chair, wet his lips, and settled back with a great air of satisfaction. "I've been busy with some detective work to help you."

"Any luck so far?" Joe asked.

"I'll say! I tried to get in touch with you yesterday, but you were always out. I've found your man Rex!"

"No kidding!"

Gummi leaned forward and gestured with his hands. "Now, I won't guarantee that this is the guy you really want. He's an old seaman who's out on a fishing trawler called the *Svartfugel*—it means blackbird."

"How do we get in touch with him?" Frank asked.

Gummi explained that the trawler was at sea but that he had found out where the *Svartfugel's* skipper lived. "His name is Rensson. Perhaps his wife can tell us something about this Rex," he added.

"What are we waiting for? Let's scram!" Joe said excitedly. They hastened down to the lobby, hopped into Gummi's jeep, and drove to a neat yellow house near the waterfront.

Gummi knocked, and a tall blonde woman answered. The youth questioned her in Icelandic. "*Ja, ja,*" she replied. "Rex Mar."

"*Tack, tack,*" Gummi said and continued the interrogation. After they had left, Frank said, "What's the pitch, Gummi?"

The boy explained that Rex's name was Mar.

"Like the sea?" Joe recognized the word.

"Right. Rex is supposed to be an old salt, and full of sea stories."

"And where is he now?" Frank questioned.

"Somewhere off the northwest coast."

"We can't overlook any possible clue," Joe mused. "Maybe he changed his last name because it was too long." The boys had learned from their detective father that even the slightest clue can sometimes solve a difficult case.

Gummi dropped the boys off at the hotel and said goodbye. He would see them later.

Frank checked the desk for any messages. There were none. Then he and Joe went up to their room.

"I'm really getting worried," Frank said. "Joe, I think we ought to contact Dad and tell him what happened." He set up the radio and began to send out signals. As he did, someone pounded on the door.

"Good grief!" Joe jumped up. "What's going on?" He opened the door.

Chet Morton burst in, his face flushed with excitement. "Guess who we met?"

"We can't guess!" Frank said.

"Come with me—downstairs—now!"

"Chet, have you gone wacky?" Joe asked.

Frank turned off the radio, and the Hardys followed

their friend. When they stepped into the lift, Frank tried to question his excited friend. "Did you catch the phoney Hallbjornsson?"

"You'll see!"

A few seconds later they arrived in the lobby. There was Biff Hooper chatting gaily with Steina the stewardess!

· 10 ·

The Arctic Patrol

"HELLO, Steina. How are you?" Frank said, extending a hand to the smiling black-haired girl.

Joe, meanwhile, glanced about the lobby. "Chet, I thought you found Hallbjornsson."

"No, it was Steina we found, and guess where—at the swimming pool!"

"I was glad to meet them on my day off," said Steina. Then she turned to Chet with a wink. "Tell me, have you found any Eskimos yet?"

"No, but we've had our adventures," the stout boy replied. But this time he kept his secrets to himself. They moved to the side of the lobby and took comfortable seats round a coffee table.

Biff Hooper spoke to Frank in a low voice. "Do you think Steina might be able to help us? She probably knows lots of important people in Iceland."

"Yes, she might," Frank replied and looked at the stewardess. "Steina, we'd like to contact a man named Rex Mar on the fishing trawler *Svartfugel*. Do you know how we can get in touch with him?"

"Of course," the girl answered with a wave of her hand, as if the request were an easy one.

Joe had his doubts. "You're not kidding, are you?"

"No. My uncle Oscar will help you, I'm sure."

"Your uncle Oscar?" Chet raised his eyebrows. "Who's he?"

"Head of the Icelandic coast guard," Steina replied cocking her head coyly.

"Great!" Joe exclaimed. "Will you give us an introduction?"

Without a word the girl rose, went to a wall telephone nearby, and dialled a number. After chatting in Icelandic, she hung up and returned to the boys. "Uncle Oscar Sigtryggsson is in his office. He's expecting you."

"Thanks a million, Steina," Frank said. "Can we see him in half an hour?"

"Sure. I must be going along now," the girl replied. Waving goodbye, she left in her small car which she had parked in front of the hotel.

The boys went directly to the Hardys' room, where Frank and Joe gave their friends all the new information. Then Joe flicked on their radio and began sending signals. Fifteen minutes later they received an answer. The conversation was amiable and casual. Frank told his father that the only Hallbjornsson they had found so far proved to be the wrong one, but that they had had some trouble getting rid of him.

Afterwards, Joe rapidly figured out their father's message. Mr Hardy said that the Icelandic officials now knew that his sons were working on the astronaut case. He also warned them to beware of a Felix Musselman.

The description of this man fitted the phoney Hallbjornsson to a T. Originally a Rumanian, Musselman had fake passports for several countries. "He may be tied in with the astronaut case. Exercise extreme caution!" Mr Hardy ended.

Frank returned the radio to the hiding place in the cupboard.

"Wow!" Joe said. "So Hallbjornsson-Musselman may be an agent of a spy network mixed up in the astronaut case!"

"That's probably his primary mission," Frank reasoned. "When he found out we were coming to Iceland, his second mission was capturing us in order to get us out of the way. He must have been afraid we would get involved with the case."

"Now what?" Biff asked.

"Well, we'd better go see Steina's uncle. You and Chet stay here and stand guard. Okay?"

Soon Frank and Joe arrived at the Icelandic coast guard headquarters, called by the almost unpronounceable name of Landhelgisgaezlan. Its offices were located on Seljaveg, close to the waterfront.

"The Hardy boys?" a clerk asked as they entered.

"Right. Frank and Joe, from Bayport, U.S.A."

"Captain Sigtryggsson is waiting for you. This way, please."

He ushered the visitors into an office with nautical decorations and closed the door. They were greeted by a tall grey-haired man who rose from his chair behind a long desk.

"So," he said, after shaking hands and offering the boys two chairs, "you are American detectives!"

"Yes," said Joe. "I know we're still young, but—"

"Not at all," the captain replied. "Our best men in the coast guard are young fellows like you. We start them at fifteen, and by the time they are eighteen or nineteen, believe me, they are excellent seamen. Your father is a world-famous detective and I gather he has trained you well in his profession."

Frank and Joe felt much at home in the presence of Captain Sigtryggsson. "You have a very fine niece in Steina," said Frank, returning the compliment.

"That's what the boys tell me," the captain said with a smile. "*Ja, ja.* Now tell me, what is your question?"

"We wish to speak to a man named Rex Hallbjornsson," Frank began. "He may be Rex Mar, sailing on the trawler *Svartfugel.*"

"I think I can help you," the captain said. He rose from his chair and went to a map hanging on the wall. "The *Svartfugel* is probably fishing in waters near Snaefellsjokull."

"The glacier?" asked Joe.

"*Ja.* Right here. Perhaps ten miles offshore. We will send you up there."

The boys were thunderstruck. "Really?" asked Joe. "How?"

"On the *Thor.* Are you good seamen?"

"Pretty good," Frank replied.

The Icelander walked over to the model of a ship sitting on a table beside the boys.

"This is the *Thor,*" he explained. "You know, we don't have a large navy, but it is a good one." He said that the *Thor* was setting out the next day on a fourteen-day tour of duty in Icelandic waters.

"Your Arctic Patrol—isn't that what you call it?" Frank remarked.

The captain nodded and continued. "Naturally, I don't think it will take fourteen days to find the *Svartfugel.*"

"Then how'll we get back?" Joe asked.

"We'll arrange that later. Perhaps on the *Albert*. It is a smaller boat on its way back to Keflavik from a two-week tour." The captain sat down at his desk again and looked straight at the boys. "You are working on the McGeorge case, too!"

Frank and Joe were startled. "Yes. It's top secret," Frank managed to reply.

"Of course. It is most unusual to have civilians involved. But perhaps you can be of help."

"We already have a clue," Frank said, and told about the leather glove. "It matches a similar one we got at the base in Keflavik." He explained how they had found it, and when.

"Excellent. But Major McGeorge disappeared earlier than that. We searched the area of the sulphur pit."

"Perhaps he came back," Frank offered. "Maybe his captors threatened to throw him in if he didn't tell his NASA secrets."

"A good possibility," the captain admitted. "We'll look into this."

The boys rose and thanked him, promising to be at his office at two o'clock the next afternoon.

"Captain Carl Magnusson, the skipper of the *Thor*, will be here to meet you," their host said as he ushered the Hardys to the door.

When they returned to their hotel, they found Chet and Biff brimming with excitement. "Here's another letter answering your ad in the paper," Biff said.

Frank opened it. A Hallbjornsson living in Hafnarfjordur thought that he might be a relative of the man called Rex.

Frank shook his head. "Now we've got two leads to follow."

"What did the coast guard chief have to say?"

"We're leaving on one of their boats tomorrow."

"That was fast. Well, suppose Chet and I go down to Hafnarfjordur and investigate the other guy?"

"Great idea!"

Chet and Biff departed the next morning, and at two o'clock the Hardys, travelling as light as they could, appeared at Captain Sigtryggsson's office.

There they met a tall, handsome man in his late thirties—Carl Magnusson, the skipper of the *Thor*. After handshakes, Captain Magnusson said, "Come with me, men. We're on our way."

He took them down to the harbour where the *Thor*, a spotless white cutter, was waiting.

"She's a big ship," Frank observed.

"Two hundred and six feet long—nine hundred and twenty tons," the captain explained.

As they stepped from the dock down a ladder to board the cutter, Frank and Joe noticed a 57mm gun mounted on the front of the boat. Behind the gun deck, at a lower level, lay a large rubber raft with two bullet-shaped pontoons on either side.

"We use that for transfers in rough weather," said Captain Magnusson, who had noticed the boys' inquisitive looks.

They followed the skipper up and down a maze of companionways to his quarters. A comfortable ward-room was located forward, and the captain's bunk was to the left. On the right side were quarters for the visitors.

"Make yourselves at home," Captain Magnusson said.

"Do you suppose you can find the *Svartfugel* for us?" Joe asked, putting down his bag.

"I think so, if we don't run into any foreign poachers."

The skipper explained that recently some ships of foreign registry had been sneaking through the twelve-mile limit. "But we spot them on radar," he continued, "and get them!"

"Then what do you do?" Frank asked.

"Bring them back to port and fine them. They cannot get away with our codfish!"

Frank and Joe looked about the ship. Several seamen, about their own age, were busy hosing and swabbing the decks. Some of them spoke English, and the boys chatted with them about their training and their ambitions.

Then they strolled about, looking at the colourful Icelandic coastline slipping past.

"You know," Joe said to his brother, "I'm beginning to enjoy our trip!"

"Well, let's hope we're successful," Frank replied with a grin.

About sundown, Snaefell Glacier came into view, its bare, rugged peaks bathed in orange light. Suddenly Captain Magnusson, who stood on the bridge, beckoned to the Hardys. They hastened up a ladder and were at his side a moment later.

"Look over there!" the skipper said tersely, peering through his binoculars. "A poacher! She's in our territorial waters!"

He handed Frank the binoculars, so high-powered that they brought the fishing trawler seemingly close enough to touch. She was about forty-five feet long and bore the name *Tek*.

Frank surveyed her from stem to stern. Five crewmen

could be seen on deck. Suddenly he gasped. "Joe, there he is!"

"Who?"

"Musselman. I'll bet anything!"

Over the Waves

JOE took the glasses to confirm Frank's suspicion. No doubt about it! The face was that of the bogus Hallbjornsson!

"Captain Magnusson," Frank said, "there's a wanted man on the *Tek*!"

"The entire trawler is wanted," the captain replied with a grim smile. "She's poaching in Icelandic waters."

He dispatched a radio message commanding the *Tek* to stop. Then he took the binoculars and watched. Suddenly he gave an exclamation in Icelandic. The trawler was turning about and racing towards the open sea!

"She's trying to get away!" Frank cried out.

If Captain Magnusson was startled by the poacher's action, he did not show it. Calmly he gave the order for full speed ahead.

Much to the surprise of Frank and Joe, the fleeing boat had exceptional speed. Churning up a greenish-white wake, it high-tailed straight west. But it was no match for the *Thor*. The cutter gained with every minute.

Finally the ships came side by side. Captain Magnusson, using a loud-hailer, ordered the fleeing boat to stop for boarding. "You are under arres !" he thundered.

Beckoning to the Hardy boys and two seamen, he boarded the poacher and was met by her irate skipper, who declared in broken English, "You cannot stop us. It is illegal !"

"You are in Icelandic fishing waters," Captain Magnusson replied evenly. "And you are not Icelandic."

"I am thirteen miles off your shore !"

"Only ten by my calculations. And my calculations are what count." Magnusson asked curtly, "Why did you flee when I radioed for you to stop?"

"I did not hear your message."

"Then you should get your radio repaired. What you did was dangerous; you could have been shot."

The captain accompanied the poacher to his bridge, where he obtained the fishing boat's registration and other vital details. Then Magnusson said, "I think you are harbouring a fugitive from Iceland and will conduct a search."

The poacher glared at him in rage. "How dare you ! You cannot do this !"

"But we will," Magnusson retorted. He motioned to Frank and Joe, along with his two crewmen. The four conducted a painstaking search for the fugitive, expecting to see Musselman pop out of a cupboard or jump out of a locker at any moment. But the bald-headed spy could not be found.

"Maybe he's hiding in some kind of a container," Frank said.

"You mean under the boat?" Joe asked.

"It's possible."

Although they searched the sides of the boat for any

tell-tale line leading under the water, their efforts were fruitless.

"Come on. We'll give the crew's quarters one more look," Frank said.

The bunks were thoroughly checked to see if anyone was hiding under a false mattress. Each mattress was thumped, but all were genuine. No Musselman!

The crewmen left. Frank and Joe gave the last bunk one more look. A small bit of paper stuck between the wall and the blanket caught Frank's eye. He plucked it from its hiding place.

"Holy crow! Joe, look at this!" It had been torn from an Icelandic newspaper.

"It's our ad!" Joe exclaimed. "The one Mussleman answered!"

"See, we were right!" Frank said. "He was on this boat!"

"One thing is sure," Joe muttered. "That crook isn't here now, and if he is, he certainly is well hidden."

The boys decided not to tell Captain Magnusson about their clue. When they returned to the bridge, the skipper asked, "Any luck?"

"No. We couldn't find him." Frank observed the poaching captain all the while. He did not twitch a muscle, and his eyes remained cold and angry. If he knew of Musselman's presence, he gave no indication.

Magnusson called for his first lieutenant, who vaulted over the rail.

"Hjalmar, take this boat to Reykjavik. We will follow!"

After warning his prisoners not to do anything rash, Magnusson returned to the *Thor*, with the Hardys at his heels. The coast guard cutter and its captive turned about and were under way towards the Iceland-ic capital city.

In the captain's cabin Frank and Joe talked with the skipper. "What'll happen to these fellows now?" Frank asked.

"They will be fined, and their fish confiscated."

"But what about our search for Rex Mar?" Joe asked.

A broad smile came over the captain's face. "I knew you would ask that question. Everything has been taken care of."

"How?"

"We will pass the *Albert* about two o'clock this morning. We will transfer you for the continuation of your search for Rex Mar."

"Great!" Frank said. "Thank you, sir."

"But it will not be as easy as boarding the poacher," the skipper went on. "You see how rough it is getting? We will have to transfer you by raft."

The *Thor* had begun to pitch and yaw. As night settled over the sea, the wind blew harder.

"We may be in for a little rough weather," the captain declared. "But you are good sailors, right?"

Joe hoped that neither of them would get seasick. But he felt a little queasy already. Dinner with the crew, however, settled Joe's stomach. The boys joined the young crewmen in a hearty meal of roast lamb and boiled potatoes. The coffee was black and piping hot.

When they returned to the deck again, the swell was even greater, and the ship rolled and rocked.

"Get some sleep now," the captain advised them. "We will wake you when the *Albert* comes in sight."

Frank and Joe slipped into their bunks and the

rolling sea lulled them to sleep in no time at all. The next thing Frank knew, there was a hand on his shoulder.

"Come. We have the *Albert* in sight," Captain Magnusson said. "You have your gear ready?"

"Yes, we're all packed," Frank replied as Joe rose sleepily from his bunk.

On deck the fresh wind with the bite of glacier snow assailed the Hardys' nostrils, and they were instantly wide awake.

In the distance the lights of the *Albert* bobbed up and down. Captain Magnusson gave an order, and a searchlight atop the mast shone down on the sea in a yellow brilliant cone.

"There comes the raft now," the skipper said, pointing over the sea. At first it looked like a cork; then, as it drew closer, Frank and Joe saw that it was identical to the one lashed on the forward deck of the *Thor*. Three seamen, using long oars as paddles, propelled the raft towards them.

On the *Thor* a section of rail was lifted up, and as the raft drew alongside, one of the sailors hurled a line aboard.

"Everything is perfectly safe," Captain Magnusson assured the boys.

Frank wondered. The raft rose and fell on each wave, coming even with the deck of the *Thor*, then dropping ten feet into the trough.

Clutching their bags, the Hardys waited. Up came the raft. Joe stepped in, and it went down like a lift. Up it came again for Frank. Then the line was cast off, and they were gliding over the frigid sea.

The raft resembled a small insect struggling in the

rolling waves. Overhead, a silver moon illuminated the snow-capped mountains along the shore.

The young seamen paddled hard. Their oars flashed as they dug deep into the brine.

Frank's eyes scanned the ocean. Suddenly he leaned over to Joe. "Something else is out there!"

"Where?" asked Joe, looking about in the- stiff breeze.

"I saw a wake!"

Joe peered intently, but could spot nothing. "What do you suppose it was?"

"A small boat, or a raft, maybe with an engine!"

Presently the *Albert* loomed up black beside the raft. A section of its deck rail also had been lifted, but Frank Hardy was not ready to board yet. Crouched in the raft, he looked up at the captain and shouted, "I think I saw another small boat out there, skipper. I'd like permission to look for it!"

"What? Speak slower, please. I am not too good with English."

Frank repeated his request, and the captain called back, "Wait. I will try first to find it on my radar." He went into the control room, while the raft, banging against the side of the *Albert*, rose and fell with a dizzying motion.

The seamen did their best to hold everything steady, and two more aboard the *Albert* clung to the line which had been thrown to them.

Then suddenly it happened. A huge wave bore down on them. It hit the raft while it was in a deep trough, and after it had passed over the clinging occupants, Frank Hardy was gone!

·12·

A Mysterious Offer

A HEAD bobbed to the surface beside the *Albert*, then disappeared beneath the sullen waves again. Instantly two of the crewmen sprang overboard, while the third restrained Joe from diving in after his brother.

Someone on the deck flashed a powerful light on the turbulent waters and Joe saw Frank in the firm grasp of the two seamen. His face was pale, his eyes shut.

Frank was pushed into the raft, then hoisted quickly to the deck of the *Albert*. Seconds later, on a rising wave, Joe stepped safely aboard.

The *Albert*'s captain, a square-jawed man named Holmquist, immediately applied artificial respiration to Frank, and finally the boy's eyes fluttered open. The captain helped him to his feet. "You tried to swallow all of the North Atlantic, but it cannot be done!"

"I sure did go under, like a sinker," Frank said, shivering from the icy water.

"Come down below and change into some dry clothes," Captain Holmquist said.

Still groggy, Frank followed him and Joe into a warm cabin. There he was supplied with seaman's clothes, while his own were hung up to dry. Then the three sat down at the table in the skipper's quarters.

"Did you see the other raft?" was Joe's first question.

"Something was out there," said Captain Holmquist. "But a raft—I doubt that. Probably a whale. We have them in these waters, you know."

"We can't look for it any more, then?" Frank asked.

The skipper shrugged. "There's nothing on our radar now. Anyway, our mission is to find the *Svartfugel*, right?"

"That's what we came for." Frank managed a grin. "You think you can find her?"

"I found her already. She is located on our chart. In the morning you will have your trawler served up for breakfast!"

Frank and Joe laughed at the captain's good humour and thanked him again for his help. Then they retired to their bunks and fell fast asleep.

The *Albert* was alive with the sound of ship's noises when the Hardys wakened. Footsteps sounded on gangways, and the smell of bacon and hot coffee drifted into their cabin.

By this time Frank's clothes had dried. The boys dressed hurriedly and found their way to the breakfast table. The seamen joked about Frank's ducking.

"He went down like a seal!" said one of his rescuers with a chuckle.

"More like a walrus I would say," Frank replied, and took his place at the square table beside Captain Holmquist.

"Now you will have something to tell back home," the skipper said.

The Hardys had soft-boiled eggs, cereal and milk. In the centre of the table stood a tall jug of cod-liver oil. After watching the seamen help themselves, Frank and Joe each took a large spoonful, washed down by a second glass of milk.

"Now you're all set for the *Svartfugel*," Captain Holmquist said. "She's off our port bow, if you'd like to take a look."

The boys hastened to the deck and looked across the leaden waters towards a tubby little trawler. The captain followed with his loud-hailer. In Icelandic he asked if Rex Mar was aboard.

"*Ja, ja*," came the answer.

The ocean was calm enough for the boats to pull alongside and soon Frank and Joe dropped on the deck of the *Svartfugel*.

"Take your time," Captain Holmquist said. "We will wait for you."

The small boat had only a crew of five, and its skipper called below decks for Rex Mar. The man appeared, wearing a brown sweater. Its turtle-neck set off a square, weather-beaten face, topped by a patch of flowing grey hair beneath a seaman's cap.

Frank Hardy extended a hand in greeting. Rex Mar's looked like a bear's paw in comparison.

"I'm Frank Hardy. Do you speak English, Mr Mar?"
"Yes."

Joe introduced himself and said, "There's something we would like you to do."

"No, I won't do it!" Mar said and turned down the narrow gangway.

"Wait a minute!" Frank called out. "You won't do what?"

The old fellow regarded them grimly through watery blue eyes. "I won't do what you want me to do. I was asked before. The answer is still No!"

Frank and Joe exchanged puzzled glances. Finally Frank said, "Mr Mar, we only want you to identify yourself."

Rex Mar closed one eye suspiciously. "Rex Mar is the name, and that's all."

From the rail of the *Albert*, Holmquist looked down with a slight smile of amusement on his face. In rapid-fire Icelandic he spoke with the old seaman. Instantly Mar seemed more ready to co-operate.

"What is it you want to know?"

"We are looking for Rex Hallbjornsson," Frank said.

"Why?"

"Somebody left him some insurance money."

The man's face lit up like the aurora borealis. "Rex Hallbjornsson. *Ja*, I am the one!"

Frank and Joe beamed at each other and shook hands vigorously. "Frank, we've done it!" said Joe. "We've found our man!"

But the elder Hardy boy was not convinced that the man standing before them was the real Rex Hallbjornsson.

"Tell us," he said, "how, why and when did you change your name?"

The seaman took a bucket, turned it upside down, and used it for a seat. Frank and Joe leaned against the capstan and listened to his tale.

Mar said that he once was shipwrecked off the coast of France. After he had been rescued, his name Hallbjornsson—hard to spell for foreigners—had been recorded incorrectly.

"I went to Spain," he said, "where my name was spelled wrong again. What a mess it was! The *b, j* and the *l*'s were all mixed up. I don't think anybody could sneeze the name!"

Joe chuckled at the description. "So you changed it?"

"Yes. I chose the name Mar because it means sea. You see, I had to do it. In Spain they thought I was a spy since all the names on my papers were spelled differently. And you know," he said, rubbing the side of his nose, "somebody still thinks I'm a spy."

"Who?" asked Frank.

"Two men. They came to see me."

"About what?" Joe wanted to know.

"About a job." Mar explained that someone wanted the help of a man who knew the coast of Iceland intimately. "But I didn't take it!"

The Hardys were immediately alerted by the strange request. Frank said, "If they ever come to you with that proposal again, will you let me know?"

"All right," Mar replied, glancing up at Captain Holmquist.

Convinced that Mar was indeed Rex Hallbjornsson, Frank told him that he had been named the beneficiary in a life insurance policy paying fifty thousand dollars. The old fellow's jaw dropped, and he stood up, looking bewildered.

When the name of the policyholder was given, a faraway look came into his eyes. He told the Hardys that it was a man he saved from drowning. "Now he will make my old age a comfortable one," Mar said with feeling.

Frank suggested that he come with them, leaving the trawler at once. "You'll have to sign some papers in Reykjavik, and then we'll try to get your money as soon as possible, Mr Mar."

The *Svartfugel's* skipper gave permission for his crewman to leave, and Rex Mar and the boys boarded the *Albert*.

It was late in the afternoon when the coast guard boat pulled into Reykjavik Harbour. The Hardys thanked Captain Holmquist and his crew, then stepped on to the dock. The old seaman followed. A taxi took them into town. Mar was let off at his lodgings, with instructions to await word from the boys, and Frank and Joe continued on to their hotel.

After hastening upstairs, they rapped on the door of Chet's room. No answer. They went to their own room and phoned the desk. Had Biff and Chet left any messages?

The answer nearly floored them. Their friends had checked out of the hotel the day before.

"What's going on?" Frank asked the clerk.

The man did not know, except that he had observed the pair talking with Gummi shortly before they signed out.

Instantly Joe got on the phone to their Icelandic friend. "Gummi, where are Chet and Biff?"

"You should know! They left after getting your message!"

·13·

Eavesdroppers

"WE didn't send any message!" Joe exclaimed, holding the receiver so that Frank could follow the conversation.

"Oh no!" Gummi said that Chet and Biff had returned from an unsuccessful visit to Hafnarfjordur and shortly afterwards received word ostensibly from Frank and Joe to meet them somewhere.

"Good grief! That was a hoax! Tell me, where were they to meet us?"

"They didn't say. Chet only told me it was a secret."

The Hardys were worried. Obviously this was an attempt by Musselman to split the ranks and deal with them individually.

Frank took the phone from Joe. "If we only had a clue! A single clue! Think hard, Gummi. Didn't Chet or Biff drop some kind of hint where they were going?"

"Yes, Chet did," Gummi said after a thoughtful pause. "He mentioned that he had better get some seasick pills."

"That's all?"

"Yes."

"Well, if you remember anything else, Gummi, give us a ring, will you?"

"Sure thing."

Frank hung up.

"At least we know they were going somewhere by boat," Joe said.

"Don't jump to conclusions, Joe. The deduction might be true, and it might not."

"If it were," Joe reasoned, "perhaps Chet and Biff went somewhere off the coast of Snaefell Glacier where you saw the mysterious raft!"

"There's only one thing to do now—inform the police and the coast guard," Frank said crisply. "I'll call them right away."

After he had notified the authorities about their missing friends, Frank telephoned Captain Magnusson. The skipper told him that the poachers had been heavily fined. The *Tek* was also searched again, but the only thing found was a coil of fine nylon line attached to an underwater hook. No sign of a man fitting the description of Musselman.

Then Frank told the captain about Chet and Biff.

"The *Thor* is going on patrol again tonight, Frank," Magnusson said. "If they are anywhere in the Icelandic waters, we'll find them!"

"Thanks, Captain." Frank hung up and turned to Joe. Quickly he told him the news. "Obviously the nylon line was for towing something," he concluded.

"Yes, but we didn't see any boat behind the *Tek*," replied Joe.

"I know. It's a puzzler all right."

"What's next?"

"Let's have something to eat, then we'll radio Dad."

After a quick supper the boys contacted their father. They got through to Texas immediately.

Frank reported that they had found Rex Mar, and

Mr Hardy congratulated them. Then he spelled out in detail an affidavit, which Frank was to prepare for the man to sign. The boy copied down the document, then told about Chet and Biff's mysterious disappearance.

Mr Hardy expressed his worry, and casually switched to code. He was sure that the boys' disappearance was tied in with the astronaut case.

"If you find Musselman, you will probably find Biff and Chet," Mr Hardy advised.

After their father signed off, the boys tried to map out a plan of action.

"We're really stuck," Joe muttered. "The only clue is that Chet and Biff may be on a boat, and we can't chase them on the ocean."

"The coast guard'll have to do it," Frank admitted. "But where to find Musselman? As far as he's concerned, we don't have any clues at all!"

Joe sighed. "How about going over to Rex Mar with the affidavit? There's not much else we can do tonight."

"Okay."

The boys walked the short distance to the sailor's house. He occupied a large room on the first floor.

Mar greeted them cordially, putting down his pipe on a small table to shake hands with them. He offered them chairs, then sank back on to a sofa and sent ringlets of smoke from his pipe.

"You look pretty happy, Mr Mar," Frank said jovially.

"I am a rich man."

"You will be, after a few formalities," Joe agreed as Frank produced the affidavit.

Rex Mar held it at arm's length, scrutinizing every

word, then he took the pen proffered by Frank in his gnarled fingers and scratched his name at the bottom of the paper.

"After this is processed in the States," Frank said, "you will receive your money."

"Fine," Mar replied. Then he looked at the Hardys seriously. "I have something to tell you," he said as Frank returned the affidavit to his pocket. "They were here again to see me."

"Who were?"

"The men who think I am a spy. You asked me to tell you."

"Thanks for the tip," Frank replied, leaning forward in his chair. "What did they say?"

"They want me to get a boat and help them take something out of the country illegally!"

"What did you tell them?"

"I said I wanted to think it over. They will return in an hour for my answer. I was about to call you when you rang my bell."

"Mr Mar, what did these fellows look like?" Joe queried.

"One was bald, short and heavy-set. The other was black-haired with a rather long nose. They are due here any minute."

Frank and Joe exchanged glances. There was no doubt in their minds that the men were Musselman and his pal.

"What do you want me to do?" Mar asked.

"Go along with their proposition," Frank said.

"But it is illegal!"

"That's just it. We might be able to uncover a nefarious scheme."

Frank and Joe quickly hid in the cupboard . . .

"All right. I will do as you say. You go now and I'll tell you later exactly what they want me to do."

Joe looked around. "I have a better idea. We'll listen in." He pointed to a small cupboard. "Can we both get in there?"

Mar sucked on his pipe, sending out a billow of smoke. "I think so."

He opened the cupboard, which was rank with the odour of old clothes. A few tools were stacked in one corner. The boys squeezed in. A narrow crack between the floor and the bottom of the door would allow enough air to keep them from suffocating.

"When they come, I will get them to leave as soon as possible," Rex Mar said.

Frank coughed a bit, and Joe's throat burned, as he inhaled the pipe smoke which drifted over the room like an early-morning heavy fog.

The doorbell rang. As Mar went to answer it, Frank and Joe ducked into the cupboard. Seconds later they heard Mar return with a visitor. The voice was unmistakable. *Musselman!*

Frank and Joe hardly dared to breathe, lest any sound give away their eavesdropping hideout.

"All right now," said Mar. "Tell me just what do you want me to do?"

"How many times must I tell you?" the caller replied impatiently. "I want you to hire a small fishing boat."

"And then what?"

"Are you absolutely daft, old man?" snapped Musselman. "Go to the coast near Snaefellsjokull and I'll be waiting for you there. Look, here's the spot."

Frank and Joe heard the crinkling of paper as a map was spread out on the table.

"Yes. I see it," said Mar. "But I cannot sail such a boat all alone."

"Then get yourself a crew. I will pay you well."

"How many will you pay for?"

"Three good men. It may be a rough trip."

Joe could not resist whispering to his brother. Putting his lips close to Frank's ear, he said, "Let's turn the tables on this goon! We'll go with Mar, and at the same time we can hunt for Biff and Chet!"

There came the scraping sound of chairs pushed back from the table as the caller prepared to leave.

"I'm leaving Reykjavik early tomorrow morning," Musselman said, then added, "I can trust you to take care of this assignment?"

"*Ja*."

"Then here is an advance payment. Get a seaworthy boat and do it as quickly as possible."

Joe longed for the man to depart. The stuffy air in the cupboard and the tobacco smoke filled his lungs. How good it would be to inhale some fresh air!

"Goodbye," Mar said, and the boys heard the door close. But before they could open the cupboard, the lock clicked shut.

Frank tried to turn the knob and stifled a gasp. They were trapped!

·14·

A Perfect Disguise

"Joe, we're locked in!"

"Holy crow! Were we ever fooled by Rex Mar! Frank, what are we going to do?"

The boys talked in hushed whispers.

"Let's not panic. We'll get out. Easy does it, Joe."

"Yes. But suppose they're out there waiting for us?"

"That's the chance we'll have to take," Frank replied, feeling about the dark cupboard.

"What are you looking for?" Joe asked.

His brother said that he had seen some tools. Maybe one of them would be of use. By this time it had become insufferably hot. Perspiration began to drip from their faces.

"If we had only carried a torch!" Joe muttered. He pressed his ear close to the door. There was no sound outside. If Mar was in league with the criminals, perhaps he had left with Musselman.

"Joe, I've found something!"

"What is it?"

"A jack."

"Good. Now if we had a two-by-four—" With both hands Joe rummaged on the floor of the cupboard. "Here's something—a block of wood!"

"How long?"

"Not long enough."

Frank's hand touched a large hammer. "Now I think we have it, Joe!"

Pushing the old clothes to one side, he placed the base of the jack against the rear wall of the cupboard. Joe held the block of wood and the hammer end to end between the door and the head of the jack. They fitted loosely.

Using an old spanner, Frank activated the jack. *Click! Click! Click!* Their improvised battering ram was wedged tightly between the back of the cupboard and the door. Frank applied more pressure. The door creaked a little. Could their device spring the lock?

Click! Click! Crash! The lock was forced and the door sprang open.

The room was not empty after all. There sat Rex Mar, puffing on his pipe and smiling.

Open-mouthed, Frank and Joe looked at him in amazement. "What—what—? Why did you do that?" Frank asked.

Joe's fists were clenched in anger. "You nearly suffocated us. Is this your idea of fun?"

The old sailor motioned the boys to simmer down. "You proved yourselves," he said. "I wanted to see what you would do in a difficult situation."

"Then you knew the jack was in the cupboard?" Frank asked.

Mar nodded. He went to the refrigerator and pulled out a bottle of cold water. Frank and Joe each gulped down a glassful.

Now calm after their ordeal, Frank asked, "Was that the blond man you spoke to?"

"Right. Did you see him through the keyhole?"

"How could we! The key was in it," Joe said caustically.

"Yes. I forgot."

"What was his name?"

"He did not tell me."

"How about your crew?" Frank went on.

"You two, of course," Mar replied. "I told you, you proved yourselves."

Frank and Joe nodded to each other. They would have to level with Mar.

"We'll need disguises," Frank said.

"What for?" The old seaman looked surprised.

"Judging from the voice of your visitor, he might be a member of a gang we're after. We'll get the third crewman, too, an Icelandic friend of ours by the name of Gudmundur. You can depend on him."

"Good." Mar asked no further questions. "I will look for a suitable boat. When I find one, I will call you at your hotel."

The boys agreed and bid the seaman goodbye. Even though it was very late, they stopped at police headquarters to find out if any word had been received about the missing Biff and Chet. The report was negative.

Glum and disappointed, Frank and Joe returned to the Saga Hotel. They sat quietly in their room for a while, mulling over the entire situation.

"I must confess," Frank said, "that I'm still not thoroughly convinced about Rex Mar."

"I know," Joe said. "We're putting ourselves in his hands. If he turns out to be one of Musselman's guys, we're really in for it."

"On the other hand, if he's in league with Musselman, why did he tell us about this 'illegal' job to begin with? Why did he let us know that he knew Musselman, and why did he let us overhear their conversation?"

"Search me."

"Well, with Gummi it'll be three against one on that trawler. I think we can handle the situation."

A phone call brought the Icelandic boy to the hotel early the next morning. "Any word from Biff and Chet yet?" he asked as he came in the door.

"No. But it seems we found the right Hallbjornsson."

"Great! Now your official mission is over, and once you find Chet and Biff you can have some fun in Iceland."

"Well, there's a complication," Joe replied. "The fake Hallbjornsson is trying to get the real Hallbjornsson involved in a smuggling job and—"

Gummi interrupted the boy with a gesture of his hand. "Now look, fellows! You gave me that story about being detectives on an insurance case, and I bought it. Now you're overdoing it. I'm not exactly stupid, you know. Either you level with me, or I'll exit right here and now!"

"Calm down, Gummi," Frank said. "We are American detectives on an insurance case, and everything we told you is true. But we got involved in something else—" He exchanged a quick glance with Joe, who nodded his agreement.

"Well?" Gummi still had a suspicious look on his face.

"Will you promise to keep it to yourself? It's a top-secret affair concerning both the American and the Icelandic governments."

112

"I'll keep quiet."

Frank and Joe revealed everything to their friend. When the Icelander heard the story, he eagerly pledged his support as a crewman.

"I might be able to help my country, too," he said enthusiastically. "Are you going to tell the coast guard?"

"Yes. I'll phone Captain Sigtryggsson and let him in on our plans. He knows we are working on the case," Frank said.

"When do we start?" Gummi asked.

"As soon as Rex Mar finds a boat," Joe replied.

"And you and I will have to work up disguises," Frank put in. "We'll go down to the barber-shop right now and have our hair dyed. Gummi, can you get us some old seamen's clothes?"

"Sure. I have some at home. Come on over when you're finished."

The boys parted at the lift in the lobby, and Frank and Joe went to the barber-shop in the basement, where they had their hair dyed a reddish colour. False eyebrows and cheek pads completed their disguise. Grinning contentedly, they took a taxi to Gummi's house.

"Boy, if I didn't know better, you could have fooled me," he said admiringly. "Here, put these on!" He handed them well-worn work clothes.

"Let's go down to the harbour and see if we can spot our friend Mar," Frank suggested when they had changed.

"God idea. We can try our disguise on him," Joe said.

All three scrambled into Gummi's jeep. On the way,

the Icelandic boy said, "One more thing. Don't speak English when those thugs are around!" He taught them a few Icelandic words, which, if muttered repetitively, would fool any foreigner.

They parked the car in the busy harbour area and strolled along the waterfront.

"Look!" Joe said after a while. "Isn't that Rex Mar over there?"

"Right. He's checking out a trawler!" Frank exclaimed.

Mar was haggling with a sailor aboard a small fishing boat. Then he turned, smiled and stepped back on to the dock.

"Let's go!" Frank said, and they walked directly towards the approaching seaman. Mar showed no sign of recognition. When they passed him, Frank deliberately stumbled into him. The man teetered back. Frank mumbled a few Icelandic words, and the boys walked on.

Out of earshot, Joe let out a muted whoop. "We did it, Frank! That old salt didn't recognize us at all!"

The boys turned to see Mar sizing up the trawler. She was about thirty-five feet long, broad of beam, with a squat, sturdy look. As the old fellow turned to go, the boys accosted him.

Mar's eyebrows nearly raised to the peak of his cap as Frank revealed their identity. Then Gummi was introduced. They shook hands.

"We saw you make a deal," Frank said. "When do we set sail?"

"This afternoon, if you're ready."

"We are. Okay, Gummi?"

"Right."

"We will meet on board at five o'clock," Mar said, then hastened off to lay in supplies.

At five-thirty that afternoon the little boat named *Asdis* churned out of Reykjavik Harbour and along the coast in the direction of Snaefellsjokull. Once safely at sea, Frank and Joe removed their cheek pads and eyebrows and fell to helping skipper Mar with chores on the deck.

By eight o'clock a stiff wind kicked up white-caps on the sea, and the boat began to rock. On the bridge, Mar regaled Frank and Joe with stories of Iceland.

On the wall behind the wheel was the Icelandic coat of arms. It showed a shield, which Frank recognized as the insignia on Icelandic coins. Standing on the right side of the shield was a giant, holding a staff. On the left side was a bull. Over the top loomed a dragon and a huge bird.

"What does it mean?" Frank asked.

"There's a legend behind it," Mar said, and Gummi nodded. As the storm worsened, the Hardys were told the story of a bad Viking king named Haraldur Gormsson, who wanted to conquer Iceland.

"But he realized he must send a scout to look the place over," the old seaman explained, "so he sent his lieutenant, who turned himself into a whale to swim around the island."

"Like a spy submarine," Joe said.

Leaning against the side of the cabin for balance, Gummi laughed. "There was plenty of magic in those times. Same as today."

"Do you expect us to believe that?" asked Frank.

Rex Mar made a face. "Believe what you want, but

that whale was met on the east shore by a furious dragon, breathing poisoned fire. The dragon was also accompanied by giant worms and snakes, so the whale withdrew."

Gummi took up the yarn. "Next he went to the north shore. There he found a huge bird, like a falcon, whose wings touched the mountains on both sides of a fjord. With him were other birds, big and small."

"And they scared the whale?" asked Joe.

"What else?" Mar chuckled. "On the west side, the whale was met by a bull, who came snorting and charging into the seas."

"All alone?" Joe asked.

"Oh no," said Gummi. "With him were other guardians of the island—the trolls and the hidden people. Naturally he scrammed out of there!"

Rex Mar scratched his head at the colloquial English which he had not heard before.

"On the south shore," Gummi continued, "the whale saw a giant with an iron staff in his hand. This guy was taller than a mountain, and with him were many other giants. Nothing was left on the shore now but sand, glaciers and heavy seas. So the whale withdrew and reported what he had seen to King Gormsson."

"Did the king tackle Iceland after that?" Joe asked.

"Not on your life! Today these four creatures are known as the defenders of Iceland."

The sea had become so rough by now that the skipper suggested everyone go below. He throttled back the engine and headed into the wind. But suddenly the gale shifted and the *Asdis* rocked violently.

Mar's face was impassive and showed no sign of fear, but Gummi was worried. "I've never seen a storm like this before," he said. He had barely finished speaking when the *Asdis* pitched forward. The entire crew was thrown to the deck!

· 15 ·

A Bad Break

WAVES crashed over the deck, nearly swamping the *Asdis*. The boys battened down the hatches while Rex Mar switched on the pump engine.

"I could do with some of Chet's seasick pills now!" Frank shouted above the howling gale.

The little trawler endured the buffeting by the elements for two hours before the storm let up a bit. Then the winds tapered off gradually, giving the crew time for catnaps before dawn lit up the jagged grey coastline.

After a breakfast of cold lamb, bread and milk, the boys joined Rex Mar at the wheel. "We'll relieve you for a while, sir," Frank said. "You need some rest."

The Icelander accepted the offer, but would not go below, instead he stretched out on a bench and fell fast asleep.

While Frank held the wheel, Gummi read the chart spread out on a table. "X marks the spot where we're to put ashore," he said.

Frank checked the co-ordinates. "Wow! Look here!" he called to Joe. "This is very near the place where we transferred to the *Albert!*"

The sturdy *Asdis* rode the waves for another hour,

then Gummi woke the skipper. "I think this is where we take her in," he said.

The old man stood up stiffly, looked at the map, then peered over the water at the sullen coastline. "*Ja.* There's the inlet."

Frank spun the wheel and guided the trawler towards shore. Near the mouth of the stony inlet, Joe exclaimed, "Hey, Frank! A rubber raft!" He reached for the binoculars on a shelf and whipped them to his eyes. "And it has a small outboard!"

"I didn't see a whale after all!" Frank said.

Joe moved towards the radio. "Shall I contact Captain Magnusson now?"

"No. If Musselman is listening in on our wavelength, it would give us away," Frank replied.

Mar made the *Asdis* fast to the makeshift dock in the inlet and said, "Now we will have to wait until the man contacts us."

"Meantime I'm going to check on that raft," Frank said.

While Gummi scrambled up a low ridge near the shore to keep a look-out, Frank and Joe climbed round the jagged shore to where the raft bobbed in a small rock-strewn inlet.

Joe was first to step into the craft. "It has a water-tight canopy!" he exclaimed. "I've never seen one like this before. And look, Frank, these pontoons aren't metal. They're rubber, with valves like ballast tanks."

"You're right. See these little compressed air containers?"

Joe grew even more excited. "Of course! This is the underwater gimmick we suspected. Musselman was towed by the *Tek* until they came near this landing spot. Then he surfaced and beat it for the shore!"

"At the same time we were transferring to the *Albert*. That was a close call for him!"

Frank and Joe left the raft as they had found it and returned to Gummi with their information.

"Those guys are no amateurs," the Icelandic boy said. "We'd better be careful."

They had to wait almost all day for their rendezvous.

When dusk began to settle over the ocean, the skipper took his binoculars and scanned the shore. "Here comes our man now," he said, and handed the glasses to Frank. A jeep came bouncing over the rough ground. Musselman was at the wheel.

"Into your disguises, quick!" Mar ordered.

Frank and Joe hastened below, attached their false eyebrows and padded out their cheeks. When they came on deck again, Musselman was there to greet them. Beneath his jacket bulged a pistol in a shoulder holster.

Frank chuckled inwardly at the confrontation. Disguise versus disguise! Obviously Musselman wore his to mislead Icelandic authorities, but the Hardys knew his secret. They hoped he would never discover theirs!

Now the man leaped nimbly on deck. Smooth-spoken, he complimented Mar on bringing the boat through such a fierce storm.

"You wanted a seaworthy boat, and I got one, Mr——"

Musselman grinned. "Call me Chief, that's all you have to know." He glanced at the three boys and his eyes returned to the skipper. "You will sail to Greenland for me, but we must avoid the Arctic Patrol."

"We are carrying contraband? What kind?"

A sly smile crossed Musselman's lips. "Are all Icelanders so inquisitive? Well, I'll tell you. I have three boxes of rare metal ore. A new find in this part of the world. But the Icelandic government will not let me take it out." He shrugged. "So we do it anyway. Bring your crew and follow me!"

The four leaped ashore and walked to the jeep with Musselman. It was an open-top vehicle, much like Gummi's. Mar sat in front, while the youths squeezed into the back.

The jeep banged and bounced over the rough ground, heading for the interior. Presently a trail came in sight. It was nothing more than tyre tracks which curved and undulated over the barren ground.

The driver increased his speed, and as they came to a bend round a small gully, the jeep slewed to the right and a wheel teetered over the edge.

"Look out!" Joe shouted.

The jeep banged on its rear axle before regaining the trail again. Musselman half turned his head towards the back seat.

"Did someone speak English?" he asked.

"*Nei*," Gummi replied.

"I have one bad ear," Musselman said. "I must have heard wrong."

Joe kicked himself mentally for the slip of the tongue and determined to be more careful in the future. One false move now, and all would be ruined!

Presently the ground became even rougher, and soon the jeep stopped. A hundred yards farther and halfway up the edge of a stony slope stood five ponies.

The rugged little horses had shaggy coats and waited patiently as the five travellers approached.

The ponies were saddled and the party mounted. Musselman took the lead. They trudged along and rounded a bend in the valley, then turned into a partially hidden glen, shielded by towering chunks of lava.

Behind one of these stood a large turf hut built into the hillside. A long thin antenna stuck out of the roof.

Musselman stopped, and after they dismounted led the quartet inside. The interior was sparsely furnished, yet warm and comfortable. The table, chairs, stove and other accessories were modern.

The Hardys looked round for the three boxes. None were in sight.

"Pretty elaborate set-up, Joe," Frank murmured to his brother out of Musselman's earshot.

Just then the door opened and another man appeared. *Musselman's pal—the helicopter pilot who had lifted him off the glacier!* Now for the first time they heard his name— Diran. He, too, glanced at the Hardys without recognition, then spoke in low tones with his accomplice.

After a meal of beans, bread and cold meat, Musselman dragged out some folding beds and directed the boys to turn in for the night.

Then he and his confederate slipped out into the darkness.

"Come on, Joe! Now is our chance!" Frank said.

They hastily pulled on trousers and shoes, crept across the earthen floor, pushed open the door and went out into the night.

As they rounded a large lava boulder, they heard voices. Both boys ducked down. About ten feet ahead stood the two suspects. The men spoke in a language that neither one of the Hardys had ever heard before.

Suddenly a chill of fear struck them when Mussleman mentioned the name "Hardy."

Was the boys' presence known? Had their cover been blown?

·16·

The Boxes

At hearing the name "Hardy," Frank's heart sank. No doubt the men were well armed. Making a break for it now would be foolhardy. The boys crept back into the house and whispered their discovery to Gummi and Mar.

"I wonder what they intend to do," Gummi said.

"Well, we have no choice but to play it by ear," Joe muttered glumly.

Only Musselman returned to the hut that night. His confederate remained outside. The boys concluded that he was guarding the door.

Shortly after daybreak Diran stepped in and began to prepare breakfast. He gave no sign o recognition and the boys were relieved. Perhaps everything was all right, after all.

Breakfast was a makeshift affair, with everyone eating eggs and bread in tin plates wherever they could find a place to sit.

Sidling up to Rex Mar, Frank murmured, "Ask them about those boxes."

The seaman spoke in English. "The boxes with the contraband, Chief—I do not see any. Where are they?"

Musselman put down his plate and wiped his mouth

with the back of his hand. "Not so fast, Mar. They are not here."

"Oh?"

With a crooked smile Musselman motioned to his accomplice. "Diran and I are leaving for a while. All of you stay here until we come back," he ordered. "More of my men are outside."

After they had left, Frank looked out of the small window. Musselman and Diran disappeared behind a big volcanic boulder. "Come on," Frank said tersely to the others. "Let's search this place."

"Right," Joe added. "We might come up with a clue!"

The three boys, assisted by Rex Mar, left nothing untouched. They looked into every utensil, pounded the thin mattresses, and pulled out the beds to look beneath them.

Joe was about to replace Musselman's bed when his eyes caught a thin crack in the earthen floor. "Hey, Frank, look at this!"

The boys dropped to their hands and knees. Frank pulled out his pocket-knife and worked it into the crack, which grew wider.

Following its course, the knife-point outlined a square, between two and three feet wide.

"It's a trap-door of some kind," Gummi declared.

Rex Mar stood by fascinated as the young detectives worked feverishly. Frank asked him to stand guard at the window in case the two thugs should return.

The boys prodded until they found a ring, which they pulled hard.

Up came the trap-door!

A ladder led down to a dark cellar. No light switch

was in evidence. "Do you have a cigarette lighter, Mr Mar?" Joe called out.

The man reached into his pocket and tossed a lighter. Joe flicked it on and descended.

"Holy crow, Frank! Come down and take a look at this!"

Frank climbed down the ladder, and the two found themselves standing in a small room, one side of which was literally covered with radio and electronic equipment.

"What a sending-and-receiving station!" Joe exclaimed.

Frank gasped as his eyes roved over the elaborate set-up. "This is a top-quality spy centre, Joe!"

The Hardys were skilled at radio transmission, and knew how to operate much of the equipment which gleamed in the glow of the flickering lighter.

"Frank, I wonder what this is," Joe said, and lightly touched the edge of a highly polished metal box.

Suddenly there was a sizzing sound, accompanied by blue sparks. Without a word, Joe sank to the ground. The lighter fell from his hand and was extinguished.

An icy chill ran down Frank's spine as he stood in the pitch blackness. He dropped to his hands and knees and searched about until he found the lighter. *Flick*—it failed to respond. *Flick—flick*. Finally it burst into flame again, sending its feeble light over Joe's ashen face.

Frank felt for his brother's pulse. He was breathing. "I've got to get him out of here, and quick!" Frank thought.

Just then Gummi leaned over the trap door. "What's going on down there, fellows? Is everything all right?"

"No, Joe's been shocked," Frank replied. "Come on down and give me a hand. We've got to get him up."

Gummi descended, and together they lifted Joe's limp body from the floor. Gummi climbed the ladder first, tugging at the boy's arms. Frank stood beneath his brother, shoving as hard as he could. Soon the unconscious Joe was lying on the earth floor.

Frank rolled him quickly out of the way. Gummi replaced the trap-door and patted the earth so that the cracks did not show. Then he put the bed back into place.

Frank, meanwhile administered artificial respiration to his brother. Suddenly Rex Mar called out, "Here they come!"

"How far away?" Gummi asked.

"A hundred yards."

Frank worked like fury. Joe's eyes opened and Frank and Gummi pulled him to his feet. "Snap out of it, Joe!" Frank hissed, but his brother was still groggy.

Half dragging, half walking Joe to his bed, the boys put him down, tucked his hands in behind his head, and crossed his feet, making it look as if he were napping.

By now Joe was fully conscious but still weak and his left forefinger bore a slight burn.

"They stopped to talk," Mar reported.

Frank wondered what the discussion was about. The boxes, no doubt. A thought, half submerged in his subconscious, now came to the surface strong and clear.

Three boxes and three missing people!

Frank whispered his suspicions to Joe and Gummi. Joe looked sick with fear. Were Major McGeorge, Chet and Biff "the rare metal ore" sealed in those boxes?

Gummi was more optimistic. "We haven't seen the boxes yet," he said. "Maybe they're only small ones!"

Joe had a plan. He wanted to break out of the door just as the others were entering, grab one of the ponies, and race back to the *Asdis*. "I could radio for help," he said. "I'm certain these fellows have something to do with the missing astronaut."

"No doubt," Frank agreed, but cautioned against any rash move. "Gummi's right," he said. "We have to get a look at those boxes before we do anything."

"Quiet!" Mar ordered. "They are coming now."

The door opened and the two men stepped inside.

Gummi, who stood beside Frank, quickly stepped to the other end of the room. In doing so, his foot accidentally banged into Diran's leg. The fellow cursed and hit the Icelandic boy with the back of his hand. Gummi staggered before regaining his balance, but said nothing.

"Outside, all of you!" Musselman commanded. He spoke in English, and the Hardys pretended not to understand. The chief jerked his thumb towards the door. Frank and Joe walked out behind Gummi and Mar.

Waiting behind a boulder were three carts with ponies harnessed in readiness. The two men hopped into the first one and beckoned the others to follow. Mar got into one cart with Frank.

"That fellow Diran didn't curse in Icelandic," the seaman whispered.

"What was it?"

"Some kind of Balkan language. I heard it when I was shipping in the Black Sea."

The lead pony cart wound in and out among the

boulders on a trail which slanted up the hillside. Finally the boys realized what their destination was when the yawning blackness of a cavern appeared before them.

Flashing powerful lights, Musselman and Diran drove right into the cave, beckoning the others to follow. Then Musselman stopped and everyone jumped down.

"Follow me!" ordered the chief.

They walked deeper into the volcanic cave until the light revealed three rectangular boxes in one corner. They were made of fresh wood and stood against the wall like oversized coffins!

E

· 17 ·

Shut In

THE sight of the three boxes propped against the wall of the cave struck fear into the hearts of the boys. Joe gulped and looked about for a possible clue. His eyes lit upon a khaki jacket crumpled on the hard floor. It bore the U.S. insignia of major!

No doubt any more. The astronaut must have been here! Frank also spied the jacket and glanced at Joe. Both had the same plan in mind. With Gummi and Mar they would make a break out of the cave at any cost, and try to get back to the *Asdis*.

Joe signalled Gummi, and Frank motioned to Rex Mar. Then Joe let out a bloodcurdling war whoop and made a dash towards the daylight at the mouth of the cave.

Frank and Gummi raced after him, but Mar had no chance to escape. Musselman had blocked his way the very instant Joe let out his cry.

Just as the three youths dashed into the open, the cave echoed to the crack of a pistol shot. Two men, lying in wait outside, reacted to the signal.

They jumped Frank and Gummi and sent them flying. Joe whirled round to join the fierce fracas which followed. Fists flew. Gummi was downed by a blow to the head, but Frank staggered his opponent with a right cross to the jaw.

Then Musselman and Diran plunged into the fray. A swinging pistol butt sent Joe Hardy to the ground. Frank was seized, and it was all over.

Pulling stout cords from their pockets, the men tied the boys' hands behind their backs.

Just then Rex Mar, looking bewildered, walked out of the cave. "What are you doing to my crew?" he demanded.

"Quiet!" Musselman snapped.

The three were dragged to their feet, still reeling under the impact of the assault.

"These boxes will be of good use after all," Musselman said and nodded towards the cave. Then he laughed loudly.

"The major and that fat kid would have been awful heavy anyway," one of his henchmen said.

"So would his friend, the tall one," said the other.

Musselman looked grim. "That is not the point. Bring the boxes out. We will go back to the hut and await instructions."

The two fellows went inside and carried the boxes out one by one. Then they stacked them on one cart. Musselman ordered the three boys into the second cart, which he drove himself, while Diran and Mar took the third.

Soon they were back at the hut. Frank, Joe and Gummi were pushed inside and shoved on to the beds. Mar followed and fell into a chair.

Musselman and Diran sat down also, while the other two men lifted the trap-door and disappeared into the radio room below.

"So we have captured the Hardy boys at last!" Musselman sneered.

"How did you recognize us?" Frank demanded.

"Your brother spoke English in a moment of danger. It was not very smart!"

Joe gritted his teeth. "You won't get away with this, Musselman!"

His captor merely smiled and went on quietly, "We have got away with it already. And it was not easy. You slipped through our net in Bayport, but we caught the little sardines in Iceland!"

"Let us go!" Gummi hissed. "I'm an Icelander. My countrymen will find us and you'll pay for it, you dirty foreigners!"

Colour rose to Musselman's face. He pointed to Diran. "Mr Ionescu and I happen to have Icelandic passports."

"Fake ones, of course," Joe said sarcastically.

"Why did you try to get rid of us?" Frank asked.

"We knew your father was working on the astronaut case and suspected he sent you up here to help."

Frank stiffened. So the spies had known all along that his father was involved in the case. Would they try to capture him, too—or perhaps had done so already?

"Then you tried to pose as Rex Hallbjornsson to get the fifty thousand dollars," Frank went on.'

Their captors snapped his fingers. "Fifty thousand dollars! It is worth nothing compared to our real prize. We wanted you—as a ransom to get your father off the case, but now it is too late. You are expendable."

Diran Ionescu pointed a finger at his superior. "But you almost did not catch them. They slipped away at the airport, and they got off the glacier, too!" He laughed.

Musselman snarled, "Quiet! If you had had that plane's engines tuned up, I could have flown them to the east coast and then to our—"

He was interrupted by one of his henchmen, who poked his head through the trap-door. "I just made contact. Plan B is in operation. They are on their way."

Musselman smiled. "Excellent. We are ready."

"Ready for what?" Frank thought frantically. He tried to stall further action by taunting their enemies. In a sarcastic voice he said, "You think you're clever. But we know you got Major McGeorge and threatened to throw him into the sulphur pit unless he gave you NASA secrets. And the Icelandic authorities know it, too!"

Musselman looked startled, and Frank went on, "But he wouldn't talk, would he?"

"He'll talk when we get him out of this country," Ionescu boasted. "Then we will have the facilities to make him talk!"

"And what is your Plan B?" Gummi spoke up.

Musselman shook his head and said, "You will never know."

Just then the sounds of a radio broadcast issued from the trap-door. It was from the American base in Keflavik. In terse, short sentences the announcer broke the big story:

"Major McGeorge has vanished on his trip to Iceland. A force of Marines is prepared to comb every nook and cranny of the island. . . ."

"Shut it off!" Musselman screamed and went below. The boys heard him send a message. When he reappeared, he said, "Into the boxes with them!"

The three boys were led outside. Despite the pleading

of Rex Mar, they were roughly tossed into the boxes. They struggled, but it was of no use. The criminals shut the lids and secured the latches. Frank, Joe and Gummi were sealed inside to meet their fate!

Mar was forced to help move the boxes on to the carts and the ponies started off. Joggling and bouncing, Frank looked about the dark interior of his prison. He detected a thin crack of light. At least there was enough air coming in to keep him alive, for the present.

He judged that they were halfway to the place where the jeep had been left. Suddenly he heard Ionescu cry out in fright. "There it is! It's coming for the ponies!"

"Or us!" Musselman shrieked.

Frank heard Rex Mar shout the Icelandic word *isbjorn*.

Ice bear—polar bear! Several of the beasts were known to be in the area. If they were hungry, they would attack anything!

Frank pressed his eye to the crack and saw a large white form advancing. The horses reared and his box was almost jerked off the cart.

There was the crack of a rifle, then another, followed by a fierce growl and a snarl amidst the panicked neighing of the ponies.

"Ionescu, you fool!" came Musselman's voice. "You only wounded him. Run—run for your life!"

Rapid footsteps could be heard as the men ran for cover. Frank hoped his frantically galloping pony would not throw off the box and braced himself during the short but violent ride.

Then all was silent. Suddenly Rex Mar's voice sounded above Frank's box. "The bear is after them!" he said hoarsely and opened the lid.

The helpless boys were bundled into the boxes.

Frank jumped out and helped the seaman free Joe and Gummi.

"Why didn't you run away?" he asked Mar.

"The bear jumped over me and knocked me down. When I came to, they had already fled, and the beast was after them."

"If they escape the bear, they'll come back for us," Joe said. "We'd better scram."

"But then we'll never catch those spies!" Frank said. "I say we fill the boxes with rock. Would you be willing to stay and pretend we're still in there, Mr Mar? Meanwhile, we'll make a run for the trawler and radio for help."

Mar nodded grimly. "They will not get away with this. I will stay!"

Quickly they collected chunks of lava, wrapped them in their jackets and put them into the boxes. Then they shut the lids. The men were still out of sight.

One had dropped his gun. Mar picked it up. "Just in case the bear comes back," he muttered. Then he lay down on the ground about ten yards away from the carts. "I will pretend to be unconscious," he declared. "This way they will not be suspicious. Now run and radio for help, quick!"

· 13 ·

Divide and Conquer!

THE trio set off at a fast trot. If they could reach the *Asdis* before Musselman and his gang, they had an outside chance of trapping the spies.

Frank took the lead for a while. The three ran, Indian file, dodging in and out behind the grotesque volcanic formations. Then Gummi took the lead until they came in sight of the jeep.

"Now we can ride the rest of the way," Gummi panted jubilantly. He sprinted and leaped into the driver's seat. But before he could start the motor, Frank ran up to him. "No, Gummi, that won't do!"

"Why not?"

"If the jeep's gone, they'll know someone took it."

"Frank's right," Joe stated. "We don't want to alert them."

"But when they reach the jeep, they'll overtake us," Gummi protested.

"I think not," Frank replied. "Don't forget they're carrying those three big boxes, and they wouldn't fit on the jeep, along with four men!"

Gummi reluctantly admitted that the Hardys were right. He hopped out of the vehicle and lifted the hood.

"What are you going to do?" asked Joe.

"Disconnect one spark plug. That ought to give them a little more trouble."

Then the three set out again. The short rest had relieved their aching muscles, and the smooth rhythm of their bodies carried them swiftly towards the shore.

Finally they came to the crest of a small rise, and halted to gaze down at the sea, churning and foaming on the rocks below. There, at the crude dock, bobbed the *Asdis*.

"What a welcome sight!" Frank called out.

The boys raced down the hill and on to the trawler. Joe's first reaction was to radio the Icelandic coast guard for help, but Frank opposed the move.

"If Musselman's crew has a radio, they might intercept our call."

"Then they'd have to change their plans again," Gummi said, adding, "That would be the end of poor Rex Mar."

"Then ambush is our only choice," Joe declared.

Frank grinned. "Divide and conquer!"

"How will we work it?"

"Let's talk about it over some chow. I'm starved," Frank suggested.

The boys quickly refreshed themselves with food and water, all the while discussing the best way to seize the enemy. By the time they had finished their snack, a basic plan had been worked out.

Frank was to hide in the lifeboat, whch swung gently on its davits. Joe would secrete himself in a locker on the bridge, while Gummi would hide in the captain's quarters.

"It's going to be mighty rough," Frank said. "We'll have to take them one at a time."

"Suppose one of us gets into trouble—more than he can handle?" Gummi asked.

"Then we'll give a rebel yell," Joe suggested

"It'll be all for one," Frank said. "Let's each get some rope so we can tie up our friends."

They found rope in a locker, then gathered on the bridge. Gummi took the binoculars and scanned the forbidding coastline.

"What if they don't come?" he asked nervously.

"Don't worry," Frank replied. "This caper is too big for them to drop it now."

"So we catch them. Then what?"

"We'll go back and search the cave. I have a hunch that someone is still there."

"Like who?" Gummi put the question without removing the glasses from his eyes.

"It could be that—"

"Here they come!" Gummi interrupted.

On the brow of the hill appeared a strange-looking caravan. In the lead was the jeep, occupied by four men. Tied to the back of the jeep were the pony carts. Two boxes were laid across one of them, the remaining box was in the second cart, along with Rex Mar.

"Okay, fellows, to your places!" Frank said.

Joe remained on the bridge. He opened a vertical locker, which contained only the captain's coat, squeezed in, and closed the metal door until only a crack remained.

Gummi hastened to the captain's quarters, where he hid behind the bathroom door. Then Frank, making sure to keep himself shielded from view, lifted one end of the lifeboat cover.

He crept inside and peered out from beneath the canvas. Musselman's caravan bounced along.

"We've got them fooled so far," Frank thought as he watched Diran Ionescu brake the jeep to a halt by the dock.

Musselman turned to address the boxes behind him. "Here we are! Ready for the big ride?" He laughed and turned to his lieutenant. "They are not talking!"

"I suppose they know when they are defeated," Ionescu said. "All right, men, on to the boat with them!"

The three boxes were lugged on to the deck and placed alongside the rail. Then Musselman ordered his crew to cast off. The engine was started and a low throbbing vibrated through the *Asdis*.

"On to the bridge, Mar!" Musselman commanded.

"What do you want me to do?" Mar protested as Musselman shoved him roughly towards the wheel house.

"Head for Greenland! Once we are past the twelve-mile limit, over go the boxes."

"You are going to kill them?" Mar asked as he steered the boat out of the little cove.

Taking in every word, Joe Hardy shuddered at the thought of the fate that might have overtaken them.

"But what about me?" The old seaman sounded frightened.

"We will take care of you when we get to Greenland."

The spy stepped backwards. Should Joe attack now? He could fling open the door hard, but before he could act, Musselman quickly left the bridge.

Joe opened the door wider. "*Psst!* Captain Mar!"

The skipper whirled around in astonishment, then an expression of relief came over his face.

Joe put a finger to his lips. Quickly he told where the other boys were stationed and added, "The next guy who comes on to the bridge will get it!"

Mar nodded and smiled.

Frank, meanwhile, peered out from beneath the lifeboat cover. One of the two henchmen walked casually past and leaned on the rail to look over the sea. Silently Frank crept out of his hiding place. The davit rocked and squeaked, causing the thug to turn round. But Frank had already launched himself. He collided with the man in mid-air and together they sprawled on the deck.

The thug wore a look of complete amazement as he scrambled to his feet. Frank got in the first blow, a crushing right hand to the solar plexus!

"Umph!" His opponent doubled up, just as Frank delivered a stiff left to his chin. The man went down like a sack!

Quickly Frank bound his hands and feet. Then, struggling with all his might, he lifted him up and dropped him into the lifeboat. One down, three to go!

The boy stalked the deck, then ducked behind a stanchion as the second henchman came by. Swiftly Frank put his foot forward. The man tripped, landed on the deck, and turned, wild-eyed.

Frank grappled with him, but the wiry henchman wriggled from his grasp and ran along the deck, shouting, "They're out! Musselman, they're out!"

Instantly the chief and his lieutenant appeared. Musselman reached for his gun, but Frank bulled into him, head lowered. At the same time, he let out a bloodcurdling rebel yell.

Hearing, it, Joe dashed out of the locker and down

the deck. Gummi came out of hiding and raced up the deck. The mêlée that followed was a bone-crushing battle. Each of the boys took an opponent.

Frank struggled to subdue Musselman, while his brother exchanged blows with Ionescu. Gummi had his hands full with the third man. They rolled over on the deck, scrambled up, and fought along the rail.

Suddenly Gummi was seized by the shirt front and lifted halfway over the rail. Another few inches and he would be cast into the cold sea!

Just then Rex Mar raced over and grasped the thug around the throat with his huge paw of a hand. Together, he and Gummi tossed the man over the rail. With a splash he hit the water and screamed for help.

Gummi grabbed a life jacket and threw it to him. The fellow clung to it, then disappeared far behind the boat in the wake.

Joe, meanwhile, was near exhaustion, battling the powerful Ionescu. Gummi came to his aid, distracting the spy for a split second. It took Joe only a moment to deliver a chop to the forehead. Ionescu went down.

Now Mar and the boys turned their full attention to Frank's fight. But Frank needed no help. He had Musselman on the rail, flailing him with rights and lefts.

The man's knees sagged and Rex Mar rushed over to seize him. He lifted Musselman overhead like a sack of grain, and threatened to drop him into the sea. Musselman screamed for mercy and Mar dropped him to the deck.

"So you were going to murder these boys!" he shouted. "Frank, Joe—tie him up. The captain is in command of his boat again!"

Mar went back to the bridge and radioed the coast guard for help. Then he turned the boat round. A few minutes later they picked up the man bobbing in his life jacket.

With all the criminals safely tied, Mar headed for the old dock. When he pulled up, Frank and Joe jumped ashore.

"Captain Mar, will you and Gummi wait here for us?" Frank asked. "We'll go back to the cave and search the place thoroughly."

"We sure will," Gummi replied, grinning. "The coast guard should be here shortly to take care of these jerks!"

"We should put *them* into the boxes and drop them in the ocean," Mar growled.

"We'd better leave their punishment up to the authorities," Joe said. "Well, keep your fingers crossed that we find Major McGeorge and the fellows!"

The boys waved, disengaged the pony carts, and set off in the jeep. Soon they reached the place where the ponies had been left. Each mounted one of the rugged little horses and rode to the hut.

Reaching it, they cautiously looked about in case any of Musselman's men was around. There was none. Joe found a flashlight in the hut, then they hastened to the cave. Inside, it was dark and gloomy.

"This is much bigger than I thought," Frank murmured as they made their way cautiously into the farthest recess. At the end, their beam illuminated a figure, bound and gagged, lying face down.

"Major McGeorge! Is that you?" Frank cried out as he raced ahead and bent over the man. There was no reply. "Here, let's roll him over, Joe!"

They grabbed the shoulder of the husky figure and rolled him face up. Their light shone upon a pale face with eyes closed.

It was Biff Hooper!

·19·

Hijackers!

WORKING speedily, Frank and Joe untied Biff, then carried him out of the cave into the daylight.

"He's in bad shape," Joe said worriedly as he glanced at the peaked countenance of their once-rugged friend.

"Come on. We'll give him a good massage," Frank suggested.

After the Hardys had stimulated Biff Hooper's circulation, their pal opened his eyes. He tried feebly to rise, but fell back on to the ground.

"Easy now," Frank said. "You're very weak, Biff. Where are Chet and Major McGeorge?"

With a blank expression, Biff looked straight ahead, as if not seeing the Hardys at all. Joe patted his face vigorously.

"Biff! Wake up! Tell us what's been going on!"

Biff's lips moved wordlessly. Finally with great physical effort, he whispered, "Bomb—bomb set to—"

"Good grief, Joe! Let's get out of here before the cave blows up!"

Frank and Joe lifted Biff upright, with an arm over each shoulder and ran as quickly as possible.

Well away from the cave entrance, the boys stopped and glanced back. They had reached their ponies, but needed another one to carry the injured Biff.

"Look, Joe," Frank said, pointing to the side of the cave, "there's another pony grazing." The boys called to the animal, but it paid no attention to them.

"I'll go and get him, Frank!"

"No! The whole place might blow up in your face! We'd better wait until—"

But Joe had already dashed towards the pony. If this had been the running track at Bayport High, he thought grimly, he would have set a new record for the 440 yards!

He reached the pony, grabbed its tether, and pulled. The little horse responded instantly, running by Joe's side as he hastened with eyes half shut, anticipating the bomb explosion.

Perspiration streaming down his face, he returned to the others. Frank had helped Biff on to one of the ponies, but he leaned forward groggily over the animal's neck.

"We'd better tie him on," Joe panted as he pulled some rope from his pockets. Frank helped him, then they mounted their own ponies and rode on either side of Biff.

They set off at a brisk pace, but their backs were turned to the cave no more than a minute when a terrific *boom* shook the ground.

The concussion nearly knocked the three boys off their ponies, and Frank and Joe struggled hard to keep Biff upright. The animals reared in fear, but finally the Hardys regained control.

Joe glanced back over his shoulder to see a gaping, smoking hole where the small knoll once had been. "I hope Biff can explain everything," he thought as they plodded on.

Once they were in the jeep, their task was easier. Joe, at the wheel, started the engine, while Frank clung to Biff to keep him from bouncing out.

Joe handled the wheel like a race driver, cutting in and around the volcanic boulders. Finally he came to the rise of ground which overlooked the sea.

There, below them, lay two boats! The *Asdis* had been joined by the coast guard ship *Thor*. There was much activity on both decks. By the time the jeep reached the dock, Captain Magnusson and his men were there to meet the arrivals.

"We got Biff Hooper!" Frank called out. "He can't talk. Here, give me a hand with him!"

Crewmen from the *Thor* raced for a stretcher and carried Biff below decks where a medical orderly worked to revive him. The skipper, meanwhile, lauded the Hardys for their catch.

"The president of Iceland should give you a medal for this!" he said, pumping their hands. "That Musselman's a bad one. Gummi told us how you bagged all four of them!"

Captain Magnusson had just finished telling the boys that the prisoners were now secured in chains on the *Thor*, when a helicopter appeared out of the blue. Moments later it landed neatly on the *Thor's* afterdeck. The door opened, and out stepped Mr Hardy.

"Dad!" Joe cried out as the boys ran to greet their father.

"Am I glad to see you two alive!" the famous detective said. "You were playing with dynamite. Musselman is known to be a ruthless international spy!"

"Dynamite is right," Joe said. "He nearly blew the three of us to kingdom come!"

The helicopter pilot, who had stayed with his craft, waved goodbye and the chopper slid into the brisk air.

After introductions had been made all round, Captain Magnusson led the Hardys and their friends to his quarters. Everyone sat down, and conversation crackled with vital news.

Mr Hardy's quest in Texas had turned up a clue which had led to the unmasking of one of Musselman's accomplices.

"This man actually had an important job with the National Aeronautics and Space Administration," the detective reported. Interrogation had led to information that Frank and Joe were in grave danger.

"I hurried here as quickly as possible," Mr Hardy continued, then added with a grin of satisfaction, "But you fellows got the job done before I arrived."

"It isn't finished yet, Dad," Frank spoke up. "And Biff may have the key to the riddle, if we could only get him to talk."

Just then the *Thor's* first lieutenant came in with the news that the American boy was regaining full consciousness.

Frank and Joe went to Biff's room and found him greatly improved. But he still seemed unable to give a coherent story.

Captain Magnusson, who had followed the boys, suggested they let Biff rest for a while and have dinner. Soon everyone was seated round the large table, enjoying a hearty meal. Everyone but Rex Mar— who had been assigned three of the *Thor's* men to bring in the *Asdis*.

After supper, Mr Hardy grilled the four prisoners. They refused to answer even the simplest questions.

Meanwhile Frank, Joe and Gummi sat at Biff's side, trying hard to stimulate his memory. It was well after midnight when Biff cried out, "Frank, Joe, I think I've got it now!"

The boys, who had fallen asleep on makeshift bunks near their friend, jumped up excitedly and Frank ran for his father. Then everyone crowded round Biff.

"How about starting at the beginning," Mr Hardy suggested.

Frank put in, "Gummi told us you got a message to meet us somewhere."

"Right," Biff began. "We received a telegram from Akureyri, saying you needed help and instructing us to take a private plane from Reykjavik which would be waiting for us."

"We thought you'd gone by boat!" Joe interrupted. "Chet mentioned something to Gummi about seasick pills!"

"Well, Chet had eaten a lot for lunch that day and his stomach was upset, so he bought some for the plane trip."

Joe grinned ruefully. "That's what you call a *mis*-clue!"

"On the plane," Biff continued, "we were socked and tied up. It landed on a small strip near the cave. Obviously they wanted us out of the way, so Frank and Joe'd be easier to handle."

"Then what happened?" Gummi inquired.

"We were supposed to be shipped to Greenland in three big boxes, together with Major McGeorge. In case they had difficulties, there was an alternative solution which they called Plan B."

Frank and Joe exchanged excited glances.

"What was that?" Frank asked.

"McGeorge was to fly out together with Chet," Biff went on. "The astronaut and I are about the same size, and even look somewhat alike. He would travel under my name."

"Is that what finally happened?" Joe asked, his nerves on edge.

"I guess so. They took McGeorge and Chet away, and planted a bomb to blow up the cave. Musselman wanted to do it right away, but the guy he called Diran has a sadistic streak in him. He was going to give me a little more time!"

Frank clenched his fists when he heard of the devilish scheme of their enemies. "Those animals!"

"Well," Biff concluded, "it didn't really make much difference to me. They hadn't given me any food or water, so I was in no shape to worry about anything."

"How were McGeorge and Chet to fly to Greenland?" Mr Hardy wanted to know.

"I have no idea. I've told you everything I know."

Everyone went back to sleep again until Captain Magnusson called them for breakfast. They had hardly finished eating when the *Thor* pulled into Reykjavik Harbour. The Hardys thanked the captain and his crew, then hopped into a taxi and sped directly to the airport. Gummi took Biff to the hotel.

At the airfield the Americans hastened to passport control. Mr Hardy talked to an official who confirmed that Chet Morton and Biff Hooper had already passed through the gate.

"But that wasn't Biff Hooper at all!" Joe blurted out.

"Who was it, then? A criminal?" the man asked, perplexed.

"Anything but," Mr Hardy said. He quickly told about the spies' plan.

"We'll have to stop the plane!" the official declared. "I hope they have not taken off yet. I think the flight to Scotland is scheduled to leave at eight-thirty."

"Scotland?" Frank cried out. "Weren't they going to Greenland?"

"No," the man replied. He led the Hardys into his office. There he quickly relayed a message to the tower.

"Prevent plane to Scotland from taking off! Abort take-off. Urgent!"

Instantly the request was relayed to the plane. No reply!

The Hardys and the airport official ran out to the field. The jet stood at the end of a runway, ready to speed down the white line.

"Dad, we have to stop it!" Frank yelled. Just then an airport jeep drove past. Frank flagged it down. He looked at the official, who nodded and barked an order in Icelandic to the driver. The man jumped out. Frank and Joe instantly hopped in and raced down the runway.

As Frank sped towards the plane, the big aircraft moved forward, its engines thundering. Car and plane were on a collision course!

· 20 ·

Cool Hand Chet

FRANK realized that a crash was imminent. He swerved to the left just as the craft became airborne. It whizzed overhead, its hot jet blasts barely missing the speeding car.

The plane virtually stood on its tail, reaching for altitude as fast as possible.

Frank drove the jeep back towards the airport buildings. The official waved them in the direction of the tower. When the boys reached the airport's nerve centre, they found Mr Hardy listening to the radio report from the Scotland-bound plane.

"If anyone follows us," the voice said, "we will shoot the pilot!"

"Good grief!" Frank said. "They mean business."

"But they will not get away with it!" the tower controller stated angrily.

Mr Hardy followed the plane with binoculars until it was out of sight, then watched on radar as the blip continued in an easterly direction.

"Maybe they're going to Scotland after all!" Joe said.

"Not likely," his father replied. "The plane's veering north." After a 180-degree turn the craft headed west.

By this time, government officials had arrived in

the tower, and a plan was evolved within a few minutes. Both the United States authorities in Keflavik and the Danish Air Force in Greenland were notified. Within minutes, a dozen planes were launched from both bases.

Frank spoke up. "We'd like to be in on the chase."

"There's not much you can do now," an American officer replied. He stood next to Frank and introduced himself as Colonel S. P. Smith of the U.S. Air Force. "But we'll need you in Narssarssuaq."

"Is that the place where they are going to land?" Joe asked.

"I'm sure they don't plan to land there, but we'll try to force them down. We have them covered with an umbrella of planes."

The colonel led the Hardys out of the tower and on to the field, where they boarded a speedy military jet.

"We should be in Greenland in about half an hour," he explained.

No sooner had the Hardys fastened their seat belts than they were thrust backwards by the terrific take-off speed of the jet. It whistled into the air, banked sharply, and headed west. Now relaxed in their seats, the trio chatted with Colonel Smith.

"So far everything is going like clockwork," he said. "That plane is a fish in our net."

"But what if the hijackers should get desperate and wreck the plane?" Joe asked.

"We'll just have to play it by ear," the colonel replied.

Now a voice crackled over the plane's P.A. system. "They are closing in," their American pilot said.

He had hardly spoken when the pilot in the hijacked

plane snarled, "Stay away from us! If you try to force us down, we will crash the plane!"

Presently another of the pursuing pilots reported that the airliner suddenly had gone into a steep dive. Colonel Smith barked a brisk order "Ease off, but keep them in sight!"

"They must be madmen!" Mr Hardy said gravely. "The lives of all those people are in jeopardy."

As the colonel pondered over what action to take, another voice came suddenly from the passenger plane.

"This is Major McGeorge. Do you read me?"

Colonel Smith and Mr Hardy exchanged suspicious glances, before the colonel took the microphone.

"Your tricks won't accomplish anything!"

"It's no trick. This is really McGeorge. Chet Morton and I have everything under control. We will see you at Narssarssuaq! Over and out!"

Excitement ran high in the Hardys' plane. Soon the mountains of Greenland came into view and shortly afterwards their plane circled over the airfield at Narssarssuaq. It touched down and taxied to one side of the field.

Before the pilot could turn off the engines, Frank and Joe saw the hijacked airliner. It flew around the field once, then came in for a landing.

Two military planes followed directly behind and escorted the jetliner to the loading area. The portable stairway was quickly rolled to the rear door, and excited passengers streamed down the steps.

After all had disembarked, the three Hardys and Colonel Smith dashed up the stairs and into the plane.

Along the aisle stumbled two men, their hands tied behind their backs. One had a bruised swelling on his forehead. The other, with a puffed right eye, glared out of the window.

Behind them strode Chet Morton. "Come on there, out! Both of you!" he ordered. But when he saw the Hardys, he asked anxiously, "Hey, fellows, did you find Biff?"

"Yes. He's fine," Frank called out.

The prisoners were hustled out of the plane and taken into custody by military police. Then the crew and Major McGeorge stepped off the airliner.

Introductions were made, hands clasped, and backs slapped. Then Colonel Smith led the Hardys, Chet and the astronaut into an airport office. Here the incredible story of Major McGeorge's kidnapping was pieced together.

"I'm sure glad the government put such able detectives on my tracks," the tall, handsome astronaut said, and thanked Mr Hardy and the boys for saving his life.

"Well, the last step you did yourself," Frank said with a grin. "How'd you manage to take over the plane?"

"I was recovering from the drug they had given me," the major explained, "and signalled Chet that I was all right."

"Then I did *it*," Chet put in, blushing. "One of those jerks who boarded the plane with us was up front and kept a gun on the pilot. I gave the other one an elbow in the ribs and finished him off with a karate chop to the forehead. *Pow!* Like this!" Chet made a fast motion with his right hand, and the Hardys chuckled.

"Your hobby really paid off!" Frank patted his friend on the back.

"After that," McGeorge went on, "we used the fellow as a screen and marched him up to the cabin. The other guy was completely taken by surprise."

"And Major McGeorge took care of him real fast," Chet concluded.

"Well, thank goodness it's all over," Mr Hardy said. "Now tell us, Major, how did they ever get hold of you in the first place?"

"I was seized at gunpoint by three men after I had separated from our group at the sulphur pit to inspect the area. They put me into a helicopter and flew me to a cave."

"That's not there any more," Joe told him. "They blew it up."

"I know. A time bomb was set when they took Chet and me out. Good thing you found Biff Hooper before it went off!" The major went on to say that he was interrogated for hours, but would not reveal any NASA secrets.

"Then they took me back to the sulphur pit and threatened to throw me in," he reported.

"That's where we picked up your trail," Frank spoke up.

"Well, those devils circled round the pit, and when I still would not talk, they drove me away again."

The Hardys learned that in the early confusion following the disappearance of the major, the helicopter had made a clean getaway.

"A chopper was found abandoned on the east coast," Mr Hardy put in. "I'm sure it was the same craft."

Frank snapped his fingers. "East coast! That's where we were headed when Musselman kidnapped us in his plane."

"Could be," Mr Hardy replied. "They had a speedboat hidden in a cove. I think they planned to take you out and dump you in the Atlantic."

By mid-afternoon Major McGeorge, the Hardys and Chet Morton had returned to Reykjavik. At the Foreign Office they learned that Musselman and Ionescu still were tight-lipped. One of their men, however, was telling all he knew about the spies to save himself from a life behind bars.

It was revealed that the thugs were spies for hire. A foreign power had set up the diabolic plan to kidnap an American astronaut, then take him to their country, claiming that he had defected.

"Iceland proved to be an effective place to carry out the kidnapping," Anders Sigurdsson told them. "Our country is entirely law-abiding and nobody would ever suspect such a thing could happen here."

"But how could such elaborate preparations have been made so far in advance?" Frank asked, recalling the turf hut with all its highly sophisticated equipment.

"The agents have been here for a long time," Mr Sigurdsson explained. "They were spying on your military base and knew far ahead of time that the astronauts were scheduled to visit Iceland."

Biff Hooper, meanwhile, had recovered enough to have supper with his pals and Mr Hardy in the Saga's beautiful rooftop restaurant. They looked down over the harbour, now blinking with light, and while dining on a delicious dish of hot smoked lamb, talked with their guest Major McGeorge.

In the middle of the meal, Captain Sigtryggsson of the coast guard entered with his niece Steina. They were escorted to the Hardys' table where introductions were made.

After complimenting the astronaut and Chet on their escape, Captain Sigtryggsson said, "I'm so pleased to meet you, Mr Hardy. Your sons and their friends have been of great service to Iceland."

As the waiter pulled up a chair for the two newcomers, the door opened again and in strode Rex Mar. He was neatly dressed in a dark suit and joined the Hardys' table.

The detective shook the old man's hand vigorously and thanked him for all he had done for the boys.

"They have done something for me, too," Mar replied with a smile. "They made me rich!"

"What are you going to do now, Mr Mar?" Joe asked. "Buy yourself a fishing trawler?"

"Sure," Frank added. "You can go into business—"

"With me, for instance," came a voice from the door. Everyone cheered as Gummi walked towards the table.

"Will you be my lieutenant?" Rex Mar asked him.

"Why not?"

They laughed and chatted about their adventure, little knowing that a new one—*The Haunted Fort*—was soon to come their way.

Finally Frank rose and requested everyone to be silent.

"There's one more thing," he said. "We found something near the sulphur pit which we should return to its owner!" With that he pulled a black glove from his pocket and handed it to Major McGeorge.

The astronaut's eyes opened wide. "What detectives!" he exclaimed.

"*Yow! Yow!*" Chet agreed.

2
The Twisted Claw

The Hardy Boys in
The Twisted Claw

Contents

Just in time Frank grabbed the girder!

·1·

Shadowed!

"CONGRATULATIONS!" Frank Hardy shouted to his brother Joe as the track athletics meeting ended. "You've won the trophy for Bayport High and set a new record for the hundred-yard dash!"

"You helped, too," Joe called, jogging along the cinder track. "What about your gold medal in the 440?" he said as he came to a halt.

"Don't forget me!" exclaimed Chet Morton. He was a stout, round-faced youth and a good friend of the Hardys, "I collected a few points in the shot-put."

"You were great, Chet," Frank said with a grin.

The trio had taken part in the annual track-and-field meeting with Hopkinsville at a stadium near their home town of Bayport. The contest also marked the beginning of the summer holidays.

"Well, are we going out to celebrate?" Chet asked.

"Sure, some of the other guys want to come, too," Joe replied. "Let's go and change—"

He was interrupted by an announcement over the loudspeaker. "Frank and Joe Hardy to the telephone in the manager's office, please."

"Oh, oh. We'd better forget about the celebrations," Frank said. "Let's go, Joe."

They were met at the office door by the manager, who handed Frank the phone. "It's your father," he said.

Frank spoke excitedly. "Hello, Dad. We won!"

"Nice going." There was a pause. "Frank," Mr Hardy went on, "I'd like you and Joe to come home soon. It's important."

Within minutes the boys had showered and changed and were in their convertible, driving towards Bayport.

"I hope there's nothing wrong," Joe remarked anxiously.

"I don't think so," Frank answered. "I have a hunch it has something to do with a new case."

Their father, Fenton Hardy, had once been a member of the New York City police force. But now he was engaged in private practice as a detective and was often assisted by his sons. Working as a team, they had solved many baffling crimes and had added even more renown to the Hardy name.

"Hi, Mother," the boys called when they arrived home.

Mrs Hardy, an attractive, soft-spoken woman, greeted her sons with a smile. "How did the athletics meeting go?" she inquired.

"Just great!" Joe declared. "We won the trophy!"

"We'll tell you about it later," Frank interrupted. "Where's Dad?"

"Upstairs. He's waiting for you."

The boys rushed up the stairs and entered their father's study. He was seated at his desk. Mr Hardy was a distinguished-looking man who appeared much younger than his years.

"We came as fast as we could," Frank said.

"Thanks," Mr Hardy replied. "I wouldn't have called if it wasn't important. I'm going to need your help in connection with a new case."

"What did I tell you!" Frank exclaimed as he playfully slapped his brother on the shoulder.

"What kind of a case?" Joe asked eagerly.

"I can't go into detail at this point. Besides, I'll be leaving on a trip shortly," his father said. "Here it is briefly. Right now there is a ship in Bayport Harbour called the *Black Parrot*. I know nothing about it other than it might have some connection with my case. I'd like you to keep an eye on the freighter while it's in port. Record anything about the crew or cargo that looks even slightly suspicious."

Frank, dark-haired and eighteen, and a year older than his blond brother, looked at his father quizzically. "That sounds sort of tame, Dad."

"I know. But it could turn out to be a pretty wild case, as you boys say."

"Should we contact you if we find any information?"

"No. I'll get in touch with you."

At that instant Mrs Hardy entered the room. "Fenton," she said nervously, "I'm worried. There's a man across the street. I'm sure he's watching our house. He's hiding behind a tree, but I caught several glimpses of him."

Joe, the more impetuous of the brothers, jumped to his feet. "Let's go and have a talk with that guy. We'll soon find out what he's up to!"

"Hold it!" Mr Hardy ordered. "It's possible he has been assigned to shadow me. I don't want him to know he has been spotted. It'll put his accomplices on guard."

Joe nodded. "This *must* be quite a case. Wish you could tell us more about it."

The detective did not answer. He glanced at his

watch. "I'm due at the airport soon. Somehow I've got to get out of the house without being seen."

"How about the back door?" Joe suggested.

"No good," his father said. "Chances are there's another man posted behind the house."

"Maybe some kind of a disguise would work," Frank said.

"I'm afraid it would be a bit too obvious under the circumstances," Mr Hardy replied. "Unless someone —" His words trailed off as he reached for the telephone book, looked up a number, and dialled. "I'm going to call Mr Callahan and ask him to come over right away."

"Our plumber?" Joe asked.

The boys glanced at each other in bewilderment. What could their father possibly want with a plumber at this time?

"You'll see," Mr Hardy said with a wink.

About ten minutes later a small truck came to a stop in front of the Hardy home. Mr Callahan, a middle-aged man wearing a cap and overalls, climbed out. He had a rather large nose and bushy eyebrows.

He walked towards the house, carrying a tool-kit in his right hand. The young detectives led him to their father's study, where Mr Hardy quickly told him of his predicament.

"Now this is my plan, Mr Callahan," Mr Hardy continued. "You and I are about the same size and weight. If you'll lend me your cap and overalls for a while, I can disguise myself well enough to pass as your double—at least at a distance."

The plumber was an old acquaintance and readily agreed. They left the study and went to the master bedroom. A few minutes later they reappeared. With false nose and eyebrows Mr Hardy looked amazingly like Callahan.

"A good make-up job, Dad!" Frank exclaimed. "You and Mr Callahan could be twin brothers."

At that instant Gertrude Hardy entered the room. She was the sister of Mr Hardy. "My word! I'm seeing double!" she exclaimed. "Two Mr Callahans in this room!"

"You're not seeing double," Joe assured her with a laugh. "One of them is Dad in disguise."

"And a pretty good likeness too, don't you think?" Frank added.

Aunt Gertrude turned to face the plumber. "Fenton, what on earth are you up to now? Something to do with a new case I take it. One day something awful is going to happen. I'm sure of it!"

Mr Hardy stepped forward. "I'm afraid you're scolding the wrong man."

Aunt Gertrude shook her head and marched out of the room. The boys roared with laughter.

"Now back to the business in hand," Mr Hardy said. "I'll leave here in Mr Callahan's truck. You boys take him to the airport in an hour to pick it up. Please let me settle for your time, Mr Callahan."

"I won't think of it. It's a favour," the plumber said.

"I insist," said Mr Hardy, then addressed his sons, "Any questions before I leave?"

"No, Dad," Joe replied.

"Let's hope," the detective continued, "that our friend across the street falls for my trick."

After saying goodbye to his family, he picked up the plumber's tool-kit, took a deep breath, and left the house.

The boys cautiously peered through a window. Across the street they saw a man's head pop out from behind a tree, then vanish again as their father drove off. Obviously the stranger was remaining at his post.

"The trick worked!" Frank exclaimed triumphantly.

"Right," Joe agreed. "But I wonder how long that guy is going to stick around."

Frank chuckled. "One thing is certain. He's in for a long wait."

While Aunt Gertrude prepared a cup of tea for Mr Callahan, Frank and Joe discussed the case.

"The *Black Parrot*," Joe mused. "Sounds eerie."

"Let's go down to the harbour first thing in the morning," Frank said. "Right now we'd better keep an eye on that fellow across the street."

The boys hurried downstairs and peered through one of the living-room windows. Minutes passed.

"No sign of him," Joe muttered. "Maybe he's gone."

"Could be," his brother replied. "But let's wait a while longer, just to be sure."

While Frank kept his post at the window, Joe paced up and down impatiently. Finally he could not suppress his curiosity any longer. "I'm going to see if that spy's still there," he said and ran out of the house. He looked behind the tree across the street, then signalled Frank that the coast was clear.

When he came back Frank met him at the door. "You shouldn't have run out like that, you know."

"Sorry. I thought it was about time for a showdown."

"You might have—"

Frank was interrupted by a terrifying scream from the kitchen.

·2·

The Black Parrot

"GOOD grief!" Joe exclaimed. "That was Aunt Gertrude!"

The boys rushed into the kitchen and almost collided with their mother who had heard the scream, too.

They found Miss Hardy shaking like a leaf. She pointed to an open window. "A-a strange man was looking in at me! Call the police! Do something!"

Frank and Joe spotted a man running down the street. They dashed out of the house and gave chase, but before they could close the gap, their quarry leaped into a car and sped off.

"There were two men in that car!" Frank declared. "One of them must have been watching the rear of the house as Dad suspected. He tried to get a look inside and frightened the wits out of Aunty."

"I wonder what he was up to," Joe put in.

"Your guess is as good as mine," Frank replied.

They returned to find their mother pressing a cold wet towel on Aunt Gertrude's forehead.

"How do you feel?" Joe inquired.

"Awful! Simply awful!" exclaimed Aunt Gertrude. "Who was that cut-throat?"

"Probably just a door salesman," Frank replied, hoping not to upset her further. "Your scream frightened him more than he frightened you."

"Some nerve!" Aunt Gertrude snapped. "Imagine! Peering into people's houses."

Frank looked at his watch. "I think we can leave now," he said to Mr Callahan. "Come on. We'll take you to the airport to pick up your truck."

"Okay," agreed Mr Callahan.

As they got into the boys' convertible, the plumber said, "Tell me, is there always that much excitement at your house?"

Frank winked at his brother. "This is a rather quiet day, wouldn't you say, Joe?"

Mr Callahan shook his head and asked no more questions.

The boys retired early that night and were up at six the next morning. After breakfast they drove to Bayport Harbour. They found the area bustling with activity.

"There's the *Black Parrot*," Joe said, pointing.

They watched as stevedores pushed handcarts, loaded with wooden crates, up a gangway to the ship. A crane was putting heavier cargo aboard.

"We won't be able to get much information for Dad unless we can board the ship," Joe remarked.

Frank did not speak. Instead, he signalled Joe to follow him and walked towards a crewman who was standing at the base of the gangway checking a manifest.

"My brother and I are very much interested in ships," Frank began nonchalantly. "Do you think your captain would let us go aboard for a few minutes?"

The man glared at them in surprise. "Get outta here!" he roared.

"Why get mad at us?" Joe queried. "We were just—"

"You heard me! Get outta here before I take a club to ya!"

Joe was about to challenge the man, but Frank grabbed his brother's arm and led him away from the ship.

"That guy's about as pleasant as a rattlesnake," Joe said angrily.

"Take it easy," Frank warned. "We can't risk getting involved in a row. We've got to remain as inconspicuous as possible."

"What'll we do now?"

"Wait and hope for a break."

The young detectives watched the *Black Parrot* from a distance. Then came a stroke of luck. A crewman placed a sign at the base of the gangway announcing that more help was needed to load the ship. The Hardys were among the first to volunteer.

"So! It's you two again!" growled the man they had encountered earlier. He stared at them for a moment. "Well—you kids look pretty strong." He named a price for every crate carried aboard and told them to take it or leave it.

"We'll take it," Frank said quickly. "But what about union cards?"

"Forget the union and get movin'!" the crewman ordered. "We haven't got any more handcarts, so you'll have to bring the crates aboard one by one."

"Thanks a lot," Joe muttered.

The job was extremely hard. The boys stuck to it most of the day, hoping to learn something, but their sleuthing was hampered by the constant surveillance of the crew.

That afternoon, while carrying a crate aboard, Joe

tripped and fell. The wooden box crashed to the deck. At that instant the first mate of the *Black Parrot* appeared and demanded to know what was going on.

"Just an accident," Frank explained. "My brother tripped and—"

"I'm not interested in excuses!" the officer yelled. He gave Joe a shove. "Now pick that up. And be quick about it!"

"Pick it up yourself!" Joe retorted as he scrambled to his feet.

The first mate was about to lash out with his fist, but Frank stepped in and grabbed him by the arm. As he did, he noticed that the man was wearing a strange ring on his finger. It consisted of a heavy silver band with what looked like a red, twisted bird's claw on top.

"Let go of my arm!" the man demanded. Frank released him. "Now get your pay and get off the ship!"

"We haven't finished our work," Joe said.

Several crewmen moved towards the Hardys. "You heard him," one of them snarled. "Get goin'."

The boys had no choice but to comply.

Joe sighed. "I certainly messed things up."

"It wasn't your fault," Frank said. "Anyway, we couldn't have done much investigating with all those guys around."

As they walked down the gangway to the pier, they heard a familiar voice call out, "Hi, masterminds!" It was Chet Morton. "Your mother said you were down here," he went on. "What're you doing?"

Frank and Joe drew the stout boy aside and told him about their assignment and their adventure on board.

"And you fellows were ordered off the ship, eh?"

Chet reflected. "Let me see." He began walking towards the *Black Parrot*. "I'll get some information for you."

"Wait a minute!" Frank said. "Come back here!" His words went unheeded.

"Ahoy, mates! Make way for a real seaman!" Chet shouted to a group of crewmen as he hurried up the gangway.

"Oh, oh. Now we're really in for trouble," Joe muttered anxiously.

Chet disappeared into the midst of the group. Shortly scuffling broke out amongst the men. Before Frank and Joe could aid their friend, he came rolling down the gangway like an oversized bowling ball.

"Are you all right?" Frank cried as he and Joe rushed to Chet.

The stout youth got to his feet and began brushing off his clothes. "I'm—I'm okay. Those guys aren't very friendly."

Frank frowned. "Right now, our chances of getting back aboard the ship are nil. Let's go home and try to figure out another plan."

The boys had an early supper, then went to their father's study to discuss their next move.

Joe thought for a moment. "I've got an idea," he said finally. "Why don't we disguise ourselves as a couple of crewmen and just board the ship?"

"I don't know," Frank muttered, rubbing his chin dubiously. "Then again, it might work if we try it after dark."

"I'll dig up the caps and seamen's jackets we used on that sailing trip last year."

"Okay. But let's disguise ourselves in the car. We

don't want Mother and Aunt Gertrude to see us. They'll only worry."

The boys lost no time putting their plan into action. Within half an hour they had completed their disguise.

"You look as if you've been at sea for years," Frank said laughingly as he gazed at his brother.

Joe grinned as he started the car. "And no one would take you for a landlubber either."

It had been dark for nearly an hour when the Hardys arrived at the harbour. They were startled to find the *Black Parrot* gone.

Frank leaped out of the convertible and approached a watchman who was walking along the pier. "Where's the *Black Parrot*?" he asked.

The man eyed the young detective. "Sailed about an hour ago. Were you supposed to be on board?"

"Er—no," Frank replied. "Heard the ship was in port. Just wondered if the captain needed a couple of extra hands."

"Then you ain't missed nothin'," the watchman told him. "Strangest crew I ever did see. Weren't friendly towards nobody. You'd be better off signin' on with another ship. Try the *Nomad*. It'll be dockin' here in the mornin'."

Frank hurried back to the car. "Well, that's that." He sighed. "The ship's gone and we have nothing to report to Dad."

"This was a tough assignment," Joe commented. "If only we had had more time."

They removed their disguises and returned home. Aunt Gertrude had a message for them. "Your father telephoned while you were out. He wants you to get a book for him."

"Sure," Frank said. "What is it?"

"It's called *Essays in Criminology*, by Weaver. He said you might have some trouble finding it since it's out of print."

"We'll try. How's Dad?"

"Fine. He'll call again in a few days."

The boys spent the following day canvassing the second-hand bookshops in Bayport. Their search was unsuccessful, however.

"Let's go to New York City," Frank suggested. "If there's a copy of the *Essays* anywhere, we're likely to find it there."

That evening Joe telephoned Jack Wayne, pilot of Mr Hardy's single-engined aircraft. The plane was based at Bayport Airport. Wayne readily agreed to fly the boys to New York.

"By the way, I understand your father recently left on a trip by airline," the pilot said jokingly. "What's wrong? Doesn't he like his own plane any more?"

"Not necessarily," Joe answered with a laugh. "Maybe he thought you needed a holiday. We'll see you in the morning."

The following day was crisp and clear. Jack Wayne was already warming up the plane's engine when the Hardys arrived at the airport. Soon they were off the ground and headed for their destination. A little more than two hours later the pilot made a smooth landing at La Guardia Airport.

Frank and Joe got on a bus that took them into the city. There they looked in the classified telephone directory and made more than a dozen calls to various bookshops, but to no avail.

Finally they went to a street well known for second-hand bookshops. After hours of searching, they finally discovered a copy of the book their father wanted.

"What luck!" Frank exclaimed as he flipped through its pages.

Joe, meanwhile, glanced casually towards the rare-book section. Suddenly his eyes fastened on a certain volume. He grabbed Frank's shoulder. "Look! Over there!"

·3·

Trapped at Sea

"It's the symbol!" Frank exclaimed. "Just like the one I saw on the first mate's ring!"

The boys stared at an old volume entitled *Empire of the Twisted Claw*. The strange, red-coloured insignia was stamped on its cover. Thick glass doors with sturdy locks prevented the Hardys from examining the book more closely.

At that moment the proprietor of the shop appeared. "Find something that interests you?" he inquired.

"How much are you asking for that book?" Joe asked.

The man adjusted his glasses and peered at the volume. "I'll have to look up the exact price. But nothing on this shelf goes for less than over one thousand dollars."

Frank and Joe looked glum. Buying the book was out of the question.

The proprietor saw that they were greatly disappointed. He regarded them for a moment, then smiled. "Tell you what. Promise to be careful, and I'll let you see the volume."

The Hardys were elated. They thanked the man as he pulled the book from the shelf and placed it on a reading table nearby.

"It's dated 1786," Frank observed as he and Joe examined the opening page.

The text that followed revealed a fascinating story. It concerned the adventures of an early eighteenth-century pirate named Cartoll. The sight of his ship, the *Black Parrot*, struck fear into those who sailed the Atlantic trade routes of that era.

"Good grief!" Joe exclaimed. "Whoever named the freighter we tried to investigate must've known about Cartoll."

"Kind of weird. What do you make of it?" Frank asked.

"I don't know. Let's go back to the story."

Reading on, the boys learned that Cartoll discovered an island somewhere in the Caribbean. He used it not only as a base of operations for his pirating activities, but also for the creation of a private kingdom. Cartoll referred to his realm as the Empire of the Twisted Claw.

"Wow!" Joe declared. "He certainly was an ambitious guy."

"It says here," Frank stated as he ran his finger along the page, "that the few natives on the island were forced to become his subjects. Later, his kingdom was enlarged by bringing captives there from the ships he had plundered."

The story also revealed that Cartoll had formed an elite personal guard. Each of the men had the symbol of the twisted claw on the breastplate of his armour.

As the Hardys turned the next page, they found that the remainder of the text was so faded it was impossible to continue reading. Apparently the last section of the volume had been damaged by seawater.

"Bad luck." Frank sighed. "I was hoping we'd learn

more about Cartoll and where his island was located."

"If we could take the book to our crime lab," Joe suggested, "the rest of the text might show up under ultra-violet light."

"The owner will never go along with it," Frank replied.

"What've we got to lose? Let's try, anyway."

The proprietor flatly refused their request. He quickly placed the book back on its shelf. "You fellows must think I'm crazy!"

"Not at all, sir," Frank said apologetically. "We can't tell you why at the moment, but it's important that we see the rest of the text."

"Only the buyer of that book will leave my shop with it!" the man snapped. "Anyway, I'd never permit it to be exposed to chemicals and lights."

The young detectives decided not to press the issue any further. They paid for the volume of essays and started back to the airport.

"I wonder if there's another copy of that *Twisted Claw* book around somewhere," Joe remarked as Wayne lifted the plane off the runway at La Guardia.

Frank glanced at his brother. "The bookshop owner claimed that it's the only one known to be in existence. If there *is* another one, it could take years to track it down."

It was early evening when they arrived home. After supper Frank settled down to look at the book they had bought for their father. Joe, meanwhile, leafed through the evening newspaper.

Suddenly he sat bolt upright in his chair. "Frank! We're due for a break! This is great!"

"What are you talking about?"

"There's an item here which says the *Black Parrot* has developed engine trouble and is returning to Bayport Harbour for repairs!"

"When?"

"Sometime tomorrow afternoon," Joe replied, tossing the paper to his brother.

Frank read the article. "According to this, the captain doesn't expect repairs to take more than twenty-four hours."

"This might be our last chance to investigate the ship," Joe said. "We'll have to work fast."

The following afternoon the boys drove to Bayport Harbour, hopeful that the ship would arrive as scheduled. Their spirits soared when they spotted the *Black Parrot* easing into a dock.

Members of the crew spilled down the gangway to help secure the lines.

"Let's stick to our original plan," Frank suggested. "We'll disguise ourselves as seamen again and board the ship after dark."

"Meanwhile, I'll call Chet and ask him to meet us here later," Joe said.

As night approached, the young detectives began putting on their disguise and facial make-up. They finished just as Chet arrived. Their friend was dumbfounded when he saw his two chums.

"How do we look?" Joe asked him.

"Great!" Chet declared. "You'd fool anybody into thinking you're a couple of old salts."

The Hardys then told him what they wanted him to do. "And remember," Frank urged, "stay out of sight and keep your eyes open. Don't run for help unless we really get into a tough spot."

"Roger. You can count on me," Chet replied.

The boys braced themselves and started down the pier towards the *Black Parrot*. They climbed the gangway and stepped on to the deck.

A crewman came towards them. He stopped and glanced at the youths. "I ain't seen you guys aboard before."

Frank mumbled in double-talk.

"Better check with the first mate then," the fellow advised. "You'll find him in the forward galley."

"Thanks," Joe replied.

The crewman continued on his way. Casually the boys walked along the deck for a short distance, then dashed down a passageway.

"Whew!" Joe sighed. "That was close. I was afraid that guy would insist on taking us to the first mate."

Frank creased his brow. "There's a chance he might check later to see if we did report. We'd better not risk staying aboard too long."

"What should we investigate first?"

"The cargo hold. I'd like to see what sort of load they're carrying."

Stealthily they made their way midships, pulled open a hatch, and descended a ladder into the cargo hold. Taking out their torches, the boys began to scan the area. The room was filled with wooden crates. They carefully prised the top off one of the boxes and found that it contained a coil of electric cable.

Examination of the labels on other crates indicated that the merchandise varied from leather goods to automobile parts. Most of the shipments were marked for Iceland.

"So far," Frank remarked, "there's nothing suspicious about this cargo."

"Maybe it's all a cover-up for some kind of an illegal operation," Joe said.

As they continued their search, the beam of Joe's torch fell upon a metal enclosure. It formed a small, separate room at the far end of the hold.

"Wonder what's in there," Joe said.

"Let's take a look," Frank suggested.

The Hardys unlatched the door of the enclosure and went inside.

Joe let out a low whistle. "More crates. And they're marked 'Explosives'!"

Frank tugged at the top of a box. "We'd need a long crowbar to break into one of these."

Suddenly the area outside the enclosure was filled with light and crewmen descended the ladder into the hold.

The boys listened anxiously as one of the men shouted an order to the others. "Double check to see everything is secure!"

Frank and Joe held their breath. The door of the enclosure was partially open. They stiffened at the sound of approaching footsteps.

"Hey!" a man yelled. "Someone left the door to the special storeroom unlatched. Won't you guys ever learn?"

An instant later the door was slammed shut. The Hardys were left in total darkness.

Frank switched on his torch. "Oh, oh. Now we're in for it. There's no latch on the inside. We're trapped!"

"Wh-what'll we do?" Joe stammered.

"Either yell for help and get caught, or wait until

the hold is clear and try to find a way out. What say?"

"Let's wait."

Ten minutes later they heard the men leave.

"Okay, let's move some of this stuff to see if there's another exit," Frank suggested.

He placed his torch on the floor near the door and with Joe's help moved the heavy crates away from the walls. The work was back-breaking, but to no avail. There were no other doors!

Dripping with perspiration, the Hardys sat down on the floor and leaned against a crate to ponder their next move. As Joe made himself comfortable, his fingers touched an object and he picked it up.

"Hey," he cried out, "look what I've found!"

Frank beamed his light on a large screwdriver which Joe held in his hand.

"Maybe we can open the latch with this," Frank said. "Here, let me have it." He scrambled up and tried to ram the tool through the narrow slit between the door and the wall. No luck. The screwdriver was much too thick.

"Oh, nuts!" Joe said.

"Let's see if we can't locate something else," Frank said hopefully.

They shifted the crates again and scoured the floor. Their hands were black with dirt, and they coughed as dust choked their nostrils. But not another tool was to be found.

"I guess we'll just have to wait until someone comes down again, and then play it by ear," Joe muttered.

Presently the boys sensed a strong vibration. The engines on the *Black Parrot* had been started.

"The ship's getting underway!" Joe exclaimed.

·4·

Good Old Chet

"WE'VE got to get out of here!" Frank declared.

The Hardys tried to force the door, but their efforts were useless. They thought of Chet. Would he give the alarm? Perhaps he'd send the Coast Guard to free them.

Finally, drowsy because of the lack of fresh air, they dozed off. Hours passed before they awoke.

Frank glanced at his watch. "The ship must be eighty or ninety miles out of Bayport by now," he said weakly.

"We can't stay in here much longer," Joe answered. He was breathing heavily. "Our only chance is to let them know we're in the storeroom."

"You're right. Start pounding on the door. We're bound to attract someone's attention."

Each of the boys removed one of their shoes and used it to hammer away at the door. But no one heard them.

"It's no use," Joe muttered in despair.

They were ready to give up, when Frank suddenly whispered tensely, "Wait! I hear footsteps!"

An instant later the door was pulled open. The boys found themselves facing three startled crewmen.

"Who are you?" one of them demanded. "Watcha doin' in here?"

The Hardys did not answer. Hungrily they gulped in fresh air.

"Stowaways, eh?" the man snarled. "The cap'n will know how to deal with you!" He stared at the youths curiously. "What's that you got on your faces?"

Frank and Joe glanced at each other. They realized with dismay that the hours they had spent in the warm, stagnant air of the enclosure had caused their make-up to streak. They had no choice but to remove it completely.

"Why, they're a couple of kids!" one of the men shouted in surprise.

The boys were ordered to march off with one of the crew members leading the way to the captain. He was a middle-aged man with a thin beard and skin that looked as tough as an elephant's hide. His eyes were deep-set and piercing. The Hardys felt uncomfortable in his presence.

"Cap'n," the crewman reported, "we found these two guys hidin' in the special storeroom."

"What were you doing there?" the officer demanded. "How did you get aboard?"

At that moment the first mate appeared on the scene. His eyes widened with surprise when he saw the Hardys. "What are those troublemakers doin' here?" he thundered.

"You know them?" the captain asked.

"Yes, sir. Had to run them off the ship when we were takin' on cargo in Bayport Harbour. They asked for work and I hired them to help load. Then that blond-haired one tried to pick a fight with me."

"You've no right shoving people around!" Joe said.

"Quiet!" the captain shouted. "Now that you're

aboard, you'll stay. And you'll work without pay."

"We demand you let us off this ship!" Frank exclaimed.

The first mate roared with laughter. "It's a long swim back to Bayport!"

"What's your next port?" Joe asked. "We'll go ashore there."

"None of your business," the captain retorted. "What's more, if you give us any trouble you won't eat. Now I'm turning you over to my first mate. His name is Marik. You'll be responsible to him."

"I warn you," Frank protested. "You'll regret it if you try to keep us aboard!"

Marik stepped forward and shoved them on ahead of him. "Stow the talk and get goin'. We can use a couple of hands in the galley. Some hard work will take the starch out of you."

When they arrived in the galley, the first mate ordered the Hardys to begin scrubbing the floor. "I want the job finished before the cooks come on duty to start breakfast. That gives you only an hour."

"But we need some sleep and food!" Joe protested.

"No back talk!" Marik growled.

Frank and Joe were given brushes and pails. They finished their task just minutes before the cooks appeared.

"So you're the stowaways Marik told me about," one of the men boomed. "I've got orders to see that you're kept busy. Look lively now!"

As soon as one galley chore was completed, the boys were assigned another. The aroma of food nearly drove them mad with hunger. Finally they were permitted a few moments to eat.

When they had finished, one of the cooks shouted to Frank, "Hey, you! Take this tray of food to the skipper!"

Frank picked it up. As he approached the captain's cabin he heard voices inside. Cautiously he pressed his ear against the door.

"I don't like havin' those kids aboard, Cap'n," a man grumbled. Frank recognized the voice. It was Marik. "They might be a couple of snoopers tryin' to find out about the set-up."

"Stop worrying," was the reply. "They're just stowaways looking for a free ride. Well, that's what they're going to get. They won't get off this ship till we reach the island."

"You're takin' 'em all the way?" Marik asked. "I hope you know what you're doin'."

"Leave it to me. But just to be safe, lock the kids up in the storeroom when we put into Stormwell tomorrow morning."

"Stormwell!" Frank thought. "That's a port on the Canadian coast!" He waited a few seconds before knocking on the cabin door. Summoned by the captain to enter, he delivered the tray, then hurried back to the galley.

It was late evening before the boys had an opportunity to talk. Frank told his brother what he had overheard.

"So! They intend to keep us prisoners!" Joe said angrily.

"Yes! Somehow we've got to make it ashore when the ship docks at Stormwell!"

"Slim chance of that if we're locked in the storeroom."

G

Frank thought a moment. "We've one thing in our favour," he said finally. "The captain and Marik don't know we're on to them. And they're not planning to lock us up until the ship docks, or shortly before—"

"I get it!" Joe interrupted. "We'll wait till the last minute, then make a break for it."

Just then the boys heard footsteps. They whirled round to see Marik and four crewmen walking towards them.

"I've been watchin' you guys," the first mate growled. "You're up to somethin'."

"What do you mean?" Frank asked.

"Shut up!" Marik shouted fiercely. "The cap'n gave me orders to lock you up in the mornin'. But I'm not takin' any chances. You're goin' to the storeroom right now!"

"That's what you think!" Joe protested. He flung himself at the first mate and together they went crashing to the deck.

Frank joined in the fight. He bent low and rammed his shoulder into the midriff of one of the crewmen. Then he struck out with a blow that sent another hurtling against the bulkhead. The mêlée attracted more members of the crew. Outnumbered, the Hardys were finally subdued.

"Take 'em to the storeroom!" Marik yelled as he struggled to his feet.

The boys were marched off to the cargo hold and into the metal-walled enclosure. Then the door was slammed shut and locked.

"It'll take a miracle to get us out of this," Joe said

Though hours dragged by, Frank and Joe were only able to sleep for short periods. They were anxious abou what would happen next. Glumly they talked of Chet. Maybe something had befallen him, too. Perhaps he never had a chance to report where they were!

Frank glanced at the luminous dial on his watch. "Good grief! It's morning. Nearly eight o'clock!"

"Listen!" Joe said. "The ship's engines. They're slowing down."

"We must be putting into Stormwell."

"If only we could get out of here!"

For a while there were sounds of activity on the deck above. Then, almost an hour passed before they heard footsteps again.

The storeroom door was pulled open. A crewman ordered the youths to follow him and led them up on deck. Two Canadian policemen were standing with the captain of the *Black Parrot*.

"Are you the lads from Bayport?" one of them asked.

"Yes!" the Hardys answered excitedly.

"Stowaways, you mean!" the captain barked. "I locked them up to teach them a lesson. We were going to put them ashore later."

"Liar," Joe muttered.

The policemen ushered the boys down the gangway and towards a waiting car.

"Hello, sons," came a familiar voice from inside the vehicle. "Climb in."

"Dad!" Frank cried out, nearly speechless.

"What—what are you doing here?" stammered Joe. "How did you know where we—?"

Mr Hardy grinned. "Get into the car and I'll explain."

As they drove off, the detective told his sons that he had been working in Montreal in connection with his case. By coincidence he had telephoned home only seconds after Chet had arrived to inform Mrs Hardy that Frank and Joe had sailed off in the *Black Parrot.*

"Good old Chet!" Joe exclaimed.

"He didn't take immediate action," Mr Hardy said, "because he thought it might be part of your plan to sail with the ship a short distance, then dive overboard. But he began to worry after an hour and decided to tell your mother what had happened."

"Lucky for us," Frank commented.

Their father went on to say that he checked with Bayport Harbour and learned that the *Black Parrot* was to make a stop in Stormwell.

"And so," Mr Hardy concluded, "I requested the help of the Canadian police, just in case the captain had any ideas about making you boys permanent members of the crew."

"And he decided to turn us loose," Joe added, "rather than risk an investigation."

"That's just what I hoped would happen," Mr Hardy said.

He noticed Frank's eyelids start to droop. "Try to catch a few winks," he went on. "We'll continue our discussion when we get to Montreal."

When they arrived, the detective obtained accommodation for Frank and Joe at the hotel where he was staying. The boys slept for a few hours, then had dinner served in their room. Their father entered as they finished eating.

"Feeling better?"

"I'll say," Joe assured him.

"And now, Dad, we'd like to tell you what information we dug up," Frank began, and they described their adventures aboard the *Black Parrot*. Then they informed their father that they had found the book he wanted and about the rare volume they had looked at in the New York bookshop.

Mr Hardy was stunned. "An island kingdom called the Empire of the Twisted Claw, you say?"

"Yes," Frank answered. "It was ruled by a pirate named Cartoll."

The detective began to pace the floor. Finally he spoke. "What an amazing story. And it seems to tie in with my case!"

"How?" Frank asked.

"I'm not certain yet. But from what you told me, this might prove to be one of the strangest mysteries we've ever encountered!"

· 5 ·

Solo Assignments

FRANK and Joe waited in anticipation as their father settled into a chair opposite them.

"Boys," Mr Hardy began, "I've been engaged by the Reed Museum Association to investigate a series of thefts. Four museums have been robbed within a few days, three in the United States and the Abbey Museum here in Montreal."

"What were the thieves after? Gems? Precious metals?" questioned Frank.

"That's one of the strange facts about the case, the detective explained. "Each of the museums had a portion of the DeGraw collection on display. It was only those items that were stolen. Nothing else in the buildings was touched."

"What's the DeGraw collection?" Joe queried.

Mr Hardy explained that Elden DeGraw was a wealthy financier who took an interest in archaeology. Several years before, he had discovered a sunken galleon in the Caribbean. The ship was filled with priceless royal treasures, including sceptres, crowns, and orbs. Of particular interest were suits of armour which had red, twisted claw symbols on their breastplates."

"Wow!" Joe exclaimed. "The armour might have belonged to Cartoll's elite guard!"

Mr Hardy leaned forward. "That's why I was a bit stunned when you told me the story about the pirate and his Empire of the Twisted Claw."

"Are there any other museums that have portions of the collection?" Frank asked.

"Yes," his father replied. "DeGraw divided up the items and donated them to ten different museums—the Abbey Museum here and nine in the United States."

"Do you think the thieves will try to rob the other six?" Joe inquired.

"I'm sure of it," Mr Hardy said.

He then told his sons that he had a hunch the loot was being taken out of the country, but how was a mystery. Each portion of the collection was bulky and would be difficult to smuggle.

"I considered the possibility of a ship being involved," Mr Hardy continued. "Checking, I learned that the freighter *Black Parrot* and its sister ship *Yellow Parrot* were suspected of carrying on some sort of illegal operation. But no one has ever come up with a shred of evidence. That's why I asked you to investigate."

"Without much success," Frank muttered dejectedly.

"At least we know Dad's hunch was right," Joe put in.

"Hold it," Mr Hardy ordered with a grin. "There's lots to learn about the case before making any conclusions."

The boys accompanied their father to the scene of the recent theft. The curator of the Abbey Museum was greatly upset over the loss of the collection. "I don't understand how they could have broken into the building without setting off the alarm," he said.

"I don't either," Mr Hardy admitted. "The system wasn't tampered with and is in perfect working order."

At that moment the telephone rang. The curator picked up the instrument, then handed it to Mr Hardy. "It's for you. Mr Hertford of the Reed Museum Association."

The detective stiffened when he heard what his caller had to say. Finally he hung up and turned to the boys. "We're flying to New York immediately! The Standon Museum has been robbed. Its portion of the deGraw collection is gone!"

The Hardys quickly made airline reservations and were on their way within the hour. When they arrived at the museum, the young detectives assisted their father in searching for clues.

"Hm! This robbery is like all the others," Mr Hardy observed. "The alarm system is intact, and there's been a clean sweep of the collection."

"How does the system work?" Frank asked.

"When turned on," his father explained, "invisible beams of light criss-cross the exhibit rooms from all directions just inches above the floor. It operates on the photoelectric cell principle."

"I get it!" Joe interrupted. "Anyone walking into the room would break the light beams and set off the alarm."

"Pretty effective," Frank added. "A thief would have to be able to float through the air like a balloon to escape detection."

Mr Hardy nodded. "I'd give anything to know the gang's *modus operandi*."

After completing their investigation, the Hardys spent the night in New York, then returned to Bayport the following morning. The boys joined their father in his study to hear a plan he had in mind.

"Five museums still have their DeGraw collections," Mr Hardy said. "And we don't know which is next on the thieves' list. The local police can't spare men to be on constant surveillance, and the museum guards need help. My plan is to have each of us cover one and prevent a robbery, if possible."

"We can have Chet help us out, too," Joe suggested.

Mr Hardy appeared somewhat dubious. "Do you think he can handle an assignment like this?"

"I'm sure he can," Frank replied.

"All right." The detective unfolded a sheet of paper. "Here's a list of the museums. Four of them are in neighbouring states. The fifth is in California. I'll have Sam Radley take care of that one."

Frank and Joe had often worked with Radley, their father's assistant, and knew he would do a good job.

Then Frank telephoned Chet to tell him about the plan. The stout boy was jubilant.

"I'm ready to leave any time!" he declared. "It'll be a sorry day for those crooks if they try to rob the place with me on guard!"

By evening Mr Hardy had completed all the necessary arrangements. Early the next morning Frank, Joe, Sam Radley, and Chet met in his study for a final briefing. After reviewing his plan, Mr Hardy gave a word of warning. "Remember, we don't know where the thieves will strike next. They're clever and dangerous. So don't take any chances."

After wishing each other luck, they started out on their individual assignments. Frank was to cover a museum in Philadelphia. He arrived in the afternoon and introduced himself to the curator, Bruce Watkins.

"Ah, yes," said the scholarly-looking official. "Your father phoned that you were coming. I feel comforted that such famous detectives as the Hardys are investigating the recent robberies."

"Thank you," Frank said. "Now, if you don't mind, I'd like to see your DeGraw collection."

The curator led him through a series of exhibit rooms. It was a magnificent old building with marble columns and floors. They entered a large room filled with ancient artefacts. One section of it contained the DeGraw collection.

"Here we are," the curator announced.

Frank stared in awe at the sceptres, crowns, and orbs displayed in a large glass case. Then his attention was drawn to a suit of armour with a red, twisted claw symbol on the breastplate.

"This is our most popular exhibit," the curator said proudly.

Frank examined his surroundings. "What kind of an alarm system do you have here?" he queried.

"The windows, doors, and most of the glass cases are well-protected," the man answered. "We are planning to install a photoelectric cell just as soon as the finances are made available to us."

"What about guards at night?"

"We have four, but will get more from an agency as soon as we can."

At that moment a staff member told the curator that he was wanted on the phone. He excused himself and hurried off.

Frank returned to the DeGraw collection and examined it more closely. Then he strolled round the other

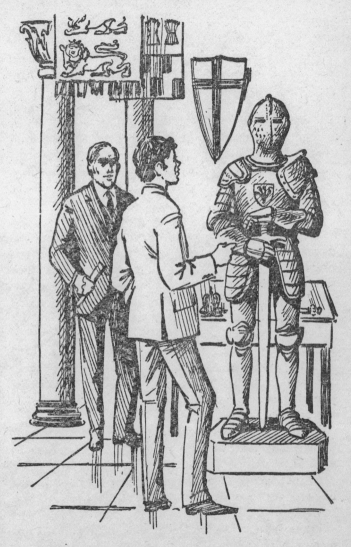

"This is our most popular exhibit," Watkins said.

rooms. He entered one which contained large monoliths from a Pacific Island, and stopped for a moment to admire the exhibit.

As he stood there, one of the stone columns behind him silently began to topple forward. Frank was directly in its path!

· 6 ·

A Desperate Moment

FRANK suddenly spotted the reflection of the falling column in the highly polished floor of the room. He gasped, and in a lightning move, he threw himself to one side.

Crash! The column hit the floor with an ear-splitting impact.

Frank was sprayed with bits of shattered rock as he tumbled across the floor. The curator, a guard, and several members came running.

"What happened?" one of them shouted.

Frank sprang to his feet. "I was almost flattened by that column," he said grimly. "It toppled over."

The curator stared in disbelief. "How could such a thing happen?"

"The column had rather a broad base," a staff member interjected. "It stood firmly in the upright position."

"Someone must have pushed it over," Frank remarked.

"Nonsense!" Watkins exclaimed, obviously startled by the suggestion. He hesitated for a moment. "Although I suppose it could be done by a man with exceptional strength."

"See here!" another staff man interrupted. "Are you

suggesting that someone deliberately toppled the column?"

"Under the circumstances," Frank mused thoughtfully, "I must consider it a possibility."

"Why would anyone do such a thing?"

"For reasons I can't divulge right now," Frank replied.

He drew the curator aside. "I have a hunch this museum is next on the thieves' list. Somehow the gang must have discovered who I am, and why I'm here. Pushing that column over could have been an attempt to get me out of the way."

"Oh, come now," Watkins retorted. "Aren't you jumping to conclusions? I'm sure the whole thing was just an accident."

"All the same, we'd better assign more men to guard the DeGraw exhibit," Frank urged.

"I've already decided on another course of action," the curator said. "The entire collection will be taken to our basement storeroom immediately. It'll stay there until this whole affair of museum robberies is ended."

Watkins ordered all available staff members to begin work at once. Nearly two hours went by before the last item of the collection was carried into the storeroom and the door securely locked by Watkins.

"I still recommend that guards be posted," Frank said. "A locked door alone is not going to stop the thieves."

"Well—all right," Watkins agreed, shrugging his shoulders. "But I can spare only two men. The rest will have to go about their regular duties."

"We can ask the local police to help," the young

sleuth suggested. "Perhaps they can spare a couple of—"

"Out of the question!" the curator declared indignantly. "Policemen attract newspaper reporters. I'm not going to risk wild rumours being circulated that something is wrong here at the museum."

Frank was annoyed by the man's attitude. Watkins was more worried about his personal image than about the protection of the collection.

"Anyway," the curator continued, "you're only acting on a hunch."

"Have it your way," Frank said tartly. "I hope you won't have reason to regret your decision."

"Hardly," Watkins assured him. He grinned. "You detectives tend to be too suspicious. I doubt if the thieves are within a thousand miles of this museum."

At that moment a tall, muscular, hard-faced man entered the basement. He was carrying a pair of shears which he placed in a tool chest. Then he hurried away. Something about the man made Frank uneasy.

"Who was that?" he asked the curator in a low voice.

"Our gardener," replied Watkins. "He takes care of the grounds round the building as well as other odd jobs."

"How long has he been employed here?"

"Less than a week, actually. We're lucky to have him. We can't pay very much and it's difficult to find someone to do the work."

The curator added that the man's name was Starker, and that he had excellent references.

After the guards were posted, Watkins invited Frank to his home for dinner.

"Thank you. But I'd better stick around here. I'll

have a quick meal at one of the local restaurants later."

As night approached, Frank had the guards help him check all doors and windows. Then he decided to have some food. One of the men recommended an eating place not very far from the museum.

Frank strolled out of the building and down the street. He had not walked very far when he realized that two men were following him.

As he quickened his pace, so did his pursuers. Gradually they gained on him. As the gap between them narrowed, Frank arrived at the restaurant and dashed inside.

"Soup's all gone, and so are the menu specials," a waiter announced as Frank quickly sat down at a table. "We're closing in half an hour."

Frank did not speak. He stared at the door apprehensively. The men did not follow him into the restaurant. Obviously they wanted to avoid being seen, and were waiting for him outside.

"How about a sandwich?" the waiter went on as he glanced at his watch impatiently. "Best I can do."

Frank made a selection and was quickly served. As he ate, he desperately tried to think of a way to escape his pursuers. He finally decided to call the police.

"Where's the telephone?" Frank asked the waiter.

"There's none here in the restaurant," the man replied. "You'll find a public booth on the corner down the street."

"But you must have a phone here somewhere!" the boy insisted.

"Sure," the waiter said icily, eyeing Frank with suspicion. "We have one in the kitchen. It's strictly for business, not for customers."

"This is an emergency! You must let me make a call!"

"Don't give me that," the man snarled. "What's wrong? Too lazy to walk?"

The situation was becoming more desperate. It was now closing time and several of the employees were preparing to leave.

Frank did not like what he was about to do, but he had no choice. "I—I don't think I could walk that far. I feel sick. It—it must have been the sandwich I just ate."

"Just a second, kid," the waiter fumed. "Don't accuse us of serving bad food. All our stuff is the best."

Frank settled into a chair. "Maybe," he groaned. "But I felt fine till now. Ugh—this is awful."

The waiter rushed off and returned with the proprietor of the restaurant.

"What's going on here?" the man demanded. "I hear you don't feel good. I've been in this business twenty years and never poisoned a customer yet!"

"There's always a first time," Frank muttered weakly. "Somebody get me a taxi."

The proprietor turned to the waiter. "Call him a cab," he ordered. "This kid must be crazy. The sooner we get rid of him the better."

Minutes later a taxi rolled up in front of the restaurant. The owner and several of his employees accompanied Frank as he trudged towards it and climbed in.

"Take me to the museum," he told the driver. As they sped off, he peered out the rear window in time to see two men leap out from a dark alleyway.

Arriving at his destination, Frank went to the basement to check on the storeroom. There the two guards were engaged in idle conversation.

"Everything okay?" Frank asked.

"Yeah," one of the guards replied. "Our only problem is trying to stay awake."

"Whatever you do," Frank warned, "don't fall asleep. I'll get a couple of the other men to relieve you in two hours."

He then hurried to the curator's office to telephone his father and report what had happened.

"You had a close call," Mr Hardy commented. "From what you tell me, I don't think the column fell over by accident either. And what about the men who followed you?"

"No sign of them," answered Frank. "But I did catch a glimpse of one man. He was tall and muscular. I'm sure he was Starker, the museum gardener."

"Get help," his father urged. "Call the police in on this. Never mind what the curator said. This could be serious!"

Just then a loud noise echoed through the museum. Frank asked Mr Hardy to hold on for a moment and quickly placed the phone down on the desk.

"Who's there?" he shouted.

No answer. Frank raced down into the basement. The two guards were on their feet, poised for action.

"We heard a noise!" one of them said excitedly. "What was it?"

Frank was about to reply when his attention was seized by a hissing noise. Then a white, odourless smoke began to filter into the room.

"What's that?" a guard shouted.

In the next instant several men wearing gas masks appeared. Frank lunged at the intruders, but his body seemed to be drained of energy. He fell to the floor, unconscious!

·7·

Mysterious Cargo

"WHAT—what happened?" Frank asked groggily as he regained consciousness. He found himself staring into the face of a police sergeant.

"You were knocked out by some kind of gas," the officer repli d. "So were all the guards in the building."

Still dazed, Frank struggled to sit up. "But how come you're here?" he inquired. "Who notified you?"

"Your father called headquarters," the sergeant explained. "He said you'd heard a noise in the museum and went to check it out. When you didn't return to the phone, he suspected something was wrong."

Frank glanced round. He saw several policemen inspecting the area. Others were helping to revive the two guards by the storeroom door.

Suddenly Frank sprang to his feet. "The DeGraw collection!" he cried. "Is it gone?"

"The storeroom is empty, if that's what you mean," the sergeant replied.

At that instant the curator arrived on the scene. "I received a telephone call to come here at once. What's —?" His words trailed off as he peered into the empty storeroom.

"The collection's been stolen," Frank said.

Watkins's face turned pale. "This is outrageous!"

He glared at Frank. "Why didn't you stop the thieves?"

Frank fought hard to control his temper. "I warned you, sir. We should have called in the police."

"Are you trying to blame me for what happened?"

Frank said nothing. He did not want to waste precious time by getting involved in an argument with Watkins. Instead, he began to search the area for clues.

On the floor he spotted a short piece of rope. He examined it closely, then showed it to the police sergeant. "Do you mind if I keep this for a while?" he asked.

The officer looked at it, then returned it to Frank. "We might need it later."

"Certainly."

"I have a couple of men coming over from the crime lab to check for fingerprints," the sergeant went on. "You get some sleep. I'll let you know if we find anything."

"Think I will," Frank agreed wearily. He went to the curator's office and settled down into a comfortable chair.

He slept several hours before he was gently shaken awake. "Hello, son," came his father's voice.

"Dad! When did you get here?"

"A couple of hours ago. I decided to let you sleep a while longer."

Frank grimaced. "Then you know about the robbery."

"It wasn't your fault. I had a talk with the curator. Never met such a stubborn man. He should have given you more co-operation."

Frank filled his father in on all the facts. Then Mr

Hardy said, "We're dealing with a shrewd ring of thieves. But they must know we're on to their game. I have a hunch the gang will wait for a while before they pull off another robbery."

"What's our next move?"

"Breakfast and then back to Bayport. I've already called Joe and the others. The local police have agreed to take over in the other towns and will guard the museums heavily for an indefinite period of time."

Fenton Hardy and Frank arrived in Bayport in the early afternoon. Joe had just come home and was in the study with Chet.

"Hi!" Chet greeted them. "Heard you had a tussle with the museum thieves."

"And they won," Frank replied ruefully.

"By the way," Joe said, "Sam Radley telephoned from California. He had trouble getting an airline reservation and won't be here till tomorrow morning."

At Joe's request, Frank repeated the story about the robbery. Then he produced the piece of rope he had found on the floor of the storeroom.

"Looks like ordinary rope to me," Chet muttered.

"It does," Frank agreed. "My guess is that it's part of the rope the thieves must have used to tie up the loot. But here's what I find particularly interesting. Notice that it's neatly spliced."

Joe shrugged his shoulders. "So what?"

"Doesn't it suggest anything to you?" Frank questioned.

Suddenly Joe's eyes lit up. "Oh, I get it. Experienced sailors are usually good at splicing ropes. Maybe the crew of the *Black Parrot* have been committing the robberies!"

"Could be," said Mr Hardy. "But I have a hunch that they're only involved in transporting the loot."

Frank agreed. "The thefts seem to be the work of a skilled gang."

Joe eagerly suggested that they try again to investigate the *Black Parrot*. Their father was reluctant. He warned the boys that they would surely be recognized by the captain and most of the crew.

"We won't attempt to board the ship," Frank explained. "We'll observe it from a distance. With luck, we might pick up some useful information."

There was a long pause. "All right, I'll go along with your plan," Mr Hardy said finally. "But you must be extremely careful."

"We will," Frank promised.

Joe was jubilant. But an instant later his enthusiasm disappeared. "Wait a minute. We've overlooked something. Where do we find the *Black Parrot*?"

"I have a hunch that the ship will be back at the East Coast sooner or later," Frank said. "Let's try all the ports up to Canada."

During the next few days the Hardys checked the shipping schedules in the newspapers, and kept in constant contact with the various harbour authorities. A week went by before Frank's prediction proved to be correct.

"You were right!" Joe said. "The *Black Parrot* is due to dock at Stormwell again the day after tomorrow."

"We'll leave for Canada in the morning," Frank decided. "Too bad we can't use Dad's plane. But Jack's flying him to Philadelphia tomorrow. He wants to have another talk with Watkins."

Chet needed no persuading to go along. They

arrived at their destination late the following afternoon and checked in at a hotel near Stormwell.

"How about something to eat?" Chet suggested.

"Okay," Frank answered, smiling. "I noticed a dining-room just off the hall."

"So did I," the stout youth admitted.

"You didn't expect Chet to miss any spot where food is served," Joe said to his brother jokingly. "He has a built-in compass that would lead him to all the restaurants within fifty miles."

"Cut it out, fellows," Chet said.

They entered the dining-room and sat down at a table. A waiter handed each of them a menu. While they were trying to decide what to order, Frank could not help overhearing a conversation between two men sitting at an adjacent table.

"The *Black Parrot* wasn't due in till tomorrow," one of them said angrily. "So what happens? The ship shows up a couple of hours ago. It's forcing me to rearrange my docking schedule."

"I don't like those *Parrot* ships, anyway," the other man commented. "There's something strange about them. Wish they'd stay away from Stormwell."

"Luckily the *Black Parrot* won't be in port long. It isn't picking up much cargo, and the crew looked as if they were in a big hurry to get underway again."

Frank leaped to his feet. Followed by Joe and Chet, he rushed past the startled waiter and out of the dining-room.

The hotel manager quickly secured them a rented car, and the boys headed for the docks.

As they approached the waterfront, Joe pointed

towards the pier, "There she is! What's that they're hauling aboard?"

"Looks like a pile of logs," Chet said. "I'd say about a dozen."

Frank's attention was focused on a trailer from which the cargo was being lifted. On the side of the vehicle was the name *Norland Timber Company, Cloud Lake, Canada.*

The boys watched as the logs were lowered into the hold of the *Black Parrot.* Then crewmen began to move round the deck. Shortly the ship's engines rumbled and a boiling cauldron of foamy water appeared at the stern.

"That was a short visit," Chet muttered as he and the Hardys watched the freighter glide away from the pier.

"Odd," Joe remarked. "Why would the ship come here just to pick up a dozen logs?"

Frank's thoughts were elsewhere at the moment. "Norland Timber Company," he said to himself. "This might be worth investigating."

The boys saw two men climb into the lorry and drive off.

"What do you make of it?" Joe asked.

"I'm not sure yet," Frank said. "But right now, I think we'd better check out that timber company."

After returning to the hotel, Frank phoned the local police.

"Yes. I can tell you something about the Norland firm," an officer said in response to his question. Actually, it's a timber mill. I hear it may close down."

"Where is it located?"

"Thirty miles north-west of here—just off the Old Pine Road."

"Thank you," Frank said. He hung up and turned to his companions. "Let's drive out to the mill."

"But it'll be dark when we get there," Joe pointed out.

"I know, but time is important."

They hurried to the car and started off. The Old Pine Road was unsurfaced and driving was difficult.

Suddenly the car began to wobble. Frank stopped and jumped out. Seconds later he gave a cry of dismay, "We have a flat!"

"Great!" Joe muttered in disgust. "Just what we need!"

He and Chet helped Frank to take out the spare tyre. While Frank jacked up the car, Chet flopped down on the spare. *Pffft!* The tyre collapsed under his weight.

"Oh, no!" Joe shook his head. "The spare's no good!"

"We're stuck," Frank admitted. He furrowed his brow. "The mill can't be more than a mile from here. Let's walk."

Chet did not think much of this suggestion, but he did not want to stay in the car, either. "I'd better go along," he mumbled. "Somebody has to see to it that you guys don't get into trouble!"

The trio trudged on. Darkness had settled over the trees and progress was slow.

Joe took out his torch and scanned the area. "Look," he said. "Tyre tracks!"

"They were made by a heavy lorry," Frank concluded. "Like the one we saw at the pier."

He motioned Joe and Chet to halt, and listened intently.

"What's the matter?" Joe whispered after a few minutes of tense silence.

"I thought I heard something in the underbrush."

"Like what, for instance?" Chet quavered.

Frank shone his light at the trees, but all was still. "Maybe it was just a squirrel."

"I think we should wait till tomorrow," Chet suggested. "This looks like trouble!"

"Why don't you walk back to the car and Joe and I'll go alone," Frank said.

Chet shifted uncomfortably from one foot to the other. "No," he said. "I'll come with you."

Proceeding cautiously, they finally spotted a small group of wooden buildings ahead. Light came from a window in one of them.

"That must be the mill," Joe whispered.

Frank nodded, then signalled to his brother and Chet to follow.

All at once the ground gave way beneath them. A split second later the boys plunged into a deep hole!

·8·

Fire!

THE boys lay stunned. Shortly, beams of light pierced the darkness from the rim of the hole above.

"We have visitors," a man's voice snarled.

"Three, to be exact," said another.

"Who are you?" Frank demanded as he struggled to his feet.

There was no response. Instead, a rope was tossed down into the hole.

"Start climbin' out of there!" one of the men ordered. "And don't try anythin'. We're armed."

Frank helped his brother and Chet to their feet. Then they hoisted themselves up out of the hole. The boys could only make out the vague images of three men holding pistols and powerful torches.

"Now talk!" one of the men growled. "What're you kids doin' here?"

"Sight-seeing," Chet said innocently.

"The fat one's a comedian!" the fellow boomed. "He won't think it's so funny when we throw them back in the hole."

They stepped closer and the tallest of the three stared at Frank and Joe. "I recognize these two!" he shouted. "They were taken off the *Black Parrot* by policemen in Stormwell."

"They're snoopers!" the man to his right exclaimed nervously. "We'd better get outta here. They might be workin' for the police!"

"Okay. But first, let's take these kids to the hut and tie 'em up. We don't want 'em trailin' us."

The Hardys and Chet were herded to one of the wooden structures and shoved inside. Then their arms and legs were tightly bound with ropes. When the job was finished, the three men left. For a few seconds they stood outside talking in the dark.

Joe rolled over and pressed an ear to the wall.

"What'll we do now?" one man whispered.

"Head for Port Manthon. The *Yellow Parrot*'s docked there for repairs," said another. "We'll board it and sail out of the country. Let's get the lorry. We can make it in three or four hours if we hurry."

When they moved on, Joe excitedly relayed the conversation.

Frank said, "Port Manthon is about a hundred miles further up the coast. If only we could get loose and—" His words were interrupted by the sound of a lorry engine being started.

"They're leaving!" declared Joe.

As the men drove off, a shower of glowing carbon sparks spouted from the vehicle's exhaust pipe. The red-hot particles landed amongst some dry undergrowth. Smoke appeared, then flames.

Unaware of what was happening, the boys tried to free themselves.

Chet suddenly yelled, "I smell smoke!"

"So do I!" Joe said.

"Fire!" exclaimed Frank.

Outside, the flames were spreading at a furious rate.

Soon the boys could feel the heat radiating through the thin, wooden walls of the hut.

"We've got to get out of here!" Joe cried. He rolled across the floor towards the door of the structure and kicked it open. "Come on!" he urged his companions.

Frank and Chet quickly followed. Outside, Joe found the sharp edge of a partially embedded rock and used it to cut the ropes binding him. Then he freed the others.

The boys looked round in horror. They were completely encircled by a raging inferno. The heat was almost unbearable.

"We're done for!" Chet shouted.

"The mill is beginning to catch fire!" Frank cried.

Desperately the Hardys sought some means of escape. There was none!

Then Joe grabbed his brother's arm. "Listen!"

A flapping noise came from the distance. As the sound grew louder, they looked up to see a Royal Canadian Air Force helicopter hovering overhead.

"Wh-what's going on?" Chet stammered weakly.

"We're getting out of here!" Frank shouted to him.

The boys waved their arms wildly. A rescue sling was lowered from the chopper, and, one by one, they were hoisted aboard.

Then the craft hovered over the site of the fire, pouring ribbons of white foam on the blaze. Another helicopter joined it, and together they extinguished the fire.

"We reached you just in time," said one of the crew members. "What were you fellows doing in the middle of a forest fire?"

The Hardys told him what had happened. They

said that they were not sure how the fire had started.

"Perhaps one of the men threw a match, either carelessly or intentionally, on the dry undergrowth," Frank concluded.

"Looks that way," the crew member agreed. "Anyway, the glow was sighted all the way from Stormwell. We were asked to help."

After several minutes the helicopter landed on a small airfield well beyond the scene of the fire. Local police were on hand when they arrived. The young sleuths identified themselves and repeated their story.

"What you fellows told us fits in with an arrest we made an hour ago," explained one of the officers. "Three men in a lorry were stopped for speeding outside Stormwell. I recognized two of them as being wanted for larceny and fraud. They're already on their way to Montreal for questioning."

Then Frank, Joe, and Chet were driven back to their hotel. They had a quick meal, after which Frank placed a telephone call to his father. Mr Hardy listened to the boys' adventure with great interest.

"You've really come up with something," he said. "I'll have Jack fly me to Montreal tomorrow. I want to interrogate these three men."

"Meanwhile, we'll go to Port Manthon to check on the *Yellow Parrot*," Frank told his father.

"Good idea," Mr Hardy replied.

Next morning Frank rented another car and arranged for the first one to be recovered. Then they started off. The trip took a little more than two hours. When they arrived in Port Manthon, they drove along a road looking down on to the water. Frank pulled into a layby and parked. Then the boys got out to scan the waterfront.

Joe spotted the *Yellow Parrot* tied to a pier.

"There she is," he said.

Frank nodded. "Port Manthon is not very big. Doesn't appear as if it could accommodate more than two or three ships at a time."

"That might be the reason she came here," his brother said. "More privacy."

The boys observed the freighter for a while. There was a gaping hole in its hull near the bow. Several crewmen were repairing the damage.

"Strangers round here, aren't you?" came a voice from behind them. "Interested in ships?"

They whirled round to see a bearded old man who had walked up quietly behind them.

"Why—er—yes," answered Joe.

"We were just passing through," Frank added, "and stopped to take a look at the port."

"Not much to see these days," the man replied with regret. "Used to be mighty active round here years ago." A smile spread across his face. "But it's always good to meet up with lads who like the sea."

"Not me!" Chet interrupted. "I'm—"

His words were cut off by a sharp nudge of Joe's elbow.

"Are you from this area?" Frank put in quickly.

"Born in Port Manthon, and sailed my first ship from here nearly sixty years ago," the man said proudly. "Name's Falop. Captain Falop."

There was an exchange of handshakes. The boys gave only their first names. Then Frank pointed towards the *Yellow Parrot* and asked, "What happened to that ship?"

"Don't quite know," Falop answered. "Never saw it in here before. Odd crew. Don't want to talk much. Different from my day." He rubbed his chin dubiously. "I asked one of 'em about the damage. Can't understand why he'd try to get away with such a lie."

"Lie?" Joe echoed. "What do you mean?"

"The fella told me their ship'd run aground," explained the man, "and that the hole was caused by a sharp rock. Nonsense!"

"Why do you say that?" Frank asked.

"The hole's well above the water-line and is too neat," Falop replied. "If you ask me, I think it was done by a shell."

"You mean the ship was fired on?" Chet questioned excitedly.

"As far as I'm concerned it was."

"Wonder how long it will take to repair the damage," Frank remarked, trying to act nonchalant.

"I'd say at least two or three days," Falop replied.

The boys continued to watch the activity aboard the *Yellow Parrot*. After a while they said goodbye to the captain and checked in at the only hotel in Port Manthon. That evening Frank telephoned the authorities in Montreal and asked if his father had arrived there. A police officer stated that he had, and gave Frank the number of Mr Hardy's hotel.

When Frank reached him there, his father said, "Hope you had better luck than I did, so far. If those three men know anything about the museum robberies, they're certainly not admitting it. I'm going to try again tomorrow."

Frank then told him about the ship, and what Falop thought had caused the damage to her hull.

H

"Hm! Very interesting," said Mr Hardy. "Perhaps I'd better request a complete investigation."

"I've another idea," Frank went on. "If it works, we might learn once and for all if the *Parrot* ships are involved in the case."

"What do you have in mind?"

"Joe and I want to sail aboard the *Yellow Parrot*!"

·9·

A Daring Plan

MR HARDY strongly objected to Frank's plan. "It's too dangerous!" he insisted. "You and Joe have been seen by crew members of the *Black Parrot*. What if some of them switched ships in the meantime?"

"I doubt it, Dad," his son answered. "Their sailing schedules were such that they never came within miles of each other during the past few weeks."

"I still don't like it."

"We'll be careful."

There was a moment of silence. "Okay," Mr Hardy finally said reluctantly. "But make sure your plan is foolproof before going ahead with it."

"We will," Frank promised.

Chet tingled with excitement as he listened to the plan. "This is going to be fun!" he exclaimed. "I can't wait to get aboard!"

Frank patted him on the shoulder. "Sorry, old friend," he said sympathetically. "No reason why you should risk your neck. You'll have to go back to Bayport."

"What?" the chubby boy shouted. "I'll do nothing of the sort!"

"We know how you feel," Joe said. "But two of us will have a better chance of getting jobs than three."

Chet's pique gradually changed to a feeling of great disappointment. He continued to plead with the Hardys without success.

"Okay, have it your way," he muttered. "When do you want me to leave?"

"After the *Yellow Parrot* sails," Frank replied. "We might come up with some useful information for Dad in the meantime. Then you can give him a report."

Next day they went to the pier and watched the ship from a distance. Repairs were progressing well. Some crewmen were working with acetylene torches, while others were positioning new metal plates over the gaping hole in the hull.

"Looks as if the job is almost finished," Joe observed.

"You're right," Frank agreed. "We'd better start putting our plan into action."

They found a general store in town and purchased work clothes, then returned to the hotel to eat and change.

"I hope there's no one from the *Black Parrot* aboard," Joe remarked as he pulled on a denim jacket.

"I'm sure there isn't," Frank said.

Chet listened quietly to their conversation. He grunted a couple of times to let his friends know he was still unhappy about being left out.

Frank and Joe had finished dressing and the three went back to the pier.

"What do you want me to do?" Chet muttered.

"Keep an eye on the ship when we go aboard," Frank instructed. "I don't expect trouble, but it'll be good to know you're around to help—just in case."

Chet could not suppress a slight smile. "You can depend on me."

"We'd better put our plan into action," Frank said.

The Hardys walked towards the *Yellow Parrot* and climbed the gangway to the main deck.

"What are you fellows doin' aboard?" called out a stocky, tough-looking man.

"We'd like to see the first mate," Joe said.

"What about?"

"Jobs."

The man laughed. "Hey, Rawlin!" he shouted sarcastically. "Here's a couple of old salts wantin' to sign on."

The young detectives turned to see a tall, wiry man march down the deck towards them. "Who are you?" he demanded.

"Frank and Joe . . . Karlsen," Frank replied.

"From round here?"

"No," Joe said. "We've been travelling and doing odd jobs. But what we really want is a chance to go to sea."

Rawlin was hesitant. "I've got to think about it first."

"Why not sign 'em on?" the crewman suggested. "The king can always use a couple of more hands—"

"Shut up!" Rawlin growled.

"King?" asked Frank. "What king?"

"Well—er—I meant the cap'n," stammered the crewman. "Sometimes I call him the king."

Much to their surprise, Frank and Joe were hired and ordered to report the next morning. Elated, they hurried to tell Chet of their success.

"Dad should be home by the time you get to Bayport," Frank told his friend. "Tell him our plan is going well. We'll try to establish contact as soon as we can."

Still disgruntled, Chet departed for home that evening. Early the next day Frank and Joe reported aboard the *Yellow Parrot*. Rawlin was the only one on deck when they arrived.

"So you two were serious about going to sea," he said. "I didn't think you'd be back."

"We wouldn't miss this for anything," Joe replied.

"I'm assigning you to general duties," Rawlin went on. "We'll be sailing in two hours." He shouted through a hatchway. "Evans! Get up here!"

A thin middle-aged man appeared. "Yes, sir?"

"Find a couple of bunks for these two up forward. Then take 'em to the cargo hold with you. Make sure everything's secured."

Evans led the boys down a passageway and into a small cubicle which was to serve as their quarters.

"Not much room," Frank observed.

"Barely enough space to breathe," Joe replied.

"Don't complain," Evans snapped. "There's a lot of things you won't like aboard this ship."

The Hardys exchanged glances. Then they stowed their gear and followed the crewman to the cargo hold.

"Look!" Joe whispered. He pointed to a pile of logs tied down at the far end of the hold. "They're just like the ones we saw hoisted aboard the *Black Parrot*."

"Start checking this stuff!" Evans yelled. "Make sure it's all battened down!"

The boys did as they were told. Gradually, during the course of their inspection, they edged their way towards the pile of logs. Frank began to examine them closely.

"What are you doing?" Evans shouted in annoyance.

"Checking the cargo," Frank answered.

"Then keep moving!"

"You want us to do a good job, don't you?" Joe retorted.

"None of your back talk!" Evans gave Joe a hard shove.

Frank stepped in and the crewman lashed out with his fists. The young detective grabbed his opponent's left wrist, and with a lightning move, pinned the man's arms behind his back.

"Let go of me!" Evans yelled.

"Not unless you calm down."

"Okay! Okay!"

Frank released him. "Now I suppose you're going to report us to the captain."

Evans was embarrassed by having been overpowered. "Naw," he growled. "I'll get even with you two later. Go to your quarters and wait for further orders."

"This should be a pleasant voyage with him around," Joe said, shaking his head.

"We'll just try to stay out of his way," Frank replied. "Trouble is what we don't want."

When they arrived at their quarters, Frank spotted a note on his bunk. He snatched it and a cold chill quivered down his spine as he read aloud:

" *'Get off this ship before it's too late!'* "

·10·

Deck Watch

"Who could have written this note?" Joe exclaimed.

"I don't get it!" Frank said. "I'm sure none of the crew knows who we are. Yet someone's trying to warn us."

The ship's engines started and the hull vibrated.

"We're getting underway," Joe observed. "That was a pretty quick repair job."

Frank stuffed the note into his pocket. "Too late to worry about this now. We'll have to take our chances."

"You kids!" came Evans's voice. "Get up on deck and help haul in the lines!"

The Hardys hastened topside, where they saw the bow of the *Yellow Parrot* swerving away from the pier.

"Come on! Come on!" Evans barked. "Get working!"

Frank and Joe assisted the other crewmen. Soon the heavy lines were pulled aboard and stacked in neat coils.

The job was hardly finished when Evans began shouting orders again. "Now get below and report to the ship's carpenter. Ask him to give you some paint. There are a few vents round here I want redone."

"We won't have time to do any investigating with him around," Joe said under his breath.

"We'll have to be patient and hope for a break," Frank replied.

The Hardys were kept busy painting. Later that day Joe was high on a ladder daubing the top of a door when his paint can slipped.

Splat! It hit the deck with a thud, spattering a grey mess in all directions.

What was worse, Rawlin walked past the spot at that very moment. He was decorated with gooey blobs.

Enraged, he looked up and shouted at Joe. "Hey, you! Come here!"

Joe quickly climbed down the ladder. Frank who had been working nearby, ran over to see what had happened.

"What's the meaning of this?" Rawlin roared.

"It was an accident," Joe said.

The man's face reddened. "I don't believe you! I think you saw me coming and dropped that can on purpose. You'll—!"

"Now wait a minute," Frank interrupted.

"Shut up! You stay out of this!" Rawlin shouted. He turned to Joe and grabbed the boy by the lapel of his jacket. "I oughta wipe up the deck with you!"

In a sudden move Joe broke away from the man's grip.

"What's going on here?" a voice boomed.

The boys turned to see a burly man of medium height approaching. He had a large greying moustache and cold blue eyes.

"Hello, Cap'n," Rawlin said. "These two kids just signed on. The blond-haired one almost hit me with a can of paint."

"That true?" the officer demanded as he glared at Joe.

"It was an accident, sir."

"That's what he says," snarled Rawlin. "And what's more, he tried to get tough with me just now."

"Oh, yeah?" the captain growled. "Lacks discipline, eh? A couple of days on bread and water in the brig will take the fight out of him."

Frank pleaded with the men on his brother's behalf. It was useless. Joe was taken to the brig below decks. It was a small enclosure with a door of metal bars. No guards were posted.

Late that night Frank secretly made his way to the ship's galley and collected some food. Then he sneaked quietly to the brig.

"Joe!" he whispered. "I brought some chow."

"Great! I'm starved."

Frank passed the food through the bars and watched as Joe ate heartily. Then they discussed the situation.

"I hate leaving you in there," Frank said. "But if you were to break out, it would only rile the captain further and possibly ruin our chances to investigate the ship."

"Don't worry," Joe replied. "I won't upset the applecart." He forced a grin. "Just keep the food coming every night and I'll be able to put up with anything."

"It should only be for a couple of days," Frank assured him. "In the meantime, I'll get our investigation underway."

"What do you plan to do first?"

"Examine those logs we saw in the hold. I've a hunch that's not an ordinary pile of lumber."

"What about the warning note? Any idea who wrote it?"

"No, not yet," Frank admitted. "But if we were recognized by someone aboard this ship, then I think the note was meant to be a friendly warning. Otherwise he would have turned us over to the captain by now."

"If you're right, I wish that that someone would come out into the open. I don't like having mystery friends for too long."

Frank agreed. "Now I'd better be on my way. See you tomorrow night."

"Good luck."

Frank began to edge his way in the direction of the cargo hold. As he rounded the corner of a passageway, he suddenly found himself face to face with Rawlin.

"What are you roaming round for?" the first mate demanded.

"Well—er—I was just getting acquainted with the layout of the ship," Frank stammered.

"Get back to your quarters!" Rawlin commanded.

Crestfallen, Frank obeyed, but decided that he would try again the following night. He fell into his bunk and was soon asleep. To him, it seemed only seconds later that he was being shaken awake.

"Up on deck!" a hefty crewman yelled.

Frank pulled on his jeans and quickly followed the man up the ladder. Dawn was just breaking as Rawlin's voice boomed through the crisp, fresh morning air.

"Everyone's to carry on with his regular duties! Frank Karlsen is to report to me!"

Frank went up to the first mate.

"I'm assigning you to deck watch," Rawlin told him. "Four hours on, and four hours off. Now report to the bridge."

Frank was bored with his new duty. But what bothered him even more was the fact that he had to remain in one spot and could not wander about to search for information.

It was well after midnight when he was relieved from his third watch of the day. He hurried off and repeated his secret journey to the brig with food for Joe.

"I thought you'd forgotten me, Frank," Joe said jokingly.

"Never, old buddy." Frank told him about his new assignment and his encounter with Rawlin the night before.

"That guy seems to be everywhere at once," Joe remarked. "When do you plan to try again?"

"Now. I noticed a storm to the east when I left watch. Rawlin is on the bridge keeping an eye on it. He won't be back this way tonight."

The ship began to roll gently. "The sea is beginning to get a bit rough," Joe commented.

"I'd better head for the cargo hold," Frank said. "There's no telling how much weather we're in for."

"Be careful," Joe warned. "And if this storm gets too rough, ask the captain to let me out of here."

Frank nodded. As he went down the passageway towards the cargo hold, he heard the clamour of footsteps ahead and looked round for a place to hide. He spotted the door of a small equipment locker, opened it, and ducked inside.

"Come on! Come on!" a crewman yelled. "Rawlin wants us forward. Looks like we're in for some real weather!"

Frank estimated that about half a dozen men rushed past his hiding-place. Fortunately they were headed away from the cargo hold.

He crept out of the locker and reached the cargo

hold. By now the intensity of the storm had increased and the ship rolled violently.

Frank took out his torch and directed its beam towards the pile of logs. As he did so, the ship lurched under the impact of the heavy sea. The logs broke loose from their bindings and came avalanching towards him!

·11·

Unknown Ally

LOUD, crashing sounds thundered through the hold as the logs hurtled across the deck.

Frank looked up and spotted a steel girder that spanned the beam of the ship. Making a desperate leap, he grabbed it and swung his body upward. The logs rolled beneath him.

Crash! Bang! They collided with the bulkhead on the portside, then tumbled back across the deck in the opposite direction as the ship listed to starboard. The cycle was repeated again and again—solid thuds with an occasional hollow boom.

As Frank clung to the girder with all his strength, the storm seemed to become even more violent.

"Can't hang on much longer," he said to himself. "But if I let go—"

The lights in the hold were turned on. Several crewmen poured in through the hatchway. For a moment they stared at the logs hurtling back and forth across the deck, then set about tying them down again.

Frank watched as they gradually brought the situation under control. Then he released his grip on the girder and dropped to the floor.

"What are you doin' in here?" shouted one of the men.

At that instant the captain entered the hold. "Everything under control?" he asked.

"Yes, sir. But we were wonderin' what this kid's up to. He was hangin' from that girder when we got here."

The captain glared. "Your place is up forward!"

Frank frantically searched his mind for an explanation. "I'd just gotten off deck watch and couldn't sleep," he said. "So I decided to take a walk."

"In this storm?"

"The weather wasn't too bad when I started out," Frank answered. "Then it got worse. I heard a lot of noise here in the hold and went to see what it was."

"Why didn't you call for help when you saw that the logs had broken loose?"

"I was going to, sir," Frank replied. "But when the logs rolled towards me, I jumped for the girder."

The captain rubbed his chin dubiously for a few seconds. Finally he accepted Frank's explanation and ordered him to return to his quarters.

By daylight the storm had subsided and the *Yellow Parrot* was churning its way through calm waters. Frank was returning from deck watch when he saw his brother walking down the passageway towards him.

"Hi, Joe!" he called out. "When were you sprung from the brig?"

"A few hours ago. But they put me to work right away in the engine room. I'm bushed."

"I don't have to be back on watch till midnight," Frank said. "Let's get some sleep. Then we'll plan our next move."

The boys slept soundly for several hours. After a late lunch in the galley Frank told his brother that he was still determined to examine the logs.

"I'm with you," Joe said. "But you've already been caught there once."

"That's a chance we'll have to take," Frank told him. "Come on."

They edged their way towards the hold and were elated to find no crewmen in the area.

"It's pitch black in here," Joe whispered as the two entered the hold and closed the hatch behind them.

"We don't want to turn on the lights," Frank said. "Use your torch."

They directed their beams of light at the pile of logs.

"Funny thing," Frank muttered.

"What's that?"

"I might have just imagined it, but when the logs rolled back and forth across the deck, some of them sounded as if they weren't completely solid. They sounded hollow."

"You mean," Joe began, "that the—" A faint noise caused him to stop abruptly.

"Switch off your light!" Frank hissed.

The boys' pulses quickened as they stood motionless and waited in the darkness. Then they heard the noise again. This time it came from a point directly behind them.

The Hardys whirled round. At the same instant they were blinded by an intensely bright flash of light.

"I'm trying to help you!" a man said. "Stop your investigation. Get off this ship as soon as you can!"

Before either boy could question the man, there was the sound of the hatchway door being slammed shut as he exited from the hole.

"What now?" Joe asked.

"We'd better get out of here," Frank said. "That

guy might've been spotted leaving. He could bring someone to check this place out."

The boys hurried to the hatch. They eased open the door, saw that the area was clear, and darted out. Back in their quarters, they discussed what had happened.

"Whoever it was," Joe remarked, "he must be the one who wrote the warning note."

"Without question," his brother replied. He paused for a moment. "But I'd like to know what his game is. If he knows who we are, why is he being so mysterious about it?"

"Could be he's holding out for money," Joe suggested. "I mean, he might be planning to demand payment in exchange for being quiet."

Frank pondered this. "I doubt it. If that was his motive, he certainly would have approached us with a deal by now."

"What's our next move?"

"Let's go on deck and take a walk round the ship. We might come up with a lead."

Strolling along in a nonchalant manner, the Hardys watched as the sailors went about their duties. As they were passing the radio room, Frank suddenly grabbed his brother's arm.

"Listen!" he whispered excitedly.

The door was partially open. Inside, two men were engaged in conversation. One of the voices belonged to the stranger they had encountered in the hold!

"Good grief!" Joe exclaimed in a low tone. "That must be the guy we're after!"

"Looks that way!"

A few seconds later the two men appeared in the

doorway, still talking. One of them looked like an ordinary sailor. The other was a lean, red-haired young man with pleasant features. Apparently he was the ship's radio operator. It was his voice the Hardys had identified.

"Okay," the crewman told him. "I'll have the antenna checked right away."

"Good." The young man turned and went into the radio room. Before he could shut the door, the boys dashed in after him.

"Hello," Frank said. "Mind if we have a few words with you?"

There was a pause before the startled operator spoke. His face had turned pale. "You—you want to talk to me? What about?" he stammered.

"What's your name?" Frank asked.

"Clay—Clay Ellis. I'm the ship's radioman."

Joe got straight to the point. "Writing warning notes and creeping round dark cargo holds must be a hobby of yours."

"I—I don't know what you mean," Ellis countered.

Frank, meanwhile, had peered round the room and spotted a camera flash gun on a shelf.

"Is this yours?" he asked, picking up the object.

"Er—no—one of the crew must have left it here," the operator said nervously.

Frank looked closely at the base of the flash and noticed the letters C.E. scratched on the metal surface. "This is a coincidence," he commented. "These seem to be your initials."

Perspiration oozed from Ellis's forehead. "All right! It's mine. So what?"

"You took our picture in the cargo hold a little while ago," Joe accused.

The young man let out a deep sigh. "Guess there's no sense in trying to lie to you," he muttered. "I didn't take your photograph, just wanted not to be seen. That's why I blinded you with the flash. You see, I know you're the Hardy boys."

"How did you learn that?" Joe asked.

"I've been interested in crime stories and the work of famous detectives for years," Ellis explained. "Photographs of you and your father have appeared in many magazines I've read. I recognized you the minute you boarded the ship."

"Why are **you** trying to warn us?" Frank questioned impatiently.

"You fellows are here to investigate the *Yellow Parrot*, I'm sure," the operator went on. "But believe me, you've walked into a lion's den. I don't want anything to happen to you."

"We appreciate your concern for our safety," Joe put in sarcastically. "What's your game? Why haven't you reported us to the captain?"

"I—I can't give you my reasons," Ellis said apprehensively.

"Are there any other crew members here who know who we are?" Frank asked.

"I'm sure I'm the only one. But don't worry. Your secret is safe with me."

"Thanks," Frank said. "Isn't there any more you can tell us about yourself, or the *Yellow Parrot*?"

An expression of fear spread across Ellis's face. "I've nothing to say," he insisted. "Anyway, you don't realize what you're getting into. Take my advice and get off this ship just as soon as you can. I'll help you."

"You seem anxious to get rid of us!" Joe stated.

At that instant a sailor entered the room and handed a folded sheet of paper to Ellis. "The cap'n wants you to send this out right away," he announced.

As he hurried off, the operator read the message. Then he walked over to the radio and flicked a switch.

"I'd better start warming up the transmitter," he said. "This message looks important."

"What does it say?" Joe asked quickly.

Ellis gazed at the boys for a moment. Then he handed them the sheet of paper. "You realize that I'm not supposed to do this," he said quietly. "But I trust you."

Frank took the message while Joe looked over his shoulder. After he had finished reading it, he said gravely, "Oh, oh. This could mean real trouble."

Ellis stared at him in surprise. "What's wrong?" he inquired. "It only says that I'm to contact the captain of the *Black Parrot* and arrange for a rendezvous with the ship tomorrow off Tambio Island."

"That's just it," Frank muttered.

·12·

Swim to Freedom

NOT without some misgivings on Frank's part, the Hardys took Ellis into their confidence, telling him briefly about their adventure aboard the *Black Parrot*.

The radioman was amazed. "This *does* mean trouble. We're bound to be visited by some of the *Black Parrot*'s crew."

"Maybe we can hide somewhere during the rendezvous," Joe suggested.

"That won't work," Ellis warned. "Any time we put into a port, or get close to a landfall, the captain double-checks to make sure all crew members are accounted for. You'd be missed immediately."

Frank began to pace the floor. "We've got to think of something. There must be a way out of this."

"You'd better go back to your quarters," the operator urged. "Meanwhile, I'll get this message off to the *Black Parrot*. Meet me in an hour on the main deck, amidships on the portside. I should have more information by then."

The boys left and made their way forward.

"What do you make of Ellis?" Frank asked.

"First impressions can be misleading," admitted Joe, "but I like the fellow and feel we can trust him. Anyhow, we haven't much choice."

"I agree. But if he *is* on our side, why doesn't he tell us more about himself?"

"He is frightened of something. I think he's being forced to sail aboard this ship."

Time passed slowly for the Hardys. Finally an hour went by, then they headed amidships for their meeting with the radioman. He was already waiting when they arrived.

"The situation is worse than I thought," Ellis announced in a low voice. "The *Parrots* are going to exchange a few crew members."

"Good grief!" Joe exclaimed. "We're bound to be recognized."

"Your only chance is to get off this ship at Tambio Island."

"And be marooned?" Frank protested.

"You won't be," Ellis assured them. "I hear there's a hermit living on the far side of the island. He's said to be friendly. I'm sure you could stay with him until you flag down a ship."

"That would be taking a long chance," Frank said.

"Your chances are nil if you don't get off this ship," the radioman warned.

"When does the meeting take place?" Frank inquired.

"Tomorrow night."

"Oh, oh." Joe sighed, eyeing his brother. "Something tells me we're in for a swim."

"I don't see any other way out," Frank admitted.

"Good," Ellis put in. "I'll meet you fellows here tomorrow night and help you get away. Make it about ten o'clock. That's when we're scheduled to arrive."

The Hardys were kept busy all the following day, and it was well after dark before they were released from duty.

Ding! Ding! came a tinkling.

"Two bells," Joe said. "It's nine o'clock."

"Only an hour to go," remarked Frank. "Let's try to get a few minutes' rest before we meet Ellis."

The boys were walking to their quarters when the first mate shouted to them. "Hey! You kids! Come here!"

"I wonder what he wants," Joe whispered apprehensively as they obeyed Rawlin's command.

"You two are spending the night in the brig," Rawlin growled.

"Why?" Joe demanded angrily. "What've we done?"

"Shut up!" He summoned four members of the crew. "Take them to the lock-up."

The men escorted the Hardys below, secured them in the brig, and hurried off.

"Now we *are* in a spot!" declared Joe. "Do you think Rawlin found out about our plan?"

"I doubt it. He's probably being cautious. He's not sure we can be trusted not to jump ship."

A few minutes later a faint shuffling sounded outside the brig. Frank and Joe made out the vague figure of a man approaching.

"Frank! Joe!" Clay Ellis whispered.

The boys sighed in relief.

"I saw what happened," Ellis went on. He produced a small crowbar. "I'll have you out in a jiffy."

The radioman prised away at the door, and it finally sprang open.

"Follow me," Ellis ordered. "The meeting is working

out slightly ahead of schedule. We're about a quarter of a mile off Tambio Island."

"Clay—thanks a lot," Frank murmured.

"Any time."

Ellis led the Hardys up on deck and to their previous meeting point amidships. At that instant the *Yellow Parrot*'s engines stopped.

A shout came from the bridge. "Let go the anchor!" There was a clatter of heavy chains, followed by a loud splash as the anchor plunged into the water.

"You'll have to swim for it," Ellis said. "The shore isn't far off. Think you can make it?"

"Easily," Joe said.

Ellis pointed to a coil of rope he had stowed near the rail. "It will be better if you lower yourselves into the water. If you dive overboard, the crew might hear you."

Frank nodded. "We appreciate all you're doing for us and won't forget it. But I think you're in some kind of trouble."

"You don't seem to belong aboard this ship any more than we do," Joe put in. "Why don't you come with us?"

"I—I can't," the radioman stammered.

Frank pulled a pencil from his pocket and scribbled something on a scrap of paper. He handed it to Ellis. "We have a radio set-up in Bayport. Can you transmit on this short-wave frequency?"

"Yes," Ellis replied. "Why?"

"We'll listen in every evening from seven to midnight," Frank told him. "If you should need help or want to give us any information about the activity of the *Parrots*, will you promise to contact us?"

Ellis hesitated for a moment. "I—I promise," he muttered finally.

The Hardys removed their shoes, tied the laces together, and hung them round their necks. Then they knotted one end of the rope round the railing and fed the balance over the side.

"Good luck!" Ellis said in a hushed voice as Frank and Joe quietly lowered themselves into the water.

They waved in response, then began swimming towards the island. In less than half an hour they were trudging up on to a sandy beach.

"Well, we made it," Joe said triumphantly.

Frank gazed silently at his surroundings. The island was covered with trees and thick undergrowth. Finding a couple of fallen branches, he handed Joe one of them. "We'd better start erasing our tracks. Otherwise they'll stand out like road signs when daylight comes."

When the job was finished, the boys walked into the undergrowth and found a clear spot where they could rest. It was not long before they were sound asleep.

Morning was ushered in by a bright, hot sun. The boys woke up to the sound of chirping birds and the rustling of palm trees stirred by an offshore breeze.

Then they became aware of another sound. Men's voices!

"Hear that?" Joe whispered excitedly.

Frank nodded. Stealthily they crawled towards the edge of the undergrowth. On the shore they spotted a dinghy. Several men were scattered along the beach nearby.

"I don't see any sign of 'em!" one of them said to his companions. "No tracks, either. I doubt that they came ashore. They're probably hidin' on the *Parrot* somewhere."

"Yeah!" said another. "Rawlin worries too much. So the kids escaped from the brig. Who cares? And even if they did make it here to the island, what's the difference? They can't cause us any trouble."

"I'm hungry!" exclaimed another man. "We had to miss breakfast because of those brats. Let's go back and get some chow."

The crewmen piled into the dinghy and began rowing towards the *Yellow Parrot*. Frank and Joe looked out to see its sister ship the *Black Parrot* anchored a short distance away.

"Those guys must've been looking for us while we were still asleep," Joe said.

"Lucky you don't snore," Frank quipped.

Eager to locate the hermit, they immediately started trekking easterly across the island.

"Shouldn't take us too long," Joe stated. "Tambio doesn't seem to be very big."

But the thick undergrowth made the going extremely rough. More than three hours passed before they came to the opposite shore. Barely five hundred yards away stood a crude hut, set well back from the high-water mark.

It looked no larger than four by four feet and its door was of sturdy oak.

"What do you think of that?" Joe asked as they came closer.

"It's strange, all right," Frank admitted.

"Should we call out?"

"No, we'd better not. If we startle the guy, he might react violently, especially if he's some kind of unstable recluse."

Frank and Joe walked cautiously round the hut. To their surprise, it had no windows.

"There's no sign of a human being here anywhere," Frank remarked.

"Maybe our hermit left a long time ago."

Frank stopped short in his tracks. "Look, Joe, footprints," he said, pointing to the sandy soil partly covered with tufts of coarse grass.

Joe bent over. "They're headed towards the beach. Maybe the fellow's out fishing!"

Frank grinned. "In that case, perhaps we could peek inside." He took hold of the door handle and pulled. It did not budge.

"Here, Joe, give me a hand!"

Joe grabbed the handle, too, and they both tugged. With a creaking noise, the door came open. It took a few seconds for the boys' eyes to adjust to the dim interior. There was nothing but a flight of steep stairs leading into the ground.

"Hey! What's this?" Joe asked.

"Come on. We'll find out."

With Frank in the lead, they carefully descended ten stairs until they came to another door.

Frank knocked gingerly. No one replied.

"Let's go in," Joe whispered.

Frank nodded and opened the door. At the same instant, lights went on in a large room. The boys gasped!

· 13 ·

Trouble on Tambio

ON the far side of the room sat a man in a huge high-backed chair. He did not move, did not even bat an eyelash.

"Hello!" Joe blurted out. There was no reply.

Joe looked at Frank. "Is he real?"

Frank shrugged, and they walked closer.

There was a frozen grin on the man's ebony face and he did not seem to breathe at all. He was attired in a red and white checked sports shirt, ragged slacks cut off at the knees, and white tennis shoes.

"Wow!" Frank whispered. "He must be right out of Madame Tussaud's Wax Museum!" He stepped forward and touched the man's face. The next moment he yelled, "Joe! He's alive!"

"Of course," said the man. "What made you think I was not?" The grin disappeared from his face and suddenly he looked menacing.

Despite their usual coolness and presence of mind, the Hardys shrank back before the recluse.

"Please do not break into my home again," he said.

With that, a trap door sprang open and the boys were dropped into a shallow pit. Half stunned, they were set upon by the powerful hermit, who sprang at them like a cat. He tied their hands with a piece of

254

*Suddenly a trap door sprang open and the boys dropped
through the floor!*

rope which he pulled out of his pocket, then brought them back into the room.

It was filled with all sorts of modern appliances. There was an electric stove, a refrigerator, ventilation system and many other devices.

After he had tied the boys by one wrist to sturdy oak chairs, their captor said, "You are impressed with my home, yes? Perhaps you are wondering how I receive the electrical power for all my treasures? Well, there is an underground generator located just behind the hut."

"Why are you holding us prisoner?" Joe asked.

"As a precaution. First let me ask what you are doing on this island," the man countered.

The Hardys did not want to tell him that they had escaped from the *Yellow Parrot*. There was a possibility, after all, that he was connected somehow with the ship.

"Er—we were sailing our ketch on a long voyage," Frank replied. "A storm came up, blew us off course, and finally shipwrecked us not far from here."

"Ah, I see," the man said. "My name is Katu."

The Hardys introduced themselves by their aliases, Frank and Joe Karlsen.

"It is not often that I have guests," Katu went on. "I am about to prepare lunch. Will you eat with me?"

Eagerly the boys accepted his invitation. They watched with mixed feelings of surprise and amusement as Katu took a package of hamburgers from the freezing compartment of his refrigerator, then switched on the electric stove.

Joe was overwhelmed with curiosity. "How did you come by all these gadgets?" he asked.

"That is not for you to know," Katu answered, displaying annoyance.

He avoided further conversation during the meal. When he finally spoke, it was to announce that they would remain prisoners until his amphibious friend returned.

"Amphibious friend?" Frank repeated. "What do you mean?"

"He flies a plane that can float on the water like a boat," Katu explained proudly, "or roll on the land with wheels."

"An amphibian aircraft!" Frank exclaimed. "It comes here to the island?"

A blank expression spread over Katu's face. He looked as if he had unintentionally revealed some deep, dark secret.

Before Frank and Joe could ask any more questions, they heard an aeroplane overhead. It passed low, then seemed to turn towards the sea. Katu left in a hurry.

"Must be the amphibian he told us about," Joe declared.

Frank sighed. "I sure hope he'll let us out of here!"

Twenty minutes later the door to the room opened. A tall, wiry man with sandy-coloured hair entered. He was wearing overalls and leather flight boots.

"Hello," he said, smiling broadly. "My name's Dan Tiller. Katu tells me you fellows were shipwrecked."

The boys nodded. "You must be the pilot of the amphibian," Joe put in.

"That's right," said Tiller. "And who are you?"

Frank and Joe introduced themselves. On a hunch they decided to play it straight and did not use their aliases.

The pilot's eyes widened in surprise. "Are you the sons of Fenton Hardy, the famous detective?"

"Yes," Frank replied. "But—"

"Say!" Tiller interrupted. "I've heard lots about the Hardys. An airline friend of mine met you and your father once. It was on one of his flights that you caught a couple of smugglers aboard the plane."

"Oh, yes. I seem to remember that," Frank muttered, hoping to avoid a lengthy discussion of the case.

"Sorry about the way you were treated. Katu was being a bit overcautious," Tiller said as he loosened their bonds. There was a worried expression on his face.

"Were you fellows really shipwrecked?" he asked. "Or did you come to Tambio to investigate me?"

"Investigate you?" Joe asked curiously. "Why? Have you done anything wrong?"

"No. At least I don't think so. But I don't pay any taxes." Tiller explained that two years before he had been caught in a storm and was blown off course. When the weather finally cleared, he had spotted a capsized dugout canoe below him. A man was clinging to the craft.

"I landed the amphibian to rescue the fellow," he continued. "It was Katu. I flew him back to my base on Cambrian Island, which is about six hundred miles north of here."

"I've heard of it," Joe interjected. "It's become a popular place for tourists, and its capital is one of the most modern cities in the world."

"Right. Katu liked it there and stayed for a year and a half. He went to school, learned English, and worked in a hotel. We became great friends and flew a lot. One day we discovered this island and decided to make it our Shangri-la, some place where we could get away from the world. It's pretty good, don't you think?"

"Terrific!" Joe said.

"But I don't know if this land belongs to anyone. This underground complex was already here, you see. We might be trespassing on someone's property. But I thought as long as we're not being chased off, it's ours."

"I don't believe you'll have any trouble," Frank assured him.

Now Katu joined them. He grinned as the Hardys praised him for his tricky defence of Tiller's hideout.

The boys took a liking to the pilot and decided to tell him about their escape from the *Yellow Parrot*.

He listened to their story with great interest. "I've never heard of the *Parrots* before," he said. "Ships are a bit out of my line."

"There's something fishy going on with those two," Joe told him. "They're anchored near the west side of Tambio right now."

"How soon will you be flying back to Cambrian?" Frank asked.

"This afternoon."

"Will you take us with you?"

"Of course. From there you can get one of the scheduled flights to Florida."

The Hardys talked a while longer to Tiller and Katu, until the pilot finally said, "Come on, fellows. I want to make it back before dark."

Katu paddled them out to the amphibian, and waved goodbye.

"All aboard!" Tiller cried as he led the young detectives through a small hatchway and into the cabin of the plane.

Then he climbed into the cockpit and started the first of the craft's two engines. When it was running smoothly, he started the second.

"Here we go!" he shouted and eased the throttles forward. The idling engines erupted into a loud steady roar. The plane bounced across the water and then lifted gracefully into the air.

As the amphibian gained altitude, Frank dashed into the cockpit. "I know you're in a hurry to get back to Cambrian," he said to Tiller, "but I just had an idea. Would you fly to the other side of the island? We'd like to see if the *Parrots* are still there."

"Sure," Tiller answered as he turned the plane to a westerly heading.

Soon they had reached the coast. A look of disappointment spread over Frank's face when he saw that the ships were gone.

"Too bad," he mumbled. "I thought we might pick up some kind of clue."

"Wait a minute," Joe exclaimed, and pointed to an object in the distance. "That looks like a ship over there!"

Tiller swung to the direction Joe had indicated. As the distance closed, Frank shouted, "It's the *Yellow Parrot*!"

As they started to circle the ship, thin trails of smoke streaked past the aircraft.

"Jeepers!" Joe cried out. "They're shooting at us!"

An instant later a column of thick black smoke began to stream from the plane's left engine!

· 14 ·

Morton's Geyser

"FIRE!" Frank exclaimed.

Tiller turned the plane sharply away from the *Yellow Parrot*. Then he pulled a knob marked "Extinguisher." Immediately faint trails of frozen carbon dioxide streamed from beneath the engine cowling. The boys were relieved to see the black smoke gradually disappear.

"Are you going back to Tambio?" Joe asked.

"No!" replied Tiller. "We can make it to Cambrian on one engine. However, it'll take longer than usual because our speed is reduced."

Hours ticked by. The young detectives were dozing off when Tiller leaned forward for a closer look at one of the instruments on the panel.

"Oh, oh," he muttered. "The right engine's starting to overheat."

"Is it serious?" Joe inquired anxiously.

"Not yet," the pilot answered. "But I'll have to reduce the power setting slightly."

As he eased back on the throttle, the amphibian gradually began to lose altitude.

"We're going down," Frank observed nervously.

"I'll let the plane settle," Tiller decided. "The air is thicker below. It will help to develop a bit more power and lift. Also, we're getting lighter every minute as the fuel burns off."

This statement was of little consolation to the Hardys. They watched the altimeter slowly unwind. Then, at 1,000 feet, the plane acquired new life. The instruments no longer indicated a descent and the engine was now operating at normal temperature.

"Whew!" Joe sighed. "For a while I thought we were going to have to paddle the rest of the way."

"We can relax," Tiller remarked with a wide grin. "The worst is over. I estimate we'll reach Cambrian in about another hour."

It was dark by the time the island came into view. The lights of its capital city twinkled like a small cluster of stars on the horizon.

"I'll use the wheels and land at the airport rather than set down on the water," announced the pilot. He contacted the control tower and was cleared for a straight-in approach.

The landing was smooth, and after parking the aircraft, Tiller obtained a ladder. He climbed up to the left engine, removed the outer cowling and inspected the damage.

"We're awfully sorry about what happened," Frank said apologetically. "It's our fault and we'd like to pay for repairs."

"Don't worry about it," said the pilot. "As far as I can see, we received one hit in the crankcase. Oil was being splashed over the engine. That's what caused the smoke."

Tiller escorted the boys to the airport terminal building. There they were told that a shuttle flight to Miami would be departing within the hour. After a quick bite to eat, Frank and Joe bade their new friend goodbye and took off on the first leg of their journey back home.

They stayed overnight in Miami and arrived in Bayport the following afternoon. Aunt Gertrude let out a cry of surprise when they entered the house.

"Mercy! It's been days and days since we've had any word from you!" she exclaimed. "Where were you? Chasing after some awful criminals, I suppose."

The commotion brought Mr and Mrs Hardy to the living-room. The boys' mother gave them affectionate hugs and Mr Hardy greeted them warmly.

"You've had me worried," he said. "I was going to notify the authorities and request a search."

An early dinner was prepared while the boys showered and changed their clothes. During the meal they described their adventures aboard the *Yellow Parrot*.

"You placed yourselves in a very dangerous position," Mr Hardy remarked with concern. "I'm thankful you decided to escape."

"And, Fenton," Aunt Gertrude interjected, "you should also tell them not to go running off for days at a stretch without letting us know where they are. Even a postcard would be of some consolation."

"Sorry," Joe quipped, winking at his brother. "There wasn't a postal service where we were."

"The situation *was* sort of grim," Frank admitted to his father. "And, the worst of it all is that we didn't come up with any real evidence to link the *Parrots* with the robberies."

"But I wouldn't say our trip was a complete loss," Joe said. "Remember, we do have a possible contact in Ellis. He might still change his mind and tell us what he knows."

The boys talked to their father about the tentative arrangement they had made with the radioman.

"We'll have to set up a listening watch," commented Mr Hardy. "Count on me to do my share. I'll stand by the radio tonight. You two get some rest."

"I'll take my turn tomorrow night," Joe volunteered.

"And we can get Chet to pitch in," suggested Frank.

The brothers retired early and slept until late the following morning. After breakfast they drove to the Morton farm to see Chet.

They were startled to see a geyser of water spouting thirty or forty feet into the air near Chet's home. A police car and an emergency van were parked nearby.

"What's going on?" Joe exclaimed as they leaped from their convertible. They were met by Iola Morton, a slim, pretty, dark-haired girl. She was Chet's sister and a favourite girl-friend of Joe's.

"I'm so happy to see you two!" she cried out. "Isn't this terrible?"

"What happened?" Frank asked quickly.

"Chet became interested in archaeology," explained Iola. "This morning he said that he was on the brink of a great discovery and began digging with a pick. I'm afraid he struck a water main!"

"Oh, no!" Joe shouted.

The boys ran to the scene. There they saw Chief Collig of the Bayport Police Department, a close friend of the Hardys. He was standing transfixed at the sight of the column of water as it gushed upwards.

"Hello, Frank and Joe. Well, your buddy really did

it this time. Lucky for him that his parents are visiting friends in Clayton today."

"Where *is* Chet?" Joe asked.

"On the other side of the geyser," Collig replied.

Frank and Joe edged their way round and looked down into the deep hole that Chet had dug. He was kneeling by the water main at the point where it had punctured, and was trying to stop the flow with his hands.

"Chet! Get out of there!" Joe yelled. "You can't stop it that way!"

Their friend looked up with a startled expression. Then he scrambled out of the hole, dripping wet.

"Hi, fellows," he said, embarrassed. "When did you get back?"

"Never mind that," Frank answered. "What's the archaeological discovery you were digging for?"

Chet glanced about sheepishly. "I—I read that there are lots of old Indian artefacts in our area. I was on the brink of finding something that would've astounded the scientific world."

"Cheer up. You might still have accomplished something," Joe said jokingly. "If that leak isn't fixed soon, you'll have created one of the greatest tourist attractions in Bayport."

"Right," Frank added. "Morton's Perpetual Geyser!"

"Aw, cut it out," Chet said.

At that instant a van from the water department rolled to a stop. The driver leaped from his vehicle.

"We're shutting the water off at the main junction!" he shouted to Chief Collig.

Then he walked towards the boys. "Which one of you is Chet Morton?"

"Well—er—I guess that's me," Chet stammered nervously.

"I understand you're responsible for this. What were you doing? Digging for gold? Or trying to sabotage the water company?"

"It was an accident," Frank interrupted.

"Just wait till his father gets the bill for repairs," the man went on. "This kid will look like an accident!"

"There goes your allowance for the next two years," Joe needled.

Dejected, Chet strolled slowly to the house and sat down on the porch steps. The Hardys felt sorry for him and followed.

"Don't take it so hard," Frank said sympathetically. "Things could be worse."

"That's what you think," Chet countered.

"Snap out of it," Joe urged. "We're going to need your help."

Chet appeared to perk up a bit. "What kind of help?"

The young detectives told him about their arrangement with Ellis aboard the *Yellow Parrot*.

"You can count on me!" their chum declared. Then he hesitated. "That is, you'd better wait until my parents come home tonight. I don't know how my father will take the water-main business. He might not give me permission."

"Well, I'm sure he will," Joe said. "This is an important assignment."

The Hardys returned home. After dinner they had just sat down to read the evening newspaper when the telephone rang. Frank answered.

"I'm off the hook!" Chet said jubilantly. "The water

company found several defects in the pipe I punctured. They said they would have had to make repairs soon, anyway."

"That *is* good news!"

"I've a good mind to charge them for services rendered," Chet went on. "After all, I did part of the work for them by digging the hole."

"If I were you," Frank advised, "I'd leave well alone."

"Okay. How soon do I begin my assignment?" Chet inquired eagerly.

"We'll let you know."

Frank hung up and rejoined his brother. Later Mr Hardy came bounding down the stairs from the study.

"I just received a phone call!" he exclaimed. "Another museum has been robbed of its DeGraw collection!"

· 15 ·

Imposters

"WHERE?" Frank asked excitedly.

"The Shillman Museum in Connecticut," his father answered. "Mr Sedley, the curator, said the guards were knocked out by some kind of gas."

"Again! Just as in Philadelphia," Frank put in.

"Right. I'll have to leave at once. I'd like at least one of you to come with me."

Joe turned to Frank. "You go," he said. "I'll stay here. It's my night to stand radio watch."

Jack Wayne was notified to have the plane ready at the airport. Soon the pilot and his two passengers were airborne.

It took less than an hour to reach their destination. When they landed, Frank and his father took a taxi directly to the museum.

"The alarm system failed to work, yet it showed no signs of having been tampered with," Mr Hardy explained on the way.

When they arrived at the museum, there were no patrol cars or policemen in the area.

"This is odd," remarked Mr Hardy. "If a major robbery took place here less than two hours ago, where are the police?"

"Strange," Frank agreed. "But there must be an

explanation. At least the curator must be here. He's probably inside waiting for us."

Father and son pounded on one of the large metal doors at the front entrance of the museum. Minutes went by before a door was eased open and an elderly guard peered out.

"What do you want? The museum closes at five o'clock," he said testily. "Come back tomorrow!"

"I received an urgent telephone call from the curator," Mr Hardy said. "We're here to see him."

"The curator? Mr Sedley?" the guard replied, eyeing the Hardys suspiciously. "He went home shortly after we closed for the day. Who are you?"

The detective produced his credentials. Suddenly the guard straightened his cap and gave an informal salute. "Mr Hardy!" he exclaimed. "I've heard of you. I'm Jeremy Turner, chief of the night guards. What can I do for you?"

Bewildered, Frank stared at the man. "Wasn't there a robbery here a couple of hours ago, Mr Turner?"

"A robbery?" the guard queried with a look of astonishment. "Is this some kind of a joke?"

"I assure you it is not," Mr Hardy answered impatiently. "I'll have to call Mr Sedley at once! Take me to a telephone!"

Turner quickly led the detectives to one of the museum's offices. There Mr Hardy pulled a notebook from his pocket, opened it to a list of telephone numbers, and began to dial. Seconds later he had the curator on the line.

"You say I called you about a robbery at our museum?" Mr Sedley said, after hearing the story. "Preposterous! I did no such thing!"

"That's all I need to know," the detective replied. "Forgive me for being abrupt, but I must leave right away."

He put the phone down, then picked it up again and dialled another number.

"What's up, Dad?"

"I'm calling home," his father told him. "I want to talk to your brother."

Joe answered the telephone. "Hi, Dad," he said. "What about the robbery? Did you—?"

"There wasn't any!" Mr Hardy quickly told Joe what had happened. "Here's what I want you to do," he went on. "Call the other museums that still have their DeGraw collections and warn them. Frank and I are flying back to Bayport right away."

"Okay, Dad. Will do."

Frank and his father hurried back to the airport. When they landed at Bayport, Joe came running towards them as Jack taxied the plane to the parking ramp.

"Dad!" he cried. "We're too late! The State Museum in Delaware was robbed of their collection round ten-thirty!"

Frank cried out in dismay.

"I was afraid of this," Mr Hardy said angrily. "As soon as I learned the call from Mr Sedley was a phoney, I suspected it was a trick to draw us away."

He turned to the pilot. "We've got to fly to Delaware right away. While you refuel the plane, I'll check with the curator and the police down there. One wild-goose chase is enough."

"Sure, Mr Hardy."

The detective rushed off to a telephone. Minutes

later he returned. "Well, this time it's the real thing!"

"May I go along?" asked Joe. "Chet's at our house standing by the radio."

"Climb in," his father replied.

The sleek Hardy plane streaked down the Bayport runway on take-off for the second time that night. After an hour plus a few minutes they landed at their destination and headed for the State Museum.

There they found the building swarming with uniformed police and plain-clothesmen. As the trio walked inside, a tall, neatly dressed man blocked their way.

"Sorry," he announced. "Only the police are allowed in here."

Mr Hardy presented his credentials and introduced his sons. A broad smile appeared on the man's face. "This *is* a pleasure," he said. "Never thought I'd have an opportunity to meet you. I'm Seth Spencer, chief of detectives."

There was an exchange of handshakes, then Frank spoke up. "Have you uncovered any leads?"

"Not yet. The thieves seem to have made a clean get-a-way."

"What about the guards?" Mr Hardy queried.

"All were knocked out. Since gas was used in the other robberies, they wore masks. But every single mask was punctured!"

"Was the alarm tampered with?"

Spencer rubbed his chin dubiously, "No," he replied finally. "And that's something I can't figure out."

"Were there any eye-witnesses?" Joe asked.

"None who saw the robbery being committed," the officer replied.

"Who notified the police?" Mr Hardy inquired.

"A passer-by became suspicious when he spotted a trailer-lorry race out of the museum driveway with its lights off," Spencer explained, "so he called head-quarters. Unfortunately he was unable to give us the licence number or a detailed description of the vehicle."

"One thing is certain," Joe remarked. "It was carrying the stolen DeGraw collection."

"Our men and the State Police are checking all trailer-lorries leaving the area," the detective chief said.

After the museum and police officials had completed their investigation, Spencer and the Hardys questioned the guards.

"That's all any of us remember," one of the guards declared. "There was what seemed to be a cloud of gas, and then—"

"By the way, how is Mr Fosten?" another asked. "Is he all right?"

Spencer looked at the man quizzically. "Mr Fosten, the curator?"

"Yes, of course."

"My men have been trying to reach him since we learned about the robbery. He's not at home and none of his friends know where he is at the moment."

The guard seemed surprised. "He was in his office last time I saw him," he said. "That was right before the robbery. He came back here about an hour after we closed for the day. Said he was going to spend the evening catching up on some paperwork."

"Good grief!" Spencer shouted. He summoned his men. "I want you to go through this place again with a fine-toothed comb. Mr Fosten might be lying un-conscious in the building somewhere!"

A thorough search, however, revealed nothing. The detective chief scratched his head in bewilderment.

"Maybe the thieves took the curator along with them," Frank suggested.

"If so," Spencer said, "they'll have a kidnapping charge added to their crime."

Nearly an hour had passed when the telephone rang in the curator's office. A policeman lifted it up, then shouted to Spencer, "You'd better take this call, Chief!"

"I'm Avery Fosten," a voice crackled from the receiver. "Just heard a TV news broadcast saying the museum was robbed. What's going on?"

"Where are you?" Spencer demanded. "We've been trying to reach you for hours!"

"My wife and I are spending a couple of days at a friend's summer home in Maryland," the curator replied.

"How long have you been there?"

"Since about seven o'clock. The drive took less than two hours."

"But one of the guards here told us he'd seen you working in your office up until the time of the robbery," Spencer said.

"That's absurd!" the curator insisted. "My wife and I left immediately after the museum closed."

"You'd better come back right away. There's something fishy going on here."

After hanging up, Spencer told the Hardys about Fosten's call.

"If he's telling the truth," Frank put in, "there's only one explanation. The man the guard reported seeing in the curator's office was an imposter!"

"You're right," his father agreed. "And a clever plan, too. Disguised as the curator, the imposter had no trouble entering the building after hours. Then he was free to let his accomplices inside without attracting attention."

At that moment a patrolman rushed up to Spencer. "Sir, a trailer-lorry was found abandoned on a side road twelve miles north of here," he said. "The crime lab has been checking for fingerprints and other clues. So far they've uncovered nothing."

Frank turned to the detective chief. "Would you issue an alert requesting a check of any trailer-lorries carrying logs?" he asked.

Spencer was a bit puzzled. "Sure—I can do that. But why a lorry carrying logs?"

"I can't explain now," Frank replied. "It's only a hunch of mine and may not amount to anything."

Shrugging his shoulders, Spencer walked to a telephone, called headquarters, and ordered a general alert.

Exhausted, the Hardys went to the curator's office and settled down into comfortable chairs. Soon they were asleep.

It was nearly dawn when a policeman awakened them. "Chief Spencer is back at headquarters," he said. "He just called. The State Police in New Hampshire stopped a trailer-lorry hauling logs outside the town of Newland. It was heading north. They checked and found that the licence number plates were phoney."

"Where's the lorry now?" Frank asked quickly.

"At the police garage in Newland. They're also holding the driver and another man who was with him."

The Hardys were driven to the airport in a patrol car.

They found Jack Wayne sleeping soundly on a sofa in the operations room.

"Jack!" Frank said as he gently shook the pilot awake. "We've got to fly to Newland, New Hampshire, right away. Is there a field nearby?"

"New-Newland, New Hampshire," Jack murmured as he rubbed his eyes wearily. "I'll check my chart."

He unfolded a map and examined it. There was a small airport located two miles north of the town.

"I'll call the police in Newland and ask if they can have one of their men pick us up at the field," Mr Hardy said. "How long will it take to get there?"

Jack measured the distance and made a quick mental calculation. "Approximately two hours."

They had a quick breakfast at the airport before taking off.

When they landed, a uniformed policeman was waiting for them. He led the Hardys to a patrol car and drove to Newland Police Headquarters.

There they were shown the lorry. About a dozen huge logs were piled aboard it.

Frank stared for a moment, then picked up a large stone and walked towards the vehicle.

"What are you up to?" Joe asked.

"If my hunch is correct," his brother replied, "you'll see in a minute!"

An Unfortunate Scoop

Frank began to hammer away at each of the logs in turn. Suddenly he struck one that gave off a slightly hollow sound. Then he found another, and another.

"They're not solid!" exclaimed Mr Hardy.

After close examination Frank gripped the end of one of the logs and began twisting it.

"Give me a hand!" he said to Joe.

Together, they worked on the log. Presently its butt started to turn like a threaded bottle cap. Soon it dropped free.

"Good grief!" Joe cried. "It *is* hollow!"

"Exactly."

Mr Hardy looked on in amazement as his sons reached inside the log and pulled out crowns, orbs, and several jewelled sceptres. Labels on the items proved they were from the DeGraw collection.

"Now we know," Frank said excitedly, "how the thieves transported their loot right under the very noses of the authorities."

"Congratulations!" his father interjected. "Your hunch has solved one aspect of the case."

Arrangements were made to place the truck and its cargo under strict guard. Then the Hardys asked to see the driver and his companion. The policeman who had picked them up at the airport led them into the interrogation room, and the prisoners were brought in.

The driver, who gave his name as Gaff Parkins, was a stocky, tough-looking man. The second man identified himself only as Miker. He was tall, lean, and the deep lines on his face emphasized his hard features. The men were asked if they wanted a lawyer, but both shook their heads.

"Why are we bein' locked up in a cell?" Parkins demanded. "We don't know anythin' about bad licence number plates. We're just a couple of hired hands."

"Yeah!" Miker added. "Tell us what the fine is and we'll get outta' here."

"You're involved in more than just a motor-vehicle violation," Mr Hardy informed the prisoners.

"What do you mean?" snarled Parkins. "We ain't done nothin'."

"Except help to rob the State Museum!" Joe snapped.

"I don't know what you're talking about!" Miker declared. "We didn't steal anything. Our job is to haul logs."

"Filled with stolen loot?" Frank put in.

The prisoners glanced at each other with startled expressions.

"I knew there was more to this than we were told," Miker addressed his companion nervously.

"Shut up!"

"I won't!" Miker exclaimed in defiance. "This sounds like big trouble, and we're caught in the middle. Before we get in any deeper, I'm for telling what we know."

Parkins settled back in his chair and sighed. "Maybe you're right," he said.

"Understand," Mr Hardy told him, "you're not being asked to give a confession. But if you help us, it'll go in your favour."

"Okay," Miker agreed. "A little over a year ago Gaff and I tried to break into the freight-hauling business. Money was a problem, and the only thing we could afford was one trailer-lorry."

He went on to explain that recently they ran out of funds and were unable to renew their vehicle licence and to pay other insurance fees necessary to operate the trailer.

"Then late yesterday afternoon we got a call from a stranger," Miker continued. "He asked if we could pick up a pile of logs that had been shipped to Wilmington. The money he offered would've put us back in business for at least a year."

"Didn't that make you suspicious?" Frank asked.

"I was too excited to think straight," the man answered. "He offered to pay us half in advance. But then I remembered we couldn't legally run the lorry. I asked the stranger if he could wait a day or two so that I could clear up the matter. He said not to worry, he would give us a special set of Canadian licence number plates that would get us through."

"I didn't like the whole thing from the start," Parkins put in. "But the guy said the job had to be done that night, or the deal was off."

"Finally we decided to take a chance because the money was just too good to turn down," Miker added. "So we picked up the logs at a dock in Wilmington."

"Where were you supposed to deliver them?"

"To Stormwell, a port in Canada. But first we were to meet a van outside of Wilmington."

The Hardys looked knowingly at one another. Frank asked what took place at the rendezvous.

"When the van arrived, some guy told us to take a walk and return in an hour," said Miker. "We started out, then doubled back to see what was going on. We spotted those guys loading things into the logs. I was ready to call the deal off right then and there."

"Why didn't you?" Mr Hardy inquired. "Since it looked crooked, you should have called the police."

"I talked him out of it," Parkins admitted. "I know hoods when I see them. Those guys would never let us quit!"

"And that's all we know," Miker insisted.

"Can you give us a description of any of the men you saw?"

"No," Parkins replied. "It was too dark."

The prisoners were led out of the room. Then the Hardys discussed the situation.

"I'll call the police in Wilmington," Mr Hardy said. "I would like to find out how the logs got to the dock." He put through a call and the police chief of Wilmington promised to track it down.

"The logs were to be taken to Stormwell," Frank said. "That means one of the *Parrot* ships must be heading there for the pick-up."

"You can bet on it," agreed his father. "And our first concern is to prevent information about this from leaking out. We don't want to alert the thieves before the ship docks."

The desk sergeant called out to the Hardys as they hurried from the interrogation room. "It looks as if you fellows are going to get your names in the newspapers today," he announced with a grin.

"What do you mean?" Frank asked.

"Ed Watts, the police reporter for the *Newland Record*, was here about half an hour ago," the sergeant replied. "He checked the police diary as he usually does. Sure got excited when he learned that you had found the museum loot inside those logs. Didn't even wait for an interview. You should have seen him dash off to make the morning edition with his scoop."

Mr Hardy rushed to telephone the managing editor of the newspaper. He pleaded with the man not to print the story.

"Sorry," the editor informed him, "but the presses are already rolling. Anyway, it wouldn't do any good. The wire services have picked it up."

The boys were crestfallen when their father told them the situation. He suggested they all return to Bayport and plan a new course of action.

The drivers were released on bail and drove away with their truck, but the logs were kept as evidence.

It was evening by the time the Hardys arrived home. Too exhausted to think clearly, they decided to retire immediately after supper, since Chet had agreed to stay on radio watch one more night.

Before they undressed, a telephone call from the Wilmington police advised that there had been no record of the log shipment. "It obviously was strictly illegal," the officer reported.

Next day the boys rose early and enjoyed a leisurely breakfast, then joined their father who was already at work in his study.

"The morning edition of the *Bayport News* came a little while ago," he said with a frown. "Take a look at the front page, third column."

Frank and Joe looked glum when they saw the headline:

HARDYS FIND MUSEUM LOOT IN HOLLOW LOGS

It read in part: "The Hardys did it again! Officials of the State Museum in Delaware were astounded to learn that the famous Bayport detectives had uncovered an invaluable collection recently stolen from the museum. The loot was cleverly hidden in hollow logs which were being hauled aboard a trailer-lorry with Canadian licence number plates. Police are looking for a possible Canadian contact. . . ."

"This ruins everything!" Joe declared angrily.

Mr Hardy picked up the phone and placed a call to the Port Authority in Stormwell. He requested any recent information they might have concerning the *Parrot* ships. From the expression on their father's face, the boys concluded that the news was not encouraging.

"You're in for another let-down." Mr Hardy sighed as he hung up the phone. "The *Black Parrot* was due to dock last night. So far there's no sign of her."

"Someone must have radioed the captain," Frank said, "and told him about our finding the loot."

"He must be making a run for it," Joe added. "And you can be sure Stormwell has seen the last of the *Parrots.*"

"If only we had more leads," Mr Hardy said. "The Stormwell authorities tried to find the location of the ship but to no avail. And where to look next is a problem, because the *Black Parrot* did not report its last position."

"Too bad Parkins and Miker couldn't give us more

information about the gang," Joe muttered. He glanced at his brother. "I wonder where the thieves are now."

"Scattered like geese in a hurricane, if they read the newspapers," Frank said glumly.

"As I see it," Mr Hardy announced, "our only hope of ending this case quickly depends upon one thing."

"What's that, Dad?" Frank asked.

"That your friend Ellis contacts us."

· 17 ·

An Unexpected Visitor

"By this time," Joe said dejectedly, "Ellis might not even be aboard the *Yellow Parrot* any more."

"Possibly," Frank agreed. "He might have decided to escape from the ship. Or the captain could have found out that he had helped us and taken him prisoner. But we're just guessing. We have nothing to lose by sticking close to the radio."

That afternoon Chet's jalopy screeched to a halt in front of the Hardy house. The stout youth leaped from his car and jabbed at the doorbell excitedly.

"What's going on?" Joe asked as he admitted his friend to the house. "You look as if you've just discovered the secret of perpetual motion."

"Everybody brace themselves for the unexpected!" Chet declared. "I'll be acclaimed by archaeologists in every corner of the globe!"

"You haven't been digging again?" Joe questioned apprehensively.

"Well—er—yes," his pal admitted with a certain aloofness. "But I made sure there weren't any water mains around."

The commotion brought Mr Hardy and Frank to the scene. It was then that Chet pulled a small, weathered bowl from his pocket and displayed it proudly.

"Consider yourselves privileged to be among the

first to set eyes upon this ancient artefact," he announced. "Study its lines closely."

"Where did you find it?" Frank asked, trying to suppress a grin.

"On the farm," Chet replied.

"How old do you think it is?" Mr Hardy queried.

"Probably dates back to the pre-glacial period," Chet replied with a confident air. "A Carbon 14 test will determine its age more exactly."

Aunt Gertrude appeared and stared at Chet's discovery curiously. "Oh, I see you've found it," she said finally.

"Found what?"

"My little sugar bowl," Miss Hardy answered. "Don't you remember? The boys borrowed it when they had a family picnic at your parents' farm."

"I remember now," Joe said. "That must've been two or three years ago. You were awfully upset when we told you it had been lost."

"Impossible!" Chet shouted indignantly.

Aunt Gertrude hurried away, then reappeared with another bowl in her hand a moment later. It was almost identical in size and shape to Chet's. "You see, it was part of a set. Mercy! Imagine finding the bowl after all this time. But, of course, it's too weathered and cracked to be of use to me now."

Chet's face turned a ruby red. "I—I don't feel too well," he stammered.

The Hardys howled with laughter. Chet dashed out of the house and sped off in his jalopy before the boys could stop him.

"Poor Chet," Joe said with regret. "He took it pretty hard."

"We'll call him up later and apologize," Frank suggested.

After supper the doorbell rang. Mrs Hardy went to answer it and came back seconds later.

"Fenton, there's a man to see you," she said. "Gertrude doesn't like his looks and is watching him from behind the front room curtains."

Mr Hardy and the boys accompanied her to the door. Standing on the porch was a man of medium height and weight. He had removed his hat and was clutching it nervously.

"Mr Hardy?" he quavered.

"That's right."

"You gotta help me. I'm in serious trouble."

The Hardys led the caller to the study and offered him a chair.

"Now suppose you tell me what kind of trouble you're in," asked Mr Hardy, "and how I can help you."

"My name is Barney Egart," the man started. He seemed reluctant to go on for a moment, but then continued. "I have got myself into a terrible mess."

"What mess?" Frank questioned.

"Going with those guys to the State Museum," Egart replied. "You've got to believe me! It was my first job with the gang!"

His statement struck the Hardys like a thunderbolt.

"You mean you were in on the robbery?" Joe exclaimed.

"Where's the rest of the gang?" Frank wanted to know.

"On their way to Canada. After the stuff was loaded inside the logs, we split up. Orders were to meet in Stormwell for the pay-off."

"Go on," Mr Hardy said quietly.

Egart shifted in his chair nervously. "When I saw all the news about the robbery, I chickened out of the Stormwell meeting. So I decided to come here."

"Why?" Mr Hardy inquired.

"I don't have any friends who can help me. No money. Nothing!" came the reply. "Your reputation is well known. You see that a guy gets a break. So when I read you were connected with the investigation, I decided to talk to you."

"How did you get involved with the gang in the first place?" Joe asked.

"I was in Wilmington a few days ago looking for work," Egart explained. "Things were pretty bleak. Then I ran into a guy I'd met in California once. Name is Starker."

Frank turned to his father. "That's the big fellow who was employed at the museum in Philadelphia as a gardener!"

"I don't know anything about that," Egart commented. "All I know is that the guy asked me if I wanted to make some easy money. Said his friends needed an extra man for a job coming up. I was too broke to turn it down."

At Mr Hardy's request, Egart gave him a description of six other men who made up the gang. He said that since it was his first meeting with them, he knew nothing about their operations, or if they had a permanent hideout.

"Do you know anything about two ships named the *Yellow Parrot* and the *Black Parrot*?" Frank queried.

The man appeared surprised by the question. "I overheard a couple of the guys talking about them," he said. "They pick up the loot and make the pay-offs. And I can tell you this. From what I've heard, the gang doesn't know any more about the ships than I do. They're hired to steal the stuff and deliver it, that's all."

"It's a safe set-up," Frank said. "Whoever wants the DeGraw collection doesn't risk getting caught at the scene."

When the questioning was over, Mr Hardy said, "I promise to do whatever I can for you. But the first thing is to turn yourself in."

"You—you mean the police?" Egart stammered.

"Yes. Otherwise there's nothing I can do to help. Also, the fact that you surrendered on your own will be to your advantage."

Reluctantly Egart agreed. The Hardys drove him to Bayport Police Headquarters, where he officially gave himself up. Chief Collig was off duty, but quickly appeared in response to a telephone call.

"I'll get this out on the teletype right away," the chief said when Mr Hardy gave him Egart's descriptions of the men.

When they returned home Frank elected to stand by the radio. He carefully tuned the receiver to the pre-arranged frequency, then settled back in his chair with a book.

It was almost midnight when a faint signal in Morse code crackled from the receiver. Frank sat bolt upright in his chair and copied down the dots and dashes. Deciphered, the message read: *Ellis 0200 GMT tomorrow.*

Frank rushed to waken his father and Joe. They gazed at the message excitedly.

"It must mean that Ellis is going to contact us at

Excitedly they gazed at the message.

K

nought-two-hundred hours Greenwich Meridian Time tomorrow," Joe concluded. "That would be nine o'clock our time."

The following day dragged on slowly for the boys. Then, as the appointed hour arrived, the Hardys crowded round the radio receiver. Soon they began to hear: *dit dit-dah-dit-dit dit-dah-dit-dit dit-dit* . . .

Frank jotted down the message: *Ellis need help. Urgent. Will transmit 200 KC 1700 CW to 2100 GMT daily. Should pick up at Cambrian. Must go.*

"He's in trouble!" Joe exclaimed.

18

A Hidden Target

FRANK transmitted an immediate reply, but there was no response from Ellis.

"Maybe our equipment isn't powerful enough to reach his receiver," Joe said. "We don't know how far away he is."

Mr Hardy studied the message. "Ellis will be transmitting on a frequency of two hundred kilocycles," he observed. "But for what reason? And I've forgotten what the CW means."

"*Continuous* or *Carrier Wave*," Frank explained. "It's the modulation of these waves that make it possible to transmit."

"Quite right."

"What it amounts to, Dad," Joe put in, "is that Ellis will be transmitting a continuous signal on which we can take a directional bearing or home in with an aircraft radio compass."

"And 'Should pick up at Cambrian'," Mr Hardy concluded, "must mean that you can begin receiving the signal in the vicinity of that island."

"Exactly," agreed Frank.

"Then there's no time to lose," his father decided. "We must go there as soon as possible."

"Shall we use your plane?" Joe asked.

"I've another idea," Frank said. "Dan Tiller's amphibian is better suited for an over-water search. We can offer to hire his services when we get to Cambrian. If he's not available, there'll be other amphibians for charter."

"Good," Mr Hardy said. "Right now, I'd better telephone the airline and make reservations. By the way, ask Chet if he wants to come along. We're going to need all the help we can get. I'll get a seat for him too."

"Great!" Frank said. "I'll call him as soon as you're finished."

Chet was still a bit huffed at the way they had laughed about the sugar bowl. But his attitude quickly changed when he heard of the proposed trip to Cambrian Island.

"When do we leave?" he shouted excitedly.

"We'll let you know just as soon as Dad has our reservations confirmed. It'll be tomorrow morning some time."

Soon the phone rang and the boys hurried to Mr Hardy's study. He was just putting down the phone. "Everything's set," he said. "We'll depart tomorrow at eight A.M. from La Guardia. Jack can fly us there."

The atmosphere at breakfast the next morning was charged with suspense. Although Mrs Hardy did not share her family's excitement regarding the trip, she gallantly took it in stride.

Aunt Gertrude, however, could not restrain herself. "Mark my words!" she exclaimed brusquely. "Don't press your luck too far. Nothing good can come of this foolish trip!"

"Where's your spirit, Aunty?" Frank teased.

"Humph!" was her only answer.

After urging the two women not to worry, Fenton Hardy and his sons drove off to pick up Chet at the Morton farm, then hastened to Bayport Airport. Jack Wayne was already waiting, and soon they were in the air, heading for New York.

"There will be a slight delay because of heavy air traffic," Jack announced as they neared their destination.

Upon landing, the Hardys and Chet hurried to the terminal building. Their flight to Miami was being announced over the public-address system. They checked in their luggage and boarded the jet.

"I didn't think we'd be seeing Cambrian again so soon." Joe remarked as the aircraft lifted off the ground.

"Let's hope we'll find Tiller there," Frank added.

In Miami, the four changed planes as scheduled and departed on the last leg of their journey.

It was mid-afternoon when the plane touched down on the runway at Cambrian. By telephone Mr Hardy made arrangements for them to stay at a new hotel located near the airport.

"Dad," Frank said, "Joe and I would like to go to the other side of the airfield to see if we can locate Tiller. We'll meet you at the hotel later."

"Certainly. Go ahead. Chet can stay with me and help with the luggage."

The boys dashed out of the terminal building and headed towards the south side of the airfield. It was in that area that Tiller had parked his amphibian after they had returned from Tambio.

"There he is!" Joe yelled, pointing.

"Boy, am I glad we found him," Frank said and called hello to the pilot.

Tiller was surprised to see the Hardys.

"What are you fellows doing here?" he asked with a wide grin. "I thought you were back in Bayport hunting criminals!"

"We were," Joe replied.

"Have any trouble repairing the engine?" Frank inquired.

"None at all," the pilot assured him. "Spare crankcases are one thing I'm not short of. It was just a matter of replacing it."

"That's great," Joe put in, "because we'd like to hire your services."

"I'm available. What is it you want me to do?"

The boys told him about Ellis's message and of the possibility of using his signal to locate the *Yellow Parrot.*

"And you say he'll be transmitting on CW between the hours of 1700 and 2100 Greenwich Time?" Tiller queried.

"Right," Frank answered. "What's the time zone difference here?"

"Cambrian is three hours earlier than Greenwich," Tiller replied. "So that would make it two P.M. to six P.M. local time." He glanced at his watch. "If your friend is keeping to his schedule, he should still be transmitting. Want to take a trial hop in my plane and see if we can pick up the signal?"

"Sure. That's a good idea," Frank said.

"I'll go and give Dad a ring at the hotel," Joe volunteered. "Be right back."

Ten minutes later they were streaking down the runway for take-off in the amphibian.

Tiller climbed to five thousand feet, levelled off, then tuned his radio compass receiver to two hundred kilocycles. There was no response.

"If the ship's a great distance away," Frank remarked, "the signal will be very weak."

Tiller increased power and eased the nose of the plane upwards. "I'll climb to a higher altitude," he said.

The amphibian was approaching ten thousand feet when the indicator needle on the radio compass began to flicker. A low, steady humming sound came from the speaker of the receiver.

"We're getting something!" Joe excalimed.

"It *must* be the signal from the *Yellow Parrot*," Frank said.

The pilot watched the instrument. "The needle is reacting sluggishly," he observed. "The ship's quite a distance away. But we can determine the direction."

"Have you any idea about how far?" asked Joe.

"No. But I'll fly a *time-distance* problem. It will only give us a rough estimate. However, that's better than nothing."

As Tiller began the manoeuvre, he explained that the procedure involved flying in a direction which would be exactly at *right angles* to that of the ship. "The heading is then maintained until the radio compass shows at least a 10-degree change in relative bearing," he said.

The boys listened eagerly as Tiller went on, "This change in bearing, together with the time flown in order to obtain it, is used in a very simple mathematical formula to get the distance to the source of the signal, or in this case, the *Yellow Parrot*."

Several minutes passed. Then the pilot jotted down some figures.

"According to my calculation," he announced finally, "the ship is from three hundred and fifty to four hundred miles away."

Joe let out a low whistle. "Does your plane have enough fuel to make it there and back?" he queried.

"Barely," Tiller replied. "But I have a long-range tank I can install in the cabin. It'll give us plenty of reserve."

"There's one snag," Joe interjected. "Won't the tank cut down the number of passengers you can carry?"

"Yes," the pilot agreed. "I'll be limited to two."

"Dad and Chet won't be happy to hear that," Frank muttered.

Tiller returned to the airport. After parking his plane, he asked, "When do you want to make this flight?"

"Tomorrow, if possible," Frank said. "But I want to be sure you realize the danger. The crewmen aboard the *Yellow Parrot* are rough customers. If we should run into trouble and get caught—"

"Don't worry about me," Tiller interrupted.

The boys rejoined their father and Chet at the hotel and told them about their flight.

"And you say the addition of a long-range tank will permit only two passengers," Mr Hardy said. "I've a feeling you'll suggest that Chet and I go and you two stay behind." He winked at Frank.

Chet let out a whoop and patted Mr Hardy on the back.

"Well, not exactly," Joe said.

"We know the *Yellow Parrot*," Frank explained. "It's better that we go."

Chet sat down, looking disappointed.

"If you locate the ship, you must promise to be careful," Mr Hardy told his sons. "Don't try boarding the freighter. Get what information Ellis has and return here as soon as possible."

"We will," Joe promised.

It was late the following morning when Tiller telephoned the boys to tell them that he had just finished installing the long-range tank.

"That's great," Frank said. "Let's plan to take off a few minutes before Ellis is scheduled to begin sending his signal."

"Okay."

Mr Hardy and Chet accompanied Frank and Joe to the airport. As departure time neared, Tiller started the engines and his two passengers climbed aboard the plane.

"Good luck!" Mr Hardy shouted above the noise of the propellers. "And remember what I told you!"

His sons waved from a side window as Tiller taxied towards the runway.

Soon the amphibian was climbing out to sea. Then it turned on a southerly heading.

"It's exactly two o'clock," Joe announced, glancing at his watch. "Ellis should be transmitting."

The pilot switched on his radio compass receiver and tuned to the proper frequency. A low, humming sound crackled from the speaker. Gradually the needle of the instrument started to seek out the source of the signal.

"A course of 165 degrees should take us in the right direction for the moment," Tiller said. "The indication will become more accurate as we get closer to the ship."

Three hours went by. The boys watched the radio compass as it grew more and more sensitive to Ellis's signal.

"I'm going to work another *time-distance* problem," the pilot declared.

He swung the plane on to a new heading, and within a few minutes, completed his calculation. "We've got about eighty miles to go," he concluded.

The boys tingled with excitement. Less than half an hour had gone by when Frank pointed directly ahead.

"Cumulus clouds!" he exclaimed. "That could mean an island or a group of islands."

"Right," Tiller agreed. "And according to our radio compass, we're headed towards them."

As they continued, small rocky islets began to slide beneath them. Ahead, a mass of larger islands came into view.

"We're getting a strong signal," the pilot said. "We must be very near the ship."

"Stay on your present course and keep going," Frank said. "If the crew spots our plane, we don't want them to know we're searching for the *Yellow Parrot*."

An instant later the needle of the radio compass whirled round and pointed towards the tail of the aircraft.

"We've just passed over the ship!" Tiller shouted.

The boys quickly scanned the islands below. They saw no signs of the freighter, but noticed an odd-shaped island with a narrow inlet that was heavily covered with vegetation.

"I've a hunch the *Yellow Parrot* is hidden down there," Joe said.

"So do I," Frank agreed. "Let's land and take a look."

Tiller continued on his original course for a few more minutes, then descended to within a few feet of the water and turned back towards the islands.

"We'll stay down low to avoid being spotted," he told them. "Then I'll land about a mile out and taxi the rest of the way."

"Okay," Frank said. "The island we want is in the centre of the group. After dark, Joe and I will use your rubber raft and paddle to the inlet we saw."

After a smooth water landing, Tiller and the boys settled down to await sunset.

Tiller reached behind his seat. "Here's some food I brought," he said.

"Am I glad you thought of food," Joe replied with a chuckle. "This flight sure stimulated my appetite!"

After they had eaten, they talked until it was dark. Then the pilot inflated the raft and eased it over the side.

"Lots of luck," he said in a hushed voice as Frank and Joe started towards their objective.

The next hour was spent weaving in and out of a series of small islands. Finally the Hardys had the inlet in sight. They could make out the vague image of a ship anchored beneath a camouflage net covered with vegetation.

"It's the *Yellow Parrot*!" Joe said excitedly.

"Let's paddle closer," Frank whispered. "But we'd better stay near the shore for cover."

They came within a hundred yards of the ship and

Frank's right hand, gripping the paddle, dipped deep into the water. Their eyes were strained at the figures moving about the deck.

"We can't make a sound," Frank whispered. "Feather your paddle in the water, Joe, don't lift it out."

"Roger. I see they have guards posted near the rail."

Just then a sharp whack hit the side of the raft. There was a swishing sound in the water, and something grabbed Frank's paddle just below his fingers.

"A shark!" he cried out. He had hardly uttered the warning when a huge dorsal fin knifed under the bottom of the raft, half-lifting it out of the water. The boys tried to hang on, but were hurled over the lip and into the briny sea.

Silence was now out of the question. Frank and Joe knew that they must kick, scream, and flail their arms in an effort to scare the shark away.

"Swim for it!" Joe shrieked.

The shark made another pass, brushing past him with a tail slap which made Joe feel as if the end of the world had come.

The Hardys were too terror-stricken to notice what was going on at the ship's deck. The noise had alerted the crew. Bright beams of light pierced the darkness and swept towards the raft.

"Do you hear something?" yelled a crewman aboard the freighter.

"Someone's out there!" shouted another. "And a shark's after him!"

"Get a rifle!" came a third voice.

As Frank and Joe struggled frantically to reach the

shore, a shot whizzed past Frank and hit the shark with a thud.

Joe, who was behind his brother, saw the monster roll belly up and stain the sea with red, in the glare of the spotlight.

An instant later the boys reached a patch of sandy beach. They scrambled ashore and glanced round for a place to hide.

"Head for cover!" Frank whispered, pointing to a clump of rocks nearby.

Before they could make a run for it, a group of bronze-skinned natives seemed to appear from nowhere. They quickly surrounded the youths. There was no escape.

19

The Pirate King

THE Hardys were seized and marched off. The group walked along the beach for a short distance, then turned on to a trail leading inland.

"Where are you taking us?" Joe demanded.

The natives did not speak. Instead, they gestured to the boys to keep moving.

After travelling about a mile, they came to a village tucked in a valley ahead. The community was comprised of small stone buildings, box-like in shape. Coconut palms dotted the area.

In the centre of the village was a mediaeval-looking structure. The boys were led towards it.

"Look!" Joe exclaimed in disbelief.

Two guards flanked a set of heavy wooden, arch-shaped doors with massive iron hinges. They wore conquistador-type helmets and breastplates, which bore the bright-red symbol of the twisted claw!

At a signal from one of the natives, the guards pushed open the doors and ordered the prisoners inside.

The interior of the building was magnificent. The walls soared upwards and met in a series of gentle arches. These, combined with towering columns and polished stone floors, gave the area a palatial appearance.

"Amazing!" Joe whispered.

"I could do without it!" Frank muttered.

They were marched towards another set of wooden doors flanked by helmeted guards. On the wall above were carved the letters ETC.

"Empire of the Twisted Claw!" Frank muttered, recalling the rare volume they had seen in the New York book-shop.

The doors were pushed open to reveal a large room which looked much like a mediaeval banquet hall. Seated at the far side on a throne was a man wearing a fur-collared red robe. His aquiline nose jutted out from between a set of dark, glacial eyes. Standing to his right was Rawlin, first mate of the *Yellow Parrot*!

The man rose and stared at the boys menacingly. "What have we here?" he shouted. "Prisoners?"

Rawlin gazed at Frank and Joe as if he were seeing ghosts. "I know those kids!" he yelled. "They're the Hardy boys!"

"Sons of Fenton Hardy the detective?" asked the man in the robe.

"Yeah!" Rawlin answered. "They sailed aboard our ship once. I didn't know who they were at the time. Then we got the message from the *Black Parrot* saying that the loot from the State Museum had been found by the Hardys."

"Tell me more!" the man in the robe said in an ice-cold voice.

"Well, I put two and two together. I asked for their descriptions and, sure enough, it checked with the kids who jumped ship at Tambio."

"News travels fast, doesn't it!" snapped Joe.

The red-robed man seated himself again in chilly

composure. "I am Cartoll, king of this island," he announced. "I demand to know how you got here!"

"You don't really expect us to tell you!" Frank shot back.

"We were sight-seeing," Joe wisecracked. "It's a nice island."

Rawlin fumed. "Let me take care of these guys!"

"Calm yourself," Cartoll ordered with a smirk. "I admire audacity. However, I've no time to question them now." He clapped his hands.

Two guards responded. "Take the prisoners to the east tower room!" Cartoll commanded.

"I still think we ought to find out how they got here first!" Rawlin protested. "There might be others!"

"It's obvious they came by boat or plane," Cartoll concluded. "Have your men conduct a search of the area as soon as it is light."

"If only there was some way to warn Tiller," Frank thought frantically as he and his brother were led away by the guards.

The east tower room was situated at the top of a long, winding stone stairway. One of the guards unlocked the door and ordered the boys inside. The other one brought some bread and a jug of water, then the door was shut behind them.

When their eyes grew accustomed to the gloom, they were startled to see an elderly man with shaggy grey hair and a beard seated at a wooden table.

"Are you prisoners of Cartoll too?" he asked in a weak voice. "I have not seen you before."

"Yes," Frank replied glumly. "And who are you?"

"Leroy Ellis."

Frank and Joe looked at each other in surprise, then

Frank introduced himself and his brother. "Any relation to Clay Ellis?" he added.

"He's my son. You know him?"

"We've met him not long ago. Why are you a prisoner?"

"Because I refuse to help Cartoll with his crazy schemes. And I'm being used as a hostage so my son won't go to the authorities."

"So that's why Clay wouldn't tell us anything," Joe said, munching on a piece of bread.

"Perhaps you can tell us what's going on around here," Frank said. "Who is this Cartoll?"

The old man explained that Cartoll was the great-great-great grandson of a notorious eighteenth-century pirate who had established a kingdom on the island.

"We read about him and his Empire of the Twisted Claw in an old book," Joe interrupted.

"If you're familiar with that part of the story," Ellis said, "I'll bring you up-to-date."

He explained that he came upon the island more than a year before while sailing his ketch round the Caribbean. He was accompanied by his son, who was on holiday from his job as radio-man for a reputable shipping firm. They were impressed with the old buildings of the village and the friendliness of the natives.

During their stay, Cartoll arrived on the island and declared himself heir to his ancestor's kingdom. He forced the natives to be his subjects and revived the Empire of the Twisted Claw.

"He's mad and must be stopped!" Ellis insisted.

"What about the *Parrot* ships?" asked Frank.

The old man scowled. "Cartoll owns the ships and uses them for smuggling purposes. It's that scoundrel's way of financing his so-called royal enterprises."

Frank went on, "Do you know why he's so determined to get his hands on the DeGraw collection?"

"It's another of his crazy quirks," Ellis replied. "The items in that collection were owned by the original pirate king. They were being brought here to the island by a galleon when a sudden storm came up and sank the ship."

"And now Cartoll thinks the stuff belongs to him by reason of inheritance?" Joe queried.

The old man nodded. "Of course the idea is absurd. But such things are meaningless to a person of his mentality."

After their talk, the Hardys' thoughts turned to the possibility of escape.

"Your chances are slim," Ellis warned. "There are too many guards inside the palace."

Joe pointed to the only window in the room. It was a small, lancet-shaped opening covered with metal bars. "Maybe we can get out through there," he suggested.

Ellis smiled. "I had the same idea once." He reached inside his sleeve and pulled out a pointed piece of metal about the size of a pencil. "I began using this to dig away the stone round two of the bars. After that, I could stick my head through and realized escape was hopeless. There's a forty-foot drop to the ground."

The boys examined the window and saw where Ellis had scraped away the stone at the base of the bars. He had cleverly filled the depressions with loose dirt to prevent his work from being discovered.

Joe pushed away the bars and gazed down. "It is quite a drop," he said.

"I have an idea," Frank put in. "We'll tie our jackets and belts together to form a line. It won't reach all the way to the ground, but at least it'll lessen the height."

"I have a blanket you can use," Ellis added.

The boys quickly knotted the articles together. Then Frank estimated its length. This will take us within fifteen feet of the ground."

"A cinch," Joe commented with a grin.

Frank glanced at his watch. "It'll be daylight within a couple of hours. We'll have to work fast."

Frantically the Hardys dug away at the stone until the lower ends of two more bars were exposed. Then they pushed and pulled with all their strength until the upper ends loosened and tore free.

"All set?" Joe asked as he secured the line to one of the remaining bars.

"I—I'd like to go with you," Ellis said shakily. "But I don't know if I can make it."

"We're not leaving you behind," Frank said firmly. "You can do it. My brother and I will go first. We'll be waiting to help break your fall."

The Hardys slid down their makeshift line, then dropped the remaining distance to the ground.

Next, Mr Ellis emerged from the window above. He gripped the line and started to descend. But at the halfway point he came to a halt. The man obviously was frightened.

"Don't stop now," Frank muttered anxiously.

There was a short pause. Then Ellis continued and finally made a soft landing with the boys' help.

"Now what?" Joe asked in a hushed voice.

"Let's head back to where the *Yellow Parrot* is anchored," Frank urged. "Somehow we've got to get hold of a raft or a boat and warn Dan Tiller."

Dawn was breaking as the trio dashed out of the village and along the rugged trail leading to the beach.

Upon reaching their destination, they were stunned by what they saw. Tied to a mooring close to the *Yellow Parrot* was Tiller's amphibian!

"Dan's been captured!" Joe exclaimed.

Frank was too shocked to speak. He stared at the plane, realizing that their only means of escape had fallen into the hands of Cartoll!

· 20 ·

Island Rescue

AT the sound of men approaching from behind, the boys and Mr Ellis quickly hid behind some bushes.

"I don't like what you're planning to do," came Rawlin's voice. "It's too risky."

"Your opinion couldn't interest me less," a second man replied.

"That's Cartoll!" Joe whispered.

"But you already have most of the DeGraw collection," Rawlin went on. "And the gang you hired has been arrested. Why take chances?"

"You don't understand," Cartoll countered. "That portion of the collection at the Norwood Museum in Connecticut is of special interest to me. The armour was made for my ancestor's exclusive use. I must have it."

"So you're bent on stealing the stuff yourself," Rawlin said in disgust.

"Not exactly. You and some of the crew are going to help me. And thanks to the Hardys, we have a plane at our disposal. We'll be there in no time!"

The men walked by the hidden trio. They halted when they reached the beach. The Hardys could still overhear their conversation.

"But I've never done anything like that before," Rawlin protested.

"There's always a first time," Cartoll said sarcastically. "Don't worry," he added. "With the gang captured, the museum will surely be off its guard. We won't have any trouble."

Rawlin shouted to a crewman on the deck of the *Yellow Parrot* and ordered him to bring a dinghy ashore. Soon the men were being rowed out to the ship.

Frank's and Joe's pulses quickened as they waited and watched. Suddenly Tiller appeared on the deck. He was being pushed along by two hefty crewmen. They ordered him over the side and into another dinghy. They they took him to his amphibian.

"Tiller's removing the long-range tank," Joe observed after a while.

"Right. He's making room for Cartoll and his gang," Frank added. "But he still has enough reserve in his main tanks to reach Cambrian and refuel before going on."

"Maybe he'll try to make a break for it there," Joe said.

"I doubt that your friend will get a chance to escape," Mr Ellis warned. "Cartoll is clever. He'll be watching like a hawk!"

More than two hours had passed when the Hardys saw Cartoll, Rawlin, and three other men leave the ship and board the plane. Then Tiller started the engines and taxied out to clear water. He applied take-off power and the craft left a churning wake behind as it sped along. Soon it rose off the water and disappeared to the north.

Frank sighed. "We're in bad shape! Tiller and his plane might never come back here, and even if Cartoll brought him back, how could we contact him?"

"Might as well resign ourselves to being hermits from now on," Joe quipped in dark humour.

Mr Ellis turned to the boys. "I've got an idea," he said slowly. "There's a good chance it might work."

"What's that?" Frank inquired.

"I have earned the respect of many of the natives, including the village leader. Their fear of Cartoll prevented them from getting together and ousting the tyrant. Now that he's away, maybe I can talk them into action!"

"If only you could!" Joe said excitedly.

"It's risky," Frank warned.

"But it's our only alternative. I'm going back to the village," Ellis declared. "At least it's worth a try."

"We'll go with you," Frank said.

"No, it's better I go alone," the man insisted. "You fellows keep an eye on the *Yellow Parrot*. Maybe you'll spot my son." He scrambled to his feet and disappeared down the trail.

The Hardys grew more impatient as the hours dragged by. All was quiet aboard the ship. Sunset was less than an hour away when the boys heard sounds of commotion from the direction of the village. They sprang to their feet just as two guards in shiny breastplates came running down the trail. The young detectives flung themselves at the men and caught them above the knees. Their opponents somersaulted into the air and crashed to the ground.

A split second later two more guards appeared. The

boys attacked. Locked in a struggle, they and the men tumbled down the trail and on to the sandy beach. A crowd of natives arrived and seized the guards.

"It worked!" Mr Ellis shouted joyfully as he pushed his way through the group. "We've got the scoundrels on the run!"

"Look!" Joe yelled to his brother as he pointed towards the *Yellow Parrot*.

Frank turned to see the ship getting underway.

"My son is still aboard!" the old man cried out. A minute later an amphibian, much larger than Tiller's, roared low overhead. It turned and landed on the water nearby.

As the plane taxied towards the beach, its aft cabin door sprang open. The boys were startled to see their father's head appear. "Hello, sons!" he shouted. "Are you all right?"

"Starved, but okay otherwise," Frank called back.

A rubber raft was tossed over the side. Mr Hardy climbed into it. Then Chet emerged and joined him. Together they paddled ashore.

"Are we glad to see you!" Joe declared with relief. "But how did you know we were in trouble?"

"I have an excellent view of the airport from my hotel room in Cambrian," the detective explained, "and happened to spot Tiller's amphibian come in for a landing. Naturally, I thought you had returned. When Chet and I went to the field, we were startled to see the plane taking off again. I knew something was wrong."

The detective said that he then contacted air-sea rescue and an aircraft was made available for an immediate search.

"Luckily," Mr Hardy added, "Ellis hadn't stopped sending his signal."

"Looks as if you've had a bit of excitement round here," Chet observed. He stared at the captured guards. "Who are these characters in the tin coats?"

Frank and Joe told him about their recent adventure. Then they introduced Mr Ellis.

"We owe a lot to you and your son," Mr Hardy told the grey-haired man.

"Thank you," Mr Ellis replied. "But Clay is still aboard the ship. What can we do?"

"Don't worry," Mr Hardy said. "I'm going to request an international alert. The *Parrots* will be seized wherever they try to put into port. Your son will be all right."

Darkness was approaching rapidly. Frank glanced at his watch. "We still have Cartoll to deal with," he interjected. "He and his men have several hours start on us. We'll have to move fast!"

Mr Ellis joined the Hardys on the flight back to Cambrian. While en route, the pilot contacted Miami on his high-frequency transmitter at Mr Hardy's request. He asked that a message, warning about the intended robbery, be relayed to the authorities in Norwood. A full description of the thieves was included.

Upon arriving at their destination, Mr Hardy and his party quickly gathered their luggage. After saying goodbye to Mr Ellis, they boarded the last shuttle flight of the evening to Miami.

"I've never travelled so many miles in so short a time before," Chet remarked wearily as the plane approached the Florida city.

In Miami, Mr Hardy telephoned Jack Wayne and instructed him to meet them at La Guardia. Then he and the boys boarded a jet aircraft and were soon speeding northwards.

The flight to New York was smooth and fast. Jack was waiting when they arrived and flew them directly to Norwood. There a patrol car was standing by to take Mr Hardy and the boys to the museum.

"We caught all but one of the thieves," the policeman announced as they drove, "thanks to the information you sent us."

"Which one of them got away?" Frank asked quickly.

"I don't know. You'll have to ask the chief," the officer replied. "They were real amateurs. Broke open a door at the rear of the museum and set off an alarm hooked up to headquarters."

"The gang forced a pilot by the name of Tiller to fly them here," Joe said anxiously. "Any news of him?"

"He landed his plane on the lake near here. Later a police officer happened to spot it anchored close to shore. He investigated and found the pilot tied and gagged in the cabin. The fellow's okay and is at headquarters."

When they arrived at the museum, several patrol cars and a police van were parked at the kerb. Inside the van were Rawlin and the three crewmen. Cartoll was missing!

"Where's your boss?" Joe demanded.

"I don't know," Rawlin snarled. "And don't ask me any more questions because I'm not talking."

Frank rubbed his chin dubiously. "Cartoll couldn't have vanished into thin air!" He turned to the police chief. "Mind if we go inside the building and have a look round?"

"Go ahead," the officer answered. "But I doubt that you'll find anything."

Joe and Frank entered the museum and hurried to the exhibit room where the DeGraw collection was displayed.

The room was dark. Frank found the switch and turned on the lights. The boys looked round. Everything was intact. On the far side of the room, armour engraved with the symbol of the twisted claw stood on a pedestal.

As they turned to leave, Joe suddenly grabbed his brother's arm. "Hold on!" he whispered. "I might be seeing things, but I'm sure that figure on the pedestal moved!"

Cautiously they walked towards the spot. Frank stepped forward and lifted the visor.

A face stared out at him. *Cartoll!* With a curse, the man sprang at the youths. A violent struggle followed. Joe screamed for help. The noise brought Mr Hardy and several policemen to the scene.

"What's going on here?" one of the officers demanded.

The boys hauled the metal-clad man to his feet. "Meet Cartoll!" Joe declared.

Frank pulled the helmet from their captive's head. "Clever way to avoid being captured. And he almost got away with it."

Cartoll was furious. "You'll regret having meddled in my affairs!" he shouted. "Too bad Starker didn't succeed in squashing you like an ant in the Philadelphia museum."

"That's another charge against you," Joe said. "Attempted murder."

As the police marched the prisoner away, Mr Hardy held up a box-shaped object. At one end was what appeared to be a photographic lens.

"What's that?" Frank inquired.

"It's the secret as to how the museum thieves avoided setting off the photoelectric alarm systems during some of their robberies," his father replied. "Rawlin and his men were carrying a supply of these when the police caught them."

"How does the gadget work?" asked Joe.

"You know that the alarm system operates by aiming a beam of light at a photoelectric cell," Mr Hardy began. "The cell and light source are on opposite sides of the room. As long as the beam is not interrupted by someone walking through it, nothing happens. But if the beam is broken, off goes the alarm."

Joe nodded. "I get it," he said. "That box you're holding is a device which produces a beam of light. If aimed at the photoelectric cell, it simply replaces the original light source across the room."

"Exactly," his father said. "Then the thieves were free to move around the area without setting off the alarm."

"Simple," Frank muttered. "But not all the museums had this type of system!"

"True, but one of the gang's members was an expert in alarm technology. They tackled each one according to how it was set up.

"Once that problem was solved," Mr Hardy continued, "the rest was comparatively easy. Some of their gang got jobs at the museums they planned to rob.

They punctured the gas masks, making sure the knock-out fumes would be effective."

"Like Starker, who worked as a gardener," Joe interjected.

"Right. In other cases they threatened the guards to let them in. They used a different approach each time, and that's what made the case so hard to crack."

"There's one more thing that bothers me," Frank said. "What caused that shell hole in the *Yellow Parrot*?"

Mr Hardy grinned. "I found that out, too. She was shot at by a Central American smuggler patrol boat one night, but got away without being identified."

At that moment Chet wandered into the museum. He had been dozing in the police patrol car and was rubbing his eyes. "Find any clues?" he asked with a yawn.

"A few," Frank quipped. "You're a little bit late."

"Why didn't you wake me up? I was supposed to help you with this case."

Mr Hardy smiled. "We're all pretty tired. Let's head for home. The mystery is ended."

The boys nodded. Frank and Joe had no idea at that time that a new case, *The Wailing Siren Mystery* would soon take up all their time.

It was morning when they arrived in Bayport. Mr Morton greeted them when they dropped off Chet at the farm.

"I'm glad to see my son back," he said. "I've lots of work for him."

"But I need a chance to recuperate!" Chet protested.

318

"Okay," his father replied. "I'll give you till tomorrow. Then you'd better start digging over the back garden."

"That should be right down your alley, Chet." Joe laughed. "You might be lucky and discover another sugar bowl!"

3
The Secret
of Pirates' Hill

The Hardy Boys in
The Secret of Pirates' Hill

The Secret of Pirates' Hill was first published
in the U.K. in a single volume in hardback
in 1972 by William Collins Sons & Co. Ltd.,
and in Armada paperback in 1979.

Contents

·1· *Underwater Danger*

"DON'T forget, Frank, any treasure we find will be divided fifty-fifty!" Blond, seventeen-year-old Joe Hardy grinned. He checked his skin-diving gear and slid, flippers first, over the gunwale of their motorboat.

"I'll settle for a pot of gold," retorted Frank.

He was similarly attired in trunks, air tank and face mask, and carried a shark knife. The brothers had anchored their boat, the *Sleuth*, off a secluded area of beach. It ran beneath a low, sand-dune-covered, rocky promontory called Pirates' Hill. The only other boat in sight was that of an old fisherman out for an early morning catch.

"Here goes!" said Frank as he plunged into the cool waters of the Atlantic. Together, the boys swam towards the bottom.

Suddenly Joe clutched his brother's arm and pointed. Twenty feet in front of them and only a short distance from the surface was another skin diver in a black rubber suit and a yellow-trimmed cap. The barbed shaft of a spear gun he held was aimed in their direction!

As the man pulled the trigger, Joe gave his brother a hard shove, separating the boys. The arrow flashed between them and drifted away.

"Wow, what's that guy trying to do?" thought

Frank. Had he mistaken them for fish? Or was he just practising?

The diver made no attempt to come forward and explain or apologize. Instead, he swam off.

"That's strange," Joe said to himself.

Motioning for his brother to follow, he swam towards the diver to find out what he was doing. But not wanting to be questioned, the spearman, with powerful strokes, shot to the surface.

Pointing, Joe indicated to Frank, "Up and after him!"

As the brothers popped above the waves, they looked about. The *Sleuth* lay twenty feet away and the old fisherman was still in the same spot. But the spearman was nowhere in sight.

Frank and Joe lifted their face masks. "Where did he go?" Frank called.

"I can't figure it out," Joe replied, treading water and gazing in all directions. "Let's ask that fisherman."

The boys swam to their motorboat and hung on to the gunwales. Frank called out, "Ahoy there! Did you see another skin diver around here?"

"What's that?" The old fellow, who was wearing a cap which shaded most of his wrinkled face, appeared to be deaf.

Frank shouted, "Did you see a skin diver wearing a black outfit?"

The man laid his pole in the bottom of the boat and cupped both hands over his ears. "Who had a fit?" he called.

"Never mind!" Joe shouted. With a wink at his brother, he said, "Guess he didn't see anybody."

Conjecturing that the stranger might have swum

slightly beneath the surface and taken off towards shore, Frank and Joe decided to resume their diving.

"Down we go," Joe said, as he readjusted the straps that held the air tank on his back. "But keep your eyes open for that spearman."

"Right."

Again the boys submerged. There was no sign of the other diver.

"He sure got away from here fast," Frank thought to himself. "I'd like to know who he is and what he thought he was doing!"

Long, strong strokes with their rubber-finned legs forced the boys downwards through seaweed gardens. Small fish swished in and out among the fronds. Seeing no interesting objects to salvage, Frank signalled Joe to head for deeper water. Air bubbles rippled steadily upwards.

Suddenly a giant form appeared before Frank. A black shark? Frank unsheathed his knife and faced the huge fish. Just then the monster swerved and Frank got a better look at it.

"A tuna!" he told himself, relieved.

As Frank turned to see if his brother was watching, he felt a sudden jar and his face mask was nearly ripped off. Frank clawed desperately to put it in place. "What's going on?" he thought as unconsciousness swept over him.

Joe, who had seen the whole episode, was horror-struck. Another shaft from a spear gun had zipped through the murky deep. From the vast number of bubbles rising through the water, Joe realized that his brother's air hose had been pierced. Water was flooding in!

With powerful strokes, he reached Frank. Towing the limp form with one hand, Joe headed for the *Sleuth*'s anchor line, dim in the distance. Working his fins as violently as possible, he fought his way towards it for what seemed an eternity.

Finally Joe reached the rope and pulled himself to the surface. When both boys bobbed into the air again, Joe tore off Frank's headgear, holding his face above the waves. Then he pushed his brother inside the boat and scrambled after him.

"Frank!" Joe cried out, laying his brother in a prone position and feverishly applying artificial respiration.

Minutes passed before Frank stirred. Joe continued his treatment until he heard a moan, then a feeble question.

"Ugh—where—what happened?"

"We were shot at again and you were hit!" Joe said, helping his brother sit up. "This time it was deliberate."

"The same diver?"

"It must have been."

"Probably hiding behind an underwater rock," Frank concluded.

At that moment the boys heard the fisherman call out, "Something wrong over there?"

Joe shook his head and the old fellow continued his fishing.

"That devilish skin diver must be a phantom," Frank said, after filling his lungs with deep draughts of air.

"I still can't figure him out," Joe mused. "Say, do you suppose he's looking for sunken treasure and wanted to keep us away?"

"I never heard anybody talk about sunken treasure

off Bayport," Frank said.

"No," Joe agreed. "Well, pal, I think you've had enough for one morning. Let's go home."

Waving at the fisherman, he pulled up anchor and started the motor. Two miles away on Barmet Bay was the boathouse where the boys kept the *Sleuth*. As they turned towards the bay entrance, Joe grinned ruefully. "I wish we could have kept that spear for a clue," he remarked, "but it passed clean through your air hose and disappeared."

"Better luck next time."

"What!" Joe exclaimed. "Better no next time at all!" Then he said, "We wouldn't know that fellow even if we should meet him again."

"I did notice one thing," said Frank. "He wore a yellow band round his black swim cap."

"Pretty slim clue. You feeling okay, Frank?" Joe asked, observing how pale his brother was.

The older boy said he had fully recovered from the shock. "Say, look!" he soon added. "Someone's waiting for us at the dock."

Drawing closer, they saw that the man was about thirty-five years old, stockily built, and had wiry, black hair. He stood motionless, his legs braced apart, looking intently at the approaching boys. Joe ran the *Sleuth* inside the boathouse and the brothers stepped ashore.

"Good morning," the stranger said. "My name's Clyde Bowden. I'm from Tampa, Florida. I assume you're the Hardys?"

"That's right," Frank replied, as the trio exchanged handshakes. "What can we do for you?"

"A detecting job."

"That's for us!" said Joe excitedly, but Frank added cautiously, "Let's hear about it first."

The Hardys, star athletes at Bayport High, were the sons of Fenton Hardy. Once a crack detective with the New York City Police Department, Mr Hardy was now an internationally famous private sleuth. The brothers often helped their father on cases and also had solved many mysteries of their own.

Their first big success was *The Mystery of the Aztec Warrior*, and only recently they had had a hair-raising adventure in tracking down *The Secret of the Caves*. Now they seemed to be heading for another mystery.

"How did you know where to find us?" Joe asked.

"I just left your home on Elm Street," Bowden replied. "Your mother said I might meet you here. I understand you're amateur sleuths."

"Yes," said Frank. "While we change from skin-diving gear into clothes, suppose you tell us about your case?"

"I hear that you fellows, as well as your father, do a pretty clever job of detecting," Bowden began.

"Mother didn't tell you that," said Frank, smiling. "She never brags about us."

"No. As a matter of fact, I heard it from your postman."

Frank and Joe grinned at each other as the three left the boathouse, then listened intently as Bowden explained the case. He was searching for an early eighteenth-century cannon known as a Spanish demi-culverin. It was supposed to be in the vicinity of Bayport.

"A Spanish cannon in Bayport?" Joe asked unbelievingly.

"I have reliable information it's around here," Bowden answered. "Although I'm not in a position to tell you how I know about the cannon, I'm certain that with your help I can find it."

As they walked towards the Hardy home, Frank asked the man for the dimensions of the cannon. Bowden described it as being nine feet long and weighing one and a half tons. "It fires an eight-pound shot," he added.

"What do you want the old cannon for?" Joe asked.

Bowden smiled. "Believe it or not, I'm helping to outfit the pirate boats in the famous Gasparilla Exposition in Tampa this year," he replied. "All the details, including the guns, must be authentic."

"That's very interesting," said Frank, as they turned a corner towards the town square. "I should think that the type of cannon you're looking for would be found somewhere around the Caribbean rather than this far north. Many Spanish ships were wrecked—"

Frank stopped speaking as a deafening boom suddenly shook the air.

"What was that?" Bowden gasped, paling.

"It came from the square," Frank replied. "Sounds like trouble. Come on. Let's find out what has happened!"

·2· A Suspicious Client

WITH Bowden following, Frank and Joe ran towards a crowd in the town square. They stood round an old

Civil War mortar on a pedestal. White powder smoke drifted from the muzzle.

"Somebody fired the old gun!" Joe cried out in astonishment. "Do you smell that powder?"

"It must have been an accident," Frank said excitedly.

As the brothers made their way through the crowd they saw local police officers Smuff and Riley being questioned by the onlookers.

"What happened?"

"Who set it off?"

"Was anyone hurt?"

Before the policemen could reply, a booming voice sounded and a grizzled old man, dressed in a Minute Man's outfit, complete to tricorn hat and leggings, walked up to the mortar.

"I cain't understand what all this here fussin' is about," he drawled.

Officer Riley stood erect and demanded, "And who do you think you are in that rig?"

The old man's weather-beaten face beamed. He said that he was Jim Tilton, a retired National Guard artillery sergeant. He had been asked by Police Chief Collig to manage the Independence Day cannon salute. "An' I think I look 'propriate for this job," he added.

"But this ain't the fourth of July!" Riley protested. "It's only the first. Why should you come round here bombardin' the town without warnin'?"

The old-timer raised his hands good-naturedly. "I'm mighty sorry I caused so much fuss. After all, I wasn't usin' a ball. I just had some powder an' waddin' in her."

Tilton showed a letter to the officers. It was from Chief Collig and the Fourth-of-July Committee, permitting Tilton to test the mortar.

"Well, there was no harm done," Riley said, "but I should have been notified. But anyway, we know the gun is ready—we and everybody for five miles around!"

Reassured, the crowd dispersed as Officers Smuff and Riley herded them off. Sergeant Tilton remained, talking with a few men. The Hardys moved closer for a better look at the old sergeant and the equipment he had been using.

Bowden also edged forward and stared with keen interest at the various markings on the gun. He told the boys that this was a Federal piece.

"It was cast at the same arsenal that turned out the famous 'Dictator,' " he said. "That was a thirteen-inch mortar used against Petersburg, Virginia, in the Civil War."

"Land sakes," Tilton remarked in surprise, "you know a lot! An' here I am, a veteran of that famous battle between the *Monitor* an' the *Merrimac*, an' I didn't never suspect anything like that about this ol' hunk o' iron."

Everyone laughed and Joe quickly calculated that for Tilton's tall tale to be true he would have to be well over a hundred years old.

As the sergeant began to clean the barrel of the old weapon, Bowden turned to Frank and Joe. "My offer to you," he said in a low voice, "is one thousand dollars if you find the Spanish cannon."

Frank and Joe were amazed. A thousand dollars for an old gun to be used in a pageant!

Sensing their thoughts, Bowden quickly added, "I'm a man of means and can well afford it."

He explained that he had already combed Bayport proper. The boys' responsibility would lie in searching the surrounding areas and nearby towns. Bowden said he was staying at the Garden Gate Motel on the state highway and could be reached there if anything developed.

"We don't charge for our sleuthing," Frank informed the man.

Bowden was astonished. "You've solved all your cases for nothing?"

Joe nodded. "If we should help you," he said, "it will be on that basis."

"Okay. But I'll make it worth your while somehow!" Then, seeing Tilton preparing to leave, Bowden hastily excused himself. "I have a few questions to ask this old codger. See you later."

"Okay, Mr Bowden," Frank replied. "We'll think about your request and let you know."

The Hardys crossed the square and headed for the police station to report the underwater attack on them. They went directly to Chief Collig, a solidly built man in his late forties. He often co-operated with the Hardys on their cases, and now listened intently to their latest adventure.

"This is serious," he said. "I'll tell the harbour patrol to look for a skin diver wearing a black suit and a swim cap with a yellow stripe."

The boys thanked him and left. As they walked up Elm Street on which they lived, their conversation turned to Bowden.

"It seems that we're back in business!" Joe remarked.

"Let's take on the case. It could be interesting."

"I'm a little worried about it," Frank replied. "The whole setup seems a bit phony."

"Your imagination, Frank. Bowden's okay."

Joe was naturally impulsive and always ready for action. Frank reminded him of the many times they had met people who had seemed to be above-board yet had turned out to be dishonest.

"But we'd still have fun looking for the cannon," Joe insisted. "What could we lose?"

"Nothing, maybe."

At the rambling stone house in which they lived, the boys were greeted by their petite mother and their tall, angular Aunt Gertrude—Mr Hardy's sister—who spent most of her time at his house. When she heard of Clyde Bowden's offer, Aunt Gertrude exclaimed tartly:

"A thousand dollars for finding an old piece of junk! There's something underhand about such a deal. Mark my words!"

Mrs Hardy's face wore a worried frown. "I wish your father were here to take the case," she said, "instead of being in Florida."

"Florida!" Joe exclaimed. "Frank, Dad could check on Bowden's credentials. Let's phone him!"

Mrs Hardy said the detective could be reached only by telegram at an address in Miami. Frank wrote it down and hurriedly sent a wire.

"A reply may take several days," Joe remarked. "I hate to wait. Why not make a start on Bowden's case? We can drop it when we like."

"Okay, but let's not get in too deep until we hear from Dad."

"I'll let Bowden know," said Joe. He dialled the

Garden Gate Motel. Bowden was not in, so Joe left a message for him. Then he turned to Frank. "What say we advertise in the newspaper for information about the demiculverin?"

"Good idea." A query was placed in the classified section of the *Bayport Times*, which had a wide circulation in the smaller outlying towns.

"Now we're getting some place!" Joe exulted. "Say, maybe Aunt Gertrude can help us."

"How?"

"As newly elected president of the Bayport Historical Society," Joe said, "she might know of some ancient cannon in the vicinity."

Their aunt had gone to the kitchen to start preparing lunch, so the boys went out there and put the question to her. After a moment's thought, Miss Hardy said, "I know of one cannon."

"Where is it?" Joe asked eagerly.

"Let me see—I think it's on the back lawn of a museum in Greenville."

"Do you know what type it is?" Frank asked.

"I think maybe pre-Civil War," their aunt replied. "Possibly Spanish. I'm not sure."

"We'll take a look," said Joe.

After lunch the boys drove to the Greenville Museum. Frank parked in front alongside the hedge, and the two walked through a gate to the spacious lawn at the back.

The cannon, a long-barrelled six-pounder, stood in the centre of the plot. Joe read the plaque fixed to the piece.

"It's a Spanish gun!"

Frank joined him and read the inscription on the

bronze plaque. It stated:

"*Pasavolante*, meaning fast action. Made in Toledo, Spain. Often called *cerbatana*, after Cerebus, the fierce dog of mythology. *Pasavolante* in modern Spanish means peashooter."

"Do you suppose this could be the peashooter that Bowden is searching for and he just got the name wrong?" Joe asked.

"I doubt it," Frank answered. "Bowden seemed sure it was a demiculverin."

"False clue," Joe sighed.

As the brothers started back across the lawn, they noticed a tall, slender man, with a swarthy complexion, entering from a side gate. Bare-headed and wearing a black cotton motorcycle jacket, he moved hurriedly towards the gun.

The boys looked back at him as they walked. Now the man was kneeling at the *pasavolante*. Frank and Joe saw him rise and run to the far side of the cannon to scrutinize it.

"Maybe he's trying to locate a demiculverin too," Joe remarked. "Let's go back and ask."

Retracing their steps, they had covered only a few feet when the man suddenly ran for the side gate by which he had entered.

"He must be goofy," Joe remarked.

The brothers turned back to the road. Then they heard a motorcycle roar into action.

The swarthy stranger, wearing goggles, sped round the corner, directly towards the boys!

·3· *A Motorcycle Clue*

As THE motorcycle roared down on them, Frank and Joe leaped aside and stumbled headlong into the hedge. The driver missed them by inches!

"Sorry!" he shouted and sped off.

The boys angrily picked themselves up.

"Did that lunatic mean he was sorry he didn't hit us?" Joe stormed.

"I'd like to get my hands on him!" Frank said. "Look at my trousers!" The sharp twigs of the hedge had made a long tear in them.

"Did you get his licence number?" Joe asked.

"No," Frank answered ruefully. "But the motorcycle looked like a foreign make. I saw the letter K on the rear bumper."

"If I ever see that fellow again, he'll have some explaining to do as to why he nearly hit us," said Joe. "And I'd like to ask him about his interest in the old cannon, too."

"He certainly acted as if he was afraid he might be noticed," said Frank.

At home they hurried into the kitchen. Aunt Gertrude was removing a batch of biscuits from the oven. She exclaimed, "No need to charge in here like a herd of buffalo!"

"We smelled the biscuits and couldn't wait to have some," Joe said with a grin, as he reached for the tray of hot ginger snaps.

This subtle flattery softened the maiden lady's stern demeanour. "Well, have one," she said. "But eat too fast and you'll get indigestion."

"Indigestion!" Frank cried out. "What did you do? Bake rocks in 'em?"

Aunt Gertrude gave her nephew a withering look. Although she would be the last person to admit it, she enjoyed the boys' teasing. But to hear her scold and correct them, a listener might think Frank and Joe were the bane of her existence. Aunt Gertrude's peppery manner, however, concealed a great depth of affection for them.

"Frank!" she sputtered. "You've torn your trousers!"

"Had a little accident," he admitted, and told her of the motorcyclist.

"I knew it!" Miss Hardy declared. "Hoodlums are after you again. Stay away from them!"

Frank suppressed a chuckle while Aunt Gertrude took another tray of biscuits from the oven. "You wouldn't want us to let 'em run around loose, would you?" he teased.

"Well, don't say I didn't warn you." His aunt sighed. "Trouble, trouble," she added to herself.

"What trouble?" Frank asked.

"The Bayport Historical Society," Aunt Gertrude replied. "What would you do with a case full of swords?"

Frank nearly choked on a biscuit. "Swords!"

"Yes, cutlasses. I'd like to keep them."

"Please, Aunty, start from the beginning," Joe begged, "and tell us about it."

Aunt Gertrude explained that the Society had recently received a gift from the estate of Senator

Entwistle. It included some lovely old costumes dating from 1812 and a case of cutlasses.

"I argued with our members," Aunt Gertrude went on, "but they insist that we present the cutlasses to the museum at the state capital."

"Too bad," said Frank, then asked, "Is it your job to have them shipped?"

"Yes," she replied. "But the cutlasses are to be moved to the basement temporarily. The museum isn't ready to receive them."

"And you'd like us to help you," the boys said in unison.

"Yes. Tomorrow evening."

"We'll be there."

Frank and Joe went to their room to plan the next move in locating the cannon.

"We can't do anything out of town today," said Frank, glancing at the table clock between the boys' beds. "It's almost time for dinner."

"There's something we *can* do," Joe spoke up. "Visit the motorcycle shops in Bayport and find out the name of the foreign make with a K."

"Good idea, Joe. We may even learn the identity of that fellow who nearly ran us down."

"What are we waiting for? Let's go!" Joe urged.

The boys had better luck than they had anticipated. The first dealer they called on explained that the letter K indicated the motorcycle was the Kesselring, a German make.

"You don't see many of them around," he said. "But they're becoming more popular."

"Do you sell them?" Frank asked.

"No."

"Who does?"

"Nobody in Bayport. And no one in town owns one, either."

"Do you know where the nearest agency is located?" Frank asked.

"Yes," the dealer replied. "In Delmore."

"The penitentiary is there," Joe remarked.

The man nodded. "The dealer mostly sells bikes, but he took on the Kesselring motorcycle agency because he is German."

The Hardys exchanged glances. Had the man they had seen on a Kesselring bought his motorcycle in Delmore? The boys thanked the dealer and rode off in their convertible.

"What say we drive over to Delmore in the morning and talk to that agent?" Joe suggested.

"We'll do it," Frank agreed. "The main road there is still closed. The detour leads past the Entwistle place where the cutlasses came from."

At home the boys were greeted by the aroma of fried chicken that their mother was preparing.

"You're just in time," she said, smiling.

The boys washed, then followed Mrs Hardy and Aunt Gertrude to the table.

"Any word from Dad?" Frank asked.

"No," Mrs Hardy replied. "But we should hear something soon."

Joe asked his aunt about the Entwistle mansion. She had heard it was deserted. "And it's such a beautiful place. A Society member hinted that there might be some valuable pieces, which the executors didn't find, in the house. He said Mr Entwistle was eccentric. They say tramps stay there sometimes."

That evening the boys decided to take a look at the Entwistle mansion.

"Maybe we can find out if there's really anything in the old place," said Frank, as they drove along the detour road towards the old estate.

"Yes—" Joe began, then broke off as the noisy approach of a motorcycle reached his ears. The next moment he exclaimed, "Hey, Frank! That sounds like the Kesselring cycle!"

His brother listened intently. "You're right. Hope he comes this way."

But the Hardys were disappointed when the sound of the motorcycle grew fainter.

"He must have turned down a side road," Joe said. "Let's try to catch up with him."

Frank was about to agree when both boys saw something that made them gasp.

"That red glow in the sky!" Joe exclaimed. "It's right where the Entwistle mansion is!"

"The place must be on fire!" cried out Frank, stepping harder on the accelerator.

Soon they came within sight of the grounds. On a knoll stood the huge house. One wing was a mass of flames!

"We must get the fire department here before the whole place goes up!" said Frank.

He backed the car round, and in a few minutes the boys reached a farmhouse, where they put in a call to Bayport reporting the fire.

Then they sped back to the scene of the blaze. Getting out of the car, they heard sirens wailing. Minutes later, several fire engines halted before the burning mansion. Shouts of firemen filled the air while they fought to restrict damage to the wing that was being consumed.

Finally, after half an hour's battle, the flames were quenched and the bulk of the big house stood unscathed. Chief Tally, after investigating the charred ruins, returned to his car. A good friend of the Hardys, he greeted the boys with a weary smile. Frank told him they had heard that articles of value might be hidden in the house.

"Could be," the fire chief said. "We suspect an intruder was ransacking the place and dropped a lighted cigarette."

Joe told him of hearing a motorcyclist racing away near the Entwistle place. "He might be the one who was here," he said.

Chief Tally smiled. "You boys are always on the job but this is the quickest I've ever received a clue. If you find out anything else about this rider, let me know."

Frank then told him about the man on the Kesselring who had nearly run the boys down. "The machine we heard tonight had the same kind of roar," he said.

"Thanks. I'll keep the information in mind." The chief nodded, then turned to speak to two firemen who would remain at the mansion, and the boys returned to their convertible.

"Frank," said Joe as they drove home, "if that rider is a housebreaker, he may be interested in the cannon for no good reason."

The boys slept well, but early the next morning the telephone awakened them. When Frank reached the hallway to answer it, he heard his mother talking on her bedroom extension. The door was open and she waved him in.

"Fenton, here's Frank now," she said. "You tell him." She turned to her son, excitedly. "That man Bowden is a fake!" she announced.

·4· *New Tactics*

"DAD! Hello!" Frank said. "How are you? . . . That's good. What about Bowden?"

"The man isn't known here in Tampa, Frank."

"Then he was lying about his pageant work?"

"Definitely. No pirate ship with a demiculverin has been entered in the Gasparilla event."

Frank whistled. "I've been suspicious of Bowden from the start. But you don't think we should stop looking for the cannon, do you?"

"No. There's a mystery connected with it. Furthermore, I'm working on a case—swindlers—that Bowden may be mixed up in. Apparently he's using an assumed name."

"Shall we notify the police or shadow him ourselves?" Frank asked.

Mr Hardy advised them to do neither. Instead, he said to stay friendly with Bowden and not let him know they had uncovered his lie.

"It's the best way to get at the truth," he said. "And let me know if I can be of any more help. I'd like to speak to your mother again."

Frank dashed to tell his brother the news.

"Hot-diggety-dog!" Joe cried, hopping out of bed.

"Frank, this is going to be fun. We pretend to play along with Bowden, but all the time we're trying to find out what he's up to!"

"Which problem should we tackle first—Bowden or the motorcyclist?" said Frank.

"Let's combine them in one trip. We'll go to the motel first, then on to Delmore," Joe suggested.

"Okay."

During breakfast with Mrs Hardy and Aunt Gertrude, they related their plan, and when they finished eating, made for the door. Aunt Gertrude stopped them and handed Joe a book.

"You boys might as well employ your time profitably while you're riding along. Joe, read this aloud while Frank drives."

Her nephew glanced at the book. "Why, this is great, Aunt Gertrude! It tells about the various types of artillery. Where did you find this book?"

"In your father's library." She chuckled. "I thought it might give you a clue to that demiculverin you're trying to find."

The boys hugged her, then kissed their mother.

"We'll be home in time to move those cutlasses," they promised.

As the brothers rode off, Joe consulted the index of the book. Then he turned to a section on culverins and read aloud:

"It derives from the Latin word *colubra* [snake]. Culverins were highly esteemed for their range and effectiveness of fire. Their thick walls, long bores, and heavy powder charges made them the deadliest of fieldpieces."

"Fieldpieces!" Frank interrupted. "Why would

Bowden want a fieldpiece on a pirate ship?"

Joe grinned. "Maybe he doesn't know any better. Score one for us!"

Half a mile farther along the highway, Frank pulled up in front of the Garden Gate Motel. The clerk was not at his desk when the boys entered, but a maid told them Bowden was in Cabin 15.

The brothers walked down a long row of rooms.

"There it is!" Joe said, spotting the number. He knocked on the door. There was no answer, so he tried again. Still Bowden did not come.

"Say, this looks like a note," Joe said, eyeing a folded paper pinned below the doorknob.

"Maybe it's for us," Frank suggested.

He and Joe peered at the printed message and opened their eyes wide in amazement. It read:

> *Bowden! Clear out before it's too late!*

"Wow! His enemy!" Frank exclaimed.

"Sounds as if he means business, whoever he is," Joe whispered.

In hushed tones the brothers discussed the threat. Why did Bowden have such a deadly enemy? Was it because of the demiculverin?

"This may drive Bowden away," Joe remarked. "Then we'll lose track of him."

Frank shook his head. "I doubt it. He wants that cannon too badly. Well, let's go to Delmore and stop here on our way back."

The detour they had to make took the boys past the farm of their friend Chet Morton. Chet was eighteen, roly-poly, good-natured, and loved to eat. Solving mysteries with the Hardys always gave him the jitters. Despite this, he was a loyal assistant and on more than one occasion had saved them from dangerous predicaments.

"Let's stop a minute," Joe suggested, seeing Chet's sister Iola near the swimming pool.

Frank grinned knowingly. Joe and Iola dated frequently. The boys parked in the driveway and approached the pretty brunette.

"Hi!" she said.

"Hi, yourself!" Joe said. "Where's Chet?"

Iola pointed into the pool. Their stout friend was under water, wearing flippers and a snorkel. He travelled slowly, the snorkel moving like the periscope of a miniature submarine.

"Ahoy!" Joe yelled, as the brothers ran to the water's edge.

Chet moved about like a walrus. Finally he emerged and removed the face mask and flippers.

"Hi, fellows!" he called. "This business is difficult. Can't get down deep enough."

"What's the trouble?" Joe asked. "That extra fat making you too buoyant?" he teased.

"Now, listen here," said Chet, "just because I know good food when I see it—"

He smacked his lips as if imagining he was about to taste something delicious. Then he changed the subject, telling them he was going to take lessons in skin diving from the same man who had taught the Hardys.

"Swell," said Joe.

"I can't start, though, until I earn enough money to buy all the gear."

"Don't let that worry you," Frank spoke up. "I'll lend you my outfit."

"Thanks. And now bring me up to date on everything that's happened lately."

The Hardys had just finished telling Chet and Iola about Bowden, the mysterious cyclist, and the skindiving attack, when a car drove in. At the wheel sat Callie Shaw, an attractive girl with blonde hair and sparkling brown eyes. She was Iola's chum and Frank's regular date.

Callie alighted, and after greeting everyone, said, "I'm glad you're all here. I wanted to talk over plans for our Fourth-of-July beach party. Tony Prito is coming with us too."

Tony, a schoolmate and fellow athlete at Bayport High, had been through many adventures with the Hardys.

"Let's have a clambake like last year," Frank suggested.

"And lobster," Joe added. "Tell you what, Chet. You can put on my diving gear and get us some lobsters."

"Not me," said Chet. "I wouldn't tangle with that human devilfish who shot at you fellows."

Iola looked worried. "Do you think he's still lurking around?" she asked.

The Hardys doubted this. "He knows we're looking for him, so he'll probably keep out of sight," Joe reasoned.

Suddenly Frank grabbed Joe's arm. "Look over there! Someone's spying on us!"

He had seen an intruder peering from behind a tree near the road. The quick glimpse of a black jacket led Frank to believe that the man might be the wanted motorcyclist!

"Come on, Joe!" he whispered, setting off.

Instantly the man dodged from behind the tree and started to run. The chase was on!

Having the advantage of a head start, the man managed to keep ahead of them. Then he jumped on a parked motorcycle and sped off.

From the silhouette of the rider and the sound of the motor, there was no doubt in the Hardys' minds as to the spy's identity.

"It's the rider we're looking for!" Joe exclaimed.

Together, the brothers ran back to their car and hurried after the suspect. They had covered nearly two miles before they caught sight of the man. Reaching the crest of the next slope, he looked back. Sensing that his pursuers were getting closer, the rider revved his machine and shot out of sight into the curving downgrade.

"Faster!" Joe urged. "He's getting away!"

Frank bore down and their car whined round the curve in hot pursuit of the Kesselring. Once again in the open, where the highway stretched out for miles, the boys could no longer see the motorcycle.

"He's turned off!" Joe said in disappointment. "But where?"

Frank's brow furrowed. "He couldn't have reached this point," Frank replied. "He must have swung into that dirt road we just passed. Let's go back!"

Screeching to a stop, he made a U turn and sped to the side road. Joe cried out, "I see a single skid track going in there! That's the place!"

Frank swung the car across the road and they plunged onto the rough, narrow, dirt lane. Fresh motorcycle tracks were clearly evident. Dust filled the air, choking the boys as they sped along.

"Stop!" Joe cried suddenly. "The track ends here!"

The car parked and locked, they ran back to where the tracks turned off into the pine woods.

"He couldn't go far through here on his machine," Frank said, as they pressed on excitedly.

"You're right!" Joe whispered a moment later. "Look!"

· 5 ·   *The Stakeout*

AHEAD of the Hardys in the deep woods stood a cabin. The Kesselring motorcycle was parked near the front door. Quietly the brothers moved into position for a better view of the one-room building. This must be the suspect's hide-out!

"End of our search," Joe whispered exultantly.

The brothers moved forward. Frank signalled Joe to cover the rear of the cabin while he went to the front door. It was open and the place appeared to be deserted. Frank strode inside. The rider was not in sight and there was no place where he might be hiding.

"He gave us the slip," said Frank as Joe joined him.

"But not for long," Joe declared. "He'll return for his cycle."

Frank suggested that they pretend to leave, then double back and stay in hiding until the man returned.

"Suppose he finds out our car is still on the road?" Joe said.

"We'll have to take that chance," his brother declared.

The boys walked off in the direction of their convertible, but five hundred feet beyond the cabin they turned and quietly made their way back. Hiding behind clumps of brush, they began their vigil. Fifteen minutes went by. Thirty.

Suddenly the quiet of the morning was broken by the crackling sound of approaching footsteps. The Hardys tensed. The person was approaching from behind them. They shifted their position.

"Get ready, Joe," Frank whispered.

The steps grew louder and a man appeared through the brush. The boys pounced on him, and they all fell on the ground. Frank and Joe sprang up immediately to look at their victim.

"Bowden!" Joe gasped.

"For heaven's sake, what ails you guys?" the man stormed, picking himself up.

"We—we thought you were someone else," Joe replied.

"Who?" Bowden demanded.

"We don't know," Frank answered.

"That's ridiculous," Bowden declared scornfully.

"Maybe," said Frank, wondering if Bowden had a rendezvous with the occupant of the cabin. "Why are you here?" he asked.

"I might ask you the same thing," Bowden retorted.

"That's easily answered," Frank said, pointing to the motorcycle. "We want to talk to the man who owns it."

"Do you know him?" Joe asked Bowden.

"Never saw the thing before," he answered.

353

M

"Now tell us what brings you here," Frank went on.

"A tip about the demiculverin." Bowden glanced about apprehensively. "It may be buried near here."

Both boys surmised this was another phony story. Bowden was carrying no digging tools, nor was he dressed in work clothes.

"Oh, I know I don't look like a digger," he said, as if reading their thoughts. "I was just looking for a likely place to excavate."

"Who gave you the tip?" Frank asked.

"I can't tell you that. The information was given to me in confidence."

Frank was tempted to ask Bowden why he wanted a fieldpiece for a ship. But recalling his father's admonition, he merely said:

"Sorry we knocked you down, Mr Bowden. And tell us if you need help to dig here."

Joe followed Frank's cue to be pleasant. "We went to the motel to see you this morning," he said. "Frank and I thought we'd talk to you a little more about the cannon you want us to find."

Frank broke in. "We saw the warning note on your door." He watched Bowden closely.

"Warning note?" the man repeated, showing real surprise. After Frank explained, Bowden suddenly laughed. "I guess those kids at the motel were pulling a joke on me. They were playing cops-and-robbers when I left." He glanced at his wrist watch. "I must get back."

He strode off in the direction of the road. Joe turned to Frank. "Do you believe that cops-and-robbers story?"

"No. there wasn't a child around that motel. I think

one of us ought to follow Bowden and send the police up here."

"Good idea. You go; I'll stay," Joe offered.

"Pick you up later."

While Joe concealed himself to stake out the cabin, Frank cautiously followed the suspect. Presently Bowden got into a car parked some distance ahead of the Hardys' and rode off.

"Wonder where he's going," Frank said to himself. "I'll bet we interrupted a meeting."

He climbed into the convertible and started it. Keeping a discreet distance behind Bowden, so that he would not become suspicious, he trailed him. Frank was disappointed when the man went directly to his motel and entered his cabin. He did not come out.

"I'll phone Chief Collig," Frank decided, and drove on to the next gas station to make the call.

He quickly dialled headquarters and talked with the officer. The police chief agreed to send two men to the woods at once to relieve Joe.

"Good work," he added.

Frank returned to the woods and proceeded cautiously to the cabin in case the suspect was hiding nearby. Joe was not in sight. But after Frank gave several birdcalls which they used as signals, Joe emerged from behind a tree.

"Anything doing?" Frank asked.

Joe shook his head, then Frank told him about Bowden and Chief Collig. Ten minutes later the boys were relieved by two plain-clothes men who took over the watch.

The Hardys hurried through the woods and drove on towards Delmore. It was nearly noon when they arrived in that town. Passing the massive stone walls of the state prison, they turned into the business section of town and located the motorcycle shop.

"Good morning," said the short, smiling proprietor who introduced himself as Mr Braun. "You wish to rent or buy a bike?"

"We're interested in your Kesselrings," Frank replied. "Do you sell them?"

"Yes, I have the agency. But I haven't sold one of those motorcycles in a long time. One's been standing in my basement for weeks. Would you like to see it?"

Frank and Joe looked at each other. Was their clue going to lead nowhere?

Joe said, "Yes, I'd like to see it."

Mr Braun opened a trap-door in the floor, flicked on a light switch, and the three descended a flight of wooden stairs. The man walked round a high pile of cartons, then suddenly exclaimed:

"*Ach, Himmel!*"

"What's the matter?" Frank asked.

The proprietor clapped a hand to his head. "My Kesselring! It's gone! Stolen!"

Mr Braun excitedly added that he had been on a vacation for two weeks and had just returned. The Kesselring had been there when he left.

"*Ach,* what will I do?" he wailed. "I never should have closed my shop!"

Frank laid a hand on the man's shoulder. "You may get the motorcycle back this very day," he said. He told of finding a machine at the cabin, and that policemen were now at the spot waiting to capture the thief. The dealer was overjoyed at the news.

Frank at once telephoned this latest development to

Chief Collig, while Mr Braun thanked the boys repeatedly. Then they said good-bye and left. After a quick lunch at a nearby snack-bar, the Hardys returned to their convertible.

"Joe, I have a hunch," said Frank. "That motorcycle thief might be a recently-released inmate of the penitentiary. Mr Braun's shop in Delmore would be a likely place for him to rob. Let's ask Warden Duckworth some questions."

"Good idea."

The warden was an old friend of Mr Hardy, and the boys had once assisted him in solving a prison break. Reaching the penitentiary, Frank called him from the main gate phone. A guard accompanied them to Warden Duckworth's office, where the official greeted them cordially.

"What brings you 'way out here from Bayport?" he asked.

Frank told him their suspicions and said, "We'd like to find out the names of men released from here within the past two weeks."

Warden Duckworth rose, walked to his filing cabinet, checked the records, and returned with some forms. "We've let six men go," he replied. "Four old-timers and a couple of young fellows. All had served their time."

"We can forget about the old-timers," Frank said. "The man we suspect is probably in his twenties. Who were the young ones?"

"One is Bob Chidsie, a car thief. The other, Hal Latsky, a safecracker."

"May we see their pictures?" Frank asked.

"Certainly." Duckworth handed over the record cards, to which small photos were attached.

"That's the motorcycle thief!" Joe said immediately, pointing to Latsky.

Frank looked thoughtful. "Don't forget, Joe, we've never seen this fellow close up without his goggles. Warden, could you tell us something more about him?"

"Yes—" The man studied Latsky's card for a moment. "Besides safecracking, he's an explosives expert. Also, he has an unusual hobby—the study of ancient cannon!"

· 6 ·　 *Profitable Sleuthing*

AT THE mention of Latsky's interest in ancient cannon, Frank cried out, "That convinces me, Warden! Latsky is the man we're after."

Once more the Hardys telephoned Chief Collig, who was even more amazed than before at the brothers' sleuthing. "We'll have you on the force yet!" he said jokingly.

He told them of the stakeout in the woods. Having learned from Braun the serial numbers of the stolen motorcycle, the chief had short-waved them to his men at the cabin. They had then made positive identification of the vehicle.

"It's the stolen Kesselring all right," said the police chief. "The thief hasn't returned yet, but we'll maintain a round-the-clock surveillance for as long as we need it. Braun has agreed to co-operate by leaving the motorcycle there awhile as bait for the thief. He might try to get it back."

Before the Hardys left, Warden Duckworth gave them pictures of Latsky. "Give these to Chief Collig," he requested.

On the way to Bayport the boys discussed the strange turn of events. If Latsky were the motorcycle rider, was he trailing the Hardys because they were searching for an old cannon? Did he know Bowden, and had the two planned a meeting in the woods? Or were they enemies, both looking for the old demiculverin?

"I'll phone Warden Duckworth and see if he can tell us anything about Bowden," said Frank.

At home, Frank immediately put in the call. The warden said he had no released prisoner on his list named Bowden, nor had he ever heard Latsky mention anyone by that name.

"I'll ask the guards and prisoners, though," Warden Duckworth promised. An hour later he called back. "If Latsky knows anyone named Bowden, he never mentioned it here."

"Thanks, anyway," said Frank, and hung up.

He was disappointed not to have uncovered another clue but turned his attention to Aunt Gertrude who had just come in the front door. She was waving three letters.

"I picked these up from the box at the newspaper office," she said, handing them over. "You forgot all about your ad. I suppose these are some answers from cranks. Well, hurry up and open them. I'm entitled to know what's inside!"

Frank smiled as he tore open the first envelope. Joe came to read over his brother's shoulder.

The writer of the first note was the amusing old artillery sergeant who had set off the mortar in the town square the day before. Sergeant Tilton said that he lived up the coast near Pirates' Hill. He had once heard of an old cannon on the hill, but it had been buried by sand in a storm many years ago—long before Tilton's birth.

"That's a swell lead!" Joe exclaimed enthusiastically.

Both boys agreed that the message should be investigated.

The second letter came from Mr Maglan, the retired custodian of the Bayport Historical Society. Frank opened it.

"Wait till you hear this, Aunty." He chuckled.

"Why, what is it?"

"Mr Maglan says three old cannons have been stored in the cellar of the Historical Society's building for thirty years! The new custodian, Mr Lightbody, evidently doesn't know about them."

"What!" exclaimed Miss Hardy. "Cannons in the basement!"

Joe roared with laughter. "Why, Aunt Gertrude, you've been sitting right above three loaded guns all these years without knowing it. I always thought you knew everything about the Bayport Historical Society building."

The boys' aunt did not laugh. "This is serious. Suppose there is powder in them! Why—"

Frank assured her that thirty-year-old gunpowder would be damp and harmless. Aunt Gertrude merely said "Humph!" and then reminded her nephews tartly about carrying the cutlasses to the basement. "Mr Lightbody says they're in the way."

"We'll go right after supper," Joe said. "And we'll investigate those old cannons as well."

The third note was of more serious import. Letters of the alphabet had been cut from newspapers and pasted on the paper to form words.

The message bore no signature—nor a mark to indicate one. It read:

Look for the cannon at your own risk. If you're smart you'll drop Bowden's case.

"Wow! Things are getting complicated!" Joe exclaimed. "The camps are lining up."

"Yes," Frank agreed. "And the writer must have found out we put that ad in the paper."

When Mrs Hardy heard about the threat, she became alarmed. Both she and Aunt Gertrude appealed to the boys to drop the case, at least until their father returned from Florida.

"We can't stop now," Frank protested. "Joe and I are onto some good leads. And Dad wants us on the case. But we will be careful."

Both women sighed. Then Aunt Gertrude said, "Well, Laura, I suppose with three men against us—and one of them my brother—we'll have to give in. But I want to go on record as saying that if you boys get hurt, you can't blame—"

The ringing of the telephone interrupted Aunt Gertrude's tirade. Joe grabbed up the phone and everyone waited tensely.

"Maybe it's Fenton," Mrs Hardy whispered.

Frank noticed Joe's jaws tighten as he listened to the message. It could not be their father.

"Frank," Joe whispered, "come here! It's Bowden. He wants to talk to you, too."

His brother put his ear close to the phone. "Hello," he said, "this is Frank."

Bowden's voice sounded scared. "Listen! You've got to help me! I've been threatened!"

"By whom?" Frank asked. "Those kids again?"

"No, no. This is for real!" Bowden's voice was shaky and faint. But suddenly it became strong again. "Fr-ank! Joe!" he cried out.

"Were you threatened by someone named Latsky?" Frank demanded.

There was no answer.

"Mr Bowden?" Frank said questioningly.

Still there was no response, but suddenly the Hardys heard a thud and the noise of a phone dropping onto a hard surface.

"Hello! Hello!" Frank kept saying.

There was dead silence for another moment. Then a strange voice said ominously:

"You Hardy boys! Drop the cannon search at once! This is your last warning!"

The threat ended with a sharp click in the Hardys' receiver as the intruder in Bowden's cabin slammed down the telephone.

Frank whirled to face his brother. "It sounds as if Bowden has been attacked! Probably by the person who just gave us that final warning!"

Joe started for the door. "Let's hurry over to Bowden's motel. We may catch the guy."

Frank thought it best to get help to Bowden immediately. "He may be seriously injured. I'll notify the desk clerk at the Garden Gate."

With frantic haste, Frank dialled the motel office number, but the line was busy.

"Come on!" Joe urged impatiently. "We can get there in a few minutes if we hurry."

THE SECRET OF PIRATES' HILL

When they reached the motel, Frank parked in front of Cabin 15. The door stood ajar and the brothers burst inside.

Bowden lay face down on the floor, unconscious. Blood trickled from the back of his head!

·7· *Mysterious Attackers*

As JOE and Frank rushed over to Bowden, the man groaned slightly and moved his arms. Frank turned him over.

"I'll get some water," Joe offered, and hurried to the bathroom for it.

He filled a glass and sprinkled some of the water against the prostrate man's neck and face. Bowden shook his head dazedly as he regained consciousness, and the boys helped him to his feet.

"How did you—?" he stammered, recognizing them. "Where's—? Oh, my head!"

Frank assisted Bowden to the bed, where Joe applied an antiseptic bandage he had found in the bathroom medicine chest. Then they began to question him. Bowden said he had not seen his attacker.

"I hadn't locked my door," he explained. "Somebody must have sneaked up from behind and hit me with a blackjack!"

"Latsky?" Frank queried, watching Bowden narrowly.

"Never heard of him," he replied.

"Who threatened you?" Joe asked.

"I don't know. An unsigned note had been shoved

under my door. It's right—" Bowden looked towards the telephone stand. "Why—" he sputtered. "It's gone! It was right there!"

"Your attacker must have taken it," said Joe.

Frank telephoned the desk clerk to report the assault. The clerk said he had not seen anybody prowling around, and promised to notify the local police at once.

As Bowden's condition improved, the brothers tried to ferret out more information from their mysterious client. "Where did you say you live in Tampa?" Joe inquired.

"I didn't say. Why do you ask?"

Joe explained that he thought Bowden's family or friends should be notified in case of serious trouble.

"Forget it," Bowden replied with a wave of the hand. "I haven't any family."

The man's reluctance to tell where he lived seemed to confirm Mr Hardy's suspicion that Bowden might be mixed up with a group of swindlers. But the brothers gave no sign of this.

"About the demiculverin," Frank went on. "I read that it's a fieldpiece and not used on ships."

Bowden was startled for a moment but regained his composure by pulling out a cigar. Lighting it, he said, "I admire your thoroughness. But I didn't want the cannon for a ship, only for a pageant—as part of the shore batteries."

"Oh," Frank said nonchalantly, "then the demiculverin isn't too important."

"What?"

"If it's just for a dummy shore battery, you can rig up a wooden one," Frank added.

"But—but, boys!" Bowden's face grew red with

excitement. "I must have the old cannon. Everything has to be authentic."

He laid a firm hand on Frank's arm. "You must help me! I'll double the reward. How about two thousand dollars?"

"It's not the money, Mr Bowden," Frank replied. "It's just that—"

"All right, I'll co-operate better," he said pleadingly.

"For example?"

"I can't reveal all my secrets, but I feel certain the cannon will be found along the shore here," Bowden declared.

"We'll do our best," Frank promised.

When the police arrived, the boys told them all they knew about the attack on Bowden but said nothing about the threat to themselves. Then they left.

"What do you make of it?" Joe asked his brother as they drove away from the motel.

"This mystery is getting more complicated by the minute," Frank replied. "Bowden has an enemy all right, and he's lying when he says he doesn't know who."

On the way home the boys noticed another convertible following them. In the rear-view mirror, Frank saw that the slender, good-looking young man who was driving was alone.

"Do you think he's trailing us?" Frank asked, as the car remained fifty feet behind the Hardys' for about half a mile.

"Why don't you find out? Slow down and see if he'll pass," Joe suggested.

Frank did so. The other driver pulled out and zoomed ahead. As he passed the Hardy car, he stared hard at the boys.

"Did you recognize him, Frank?"

"Never saw him before."

When the brothers arrived home, Aunt Gertrude told them that the Historical Society had just decided to hold a special meeting that evening. "You can drive me to the meeting and carry the cutlasses to the basement while you're there," she said.

After supper Frank and Joe accompanied Miss Hardy to the meeting place.

As Miss Hardy alighted, she pointed to a basement window which was open. "Such carelessness!" she exclaimed. "I must speak to Mr. Lightbody! Frank— Joe, please close it when you're in the basement. Humph! The whole place'll be full of stray cats!"

Her nephews grinned, followed their aunt to the front of the building, and went inside.

"The cutlasses are at the rear of that corridor," Aunt Gertrude said, pointing. "Carry them down to the basement and don't disturb our meeting!" Then she walked briskly into the auditorium.

"How about a look at the heavy artillery while we're there?" Joe said.

They looked about for the custodian to show them the basement entrance, but could not locate him. "I guess we can find our way," Frank said.

He walked over to a door and pulled it gingerly. Instead of leading to the basement, it opened into the auditorium.

Aunt Gertrude was on the dais, gavel in hand. "The meeting will come to order," she said with authority, and the ensuing bang made it plain that she meant every word.

As the members quickly quietened, Frank saw the

custodian seated in the front row. He was a small, thin man with grey hair and wispy moustache. The boys decided not to bother him.

"Let's try this door," Joe said, walking across the corridor. He turned the knob. The door yawned open into pitch darkness.

"This is the basement entrance, all right." He reached inside for the light switch and flicked it on. There was no response.

"I guess the bulb's burned out," Joe said. "I'll get a flashlight from the car, Frank."

He hurried outside and brought back a powerful flashlight which the boys carried in their car at all times. As Joe beamed it down the steps, Frank lifted the case of cutlasses to his shoulder.

"Lead the way, Joe."

Joe preceded his brother slowly down the cellar steps. "Careful, Frank," he warned. "They're steep."

The next moment Joe pitched forward. A blow on the side of his head had knocked him unconscious.

"Joe, what's happened?" Frank cried as the flashlight flew forward and rolled under a table.

In the feeble light Frank missed his footing and lost his balance. The case of cutlasses fell from his shoulder and landed with a jangling crash. Frank banged his head full force on the case and blacked out.

His outcry and the crash of the case threw the Historical Society meeting into an uproar. Mr Lightbody jumped to his feet.

At the same time Aunt Gertrude pounded her gavel for order. "Keep calm. I'll find out what's wrong downstairs. Come, Mr Lightbody! Vice-President, please take the chair!"

Miss Hardy charged to the basement door ahead of the custodian and felt her way down the steps. "Frank! Joe!" she called.

Groping in the darkness, she found the flashlight which was still lit. Waving it around, she gasped.

Dashing for the open window was a man in a motorcycle jacket, a mask over his face.

In his arms were five cutlasses, which had been hurled from the case. The sixth lay on the floor. Beyond it were the two brothers, motionless.

Quickly sizing up the situation, Aunt Gertrude reached down for the free cutlass, at the same time crying, "You scoundrel! What have you done to my nephews?"

With a flailing motion, she slapped the man's back with the broad side of the cutlass. He shoved her back.

"Oh, no, you don't!" she cried out.

Thwack! She hit him again. Terrified, the man dropped the five cutlasses with a din heard in the meeting room upstairs and leaped to the sill. As he started to crawl through the window, Aunt Gertrude whacked him again!

· 8 ·　*The Battle of Bayport*

WITH the intruder gone, Miss Hardy turned her attention to Frank and Joe.

"Where's the electrical panel, Mr Lightbody?" she asked.

"Under the stairs." He found it and reported that the

basement switch had been pulled, probably by the intruder. The custodian flicked the handle up and the place was flooded with light.

"What happened?" someone called out from the top of the stairs. "Do you need help?"

"Call the police," said Miss Hardy, as she began to chafe her nephews' wrists and the backs of their necks. They soon regained consciousness.

The only injuries the boys had sustained were bruises on their heads. Joe surmised that he had been hit with a blackjack.

After Aunt Gertrude had given a brief description of the assailant, Frank said tersely, "Sounds like Latsky. Let's check for clues to make sure."

As they searched, Mr Lightbody said the basement windows were always locked. The intruder must have forced one open.

Chief Collig arrived in a few minutes and heard the complete story from Aunt Gertrude. "Frank and Joe think it was Latsky," she concluded.

The officer agreed. But a search outside the building revealed no clues except footprints.

"Let's look for fingerprints, boys," Chief Collig suggested. With his kit from the patrol car they searched the basement with no results.

"Latsky must have worn gloves," the officer decided.

"I didn't notice," Aunt Gertrude and Mr Lightbody said together.

An instant later Frank leaned down and cried out, "Here's a button from the fellow's jacket!" On the floor near the open basement window lay a triangular black button imprinted with a motorcycle wheel. "It *was* Latsky!"

Chie Collig dropped the button in his pocket. As he started to leave, the officer said, "The motorcycle rider hasn't returned yet to the cabin. But I'm hoping he may show up there soon."

After Collig had gone, Joe turned to his aunt. "We haven't thanked you for saving us and the cutlasses." He chuckled. "You won the Battle of Bayport, Aunt Gertrude!"

"Oh, tosh!" she said, starting upstairs. "Mr Lightbody, lock and bar that window. Frank and Joe, put those cutlasses back in the case."

When Mr Lightbody and the boys came up a few minutes later, Aunt Gertrude was surrounded by members of the Historical Society, praising her for winning the "Battle of Bayport."

"It was nothing," she insisted. "Now we'll resume the meeting."

All the members followed her inside the auditorium except Mr Lightbody. "Boys, I can tell you about a real Battle o Bayport."

He explained that in reading pirate lore, he had learned that in 1756 a buccaneer ship had attacked two armed merchantmen off Bayport. One of the trading vessels had been sunk with all the officers and crew lost. The other merchantman had managed to sail away.

"The pirate ship," Mr Lightbody continued, "had had so much of her sail raked by the cannon of the merchantmen that she was unable to give chase. Instead, for some unknown reason, she sent a landing party ashore. Some time later the party returned aboard and the pirate ship limped off."

"Where did this happen?" Joe asked.

"Off Pirates' Hill," Mr Lightbody replied.

"The hill is really named after that incident."

Frank and Joe eyed each other with a smile. Maybe there *was* a basis for Jim Tilton's account of the cannon buried in the sand!

"That's quite a story," said Frank. "And now we'd like to see the old cannons in the basement."

Mr Lightbody led the way down another stairway and unlocked a door to a dusty, vaultlike room. Three old weapons, green with age, were set up in a row on oak mounts.

"All three are British pieces," the custodian said. "They're a *minion*, a *saker*, and a *pedrero*. And they are all made of cast bronze."

"What queer names!" Joe exclaimed. "Do they mean anything special?"

"The *saker* was named after the saker hawk, one of the fiercer birds used in falconry. The *pedrero*—you notice that it's longer than the others—is relatively lighter because it was used to hurl stone projectiles. Its walls are thinner than those of other guns. The *minion* is the smallest."

"They have beautiful decorations," Joe observed.

The pieces were covered with flower-and-leaf designs. Atop the *saker*, at its balance point, was a handle in the shape of a dolphin.

"This handle," Mr Lightbody explained, "was used for lashing or lifting the piece. And cannon like these often had colourful nicknames set in raised letters on the barrel. For instance, *The Terror*, *The Angry One*, or *The Avenger*."

"This first one is marked *The Wasp*," Joe remarked. The other cannons bore no names. "Thanks, Mr Lightbody."

He locked the door and led the way upstairs. Reaching the hall, Frank whispered to Joe, "That clue to the demiculverin petered out. Let's try Pirates' Hill next."

"Right. We'll go there tomorrow."

Just then Aunt Gertrude, followed by the other Society members, came from the meeting room. The boys' aunt was beaming.

"The Society has just voted to present us with one of the cutlasses," she told them.

Frank and Joe grinned in delight. "Great!" said Frank, and Joe added, "It'll be a swell souvenir of the Battle of Bayport! Let's take the one you used to scare off the thief!"

He ran downstairs to get it.

The Hardys returned home directly and Joe made a rack for the prized cutlass. Frank hung the weapon on the stairway wall.

"Looks good," Joe remarked. "I think Dad will like it."

As the brothers prepared for bed, they discussed the masked thief's reason for wanting the cutlasses. Frank and Joe could come to no conclusion and finally they fell asleep.

Next morning after breakfast the boys made plans for their trip to Pirates' Hill.

"Bowden seemed pretty sure the demiculverin's somewhere round there," Frank mused. "I'm going to try getting some more information from him before we leave."

He went to the phone and called the Garden Gate Motel. As Joe stood by, he saw an expression of disbelief cross his brother's face. A moment later Frank hung up.

"Bad news," he said. "Bowden checked out early this morning!"

Joe stared at his brother as if dazed. Then he asked, "Florida?"

"He left no forwarding address."

As soon as the boys collected their wits, they decided to postpone their trip to Pirates' Hill and instead try to find Bowden. They would go the rounds of local petrol stations, hoping to find that Bowden had stopped at one of them and might have left a clue to his destination.

They visited one after another without result. As the brothers were about to return home in dismay, Joe said:

"Frank, there's a petrol station about two miles out of town on Route 7. Bowden may have stopped there."

The boys headed for the place and a few minutes later pulled in. A boy was in attendance and they told him to fill their tank.

"Say," said Frank to him, "did a man stop here this morning in a green coupé?"

"Yep," the attendant replied.

"Was he about thirty-five years old, stocky build, and did he have wiry black hair?"

"Yep."

Frank said they were trying to find him and wondered where he had gone. "Did he happen to tell you?"

"Yep. Said he had a big business deal over in Taylorville."

Elated, the Hardys grinned and thanked the boy. They paid him and hurried off.

"Our luck has changed!" Joe remarked.

"I hope we can make Taylorville before Bowden pulls out of there too," Frank said.

At Taylorville, the Hardys began a systematic search for Bowden's car, going up one street and down another. After they had exhausted the business area, they started on the residential section.

"I see it!" Joe cried out presently.

Bowden's green coupé was parked in front of an old-fashioned house which advertised that luncheons and dinners were served there.

"Maybe he's eating," Joe remarked. "What say we park our car round the corner so he won't spot it?"

Frank agreed this was a good idea and kept going. He pulled into a secluded, dead-end street and locked the convertible. As they walked back towards the restaurant, Frank suddenly grabbed his brother's arm. "We'd better duck. Here he comes!"

"Where?" Joe asked.

"From that house down the street—the big white one."

The brothers ducked at the back of a hedge and watched the suspect. He went directly towards his car but did not get in. Instead, Bowden turned into the walk which led to the restaurant and disappeared inside.

"What a break!" said Frank. "Joe, you watch the restaurant. I'll go over to that big white house and see what I can find out about Bowden's activities."

"What'll I do if Bowden suddenly comes out?" Joe asked.

"Run for our car and give two blasts on the horn. I'll come out and join you, so we can follow him."

Frank hurried across the street, planning his campaign at the neighbouring house. "I'll pretend to be a salesman," he told himself.

A thin, white-haired man answered his ring. Smiling,

Frank asked if he were Mr Chestnut. When the man shook his head, Frank asked if he knew where Mr Chestnut lived.

"Never heard of anybody by that name round here," the elderly man said. He chuckled. "But you came close, son. My name's Ash."

Frank laughed, then said he was a salesman and wondered how he was going to find Mr Chestnut.

"Sorry I can't help you, young fellow." Mr Ash smiled. "And I can't buy anything from you. I just spent all my money. A salesman was here a few minutes ago and sold me some stock."

Frank's heart leaped. He was learning more than he had bargained for!

· 9 · Pirates' Hill

WITHOUT seeming to be too inquisitive, Frank asked Mr Ash, "Was it oil stock you bought?"

The elderly man shook his head. "It was mining stock. The Copper Slope Mining Company. Ever heard of it?"

Frank said that he had. As a matter of fact, his father owned some of the stock. So Mr Bowden was not selling phony stock!

"I'll bet Dad will be surprised at this," he thought, then said aloud, "Where could I find the salesman if I should want to buy some stock?"

Mr Ash told him the man's name was Bowden and he was staying at the Garden Gate Motel in Bayport.

"That's where he told me to phone him if I wanted any more stock."

Frank was amazed and almost blurted out that Bowden was no longer at the Garden Gate Motel. He thanked Mr Ash, then joined his brother, telling him what he had learned. Joe was also amazed and puzzled. The stock was high grade, but the transaction seemed strange.

"We'll wait to trail Bowden," Frank stated.

It was not long before the suspect came out of the restaurant and got into his car. Frank and Joe dashed round the corner and hopped into their convertible. The trail led towards Bayport, and when they reached the town, Bowden not only turned into the Garden Gate Motel, but went to Cabin 15, unlocked it, and stepped inside.

"Well, can you beat that!" Joe said.

The boys parked and spoke to the clerk who had given Frank the information about Bowden's leaving. The man looked at Frank in surprise.

"I thought you said Mr Borden on the phone," he explained. "Sorry. Mr Bowden is still in Cabin fifteen."

The boys went to see him and held a casual conversation about Pirates' Hill, saying they were going to start searching that area the next day. Did Bowden have any suggestions for them?

"No, I haven't," he replied. "But I'm glad to hear you're going to start work. I don't know how long I can wait around here."

"Are you thinking of leaving soon?" Joe asked as casually as he could, hoping for information.

"Oh, not right away," Bowden answered. "But it's

taking a lot of my valuable time to stay here tryin̦ ;o find that demiculverin."

"I understand," said Frank. "Well, we'll let you know what we find out."

Since it was too late to search on Pirates' Hill that day, the boys went home. They gathered various kinds of tools together which they would use for their digging and put them in the car.

"We'll have to take time out from the picnic to make a search," said Frank.

Shortly after breakfast the next morning, the Hardy phone rang. Frank answered the call. It was from Mr Lightbody. In a highly excited voice the curator cried out:

"The Historical Society's building was broken into late last night. The cutlasses have been stolen!"

"Stolen!" Frank cried out unbelievingly. "How did the thief get in?"

Mr Lightbody said a rear door of the building had been forced.

"Joe and I will be right over," said Frank.

The whole family was upset by the news. Aunt Gertrude declared she was going along.

"I feel a personal responsibility for those cutlasses," she said.

She and the boys set off at once. By the time they reached the Historical Society building, Chief Collig was there.

"This certainly is unfortunate," he said. "I can't understand how a thief got in so easily."

"Don't forget Latsky is a safecracker," Joe reminded the chief.

"Wait a second," Frank said. "Let's not jump to

conclusions. We don't know for certain that it was Latsky who broke in here the second time."

Chief Collig agreed with the boy. He said he would put extra men on the case and notify the state police to be on the lookout for Latsky.

"Neither he nor anyone else has shown up at the cabin in the woods," the officer reported. "I had a hunch the man would come back, but apparently I was wrong."

Hearing this, Frank asked worriedly, "But you're not going to take the stakeout away, are you?"

"No, but I believe the fellow knows we're watching the place and won't return."

Just then the old mortar boomed in the town square. Frank and Joe smiled at each other. They had completely forgotten that it was Independence Day! They had planned to watch the parade, then start off for the picnic.

It was eleven o'clock when they reached home to pack their car. Mrs Hardy had left two large cakes for them—a chocolate and an angel cake. Joe put them into the convertible while Frank consulted a book on tides in the Bayport area. Coming out to Joe, he said:

"I guess we can't take the *Sleuth* after all. The water will be too shallow near Pirates' Hill. It will be low tide in the middle of the day."

"How about asking Tony to take us in his *Napoli*?" Joe suggested. "It draws much less water than the *Sleuth*."

"Good idea, Joe. I'll call him."

"Sure, we can take the *Napoli*," Tony said. "I'll meet you at the dock."

The Hardys headed first for the Morton farm. Chet

and Iola were waiting with several baskets of food which included lobsters and a sack of clams. Their next stop was for Callie Shaw, then they drove directly to the waterfront.

"Hi!" cried Tony, grinning at his friends. The *Napoli* was chugging quietly at her berth.

"I'm glad you asked me to go along," he said. "It would be a dull day for me without a date."

As the motorboat skimmed along the bay towards the ocean, Callie suddenly began to laugh. The others looked up and followed her eyes to the stern. There stood Chet, a black patch over one eye and a bandanna round his head.

"Yo-ho-ho!" he sang out. "I'm the pirate of Bayport Bay and I'll show you in a few minutes where a vast treasure is hidden!"

The others roared with laughter and Iola added, "A skin-diving pirate! You'd better bring up a real treasure or you'll forfeit all second helpings as punishment!"

When they reached the end of the bay and turned up the coast, the young people watched for Pirates' Hill. Minutes later they saw it in the distance. The hill was a desolate hump of sand-covered stone jutting into the sea. There was not a house in sight, except one small cottage about half a mile beyond the crown of the hill.

"That must be Sergeant Tilton's place," Frank remarked.

Tony stopped the *Napoli* some distance off-shore and said he was going to test the depth with a pole before going any closer towards land.

"Say, how about my trying out the diving equipment now?" Chet asked. He removed the bandanna and eye patch. "I want to find that treasure for you."

Grinning, Frank helped Chet adjust the equipment.

"I think I'll put my gear on, too, in case Chet runs into trouble," said Joe.

He quickly strapped his air tanks into position and the two boys stepped to the gunwale.

"Hold it!" said Tony. "A guy in a motorboat over there is waving at us frantically. Wonder what's up."

"Who is he?" Frank asked.

"I've never seen the fellow before," Tony replied as the boat bobbed alongside.

Frank called out to the newcomer, a fisherman about fifty, and asked him what was wrong.

"I'm glad I got to you folks in time," the stranger replied. He spoke excitedly. "I just spotted a giant sting ray near here while I was fishing."

"A sting ray!" Frank echoed in surprise. "Thanks for telling us. We'll stay out of the water."

Tony pulled a pole from the bottom of the motorboat and asked Frank to test the depth from the prow of the *Napoli*. Then slowly he steered the boat shorewards.

All this time Joe had been casting his eyes over the large expanse of water. There was no sign of the sting ray. Finally he said aloud:

"Do you suppose that man was trying to scare us away from here?"

"What do you mean?" asked Callie.

"Well, funny things have been going on lately," said Joe. "That fellow could have some reason for not wanting us to go into the water."

He found binoculars in a compartment and trained them on the other boat which by now was a good distance away. The craft lacked both a name and Coast Guard identification number.

"That fisherman isn't alone!" Joe exclaimed. "I just saw another man's head pop out from under the tarpaulin!"

"Can you see his face?" Frank asked.

"No. He's getting up now, but his back's turned to us."

The Hardys and their friends looked at one another questioningly. Someone had been hiding from the group. Why? And who was he?

·10· *A Spy*

"LET's see who those two are!" Joe urged.

"You mean go after them?" Tony asked.

When Joe nodded, Tony made the *Napoli* skim across the water. Joe kept the binoculars trained on the mysterious fishermen. Suddenly they seemed to realize that the young people were heading directly towards them. Like a flash, the man who had remained hidden before dived under the tarpaulin in the bottom of the boat.

The other man started the engine. Then, in a roar which carried across the waves, the boat raced off.

"Wow!" Chet exclaimed. "Some speedy craft!"

"I'll say it is!" said Frank. "That's no ordinary fishing boat!"

The *Napoli* was fast but not fast enough to overtake the other boat. After a chase of a mile, the other craft was out of sight.

"Guess it's hopeless," said Tony in disgust. He turned back to Pirates' Hill.

The young people continued to discuss the men's strange actions until they were back at the beach. Then Chet said, "Let's forget the mystery. If I don't eat pretty soon—"

Joe grinned and finished the sentence for him. "You'll faint, fall in the water, and a man-eating shark will make away with you."

Everyone laughed but Chet. He frowned and added pleadingly, "What's a picnic for, if you don't eat?"

"We'll take care of that," his sister promised.

With the *Napoli* anchored in a scallop-shaped cove, they waded ashore, carrying the baskets of food. The waves lapped the beach gently.

"This is an ideal spot for a beach party," said Callie enthusiastically.

She and Iola took charge and gave orders to the boys. Frank and Tony were to collect driftwood, while Chet and Joe gathered plenty of seaweed. In a few minutes they returned, their arms full.

"What'll we do with this?" Joe asked.

"Those rocks over there will make a good place for the fire," said Callie.

She found a natural pit among the rocks. Into it the boys piled the driftwood and started a fire. Soon there was a roaring blaze. Then Frank heaped more rocks into the fire.

When the stones were glowing red and the flames had died out, the boys placed a layer of seaweed over them. Then the girls laid the lobsters and clams in rows on it and piled several more layers of the stringy green kelp over them.

"I can hardly wait," Chet groaned hungrily, as the tantalizing aroma reached his nostrils.

While the food was steaming, the rest of the lunch was brought out. The meal started with tomato juice and small sandwiches of ham and chicken. As they ate, the Hardy boys brought their friends up to date on Bowden, Latsky, and the search for the demiculverin.

"Later today, Joe and I want to climb to the top of Pirates' Hill and take a look for the cannon," Frank told them.

"We'd better go now," said Joe, grinning. "After this picnic we won't be able to climb!"

A few minutes later the clams and lobsters were ready. The young people gathered round the pit as Joe cleared away the hot seaweed.

"Right this way, folks!" he called out. "First plateful of juicy sizzling hot clams goes to Miss Iola Morton!"

One by one the picnickers came forward and piled their plates. Every clam and lobster disappeared. Then a huge water melon was cut into sections and served along with Mrs Hardy's cakes.

Forty minutes later Chet rolled over on the sand. "I can't move!" he moaned.

"Neither can I!" Joe echoed, sprawling full length on his back. "Girls, that was the greatest meal I ever ate!"

The next hour was a lazy one. Chet was soon snoring and the others stretched out for a rest. But finally they got up and walked to the water's edge. Chet was the last to join them.

"How about my doing that skin diving now?" he suggested.

"Okay," said Frank, and helped his chubby friend into the equipment.

"Isn't anybody coming with me?" Chet asked.

"I'll follow you," said Joe, and started putting on his flippers.

Chet waddled into the sea, and quickly made his way to deeper water, but he did not submerge.

"Chet's so buoyant he can't go down," said Frank. "Joe, you'd better weigh him down some more. Take an extra lead-filled cartridge belt with you and put it on him."

Joe grabbed the belt and splashed into the surf.

Reaching Chet, he attached the extra equipment. Almost at once the stout boy vanished beneath the water. Joe, too, submerged.

Ten minutes later Chet emerged, and swaying from side to side, sloshed to the beach. He removed his face mask and grinned.

"Brought you some souvenirs, girls," he said, and laid a large handful of unusual shells streaked with mother-of-pearl on the sand.

"Oh, they're beautiful!" Callie exclaimed.

Iola clapped Chet on the shoulder. "I'm proud of you, brother. Hope there's a pearl among these."

"How far down did you go?" Tony asked him.

"About twenty feet," Chet stated proudly. "I'll go deeper next time. And here's something else I found."

From one of his belts he brought out what looked like part of a rusty ice pick.

Tony grinned. "I suppose a whale dropped this. He likes his drinks cold and chips off the icebergs with it."

Chet ignored him. "I don't think this is a new ice pick," he retorted. "It's old and valuable."

"Sure," said Tony. "It probably belonged to that famous pirate Edward Teach."

"Do you think so?" Chet asked innocently. "I'm going to keep it as a souvenir!"

The picnic group played baseball for twenty minutes, then Frank said, "It seems to me Joe should have come back by this time."

Everyone looked out over the water. Chet scanned the area with the binoculars which Callie had brought ashore in the picnic basket. There was no sign of the diver. Frank became uneasy.

"I'm going to look for Joe," he announced.

Putting on his gear, he hurried into the water and soon was lost to sight. Frank swam up and down the coast off Pirates' Hill but did not see Joe. A sinking feeling came over him. Suppose his brother had been stung by the ray!

Then a more alarming thought struck Frank. He suddenly recalled the black-garbed skin diver who had deliberately aimed a spear at the boys earlier that week. Perhaps the man had returned!

Frank struck out faster and peered around anxiously. Suddenly above him he saw a swimmer whose body extended upright. He was clinging to a boat.

"Joe!" he thought, and hurried towards him.

His brother was grasping the gunwale of the *Napoli*, his face mask removed. Frank pulled up alongside of him and removed his.

"Good grief!" Frank cried out. "You gave us a scare. Where have you been?"

"Sorry, old man," Joe replied. "I was lying in the bottom of the *Napoli*."

"Why?" Frank asked in amazement.

"I've been spying on a spy," Joe replied. "Look up to the top of Pirates' Hill! See that figure silhouetted up there? He's been watching every move you've been making on the beach!"

· 11 · *Strange Footprints*

"THAT man's doing more than looking at us," said Frank, staring at the lone figure on the summit of Pirates' Hill. "He's digging!"

From where the Hardys were clinging to the *Napoli*, it certainly looked as if the man were turning up the sand. He held something resembling a blunt shovel.

"He didn't have that before," said Joe. "Maybe he thinks it's safe now for him to dig for whatever he hopes to locate."

"You mean, because we didn't climb the hill?"

"Yes."

"Well, let's climb it now and find out just why he *is* there!" Frank urged. "It's possible he's burying something, not taking it out."

The brothers donned their masks and swam underwater to shore. They told the others about the man and their desire to see him closely.

"I suggest we separate and start looking for driftwood," Frank said. "Then Joe and I will quietly leave you and sneak up the hill."

The others promised not to alert the man by looking up. Joe indicated a circuitous route to the top which would not be seen from above.

"You take that way, Frank. I'll wander down the beach and go up from another direction. We'll try a pincer movement on the fellow."

"Okay. I wonder if he's Latsky."

"Maybe he's Bowden."

The picnickers began gathering the wood, calling out in loud voices which they hoped would carry to the mysterious man.

"A prize to the one bringing in the most unusual shaped piece of driftwood," Callie offered.

"Bet I'll win!" Chet yelled.

Minutes later the Hardys were on their separate ways up the dune. They slipped and slid in the heavy sand. Progress was slow, but finally both boys reached the crest. Frank and Joe were about three hundred feet apart as they poked their heads above the top and looked around.

The man was nowhere in sight!

"Where'd he go?" Joe asked in disgust. "Do you suppose we scared him off?"

Frank shrugged. "There ought to be footprints. Let's see where they go."

The boys searched and finally found them. The prints were large and far apart, indicating that they had been made by a tall man.

"They go off across the dune in the direction of Sergeant Tilton's house," Frank noted. "But the marks can't be his—he isn't that tall."

The marks might belong to Latsky or Bowden, the brothers decided. Mystified, the boys followed the prints. Suddenly Joe grabbed Frank's arm.

"If it was Latsky, and if he was the one who stole the cutlasses, maybe he was burying them here until the police alert is over."

The boys turned back and dug with their hands as best they could round the area where the stranger had been standing. But nothing came to light.

"Let's go," Joe suggested. "We're giving that man too much of a head start."

The Hardys hurried along the trail of fresh prints in the otherwise smooth sand. The tracks veered suddenly and headed directly for Sergeant Tilton's cottage!

"Maybe we're closing in on the cutlass thief!" said Joe tensely. "This may be his hide-out!"

"You don't mean Tilton?"

"No. But the thief may be boarding with him."

As the boys approached, Frank exclaimed. "The footprints lead right to the door!"

Watching to see if anyone might be looking from a window, Frank and Joe walked up and knocked at the door. There was no answer. Frank knocked again. This time someone within stirred. Footsteps sounded and a moment later Sergeant Tilton opened the door. He was dressed as an officer of the Revolutionary War.

"Well, this seems to be visitors' day round here! Welcome! Come in, boys!"

"Did you have another visitor?" Frank asked, feigning innocence after he had recovered from the surprise of Tilton's appearance.

"Yep. He's gone now."

Sergeant Tilton explained that only a short time

before, a stranger had also stopped at the cottage.

"Where is he now?" Joe asked quickly.

"Oh, he seemed to be in a hurry," Tilton replied. "He was just askin' the best way back to Bayport."

"Who was he?" Joe prodded, trying not to appear too eager to find out.

"Don't rightly know," Tilton answered. "He never said."

"What did he look like?" Frank asked.

"Tall young man. Right nice face. Kind o' greenish eyes an' brown hair. Say, why are you two fellows so all-fired interested in this guy?"

The Hardys laughed. Then Frank said it was because of their advertisement for information about cannon which he had answered.

"So if any people are going to dig for it on Pirates' Hill," he added, "Joe and I want to be the ones."

Tilton chuckled. "Can't say I blame you."

Frank now told Sergeant Tilton about Mr Lightbody's account of the Battle of Bayport. "Do you think there could be any connection between that battle and the cannon you think is buried somewhere up here?"

"I sure do," Tilton replied. "There were some crooked dealin's between those old pirates an' certain folks on land in those days. I figger mebbe somebody ashore was tryin' to sell the cannon or trade it fer the buccaneers' loot."

The artillery sergeant suddenly grinned impishly. "Guess you wonder why I've got this getup on," he said. "I like to dress up in different uniforms. I've got a collection of 'em up in my pirate den. D'you want to see 'em?"

"Pirate den!" Joe exclaimed.

"Yes sirree!" the elderly man replied. "Just follow me."

Though the Hardys felt they should hurry off and try to overtake the young man they wanted to interrogate, they were tempted by Tilton's invitation. Furthermore, they might pick up some valuable information among his treasures.

"All right," said Frank.

Sergeant Tilton led the boys to the kitchen. From an opening in the ceiling hung a rope ladder. The old man grabbed it and thrust his foot into the first rung.

"Up we go!" He laughed. "This is a real gen-u-wine freebooters' cave I got fer myself up here."

Frank and Joe clambered up after the elderly man who disappeared into the darkness of the room overhead.

Tilton switched on a ship's lantern in a corner of the room. The first thing the boys noted in its dim glow was a pair of cutlasses. For a moment they wondered if the weapons could be part of the stolen collection. But just then Tilton blew a cloud of dust off them, in order to show the cutlasses to better advantage. They had definitely been in the den a long time!

"Look at those treasure chests!" Joe cried out. "And all those guns!"

The room contained an amazing collection of corsair relics. Coins, rusted implements, old maps, pirate flags and costumes, and faded oil paintings of famous buccaneers decorated the walls and tables. On a rack in one corner hung a variety of old Army uniforms.

"This is great!" said Joe, and Frank added, "I wish

we had time to examine each piece. I'd like to come again, Sergeant Tilton."

"You're welcome any time," the man said.

The boys preceded him down the ladder. As the Hardys were about to leave, the man said, "You know, I plumb forgot to mention something to you. Mebbe it's just my fancy, but it seems kind o' strange at that. The young fellow what was here a little while ago—he's lookin' for a cannon, too!"

"He is!" Frank exclaimed. "Did he say what kind?"

"A Spanish demiculverin," Tilton replied.

Instantly the Hardys were sure that they should talk to the stranger. They *must* find him!

"Thanks a lot, Sergeant Tilton," Frank said. "You've been a big help."

"Don't mention it, young fellow," the artilleryman said heartily. "An' hurry back fer a real visit."

Frank and Joe smiled and nodded. Then, following the large footprints that led away from Tilton's cottage, the boys hurried on. The marks led down the side of one dune and up another, but Frank and Joe did not spot their quarry.

At last they reached a point as high as the one on which Tilton's house was situated. Suddenly Joe stopped and gripped Frank's arm. He pointed to a figure in a depression between dunes.

"There's our man!"

·12· *A Friendly Suspect*

"DON'T let that man get out of sight!" Frank urged, running in a westerly direction through the tall grass on top of the dune.

"He'll have to evaporate to get away this time!" Joe declared, matching his brother step for step. "The fellow's just walking, so we can catch up to him easily."

But this was difficult. He was taking long, fast strides. They ran faster and finally seemed to be nearer the stranger. He was now in full view, only three hundred yards away.

"We might call to him," Joe suggested.

"No," Frank advised. "If he doesn't want to talk to us, he may run and we won't catch him."

At this moment the stranger entered the first of a series of deep dips in the sand. The abrupt rise of the knoll between him and the boys blocked the man from view temporarily.

"Oh!" Joe cried out suddenly.

Unfortunately, at that moment, his right foot had slid into a hole in the sand. As he pitched forward, the boy felt a searing pain in his leg.

"Ouch!" Joe cried out. He got up, grimacing.

Frank had turned at his brother's outcry and now came back. "Hard luck," he said. Kneeling beside Joe, he felt the injured ankle joint. "You've sure wrenched it. Better not step on that foot. Lean on me."

"Okay," said Joe, annoyed at himself. "That ends our little posse. We can't catch him now."

"Never mind," said Frank. "Put your arm round my shoulder," he suggested. "We'll attend to your ankle back at the beach."

With Frank helping him, Joe hopped clumsily through the hot sand. In their concern over Joe's ankle, both boys had stopped looking for the man. Now they peered across the wind-swept sand hills, but did not spot him.

"I hate to lose that fellow but it couldn't be helped." Frank sighed.

Moving as fast as Joe's injured ankle would permit, the brothers presently neared the picnic spot. A fire was blazing. The Hardys smiled to see Chet holding two forks in each hand, cooking frankfurters.

"Our friend must have a vacuum for a stomach," Joe remarked. "*Where* does he put so much food?"

Frank did not reply. He was gazing intently at a strange young man who was watching Chet and chatting pleasantly with the girls. The man, about twenty-eight years old, was very tall, and had a determined, jutting jaw. Under his left arm he carried a small canvas sack.

"Joe," said Frank excitedly, "unless my eyes deceive me, the man we were chasing has walked right into our camp!"

"You're right! And carrying his collapsible shovel too."

"One thing's certain," said Frank. "He's not trying to avoid us. But of course he may still be hoping to find out whether we came here to look for a cannon as well as to have a picnic."

"We'd better be careful!" Joe warned.

As the brothers drew closer, Iola handed the stranger

a frankfurter on a roll. A moment later she looked up and saw the Hardys. "Why, Joe, what happened to your foot?" she cried out solicitously and ran towards him.

Joe explained that he had twisted it. He himself was too interested in the stranger to care much about his throbbing ankle.

"I'm sorry you wrenched your ankle," Iola said, adding, "This is Tim Gorman."

"Hi!" said Joe, shaking hands with the easy-mannered stranger.

"And this is Frank Hardy," Iola continued.

Frank, too, shook hands with Gorman, then the brothers exchanged meaningful glances. Tim Gorman was the man who had passed the brothers in a car the day before yesterday and had gazed so intently at them!

The stranger must have guessed their thoughts, for he soon mentioned the incident. "I was looking for someone with the same kind of car as yours," he explained. "Sorry I seemed so rude."

Frank and Joe nodded. At the same moment Callie remarked, "Tim Gorman tells us that he has just been to see Mr Tilton."

"Yes," the visitor said, "I had a very interesting talk with the old artillery sergeant."

"We know that," Frank told him. "We were up there too."

"And I just about broke my leg trying to catch up with you on the dune!" Joe declared. "You certainly crossed it in a hurry."

"Really? Why didn't you call?" Gorman replied. "I didn't see you."

The Hardys' suspicious attitude softened considerably.

Frank steered the conversation back to Sergeant Tilton. Gorman talked freely, laughing about the amazing pirate den in the attic and the talkative old man's preposterous stories. But he did not mention the cannon, nor give any inkling of why he had been on Pirates' Hill.

Finally Joe bluntly said, "We understand you're looking for a cannon."

Gorman's face clouded. "I suppose Tilton told you that," he said, his jaw set and his eyes flashing. "That man talks too much. I asked him to keep it to himself and he told me he would."

"Is it a secret?" Chet asked.

Their visitor looked annoyed, but he regained his composure quickly. "I suppose you might say so," he replied, looking off into space as if trying to decide whether or not to reveal it.

A sudden quiet descended upon the group. The Hardys' friends waited for the brothers to carry on any further conversation.

Tim Gorman relaxed a little and said, "I may as well admit that I'm looking for a cannon." He paused. "But I'd rather not discuss it."

"As you wish," said Frank politely. "But we might be able to help each other. Joe and I have been reading about cannons."

"They sure have," Chet spoke up. "They know a lot about them."

Gorman smiled and said, "That's very interesting. But, after all, we're perfect strangers. I feel it best that I keep my business to myself. Perhaps later on I could discuss the situation with you. For the present I'd prefer not to."

The pleasant way in which he made the latter statement and the smile which went with it tended to disarm all of the group except Frank and Joe. Though Gorman was friendly, they still felt he was somewhat suspect. Not once had he mentioned a demiculverin, though that was, according to Tilton, what he hoped to find. He also did not reveal the contents of the canvas sack.

"We'll probably see one another from time to time," Gorman announced. "I'm staying in Bayport. Perhaps later I'll be in a position to discuss the cannon with you."

The others made no comment. Tony Prito, however, asked Gorman if he would like to go back to Bayport with them in the *Napoli*.

"Thanks," Gorman answered affably. "But my car is parked on the shore road."

He started to say good-bye to the picnickers then suddenly stopped and stared at an object in Iola's hand. It was the ice pick Chet had found.

Gorman stepped forward. "Where did you get that?" he asked intently.

Chet proudly informed Gorman of his underwater discovery as Iola handed over the pick. Gorman examined it closely.

"Is it an antique ice pick?" Chet asked him.

Gorman swung about, his face flushed with excitement. "This is not an ice pick. It's a gunner's pick! There *was* a cannon near here!"

· 13 ·   *Overboard!*

Tim Gorman's announcement sent a thrill of excitement through the Hardy boys. There was no question now that a cannon had been on Pirates' Hill. But what was more important, was it still buried deep under the sand? Or had the old cannon by this time been washed into the sea?

Frank spoke first. "Have you any idea, Tim, what kind of cannon it might have been?"

They waited impatiently for the young man's answer, but were disappointed in it. "There's absolutely no way of telling," he replied.

The brothers wondered if it could have been a demiculverin, but did not mention this.

Chet had walked up to face Gorman. "How did you know this was a gunner's pick?" he asked.

"Like Frank and Joe, I've been reading a good deal about artillery," the young man replied. He turned the pick over in his hands and continued, "This is part of an eighteenth-century gunner's equipment. It's one of eleven important tools a gunner needed."

"How was this pick used?" Chet inquired.

Gorman explained that by the eighteenth century, powder bags had come into wide use, replacing the loose powder which had formerly been ladled into the bore of a cannon.

"This made it necessary to prick open the bag so the priming fire from the vent could reach the charge."

"Then what?" Chet asked expectantly.

"That's where the gunner's pick came in. It was plunged into the vent far enough to pierce the bag. It's sometimes called a priming wire."

Callie suddenly chuckled. "It sounds complicated to me. I'd need several lessons to get this through my head."

"I would too," Iola confessed.

Gorman smiled. "I'll be glad to give you girls cannon instruction any time you say."

Chet and Tony chuckled, but the Hardys shot the man dark looks. They did not want their friends dating any person who was a suspect!

Callie and Iola guessed the boys' thoughts. To tease them, Iola said, "We'll let you know, Tim."

"Don't forget," Gorman said, grinning. "Well, I must be off now."

He shook hands with everyone and said good-bye. When he was out of sight, the boys discussed the man's contradictory manner.

The girls did not agree with the boys. "I think he's charming," said Iola.

Callie added, winking at her friend, "And *so* good looking. But you boys needn't be jealous," she added impishly.

"Who's jealous?" Joe stormed.

The girls giggled. Then they became serious and all discussed the possibility of the demiculverin being hidden on Pirates' Hill.

"You'd better dig for it pretty soon or Gorman will find it first," Callie advised.

"Let's start right now," Frank urged.

Acting as leader he assigned the others to various spots and for an hour the beach and hillside were beehives of activity. Various small objects were dug up but there was no sign of a cannon

"I guess we'll have to quit!" Tony called out to Frank. He explained that he had promised to be home for supper by seven and take his parents in the *Napoli* later to see the fireworks.

"We're all going to see them," said Iola. "Sorry you can't join us, Tony."

The tools were collected and carried out to the boat with the picnic baskets. After everyone was seated, Tony set off for town. Frank and Joe sat alone in the prow for a while discussing Gorman. Frank was convinced the young man was above board, but Joe was still suspicious.

"He may just be a very smooth operator," Joe remarked. "Why, he might even be in league with Latsky!"

"What gives you that idea?" Frank asked.

"He certainly knows a lot about the history of ancient artillery."

The boys were interrupted in their discussion by a call from Callie. "Oh, look, everybody!"

The *Napoli* had turned into the bay and was running close to shore where an area of the water had been roped off for the evening's display of fireworks. A small grandstand had been erected along the bank. In the water two large scows contained the set pieces and the rockets which would be sent skyward in the evening's celebration.

"Looks as if it'll be a good show," Tony remarked.

Chet proposed that his group come early in the *Sleuth* and anchor near the two barges to get an excellent view of the performance.

"Suppose we meet at the dock at eight-thirty," Frank suggested. "The fireworks start at nine."

This was agreed upon. Iola suggested that when they arrived in Bayport they should transfer the picnic baskets to the *Sleuth* and use the food that was left for a late snack.

"That's using your head, Sis," Chet said approvingly.

Iola had stood up to see the set pieces of fireworks. As Tony steered back to the centre of the bay, she sat down on the gunwale of the boat. She began to croon, "Sailing, sailing over the bounding main," and the others joined in.

When the song ended, Frank sang lustily, "Oh, my name was Captain Brand, a-sailing——"

Suddenly the *Napoli* hit something in the water. The boat gave an abrupt lurch, causing Iola to lose her balance. She fell, banging her head on the gunwale, then toppled into the water.

"Oh!" Callie screamed. "She's hurt!"

Everyone jumped up as the boat rocked dangerously. Instantly Joe kicked off his sandals and dived overboard as Iola disappeared under the waves thirty feet astern of the *Napoli*. With strong strokes Joe reached the spot and surface-dived, while Tony circled the boat back at reduced speed.

As the group watched with worried expressions, Joe's head popped to the surface for a second. He sucked in air, then went under again.

Without a word to his chums, Frank donned his skin-diving gear and was about to plunge over the side when his brother appeared again. This time he had an arm round the girl.

Iola was limp. Apparently she had been unconscious before falling into the water.

She was pulled aboard and Chet applied first aid. There were a few anxious moments before Iola's eyelids opened and she began to breathe normally. Frank told her what had happened.

"You sure you feel okay?" Chet asked solicitously.

"Yes—thanks to you and Joe," Iola said gratefully.

As soon as Tony was sure Iola was all right, he dived overboard to inspect his craft. Fortunately it had not been damaged by the large log which was now floating nearby. Tony climbed aboard and reported this to the others.

"It was a close squeak," Joe remarked.

As the *Napoli* proceeded to the Hardys' dock, Iola insisted that she felt fine. But she did promise to go home at once and rest until it was time to attend the fireworks display.

At the dock, Chet transferred the picnic baskets to the *Sleuth*. Then they said good-bye to Tony and drove off. They went directly to the Mortons'.

At eight-thirty Frank and Joe drove their mother and aunt over to some friends with whom they were to attend the fireworks display and spend the evening. Then the boys went to their dock where Chet and the girls were waiting. Soon the group was aboard the *Sleuth*, heading out to the area where the fireworks were to be displayed. Nearing it, they could hear spine-tingling band music from the grandstand on the shore.

Frank guided the *Sleuth* close to the roped-off area. Floodlights set up on the scows made the scene as bright as day.

As Frank turned off his motor, Joe, seated beside him, suddenly grabbed his brother's arm.

"What's up?" Frank asked, turning. He noticed a worried look on his brother's face.

"The man in charge of the display is the one who warned us about the sting ray!"

Frank gazed ahead and nodded. "I wonder if the fellow who was hiding in the bottom of his boat is here too."

"They're going to start!" Chet called.

A moment later there was a swish and whine as the first rocket was set off. It shot high into the dark sky above the harbour and a fountain of cascading diamonds burst into life. Ohs and ahs echoed from the onlookers.

A second and a third rocket swirled heavenwards. Red and blue sparkles gleamed brilliantly after the sharp explosions.

"This is wonderful!" Iola cried out.

"Oh, they're going to set off one of the figures!" Callie said excitedly. "Look, it's a man pedalling a bicycle!"

A twenty-foot figure, sputtering a yellow-white smoke, appeared to be cycling across the barge.

"There goes another figure!" Chet cried in delight as a multicoloured clown began to dance with slow, jerky motions.

Just then a hissing sound attracted the attention of the Hardys and their friends. The next moment a terrified shriek went up from the girls.

A rocket had been fired horizontally and was streaking directly towards the *Sleuth*!

· 14 ·   *The Elusive Mr X*

TERRIFIED, everyone sprawled flat, as the rocket skimmed over the waves like a guided missile!

Whack! The boat shook as the rocket glanced off her bow. A thundering blast followed when the missile exploded ten yards off the starboard side.

Streamers of white light ribboned across the motorboat, but the hot rocket itself sizzled on the surface of the water and then died out in a cloud of acrid smoke.

"That was too close for comfort!" Joe cried out, jumping up.

Frank leaped to the wheel as Chet and the girls peered over the gunwales towards the barge.

"That was no accident!" Frank stormed. "I'm going after the man who set off the rocket!"

"Start the engine!" Joe shouted.

The motor roared to life and the propeller kicked up white foam as the *Sleuth* shot ahead and ducked under the rope of the danger zone.

Closing in rapidly on the barge, the Hardys noticed that one of the Bayport Police Department launches was approaching from the opposite side. Its two powerful spotlights were raking the fireworks platform and the officers were shouting that there was to be no more firing.

"Look!" Joe cried. "That one man isn't paying any attention!"

A stranger to them, he grabbed a lighted torch from the head man and went to a rocket.

"He'll blow us all up!" Callie cried in terror.

A second later the young people saw him run from fixture to fixture, touching his torch to the fuses of the entire remaining display.

Frank did not wait. He put the *Sleuth* in reverse, and the motorboat ran rapidly backwards.

The next moment, the bay shook with the din of the exploding fireworks. Rockets burst forth in all directions with thunderous detonations.

The danger of being struck by the flying rockets also drove the police launch back from the barge towards the centre of the bay. There were anxious moments as the bombardment continued.

Hot fragments from the bursting rockets sprayed the deck and cockpit of the *Sleuth*, but finally Frank got beyond their range.

The din aboard the barge ended as abruptly as it had begun. One glowing wheel continued to turn slowly, but the rockets had spent themselves.

"What a crazy thing to do!" Joe exclaimed.

"Thank goodness we're all right!" said Callie. "Frank, you're a wonder!"

"I'm nothing of the sort," he replied, "and I'd like to punch whoever set off those rockets."

"Not so easy," Chet declared. "All the men on the barges are now swimming to shore."

"I can try!" Frank declared.

He turned the boat and headed for the beach. The stranger who had caused the uproar was not in sight but the man who had warned them of the sting ray was still in the water. Frank drew alongside of him and throttled the engine.

"Climb in!" he called.

The man pulled himself aboard. At the same time the police launch picked up several other swimmers. Not one of them was the man the Hardys wanted to interrogate. But they began to question their own new passenger.

"Who was the man who started that explosion?" Joe demanded.

"I don't know."

"What do you mean? You were in charge of the fireworks, weren't you, Mr—er?"

The man scowled. "The name's Halpen. I was only in charge of the timing," he answered. "The fellows lighted the fuses when I told 'em to. I don't know the name of the guy who disobeyed orders. He just came round before we were ready to start, and I supposed somebody had hired him. It wasn't any of my business."

Frank was not satisfied with the explanation. He hailed the captain of the police boat and asked if he might speak to the men they had picked up.

"Sure thing, Frank," said the officer.

Frank asked them the name of the worker who had set off the rockets. No one knew.

Their own passenger grunted. "I guess the guy just butted in for a good time," he remarked. "Unless," he went on, "he was an enemy of yours."

"If he was, we didn't know it," Joe retorted quickly.

"But he sure is now. He's in for a lot of explaining when we catch up with him!" said Frank grimly.

At the moment there seemed little possibility of this. The man had disappeared and the boys assumed he had swum up the shore line and come out on the beach some distance beyond the crowd.

"I'm getting cold," said Halpen. "Put me ashore, will you?"

"Okay, but first I want to ask you a few questions," Joe spoke up.

"Well, make it snappy!"

"Who was the man hidden under the tarpaulin in your boat the other day?" Joe shot at him.

Halpen's jaw sagged, his composure gone completely. He did not answer at once. When he did, they felt sure that it was not the truth.

"So you saw him, eh? You have good eyesight. Well, he was a stranger to me. His boat capsized and I picked him up. He didn't tell me his name."

"But why did he hide under the tarpaulin?" Joe persisted.

"Afraid of the sun," Halpen answered bluntly. "And he fell asleep."

Frank asked, "Why did you race off in your speed-boat when we tried to overtake you?"

Halpen glared at the boy. "You're a wise guy, aren't you? I wasn't running away, or that stranger, either. It was late. My wife was waiting for me. And now, take me to a boat so that I can get to my car."

The Hardys felt frustrated, but there was nothing more they could do. Frank let the man off, then proceeded towards his own dock.

Iola grimaced. "I don't believe one word that man said."

They all agreed. Joe said he would find out who Halpen was and what he did for a living.

"I'll bet it's nothing much," Chet spoke up, opening one of the picnic baskets. "Who wants a sandwich and some soda?"

Everyone did and soon all the food had been consumed. Chet said that he was still hungry, so at the Hardy dock they left for a spot frequented by teenagers which bore a sign:

Bill's Burgers
Biggest on the Bay

Immediately the Hardys' friends went to phone their families that they were all right. Then Joe called the chairman of the fireworks committee, Mr Atkin. He had just reached home.

"Halpen's harmless but a ne'er-do-well," Atkin said in answer to Joe's question. "He manages to get along somehow, doing odd jobs. He once worked in a pyrotechnics factory and understands fireworks. He's had the job of setting off the Bayport rockets and set pieces for the last several years. I can't understand what happened tonight."

"It scared the wits out of us," said Joe, then asked if Halpen owned a speedboat.

"Oh, no. But he manages to borrow boats from people he knows."

Joe now inquired how many men had been engaged to set off the fireworks display.

"Let's see," said Mr Atkin. "Five. Yes, there were five."

"I counted six," the boy told him.

"What!" the man exclaimed. "Then one of them was there without being hired. He probably was the one who caused a near tragedy."

"I'm sure the mysterious Mr X was to blame," Joe agreed. Returning to the group, he told them that so far Halpen's story fitted. "It's a puzzle, though. I don't trust the man."

Frank remarked that he was more worried about the mysterious man who seemed to have aimed a rocket at them.

"You think he did it on purpose!" Callie exclaimed fearfully. "But why? He couldn't have known we'd be there."

"Of course not," Frank agreed. "But when he did spot us, he grabbed the opportunity."

Chet leaned across the table, his eyes bulging. "You mean that guy's mixed up with the cannon gang and wanted to bump us off?"

"It's hard to decide," Frank replied.

At midnight when the Hardys returned home, Mrs Hardy and Aunt Gertrude were worriedly waiting.

"We saw the wild ending of the fireworks display and have been disturbed ever since," said the boys' mother, "even though we called the Mortons and learned no one was hurt. Thank goodness you're really all right."

"But no credit to you two," Aunt Gertrude spoke up tartly. "It's shameful how you always attract danger. If I were your mother—"

"But, Aunty, we're here in one piece, so what's the difference," Joe interrupted. "Now if we had come walking in here minus our heads—!"

"Oh, stop your nonsense!" their aunt ordered. She started up the stairs, calling, "Good night, everyone. You'd all better get some sleep."

The next morning, while the boys were dressing, Frank said they should get in touch with Bowden before searching further. "Since both he and Tim Gorman are looking for the demiculverin, I'd like to know if they're acquainted."

"Let's go!"

"We'll tell him Chet found a gunner's pick on the shore, but don't mention Pirates' Hill."

"Right."

After breakfast, the boys phoned Bowden and asked if they might call on him. "Sure, come on over," he replied. "I'll be waiting for you."

The man seemed a bit less friendly than usual when they arrived. Was he suspicious of them? But when the boys had told their story, he miled. "You're making progress, I can see that. Keep it up. Time is precous."

Bowden had no news. The police, he said, had no clues to the person who had left him the warning note and later attacked him.

Presently Frank asked, "Do you know a man named Tim Gorman?"

Bowden was visibly disturbed by the question. "Gorman!" he exclaimed, his face flushing. "I'll say I know him, but I'm not proud of it."

"What do you mean?" Joe asked.

"He's no good!" Bowden told the boys that Gorman went about posing as a naval man and was wanted by the police for swindling.

"That's hard to believe," Frank said.

Joe, on the other hand, arched his eyebrows and gave his brother a look, as if to say, "I told you so."

Bowden asked the boys how they happened to know Gorman. Guardedly Frank told of meeting him on the beach. Bowden listened intently. He interrupted the narration several times to ask about details. There seemed to be something he wanted to know, but would not ask point-blank.

Finally, he blurted out, "Did Gorman mention the cutlass?"

·15 · *An Alias*

BOWDEN'S unexpected question caught Joe off guard. Instead of giving a counter query which might have netted the boys some valuable information, he asked bluntly, "One of the stolen cutlasses?"

Joe's thoughtless remark made Frank wince, and his brother immediately realized his mistake. Their father certainly would not approve of such careless detective work! If Bowden had anything to hide concerning the stolen cutlasses, he now was forewarned.

"Stolen? No, of course not," the man said flatly.

"Then what cutlass are you talking about?"

"Forget it."

Joe, annoyed at his own blunder and Bowden's reluctance to talk, said grimly, "Mr Bowden, we can't have you playing hide-and-seek with facts and still do a good sleuthing job for you."

The man smiled patronizingly. "No need for you to get hot under the collar. Gorman's obsessed with finding a miniature cutlass—says it's a lost heirloom or something of the sort. He puts the question to any new acquaintance."

The Hardys felt this was an unlikely story. "Are you sure?" Frank asked.

"Positive. But he may pretend it's a real one just for effect. Gorman's not given to telling the truth."

Frank and Joe suppressed smiles at this remark. Neither was Bowden noted for sticking to the facts!

The boys then took their leave, saying they planned

to continue their search for the cannon. Bowden waved good-bye from the motel entrance, urging them to speed up their work.

"I wish Dad would hurry back from Florida," Frank remarked, as they rode along. "This case is getting knotty."

Joe nodded. "It sure is—as knotty as a pine board!"

Frank grinned. "I wish we could look through one of those knots and see the answer." Then, after a few moments, he added thoughtfully, "Joe, this case had me baffled until just now. But I believe I have the answer."

"What is it?"

"It migh sound far-fe ched," Frank replied, as the car hummed closer to Bayport, "but the combination of cannons, cutlasses, and the story about the pirates' fight all lead in one direction."

Joe smiled. "I get it. You mean hidden treasure."

"Right."

His brother's face broke into a wide grin. "If there's treasure around this territory, let's locate it!" he said with enthusiasm.

"We'll have to dig up more clues, though, before we can dig up any treasure," Frank said.

Since the boys had to go near their home to take the road to Pirates' Hill, Frank suggested that they stop and see if there was a letter or phone message from Mr Hardy. He turned onto Elm Street and pulled into their driveway.

The Hardy telephone was ringing persistently as the brothers entered the house. "Nobody's home," Frank said. "Grab it, Joe."

The boy picked up the instrument in the front hall.

"Yes. This is Joe Hardy. . . . Who? I didn't get the last name. . . . Oh, Smedick. Why do you want to see us, Mr Smedick?" Joe listened for a moment and added, "All right. Frank and I will come immediately."

Joe hung up and turned to his brother. "A guy with a strained voice, named A. B. Smedick, wants to see us at the Bayport Hotel. Room 309. It has something to do with the cannon mystery. Let's go!"

"Who is he?" Frank asked cautiously.

"He didn't explain."

"We'd better watch out. This may be a trap. I suggest we stay in the hall and talk to this fellow."

Frank left a note for his mother telling of their change in plans. A few minutes later the boys parked their convertible in a car park near the hotel. The elevator in the lobby took them to the third floor and the young sleuths stepped out. Joe buzzed 309 and the boys waited. Presently the door opened. The brothers gasped. Tim Gorman stood there!

"What's the idea of this?" Joe asked.

"Please step in," Gorman invited. "I'll explain."

"We prefer staying here," said Frank coolly.

Quickly Gorman reached into his coat pocket, extracted a wallet, and took out a paper and a card. He handed them to Frank.

"This one is my honourable discharge from the Navy," Gorman said, "and the other my naval identification card."

On the card the boys saw the small photograph of the man in a Navy uniform. Joe inspected it closely to see if any touching up had been done.

It was Gorman, all right, beyond any doubt. The paper was a statement of the man's honourable discharge from the United States Navy two years earlier.

"Please come in," Gorman said, and the brothers entered the room. Their host locked the door and they all sat down close together.

"I'm using the name of Smedick here for protection against certain people in Bayport who would like to see me harmed. They know me by name only."

Without explaining further, he went on, "I've investigated you boys thoroughly and know you're trustworthy. I'm very eager to have you help me solve a mystery."

"We're pretty busy right now on another case," said Joe, who still felt sceptical about the man.

Gorman looked disappointed. "I'm sorry to hear that. I really need your help."

Frank suggested that Gorman tell them what the mystery was. Perhaps they could work on it along with their other sleuthing.

Fully expecting to hear that the man was looking for a demiculverin on Pirates' Hill, the brothers were surprised when Gorman pulled a pad and pencil from his pocket and wrote:

Meet me tomorrow at 2 P.M. in the brown shack on the dune a mile north of Pirates' Hill. I'll tell you then.

The boys read the message. Frank nodded but Joe, suspicious, took the pad and wrote:

How do we know this isn't some kind of trap?

Gorman seemed disturbed by the boys' lack of faith in him. But he smiled at the Hardys and wrote a note suggesting that they use the word Collado—the name of a Spanish artillery expert of 1592—as a challenge, and, for a countersign, the name of Hotchkiss, an American artillery expert.

Joe looked annoyed. "How many people will know about this?" he asked aloud. "And before we go any further, suppose you tell us what you know about cutlasses."

The boy's remark hit Gorman like a bomb-shell. He sat bolt upright in his chair, and his face flushed. "Please, not now," he said in a strained voice. "Tomorrow. I'll tell you then. I'll be waiting for you."

He rose, took a lighter from his pocket, and burned the notes. Then Gorman walked to the door, unlocked it, and ushered the boys out.

"I'll see you tomorrow," he said, closing the door.

The Hardys did not speak until they reached their car. Then, as they drove, Joe burst out, "What do you make of all this?"

Frank said his curiosity was aroused and he would like to go to the cabin. "But I'll watch out for any double-crossing."

Joe declared he was going to check with the Navy Department in an effort to learn what Gorman had been doing since his discharge. "Do you realize he didn't tell us, Frank, and the man could have become a real phony since that time?"

"You're right. But I doubt that the Navy Department can give you much help on that score."

Nevertheless, he turned towards their house so that Joe could put in a phone call to Washington and make his request to an officer. He made the connection, but the answer, though polite, was discouraging.

"It takes us some time to make a check once a man has been discharged. It might take weeks."

Joe thanked the officer and hung up. 'You were right, Frank," he admitted. "I guess we'll have to carry on without the information. Well, let's get started for Pirates' Hill."

"Let's borrow Dad's magnetometer," Joe added. This was an electronic mine detector for locating metals under sand. "Shall we drive or take the *Sleuth*?"

"Both," his brother answered. "This gear is heavy. Let's drive to our dock and go on by boat."

Once more Frank left a note for Mrs Hardy, while Joe got the magnetometer, then they drove off in the convertible. Joe, thoughtful a few minutes, said, "Frank, we might even unearth the pirate treasure if there is one!"

"Sure," his brother said, grinning. "But we'd better stick to looking for the demiculverin."

The day was overcast and the brothers found the bay fairly choppy. Frank tied a rowboat to the stern to avoid wading ashore with all their gear. By the time Joe anchored the *Sleuth* off Pirates' Hill, a rough surf was churning onto the beach and the rock ledges.

"Let's do our searching systematically," Frank said. He proposed that they mark off sectors and work along the beach and the dunes, moving slowly up the hill.

They worked steadily until one o'clock. The magnetometer had indicated nothing of importance. The boys sat down to rest and eat the sandwiches they had brought. It was ebb tide and the beach was deserted.

As soon as he and Joe had finished eating, they resumed their work with the magnetometer. Whenever it indicated a metal object under the sand, the boys dug hopefully. As time passed they discovered a battered watch, a charm bracelet and a cheap ring, along with a tobacco tin and an old, rusty anchor.

"Say, we could open a second-hand store," Joe quipped.

"And a junk yard, too."

By five o'clock the beach and part of the hill were full of excavations but the boys had not found any artillery. Unfortunately, the magnetometer short-circuited. It would take some time to repair it, they knew. Weary, they gave up the search.

"At this rate it'll take us all summer to cover Pirates' Hill," Frank remarked, flopping down on the sand to rest.

"Yes, and Bowden's in a hurry," Joe answered with a grin.

They rowed back to the *Sleuth* and started homewards. Soon after supper the Hardy phone rang. It was Chief Collig calling the boys.

"I have some important news for you," he told Frank, who had answered.

"What's up, Chief?"

"First, I want to tell you that we still have the stake-out posted at the cabin in the woods, but no one has showed up yet."

"Too bad," said Frank.

"That's not the only thing I called you up about, though. The departmen has been working on the fire-works case. Since you fellows are interested in finding that phony helper I thought you'd like to know we've traced him to a rooming house."

"Where?" Frank asked.

"Right here in Bayport. His name is Guiness. He

skipped out just before we got there, but we picked up a clue that may help us locate him. Patrolman Smuff found it in a wastebasket in Guiness's room."

Frank gripped the phone excitedly. "What is it?"

"An address on a scrap of paper," the chief replied. "It reads *A. B. Smedick, B. H.*"

· 16 ·   *A Surprising Search*

STUNNED by the information, Frank echoed in amazement, "A. B. Smedick, B. H.!"

"Right," said the police chief. "What do you think B. H. stands for?"

"I'm sure that it means Bayport Hotel," Frank replied. "We spoke to such a person there."

"What! Well, then, maybe you can tell us where Smedick is now. He checked out."

Frank, amazed, said he had no idea. "Joe and I are to meet him tomorrow afternoon along the shore. He probably won't show up. But if he does, I'll try to find out where Guiness is."

"Do that," said Chief Collig and hung up.

Frank rushed to tell his family the news.

"That man who tried to blow us up is either an enemy or a friend of Gorman or Smedick or whatever our Navy man's name is," Frank reeled off in a single breath. He related quickly the message from Chief Collig.

"It sounds to me," their aunt said firmly, "as if everybody connected with this Pirates' Hill mys-

o

tery is a criminal. You should quit the case."

"And not apprehend any of them?" Joe protested. "Oh, Aunty, we can't stop now!"

"Dad will be disappointed in us if we don't solve this mystery," Frank added. He turned to Joe. "At this point I can almost share your suspicions about Gorman."

Joe grinned. "I thought you'd agree sooner or later, but it took the police to convince you."

"Hold on! I didn't say I'm entirely convinced. I'll let you know after we talk to Gorman at that shack tomorrow afternoon."

"If he shows up," Joe added.

Next morning it was raining heavily. Closing the bedroom window, Frank remarked, "No wonder the bay was kicking up yesterday. This storm was on its way then. It doesn't look as if we'll be able to do any searching at Pirates' Hill today."

During breakfast the boys decided to do some morning sleuthing on the stolen cutlasses. Perhaps they would give an important clue.

"Perhaps they have turned up at some of the curio shops and pawnbrokers by now," Frank observed. "Let's look at those places."

The boys' first stop was a curio shop near the Bayport railroad station. The owner lived alone in two rooms in the rear of the store. Frank gave the old-fashioned bell-pull several tugs. A few moments went by before the proprietor appeared at the door. There was soap lather on his chin.

"Step right in, boys," he said eagerly. "You're early. Just look around while I finish shaving." He returned to the back room.

"This man has got a lot of interesting looking weapons," Frank said presently, after walking round. He eyed an old-time flintlock hanging on the wall. "But," he added, "none of them has any special mark such as the authentic pieces have. These must all be imitations."

"Shall we leave?" Joe asked his brother. "We're probably wasting our time."

Though his voice was low, it carried to the rear of the shop. The proprietor came running out, pleading with the boys not to go until he had shown them the weapons.

"Sorry, we're looking for antique cutlasses," Frank told him.

"What difference does the age make," the man asked, "if you want a cutlass? If you don't have much money, I can rent you a sword."

Joe grinned. "If you can rent me a white Arabian horse along with the cutlass, it's a deal."

The dealer, realizing that he had been trying a little too hard to sell, smiled and told the boys to come back some other time.

"Well, score zero for us on that call," Joe sighed as they climbed into their car.

The Hardys drove across town to a shabby antique shop, owned and operated by a Mr Dumian.

"Yes, I have cutlasses," the dealer replied to Frank's question. He eyed the boys with curiosity over his bifocal glasses. "It's funny you're wanting them. Recently a boy named Gil Fanning—about eighteen years old—sold me five cutlasses. Told me they were family relics."

"Is he a local boy?" Frank asked, interested.

"Yes. He lives in Bayport," Mr Dumian answered.

"On Central Avenue. I paid him twenty dollars apiece—a pretty steep price, but they were the real thing. Beautiful cutlasses."

"May we see them?" Frank asked eagerly. The thought that they might be the Entwistle relics caused his heart to beat faster.

"I'm sorry," the dealer replied. "Right after Fanning brought the weapons in, a swarthy-looking fellow in a black motorcycle jacket came into the shop and bought every one!"

The Hardys shot chagrined looks at each other. It appeared that Latsky had beaten them to the draw! Furthermore, the Hardys were dumbfounded by the appearance of Latsky at the shop—assuming that the man in the leather jacket was he. It certainly looked now as if Latsky were not the person who had taken the cutlasses from the Historical Society's building. Could Gil Fanning have been the thief?

"That's not all," the man continued. "Last evening, just as I was closing up shop, a stout boy came in here looking for cutlasses. And now when you fellows come in asking for the same thing, I begin to wonder if there—"

"Did this stout fellow give his name?" Joe broke in.

"Yes," Mr Dumian said, turning to a spike of notes on his desk. "He wanted me to get in touch with him if any more cutlasses came in. Here it is." He tore a slip of paper off the spike and handed it to Frank.

The paper bore the name Chet Morton!

"Chet Morton! We know him," Joe burst out. "What would he want with the swords?"

"Search me," said Mr Dumian.

The boys thanked him and left the shop. Once outside, they decided to talk to Gil Fanning, then go and ask Chet why he wanted cutlasses.

"What a muddle!" Frank exclaimed, as the brothers went into a drugstore to look up the name Fanning in the Bayport telephone directory. One was listed at 70 Central Avenue.

Frank and Joe drove there in the downpour and found that Gil, an orphan, lived with his grandparents. Tearfully the elderly woman said the boy had not been home for a week.

"He's always been hard to manage," she said, "but we knew where he was. This is the first time he's ever stayed away without leaving word."

"Have you notified the police?" Frank asked.

"Oh, no," Mrs Fanning replied. "Gil phoned he'd be back in a while—had a job. We were not to worry." Suddenly she asked, "But why are you here? Is our boy in some kind of trouble?"

"Not that we know of," Frank answered. "Mrs Fanning, did you give Gil permission to sell any of your heirlooms?"

"Cutlasses," Joe added.

A frightened look came over the woman's face. "You mean swords? We never had any swords. You must be mistaken."

"No doubt." Frank smiled, not wishing to disturb the elderly woman any further. "Well thank you," he said. "I hope Gil returns soon."

Frank and Joe left, puzzled by the information. Where was Gil Fanning?

The rain was now torrential. Driving carefully, Frank made for Chet Morton's. Presently he came to a sharp bend in the road.

"Better slow down," Joe advised. "This is like a hurricane!"

Hugging the right side of the road, the boys suddenly heard and saw through the torrential rain a car racing into the curve from the opposite direction. It swung awkwardly and skidded, then sped almost side-on towards the Hardys' car!

"Look out!" Joe yelled.

Frank swung to avoid a collision. But in doing so, the convertible veered towards a deep ditch!

· 17 ·   *A Missing Pal*

THE boys felt a terrific lurch as the wheels on the right side of the car dropped into the soft, rain-soaked ditch. The car tilted dangerously, and Frank fought hard to get it back on the road.

Just when it seemed as if the car could not possibly stay upright, the muddy front wheel leaped onto the hard surface. Then the rear one pulled up.

"Golly!" Joe exclaimed. "I thought we were goners!"

Frank heaved a sigh, then muttered angrily, "That crazy driver ought to have his licence revoked!" He hopped out to inspect the wheels, but no damage had been done.

As he started off again, Joe said, "Say, do you suppose he tried to force us into the ditch on purpose, hoping we'd overturn?"

"You mean the driver was one of our enemies?" Frank smiled ruefully. "If he was trying to cause an accident, he nearly succeeded."

On reaching the farmhouse, Frank and Joe learned from Iola that about an hour ago Chet had taken his flippers and snorkel, and gone to their swimming pool to practise skin diving.

"Chet still wants to buy an outfit like you boys have," said his sister. She smiled. "He says he can't earn enough money for it by working on the farm, so he's going to look for another job."

Frank and Joe chuckled. Their stout friend had never shown any interest in work. Over the years Chet had had to be cajoled by his family and the Hardys to finish jobs he had started. Seldom had he been known to look for work!

"Chet sure must want that diving equipment bad," Joe remarked.

Iola said her brother was intensely interested in skin diving. "Ever since he found that gunner's pick, he's had a great desire to dive for treasure."

Frank and Joe told Iola about their search the day before, then went to the pool to talk to Chet about his visit to the antique store. They wanted to know why he was looking for cutlasses.

To their surprise, Chet was not in sight. At the edge of the pool lay his snorkel and flippers. The Hardys walked round the pool, peering down into the water. Chet was not there.

"He must be off earning some money," said Joe with a grin.

The brothers returned to the farmhouse and told Mrs Morton and Iola that Chet was not around. Both looked concerned. Mrs Morton said that Chet never left the farm without saying where he was going.

"Perhaps he went off with that boy who was here,"

Iola suggested. She told the Hardys that about half an hour ago a youth about Chet's age had strolled in and asked for him. They had directed him to the pool.

"Who was he?" Frank asked.

"We'd never seen him before," Iola answered. "He said his name was Gil. He didn't give his last name."

At this announcement Frank and Joe stared questioningly at each other. Was he Gil Fanning, the boy who had brought the cutlasses to Mr Dumian's shop to sell?

"What's the matter?" asked Iola, noting the boys' puzzled expressions.

Frank told her and Mrs Morton the whole story. Both of them looked worried and Mrs Morton said, "Oh, dear, I hope nothing will happen to Chet!"

Frank and Joe tried to reassure her that he knew how to take care of himself, but secretly they, too, were greatly worried.

"If the boys went off together walking, they probably haven't gone far," said Frank. "We didn't pass them on the road, so they must have headed in the other direction. We're driving that way, Mrs Morton, so we'll look for Chet."

"If you don't find him, will you please telephone?" Mrs Morton requested. "If Chet isn't home within an hour, or if I don't hear from him, I'm going to call the police."

The Hardys hurried off. As they rode along, their eyes constantly swept the landscape, hoping to catch sight of their chum. They went for three miles without passing a car or seeing anyone walking along the road. Presently they came to a combination country store and petrol station.

"I'll go in and phone," said Frank, getting out of the car.

Joe decided to go along, eager to learn any news of Chet The Hardys spent fifteen minutes trying to get the Morton home. The line was constantly busy!

"I hope it's Chet calling his mother," Frank said.

But when he finally reached Mrs Morton he was disappointed. Their pal had not returned home and the family had not heard from him. They, in turn, were disappointed that the Hardys had not seen Chet, and Mrs Morton declared that she was going to get in touch with Chief Collig at once.

When the conversation ended, Frank turned to Joe. "What do you think we should do? Keep hunting for Chet, or go on to the shack?"

"Let's go on," Joe replied. "Chief Collig will do everything possible, and we might pick up a clue to Chet's whereabouts by keeping our date."

Frank agreed. They bought two bars of chocolate from the old man who ran the store, then went outside. As they approached their convertible, Joe gasped and grabbed Frank's arm.

"Oh, no!" he cried out, pointing to the two rear tyres. Both were flat!

The brothers rushed over to the car. Not only were the tyres flat, but to their dismay there were huge slashes in them!

"Someone deliberately cut our tyres!" Joe exclaimed.

Frank's face turned white with anger. "Now, what do we do?" he exclaimed.

It was evident that whoever had done the mischief had come there quietly. The boys did not recall hearing a car go past. They wondered whether the tyre slashing had been the malicious mischief of some prankster, or whether one of their enemies was pursuing them and doing everything possible to keep the boys from meeting Gorman.

"We have only one spare," Joe remarked with a groan. "Where can we get a second?"

"Maybe the storekeeper sells tyres," suggested Frank, and returned to the shop.

Fortunately, the old man kept a few seconds in his cellar. Frank found one that fitted the car and brought it upstairs. The kindly shopkeeper, feeling sorry for the boys and disturbed at what had happened, sold the tyre to them cheaply. Working together, they soon replaced the slashed tyres.

"It's 'way after two o'clock," Frank remarked, as they went to wash their hands. "I wonder if Gorman will wait."

Joe reminded his brother that the stranger might not be at the shack at all. He still mistrusted the man and was sure a trap had been laid for the Hardys.

"Maybe," said Frank. "Anyway, we'll approach with caution."

Two miles farther on they reached a side road which they figured would take them near the shack. It was a sandy, single-lane drive which twisted through the scrub pines. In places it was so narrow that the rain-soaked branches brushed against the side of the car.

Presently the road ended and Frank braked the convertible to a stop.

"There's the shack!" Frank pointed to their right, as he put the car keys in his pocket.

The ramshackle old building, badly weathered and sagging, stood between two dunes. The boys trudged towards it through the wet sand, a fine spray from the wind-swept sea stinging their aces.

"What a dismal place!" Frank exclaimed.

Joe smiled grimly. "Perfect spot for a trap!" he muttered.

"I don't believe Gorman's here," Frank said as the boys pushed on, their hearts pounding with excitement. "There's not a footprint leading to the place!"

As they approached the shack, the boys were amazed to see that the front door was w de open. They concluded no one could be inside, for certa nly any occupants would have closed the door against the terrific wind.

Nevertheless, Frank cried out lustily, *"Collado!"*

The boys stood outside, waiting for an answer. The countersign which Gorman had suggested was not given nor did anyone appear.

"It's apparent Gorman's not here," sa'd Joe. "And if this is a trap, we're not going to walk into it. Let's go!"

At that moment the boys heard a muffled cry from inside the shack. Someone must be in trouble!

Their minds intent on helping the person, the Hardys forgot that they had planned to be cautious. Without a moment's hesitation, the boys rushed into the building.

The next instant they were seized by two masked men!

AMBUSHED by the two masked men, Frank and Joe fought like wildcats. The assailants were much heavier in build and held the boys with grips of steel. Neither man relaxed his vice-like hold for a moment, despite a hard, occasional punch which the Hardys managed to land.

As the boys fought desperately, the face masks slipped off the men—strangers to the Hardys.

Joe wrested his right arm free and sent a vicious punch to his adversary's jaw. The man fell back, groggy. Joe could escape.

"Here I come, Frank!" he yelled.

But in the same instant a kick from the other desperado sent Joe sprawling. In a flash his own antagonist was on top of him. There was little punch left in him but his great weight held the boy down. With the man sitting on his chest and holding his arms, Joe could hardly breathe.

At this point Frank was giving his opponent a rough time. The man was now gasping for breath. "I'll get him really winded," the boy thought, wriggling even harder to break loose.

"Hold still or I'll finish you for good!" the man threatened.

"Just try it," Frank grunted defiantly.

He gave another violent twist and almost broke loose. But the man retained his powerful hold. An unexpected downward swipe with his stiffened hand caught Frank on the back of the neck and the youth slumped to the floor.

The man turned his attention to Joe and helped his pal pin the young sleuth to the floor. He bound and gagged him, then trussed up Frank and tied a handkerchief across his mouth. The men held a whispered consultation, then one of them went into a back room. He returned a moment later dragging something in a canvas sack. He slid it into a corner and both men left the shack by the front door. The boys heard a muffled groan.

A human being was in the sack!

The Hardys concluded it must be Gorman. He, too, had been ambushed! Were the attackers enemies of Gorman working on their own or were they in league with Bowden? Or perhaps Latsky?

Desperately, the boys tried to loosen their bonds. Frank found that by wriggling his jaw and rubbing the gag against his shoulder he could loosen it. At once he cried out:

"Gorman!"

As the bundle in the corner moved feebly in reply, both boys were horrified to see their assailants rush back into the shack. They had heard Frank's outcry. Without a moment's hesitation, they knocked both boys unconscious.

Some time later Joe revived. He was amazed to find that he was outdoors and dusk was coming on. He saw Frank not far away and on the other side of him the person in the canvas sack.

"We're in a gully," Joe thought, as he struggled to rise.

His arms were still tied behind him and the gag was

in his mouth. Every part of his body ached. He was lying face up in a puddle of rain water and was soaked.

Frank, still unconscious, was also bound and gagged. His position was precarious: he lay in a deeper part of the ditch with rushing water only inches from his face. The stream, swollen by heavy rain, was tumbling along in torrents.

"Frank will drown!" Joe thought in horror. "I must get him out of here!" He struggled desperately and finally by twisting and turning, slipped his own gag off. But his bonds held firmly.

"Frank!" he shouted. "Sit up! You'll drown!"

At first there was no response, then his brother made a feeble effort to rise. Frank raised his head a few inches and tried to pull himself up, but he lacked the strength. Exhausted, he slumped back into an even more dangerous position.

"I must rescue him!" Joe told himself.

He dragged his body through the mud to Frank. Rolling onto his side, he was able to clutch his brother by one leg with his tied hands. Getting a firm hold, he pulled Frank inch by inch from the threatening stream.

It was an agonizing task. The sharp gravel on the edges of the gully scraped Joe's cheeks, but he finally dragged his brother to a safe spot. He managed to remove the gag, but the knots on Frank's bonds defied him. And Frank could not get his brother's untied.

"We'd better give up," said Joe, "or I may be too late to save Gorman."

"Go ahead," Frank said feebly. His own arms had no feeling in them.

The canvas sack lay only slightly out of water. "Those thugs must have figured on having the three of us drown in the stream. They evidently sent us rolling down the bank, but we didn't go far enough."

Redoubling his efforts, Joe crawled to the sack and tried to secure a hold similar to the one on his brother. But the embankment here had a slimy, muddy surface. With each attempt to haul the sack away from the water, Joe slipped. His own body, instead of catching on the coarse gravel to give him traction, went backwards.

"I'll never get Gorman out this way!" Joe groaned. "I'll have to get my hands free."

The bonds were as tight as ever. Joe decided to crawl back to Frank and have him work on the knots again. Halfway to his goal, he heard the sound of an approaching car. Apparently there was a road above the gully!

"Help! Help!" Joe cried out.

The car went by and the boy's heart sank. He yelled even louder. Then, to his immense relief, he heard the car slow down. Then it stopped.

A door slammed, and Joe continued his cries for help. Someone came running and a man leaned over the rim of the gully.

Bowden!

"Joe Hardy!" the man cried out. "Good grief! What happened to you?"

"Come down here, quick!" Joe yelled, "and untie me! And we must get the others out!"

Bowden slid down the embankment.

"There's a penknife in my pocket," Joe told Bowden. "Get it out and cut me loose."

Bowden did so, and together he and Joe freed Frank and assisted him to his feet.

The canvas sack moved. Bowden jumped back, startled. "For Pete's sake, what's in there?"

"It's—" Joe started to say, when Frank gave his brother a warning look.

"We don't know," Frank spoke up, "but it's probably a man. Two thugs knocked Joe and me out. They must have put all three of us here."

He and Joe went to the sack. Both were wondering what Bowden's reaction was going to be when he and Gorman faced each other.

With the penknife Joe slashed the cords that bound the sack and yanked it open. A cry of astonishment burst from the Hardys. *The prisoner was not Gorman! He was Chet Morton!*

The stout boy, bound and gagged, and wearing only bathing trunks, gazed at his rescuers stupidly. He was weak and in a state of shock.

"Chet!" the Hardys exclaimed, removing his bonds.

As their pal took in great draughts of fresh air, Bowden asked, "Is he a friend of yours?"

"Yes," Joe replied. "We must get him home at once."

"I'll take you there," Bowden offered.

"Thanks. Where are we, anyway?" Frank asked him, slapping and swinging his arms to restore the circulation.

"On the shore road about ten miles from Bayport. Say, where did you fellows get slugged?"

"Somewhere up on the dunes," Frank replied off-handedly. He felt in his pocket. "The car keys are gone. I suppose those guys stole our bus."

Bowden preceded the boys up the steep embankment. Frank and Joe assisted Chet, who could hardly put one foot in front of the other.

"You'll feel better, chum, as soon as we get you something to eat," Joe told him.

Chet nodded. "Awful hungry," he admitted.

Out of earshot of Bowden, Frank whispered to Chet, "We thought you were Gorman."

"Yes," said Joe. "That guy double-crossed us." He looked at Frank. "I guess you're ready to admit now that Gorman is a phony!"

·19·   *Chet's Kidnap Story*

As THE three boys followed Bowden to his car, the man's denunciation of Tim Gorman came back to them. Bowden probably was right, but where did he himself fit into the picture? The Hardys wondered if there were any significance to the fact that he happened to be passing this spot when the boys were in the gully.

"The less we say the better," Frank warned the others.

Joe got into the car's front seat, ready to grab the controls should Bowden drive off the main road and lead them into any more trouble. But the man drove along normally and in silence.

Suddenly Joe cried out, "There's our car just ahead!" It had been pulled into the side of the road. "Our attackers didn't steal it after all."

Bowden stopped and waited as the Hardys examined the car. The keys were in it. No one was inside, the boot contained only the two damaged tyres, some tools, and two pairs of old swim trunks. It started at once and purred softly.

"Well, thanks again, Mr Bowden," said Frank, as the three boys transferred to the convertible. By this time it was almost dusk. "We'll have to show our appreciation to you by working harder than ever to locate the demiculverin."

Just then they were startled by a sound that resembled a low, muffled groan.

Frank looked round quickly. "What was that?"

"Just the wind in the trees, I guess," Bowden replied as he waved and drove off.

"Well one thing seems certain," Frank said, pulling out onto the road. "I'm sure that Bowden knew nothing about the attacks on us."

"Maybe not," said Joe. "On the other hand, he may have employed those thugs and was driving out here to see if they had followed orders."

"If you're right," said Frank, "he sure got a surprise. And say, what about Gorman? I guess he didn't come to the shack after all."

"But sent those thugs instead," Joe said.

"Listen, you just said it was Bowden."

"Sure I did. I don't know what's going on. I'm completely baffled. Chet, tell us what happened to you. When were you brought to the shack?"

"Shack? Was I in a shack? To tell you the truth, I don't know where I was."

"Don't you remember hearing me call out to Gorman?" Frank asked.

"No. I was unconscious a long time." Chet paused, looking into space. "Here's the story. It all began when I put an ad in the paper."

"For what?" Joe asked.

"Skin-diving equipment. I wanted to buy some second-hand. You know how I like to pick up a bargain."

"Yes, we know," Frank said, smiling. "Get on with your story, Chet."

"Well, this morning a fellow my age came out to the farm to see me."

"Called Gil," Frank said. "Iola told us when we went to see you. What was his last name?"

"Gosh, I don't know. I didn't ask him," Chet said. "I was too excited."

"You mean about getting the skin-diving equipment?" Joe asked.

"That's right. You see, he told me he represented a man who was willing to sell his equipment cheap."

"What happened then?"

"I was out at our pool when he arrived. His car was parked down the road and he offered to drive me to the man's house to look at the gear. Since he was in a hurry, I hopped in without waiting to change."

"What then?" Frank asked.

"This fellow was a crazy driver, believe me," Chet went on. "He was off like a racing driver. On the highway we missed a car by inches as we came into a sharp turn."

The Hardys looked at each other and whistled. "So you were the one in that car that nearly hit us!" Frank exclaimed.

Chet gulped. "It all happened so fast I didn't have time to see who was in the car. My gosh, what if we had crashed!"

"Where did this Gil go then?" Frank prodded.

Chet said that the boy had finally stopped the car in a wooded section which he said led to the house. "As soon as I stepped out, a stocky, masked man jumped from behind a tree. In a flash he had me tied up and blindfolded."

"Then what?" Frank asked.

"While I was lying there in the rain, he said, 'What did you do with the cutlass?'

"'Which cutlass?' I asked. And fellows, what do you think he did? Kicked me and said, 'You know which cutlass I mean.'

"I told him that I had been to an antique shop to buy one but had arrived too late. The man didn't have any left. I sure didn't want to tell him about the one you fellows have."

"I'm glad you didn't," said Joe. "Chet, we were at that shop and heard the story. We think the fellow who bought all the cutlasses was Latsky."

"Honest? Good grief! That sure complicates things."

"Why did you go to the shop?" Frank asked.

Chet smiled wanly. "I was hoping to get a clue for you fellows on the cutlass Gorman and Bowden know about."

"Good try," said Joe. "Go on with your story."

Chet scowled angrily at the recollection. "When I wouldn't tell that guy anything, he flew into a rage. I don't know what he hit me with but he sure put me out. From that time on I don't remember a thing until you found me in the gully."

Just then the car reached the side road which led to the shack where Frank and Joe had been ambushed. Frank turned into it.

"Hey, where are you going?" Chet asked. "I thought you were going to get me something to eat. I'm weak."

"Ten minutes won't make any difference," Frank replied. "I've just had an idea."

"Well, it had better be good," Chet grunted.

Frank said it was possible that the figure in the canvas sack at the shack had not been Chet. Why would his attackers have bothered to take him there and carry him off again?

"The prisoner was probably someone else—maybe even Gorman," Frank declared, "and he may still be there."

"So we're about to make a rescue," Joe spoke up. "But I'll bet you the person is not Gorman."

"Listen, f-fellows," Chet quavered, "I d-don't want to be c-captured again."

"You won't," said Frank. "You'll take the car key and hide in the boot. You can act as lookout and give us the old owl whistle if anyone approaches."

Frank parked in the same spot as before. The brothers put flashlights in their pockets and got out. The area ahead was in semi-darkness, with the shack standing out like a black block silhouetted against the sky.

The Hardys moved cautiously, in order not to step in the footprints that came away from the shack. Mingled with them were drag marks, no doubt made by the unconscious boys' feet as they were removed from the building.

"You take the front of the shack, Joe, I'll go round the back," Frank suggested, as the boys approached it.

The brothers separated. Finding no sign of an occupant, they finally beamed their flashlights through the windows. The shack was empty.

In swinging his flashlight back, Joe became aware of something interesting in the sand a few feet away. Quickly he summoned his brother and pointed out a depression in the damp sand.

"Someone was lying there," he said, "face down."

"Well, it wasn't Chet," Frank surmised. "Or Bowden or Latsky." From head to toe the length was a good six feet.

"Look!" Joe exclaimed. "There's an initial here!"

The boys bent over a spot near the face mark in the sand. Scratched faintly was a letter.

"It looks like a *C*," Joe commented.

"Or perhaps a *G*," Frank said. "It could stand for Gorman."

The boys assumed that the man, bound and gagged, had made the impression with the tip of his nose. A more careful search of the area on the beach side of the shack revealed footprints and drag marks that indicated he had first been taken into the shack, probably in a sack, then later pulled down to the beach and carried off by boat.

The boys trudged back to the shack and again looked at the impression of a face in the sand. Frank felt sure it belonged to Gorman.

"I wish we could make sure," Joe said.

"I think we can," Frank replied, looking down. "Let's make a mould of this face."

The Hardys often made plaster moulds of footprints and handprints. They kept the equipment for doing this in their workshop over the garage.

"We'll have to come back and do it later," Frank said. "In the meantime, we'll protect this impression in the sand."

He went inside the shack and looked about for something to use. In one corner was an old box. Carrying it outside, he placed the box firmly over the sand impression so that the wind would not disturb it.

"Let's go!" Joe urged.

As they started back across the sand towards their car, the stillness was suddenly shattered by the mournful hoot of an owl. Chet's signal that something had gone wrong.

The Hardys broke into a run!

·20· *An Impostor*

THE hooting was not repeated and the brothers wondered if Chet were in trouble. They raced to the convertible. No one was in sight.

Joe pulled up the lid of the boot which was open an inch. Chet, inside, looked relieved.

"Did you hoot?" Joe asked him.

"I sure did. A couple of guys were here. I heard them coming through the woods, so I gave the signal."

"Where are they now?" Frank demanded.

"Both of them ran back through the woods when they saw you coming."

"Who were they?"

Chet said he did not know. It was too dark to see them well, but neither was the man who had knocked him out. From Chet's description the Hardys concluded they might be the men who had attacked them in the shack.

"They didn't use any names," said Chet, "but they talked a lot." He added that upon seeing the car, they had seemed worried, wondering how it got there. "They decided that perhaps the police had brought it as a decoy. Just then they saw you coming and beat it." Chet laughed softly as he climbed out of the boot. "I guess they thought you were the cops!"

"It's a good thing they did," said Frank, "or we might have had another battle on our hands."

As the three boys drove home, Chet was very quiet. Joe teased him about it. "So weak from hunger you can't talk?" he asked.

"I'm worried, fellows," Chet said. "I wasn't going to tell you, but maybe I should."

"What's bothering you?"

"When our attackers find out we're still alive, they're really going to make it tough for us!"

Frank declared they could not make it much tougher, but agreed all of them should be on the watch for trouble.

Chet gave a gigantic sneeze. "Those guys'll kill us one way or another," he complained. "But I'll probably die of pneumonia."

Joe wrapped a blanket round Chet's shoulders, but he sneezed all the way to the farm. By the time they pulled into the Morton driveway he was feeling chilled.

"Sorry," said Frank, his conscience bothering him a bit that they had not brought their pal home sooner.

"Look!" Joe exclaimed as they pulled up behind a police car. "Chief Collig's here now."

Mrs Morton and Iola were overjoyed to see that Chet was safe. Callie, who was spending the night, and the officer expressed their relief also.

Chet's mother at once insisted that he take a hot shower and go to bed. She prepared a light supper, topped off with steaming lemonade.

In the meantime, the police chief, along with Callie and Iola, listened in amazement as Frank and Joe related their experiences.

Chief Collig agreed that the case had become serious. "Take it easy, fellows," he advised. "I'll notify the state police about that shack. I'm sure they'll want to station a man there."

"Joe and I plan to make a plaster cast of an impression we found in the sand by the shack," Frank told him. "It might be a good clue."

"I doubt that it will work," said the chief. "But good luck. When do you plan to do it?"

"Very early tomorrow morning."

"I'll tell state police headquarters."

The chief said he himself would put more men on the case and station a plain-clothes man near Chet's farm. As he left the house, Mrs Morton bustled into the living-room to report that Chet had finally stopped sneezing. "He'll be asleep in a few minutes," she said.

Before Frank and Joe left they telephoned their home. Mrs Hardy answered and was happy to hear that the boys had suffered no ill effects from their experiences that day.

At home, Aunt Gertrude greeted them at the back door with rapid-fire words of advice about staying away from mysterious shacks.

"We might never have seen you again!" she told her nephews. "I've read about gangsters putting victims into barrels of concrete and throwing them into the sea."

"Ugh!" said Joe, then added with a grin, "That sure would be concrete evidence against them, wouldn't you say, Aunty?"

"Oh, tush!" she said, and went to the stove to remove a panful of warm milk, which she poured into glasses for the boys. "When you've finished this and the supper your mother has prepared, go to bed and get a good night's sleep."

"I guess we'd better," said Joe. "Frank and I have a date at six tomorrow morning." He told her what it was.

Both Aunt Gertrude and Mrs Hardy sighed, and the boys' mother said, "I suppose it won't be dangerous for you to go if a state policeman is there."

"I'll call you," Aunt Gertrude offered.

Next morning at five-thirty she roused her nephews. "Hurry!" she commanded. "Breakfast is ready and cold eggs and toast are no good."

The brothers dressed quickly and went downstairs to find that their mother and aunt had prepared hot cereal, scrambled eggs, and cocoa.

"The sooner you solve this mystery, the better!" Aunt Gertrude said. "It has me on pins and needles."

"Too bad," said Joe. "But I think we'll be closer to a solution when we make this death mask."

"What are you saying? Goodness! Oh, dear! I didn't know someone was—"

The brothers laughed and calmed their aunt's fears. Then, becoming serious, Frank said he hoped the person whose face had made the impression in the sand was still alive.

Joe, pushing back his chair, said, "I'll carry the equipment from our lab, Frank, while you get the car out."

Shortly after six o'clock the boys started off, promising to report back home by lunchtime.

"I shan't be here," said Aunt Gertrude. "I'm going over to the state museum to a lecture. While there I'll explain about the cutlasses. The trip will take me until ten tonight."

"Happy landing, Aunty!" Joe said, smiling.

It was a pleasant ride in the fresh morning air and the sun had risen when the boys arrived at the dunes. At once they were challenged by a state trooper who stepped from the woods. Frank showed his driver's licence and introduced his brother. The man gave his name as Williams.

"Chief Collig said you might come," the officer told them. "Go ahead. There's another officer, named Winn, at the shack."

Lugging the equipment for making the mould, the Hardys walked over and introduced themselves to State Trooper Winn. He said no one had been there since he had come on duty.

The box was still in place over the imprint of the face in the sand. Joe lifted it. The impression was intact.

"That was a good idea," Trooper Winn said. He watched intently as the boys worked.

First, Frank used a spray gun and covered the impression with a quick-hardening fluid. While he was doing this, Joe mixed the plaster in a pail. Then he carefully poured it into the sand.

"When that sets, I hope we'll have a replica of the face, clear enough to be recognizable," Frank remarked.

When the mould was hard, Frank lifted it from the sand and turned it over. The result was an indistinct blob. Only the chin line was clear.

"Tough luck," the trooper said. "The sand dried out too much during the night."

"Still, I'm certain it's Gorman!" Frank said, pointing out the solid, jutting jaw. "He's a victim of those phonies!"

Quickly Joe explained the circumstances to the trooper. "He was attacked by thugs working for higher-ups," he stated.

"Will you tell all this to Williams?" the officer requested. "He'll send out an alarm over the radiophone in his car."

"Let's go!" Frank urged.

The brothers gathered their implements and hurried back to the car. Frank told Trooper Williams of their discovery and he notified state police headquarters from his car, well hidden in the woods, to start a search for Gorman. When he finished speaking, Williams let Frank use the radiophone to contact Chief Collig. The officer said he would order a local search at once for Gorman.

"I'll let you know if we have any luck, Frank," the chief promised.

Frank joined his brother, then the Hardys said good-bye to the trooper.

"What do you say we stop at Chet's?" Joe proposed as they reached the main road.

"Good idea. I'd like to know how he is. And he'll want to hear the result of our experiment."

They found Chet in bed. There was no doubt he had a cold, but fortunately there was no sign of pneumonia.

"Maybe it pays to be fat," he said, smiling. "Keeps the cold out."

The Hardys stayed with him an hour and told him of their morning's activities.

"Golly," Chet exclaimed, "where do you suppose Gorman is?"

Frank shrugged. "A prisoner some place of either Bowden or Latsky. I hope the police find him soon. It may solve a lot of problems."

Joe, eager to continue his own sleuthing, rose and said, "Take it easy, Chet. We'll let you know if anything new turns up."

It was noon when the brothers reached home. Mrs Hardy had a delicious luncheon ready and suggested afterwards that they rest awhile. But the boys were eager to continue their search for the demiculverin.

"I'd like to stay out on the dunes until it's too dark to dig," said Joe. "Let's take some supper with us."

Frank agreed. They kissed Mrs Hardy and said they hoped to be back by nine. Working in the damp sand proved to be a hot, arduous task and just before they ate, the brothers went swimming. When the sun was about to set, they packed their tools and left.

"Not one clue to that demiculverin," said Joe in disgust.

"But we're not giving up!" Frank declared.

At nine o'clock exactly the Hardys' car hummed up Elm Street and Frank turned into their driveway. The boys noticed a dark-blue saloon parked in front of their home.

"A caller," Joe said. "I wonder who it is."

Pulling up in front of their garage door, the boys got out and and went in through the kitchen entrance.

Mrs Hardy greeted them. "You've just missed a friend."

"Who was it?" Frank asked.

"Tony Prito's cousin Ken," Mrs Hardy stated. "He came for the cutlass, as you requested."

"What!" Frank cried in alarm.

Mrs Hardy explained that when the stranger had come to the door, he had told her that Frank and Joe had been at Tony's house telling them about the cutlass. "Tony phoned and said his cousin would pick it up in a few minutes," Mrs Hardy concluded, "so I wrapped the cutlass in newspaper and gave it to him."

"Mother!" Joe cried. "That man was an impostor! We weren't there and Tony has no cousin Ken!"

Mrs Hardy sank into a chair. "Oh, boys, how dreadful!" she wailed. "I'm so ashamed!"

Frank put an arm round her. "Don't worry. But I guess we'd better find that man, Joe."

The brothers dashed to their convertible and sped after the thief.

"There he goes!" Joe cried as Frank turned the next corner.

The convertible leaped ahead. Five blocks farther on, the driver of the blue saloon, apparently unaware that he was being followed, stopped for a red light. Frank and Joe quickly pulled alongside on his left. The man at the wheel wore a black motorcycle jacket.

"Latsky!" the brothers exclaimed.

On the seat alongside him Joe saw a narrow, newspaper-wrapped package. The stolen cutlass!

As Joe flung open the door and hopped out, the man turned to look at the boys. His swarthy face twisted into an ugly sneer.

"We've got you, Latsky!" Joe cried out, quickly reaching for the door handle.

But the ex-convict was quicker. Revving his engine, he shot across the street against the red light. Joe was flung to the pavement.

· 21 · *The Wreck*

BRAKES screeched as oncoming cars tried to avoid Latsky. Joe picked himself up and jumped into the car. Frank, gritting his teeth impatiently, waited for the signal to change. When it turned green, he took off in hot pursuit of the fleeing saloon.

"I hope Latsky sticks to the main highways," Joe said, peering ahead for a glimpse of the fugitive. "With his head start, we'll have a tough time catching him if he goes into a side street."

Reaching the outskirts of the older section of Bayport, Frank increased his speed. Suddenly, going over a small rise, the boys saw the red glow of rear lights. A car swung to the left into a T-intersection highway that circled wide to the right, by-passing the outlying residential section.

"It's Latsky!" Joe shouted.

At almost the same moment, the boys heard the wailing of a siren close behind them. As Frank made the turn, Joe glanced back.

"A police car," he said. "I guess the officer thinks we're speeding. Slow down, Frank."

The boy eased his foot off the accelerator and the squad car pulled alongside. Chief Collig was at the wheel. "Where's the fire, boys?" he grinned.

"We're after Latsky," Frank explained, and quickly told of their chase.

"I'll lead the way!" the chief said, and raced off, the Hardys following.

Though the officer drove a special high-powered police car, Joe doubted that he could catch the fleeing car. Latsky had too much of a head start. "Frank," he suggested, "what about the short cut past the old Pell farm? Maybe we could cut back onto the main road and make a road block."

"Great! I'll try it."

Frank turned right at the next lane, roared over a narrow macadam road for a mile, and turned left into another dirt lane. Minutes later he zoomed onto the main highway again.

"Here he comes!" Joe cried out, as two headlights flashed over a low hill behind them. In the distance the whine of the police siren sounded.

Frank slammed on his brakes and angled the convertible across the road, so that the red tail-lights blinked a warning to stop. Both boys jumped out, concealing themselves behind a tree along the roadside.

"Wow!" Joe whispered. "Latsky and the chief must be doing ninety!"

Suddenly there was a squeal of rubber on concrete. Latsky had seen the road block and braked. His car swayed from side to side.

"He's out of control!" Frank cried, as the oncoming car headed wildly for the tree behind which the brothers had taken cover.

As the boys ran, the car bounced off the tree, screeched across the road into a field, and overturned.

"Whew!" Joe gave a low whistle as he and Frank sped towards the wreck, torches in hand.

While they were still some distance from it, they saw Latsky stumble from the car. Dazed for the moment, the man staggered, but quickly regained his balance and sped off into the darkness of woods beyond.

At that moment Chief Collig roared up and stopped. Seeing the torches he got out and hurried across the field. The Hardys were trying to pick up Latsky's footprints.

"Am I seeing things?" the officer cried out. "How did you get here? And what's going on?"

"Short cut," Joe said. "We set up a road block and stopped Latsky, but he ran into these woods."

Swinging the bright beams of their lights in the woods, the trio of pursuers followed the footprints. They led to a wide brook.

"Latsky's clever," Chief Collig remarked. "He must have entered the water and walked either up or downstream."

The brothers offered to take one direction while Chief Collig took the other.

The officer shook his head. "No use. I'll radio from my car and have the place surrounded."

The three left the woods. While Chief Collig went ahead to phone from his car, the Hardys paused to look over the wreck of Latsky's car.

"He's dropped the cutlass!" Joe cried out excitedly as his flashlight picked up the glint of the shining steel blade.

Grabbing it, they hurried to the police car. Chief Collig was delighted that the boys had retrieved their ancient sword, then said, "My men are starting out now to track down Latsky. By the way, that wrecked car was stolen. Too bad."

Soon a tow truck arrived to haul the smashed saloon back to the police garage. The Hardys said good-bye to the chief, and started home to give the cutlass a close examination.

After telling their mother and Aunt Gertrude, who had returned, that they had the weapon, the boys went directly to their laboratory over the garage. Under the powerful work lamp, they found that on one side the blade had the name of the maker, *Montoya.*

"There's probably more," said Joe excitedly, getting out bottles of chemicals with which to clean off the metal. Every inch of the fine Damascus steel blade was inspected for other markings or hidden writings. There were none.

"The maker of this cutlass must have considered it too fine to mark," Joe said. Old as it was, the sword still had a keen edge.

Next, the handle was cleaned. Every seed pearl in the design was intact, and the gold leaf was still in place.

"Let's examine that handle closely," Frank suggested, getting a magnifying glass.

There was a heavy, richly encrusted leaf scroll pattern. The boys scrutinized this to look for any gems or contraband. Until almost midnight they continued the inspection, unsuccessfully.

"I still think there might be something in this handle," Frank said stubbornly. "Let's try that special magnifying glass of Dad's."

"Good idea!" said Joe. "I'll get it."

He ran back to the house and in a few minutes returned with the extremely powerful glass.

Frank focused it over the handle inch by inch. Suddenly, he smiled in triumph. "Look here, Joe!" he exclaimed.

Following Frank's finger, Joe saw a tiny line which had been cleverly worked into the leaf pattern. "Do you think it's an opening!" he asked.

"Yes."

With the thin blade of a knife, Frank tried to force open the crack, but this proved impossible.

"Maybe there's a spring hidden somewhere in the handle," Joe suggested. "Let me try it."

Frank handed the cutlass to him and Joe bent over it intently. He pressed each tiny leaf with no success. The crack did not widen.

"Maybe it has some connection with the blade," Frank mused. "But how?"

"The spring could be rusted after all these years. I'll try hitting it on something," Joe said.

He looked round the laboratory and found a slab of stone left over from a previous experiment. Grasping the handle of the cutlass firmly, he jabbed the tip against the hard surface.

Click! The crack widened a full inch!

The boys were jubilant. Frank knelt and quickly but gently picked up the sword.

"The tip contains a tiny mechanism," he said after a moment's scrutiny. "It extends through the blade all the way to the handle."

He inspected the opening and reached into it with his thumb and forefinger.

"Anything there?" Joe asked, holding his breath.

Frank nodded. Gingerly he pulled out a piece of ancient parchment.

"There's writing on it!" Joe exclaimed excitedly.

Frank smoothed out the parchment so that the boys could read it.

·22· Gunner's Tools

"FRANK, this is written in a foreign language," Joe said, disappointed that he could not read it.

The words were not modern Spanish, but, they thought, possibly an old version of t.

"Whatever it says must be mighty important," Frank concluded, "or the writer wouldn't have hidden the message."

"And Bowden and Gorman and Latsky must think so too," Joe added. He grinned. "Frank, we've beaten 'em all!"

Happy but weary, the boys went to bed, the cutlass safely tucked under Frank's mattress.

At breakfast they showed the old parchment to their mother and Aunt. They were all bending over it excitedly when Chet walked in.

"Wow!" he said when he heard the newest development in the mystery. "You boys sure are good detectives."

"We're not good enough to read this," Frank admitted. "It must be translated right away."

Just then the phone rang. "I'll take it," Joe offered, hoping it would be Mr Hardy.

The other boys stood near as he spoke.

"This is Joe," he replied to the speaker. The caller

spoke for some time. Placing his hand over the mouth-piece, Joe whispered to Chet and Frank, "Come here. It's Bowden!"

He held the receiver a distance from his ear to let the others hear the conversation. Bowden said that Gorman had just been arrested in St Louis while travelling under an assumed name.

"Good grief!" Joe exclaimed, then asked Bowman how he had received this information.

"A friend of mine on the St Louis police force, knowing I was interested, just phoned me," Bowden replied. "I guess we can go about our job of locating the cannon without any further interruption from fakes like Gorman."

The boys were sceptical of the story. It certainly did not ring true.

To Bowden, Joe merely said, "Thanks for the information. We're working on the case."

The man told Joe he would let the Hardys know if anything further developed. He was about to hang up when Chet burst out:

"Tell him we've found the clue in the cutlass!"

Frank gave Chet a warning look, but too late. Bowden's next words were, "I heard what someone just said. Congratulations, Joe!"

Before the boy could make any comment, Bowden went on to say that he had planned to tell the Hardys of the cutlass clue, which he had heard about several months ago.

"I had a feeling, though," he said, "that it might be just an old rumour, so I kept the story to myself. And besides, I figured that being such clever detectives, you and your brother would discover the truth, anyway."

"I see," replied Joe noncommittally. Then he said good-bye and hung up.

Chet apologized for revealing the news about the cutlass. The brothers were disturbed but assured him that by working fast they would get to the bottom of the mystery and no harm would result from Chet's slip.

"Now if only we could think of someone who might translate the message on the parchment," Frank said thoughtfully.

"Let's try our Spanish teacher, Miss Kelly," Joe suggested. "If she—"

At this moment the doorbell rang. Aunt Gertrude went to answer it and was given a telegram.

"It's for you boys," she said, handing over the message to Frank.

"This wire is from Dad!" the boy said, as he unfolded the message. "Say, Joe, it's in code!"

The brothers dashed up to their father's study and removed Mr Hardy's code book from his filing cabinet. Quickly they unscrambled the message. Their jaws dropped as they read:

BEWARE DOUBLE-CROSSING OF BOWDEN!

"Double-crossing!" Frank echoed. "Dad must have further information about Bowden."

"I wish he had told us more," Joe said, as the brothers returned to the first floor with the news of Mr Hardy's message. Instantly their mother and Aunt Gertrude became alarmed.

"After all that has happened," said their aunt firmly, "I think you should leave town for a while. You can take me on a trip in the car."

The boys were fearful they might be forced into

making the trip. Both instantly promised to take extra precautions from now on.

"If Bowden doesn't suspect that we mistrust him," Frank said, "we'll have the advantage."

"Which we hope to hold till Dad returns," Joe added.

Chet whistled. "Well, count me out of any more trouble," he said. "I'm off home. Let me know what that foreign parchment says."

After Chet had chugged off in his jalopy, Frank suggested that they call on Miss Kelly and see about having the parchment translated.

"Let's stop at police headquarters on the way," Joe said. "We'll check Bowden's story about Gorman's arrest."

With the parchment tucked securely in Frank's inner pocket, they drove to the police station. There the sergeant in charge promised to check with the St Louis police about the alleged arrest of Gorman. Before leaving, Frank asked if the man named Guiness who had exploded the fireworks had been caught. The officer shook his head.

"Please let us know what you find out about Gorman," Joe said as they walked out.

Frank drove across Bayport to the small cottage where Miss Kelly lived. She was a pleasant, middle-aged woman, well liked by her students.

"We wondered if you could help us solve a mystery," Joe said, as they all sat down in her cool, attractive living-room.

"By the expressions on your faces I thought you must be working on one," Miss Kelly said. "What is it?"

Frank produced the parchment. "Is this Spanish, and can you translate it? We're stumped."

The teacher studied the scrawled writing for a moment. "No wonder," she said. "This is written in Portuguese—old-fashioned Portuguese at that."

"What does it say?" Frank asked eagerly.

"I'm sorry, but I can't translate it," the woman said slowly. "But a Mrs Vasquez I know might help you."

Handing back the parchment, Miss Kelly explained that the elderly Mrs Vasquez was Portuguese and the mother of a fishing boat captain.

"Mrs Vasquez isn't well and doesn't get up until afternoon," Miss Kelly explained, "but I'm sure if you went to see her after lunch, she would help you. I'll give you her address." She looked in the telephone directory and wrote it down. The boys thanked her and left.

"If we can't get the message translated until after lunch," Joe urged, "let's go out to Pirates' Hill and call on Sergeant Tilton. Maybe he can give us some idea of where to dig."

"Okay," Frank agreed. "We haven't had any luck ourselves." He drove out to the sand dunes.

The boys went directly to Tilton's cottage. Dressed in dungarees and a coonskin cap, the sergeant was working in his small flower garden.

"He probably doesn't have buckskins to match the hat!" Joe whispered.

The man was in high spirits. "Hi there, boys!" he yelled.

"Good morning, Sergeant," Frank replied, "We've come to do some more digging for that cannon."

"I see."

"We thought maybe you could show us where you think it should be," Joe added.

"Well, now, let me see," the man drawled as he came towards them. "Suppose I walk round the place with you." He grabbed up a folding canvas chair.

When they had gone about fifty yards along the dunes, he stopped and scratched his head. "Accordin' to my system of reckonin', the gun must have been located just about—No." He moved a few steps to his left. "Just about here."

While Sergeant Tilton lighted an old pipe and seated himself comfortably on his folding chair, the boys started digging. The ex-gunner told them story after story of his Army adventures while they dug deep through the white sand.

"Hold everything!" Joe called some time later. He was standing waist deep in a hole. "I've found something!"

He bent over and came up with a queer-looking gadget. "What would this be?" he asked, handing it to the sergeant.

Tilton examined it carefully. "This here's a gunner's scraper!" he replied.

"Probably belonged to the same gear as that primer Chet found the other day," Frank whispered to Joe.

Protected by sand, it had withstood the ravages of time better than the primer had.

"The cannon's just *got* to be near here!" Joe declared excitedly.

"That's right, my boy." The sergeant wore a knowing look as he handed the scraper back. Puffing on his pipe, he blew out a small cloud of smoke. "Don't stop diggin', lads."

Ten minutes later Frank uncovered a six-foot long wooden pole fixed at one end with an iron blade. As he handed it to Tilton, the old ordnance man exclaimed, "It's a handspike! You must be gettin' close!"

· 23 · Guarding a Discovery

THOUGH eager to dig quickly, Frank and Joe paused to stare at the strange-looking pole.

"What was it used for?" Frank asked Tilton.

"To manhandle the heavy cannon," he replied. "With this tool, the gunners could move the carriage, or lift the breech of the gun, so's they could adjust the elevatin' screw."

"Boy! We're getting hot!" Joe exclaimed triumphantly. "The cannon will be our next find!"

Jubilantly expectant, the Hardys dug deeper into the sand. But nothing further came to light.

Finally Frank straightened up with a sigh. "Joe," he said, "it's noon. We'd better stop now. You know we have an errand in town."

· Joe had almost forgotten their plan to call on Mrs Vasquez and have the parchment translated. "You're right, Frank." He asked Tilton to keep the spike and pole until they called for them. Then the brothers quickly refilled the hole, took their tools, and started back to town.

After stopping at a diner for a quick lunch, the Hardys drove directly to the dock area, where they easily found Mrs Vasquez's modest home. When Frank explained the boys' mission, her daughter-in-law ushered them inside.

A white-haired old lady with black eyes stared curiously at the Hardys from a rocking chair. She smiled, adjusted her black shawl, and motioned for them to be seated.

"Mother doesn't speak much English," the daughter-in-law said, "but I'll translate for you."

The Vasquezes spoke rapidly in Portuguese, then the old lady leaned back and read the parchment. When she looked up, more words in Portuguese followed between the women.

"What is she saying?" Joe asked eagerly.

"Mama says this message gives directions."

"For what?" Frank's heart pounded.

Again there was a rapid exchange of words in the foreign tongue, then the younger woman smiled. "Directions to a cannon. Is that right?"

"Wow! I'll say it is!" Joe could not contain himself. "Frank, this breaks the case wide open!"

The older boy remained calm. He asked, "Does it say where the cannon is located?"

"Yes. I'll write it all down."

"In English, please!" Joe requested.

As Mrs Vasquez spoke, the younger woman translated and wrote:

On high rock Alaqua Cove due east setting sun first day July is treasure cannon. Demiculverin.

The woman smiled. "Does this mean anything to you boys? Where is Alaqua Cove?"

"That was the old Indian name for Bayport, I think," Frank replied. "Thanks a million. And please, keep this a secret—for a while at least."

"Oh, yes. Mama and I will say nothing until you tell us we can. I'm glad we could help you."

Frank and Joe bowed to Mrs Vasquez, then left. They were grinn ng ecstatically.

"At last we're going to solve this mystery!" Joe exclaimed jubilantly.

"The time of year is perfect," Frank said. "If we're wrong, we're no detectives."

"Right."

On reaching Pirates' Hill with their digging tools, Joe became uneasy. "I hate to wait until sunset. Can't we start?"

"Sure. I've been here so much in the past few days that I can tell you exactly where the sun will set." Frank pointed to a distant church spire. "Right there." He took a compass from his pocket and moved until his back was east of the spire. "The cannon should be somewhere along this line." He shuffled through the sand.

"The directions said 'high rock,'" Joe reminded him. "There are rocks under this sand. Let's try the highest point on this line."

The boys set to work. For half an hour they dug furiously. Finally, Frank's spade struck metal!

"J-Joe!" Frank exclaimed. "The cannon!"

A moment later they uncovered the curve of a barrel, and judging from its dimensions, they were convinced that this was the Spanish demiculverin for which they had been searching.

"Success!" Joe cried, thumping Frank's back.

Frank wore the broadest grin his brother had ever seen. "This is super!" he exclaimed.

With their shovels the boys quickly concealed the valuable discovery until they could return the next day and uncover it completely. Then, to bewilder any prying eyes, the Hardys decided to make small excavations elsewhere. They wandered off and started to dig at random.

A short time later two figures appeared over the dunes. Chet and Tony Prito!

"We came out in the *Napoli*," Tony said. "Thought you'd be here. We called your mother who said to give you a message."

"About Gorman," Chet added. "The police left word that he's not in St Louis."

"Just as we suspected," said Frank. "I wonder if Chief Collig has any news about Gorman."

"No," said Chet. "He phoned to say that there was no progress on that score. Say, have you fellows had any luck out here?"

Frank, in a low voice, told him about finding the demiculverin. "Yee-ow!" Chet exploded.

Tony congratulated his friends and asked what the Hardys' next move would be.

"We'll dig up the whole cannon tomorrow," Frank replied.

"I wish we could stay here tonight and get an early start," Joe said. "How about camping out to stand guard over the cannon?"

"Swell idea," said Frank. "Remember Dad's warning about Bowden—he may double-cross us. And that could happen any minute."

Tony offered to go back to town and pick up a tent, sleeping bags, and food. "I'll call your folks and tell 'em, fellows," he promised.

The camp on Pirates' Hill was ready by nightfall, the tent pitched on the cannon site. As the stars came out, the Hardys and Chet crawled into their shelter. Tony was to stand guard first and posted himself outside the tent flap.

At ten o'clock Tony became aware of an approaching figure. Instantly he wakened his sleeping pals. They waited tensely until the person was almost at the tent.

"I'll get him!" Joe cried.

The campers lunged out of the shelter and Joe was about to tackle the oncoming figure when they recognized him.

"Sergeant Tilton!" Frank exclaimed.

The boys smiled at the man's clothes. He looked enough like a pirate to be one!

"So it's you," drawled the elderly man. Sergeant Tilton explained that he had spotted their flashlights and come to see who his new neighbours were. "I was just tryin' on this outfit from my pirate collection when I saw the light."

Knowing that the old man was inclined to gossip, the boys decided to keep secret their finding of the cannon. They chatted casually with Tilton, telling him they had set up camp to be ready for some sleuthing early in the morning.

"Well, boys," the sergeant said finally, "I'd better git back to my shack. I suspect you'll all be snorin' soon." Chuckling, he walked off.

The rest of the night passed quietly, with the boys rotating the watches as they had planned earlier. By six o'clock they were preparing breakfast, after which, Frank, Joe, and Tony started work under the tent, with Chet as lookout.

Within an hour the three boys had dug a deep pit and uncovered the entire demiculverin. The old field-piece appeared to be in good condition.

"What a beauty!" Frank exclaimed.

"And look at this number on it!" Joe cried out. On the barrel were cut the numerals 8–4–20. "It must be a code for this type. Let's find out what it stands for."

Leaving Chet and Tony on guard, the Hardys drove home to inspect their father's books on cannons. Joe's hunch that the numerals might be a code was in vain. They read on.

Suddenly Frank exclaimed, "I get it! An eight-pound ball and four pounds of powder."

"And twenty degrees of elevation!" cried Joe.

Hearing the excited talk of the boys, Mrs Hardy looked into the room and asked, "Have you found out something interesting?"

"Sunken treasure!" Joe exulted. "A ball shot from the demiculverin probably marks the spot where the old merchantman was sunk by the pirates in that Battle of Bayport!"

Mrs Hardy was astounded. She started to praise her sons when the front doorbell rang. Frank hurried down to answer it. Opening the door, he blinked in amazement.

Bowden!

As Frank recovered from his surprise, he said, "Come in," and called loudly over his shoulder, "Joe! Mr Bowden's here!"

Joe came down the stairs like a streak of lightning. "What's up now?" he wondered.

Bowden smiled. "Can't stay but a few minutes. Good news travels fast. I understand you've located the cannon I asked you to find!"

The Hardy were dumbfounded. They stared speechlessly.

"I'll soon pay you for solving my case," Bowden continued. "A truck will come out to the dunes to-morrow to pick up the cannon."

· 24 ·   *Human Targets*

THOUGH looks of dismay showed on the Hardy boys' faces, they did not affirm Bowden's statement that they had located the demiculverin. Neither did they deny it.

"Where did you hear that we'd found a cannon?" Frank asked.

The man's reply proved to be another bomb-shell. "I was out there and your friends told me."

Frank and Joe were too astonished to make an immediate comment. They exchanged quick knowing glances. Whatever Bowden's real reason was for want-ing the ancient cannon, they were going to try keeping it from him until they heard from their father or the police.

Bowden smiled. "I now own Pirates' Hill."

As the boys watched, thunderstruck, he took several impressive-looking documents from his pocket and showed them to the boys. One was a certificate of sale, another a government release, and the third a letter with a notary-public seal. This stated that Bowden had a right to anything found on Pirates' Hill.

"They certainly look authentic," Frank said, but realized the papers could be clever forgeries.

Mr Hardy's dire warning to his sons indicated that Bowden was probably a confidence man. It was possible that his accomplices could imitate signatures and even print fake documents.

Suddenly an idea came to Frank. The stock certificates of the Copper Slope Mining Company which Bowden had sold to Mr Ash in Taylorville might be counterfeit!

"I must get in touch with Dad about this," Frank concluded.

"It looks as if the hill is yours all right, Mr Bowden. If there's a cannon on it, there may be other treasures, too."

Frank's assurance pleased Bowden. "I hope you're right. And I'm glad you boys see the whole thing my way. To tell you the truth, I thought you might want the old cannon yourself. Accept my congratulations for a grand job!"

After he left, Frank went into a huddle with his brother and told him about the possibility of the stock being counterfeit. Joe whistled and suggested that they compose a telegram in code to their father telling him this, and mentioning the fact that the cannon had been found and Bowden was claiming it. Frank phoned the message to the telegraph office.

"I hope this information will bring Dad up here," Joe said. "Frank, this fellow is crooked. We can't just hand him the cannon!"

"Of course not. Don't forget, Joe, digging out the sand round the demiculverin so that it can be lifted, and lugging the two tons of iron over the sand will be no child's play. It may take days. Maybe something will happen in the meantime to stop Bowden."

"Let's hope so," said Joe. "Well, what do you say

we do some computing on those numbers we found on the cannon?"

He felt that they would indicate where a ball would land if it was shot from the cannon when the gun barrel was raised to the 20 degrees o elevation. The boys discovered that they were unable to solve the gunnery problem exactly.

Frank suggested that they drive over to see Mr Rowe, head of the mathematics department at Bayport High School. "He's teaching summer school, and I'm sure he'll be there now."

The boys set off for Bayport High and found that fortunately Mr Rowe was having a free period. Intrigued by the problem, he went to work, filling several sheets of paper with calculations. At last he said:

"The cannon ball would land two thousand yards away, if trained and elevated at precisely the angle given in the figures."

Frank and Joe thanked the teacher, then hurried to their car. On the way back to the dunes, Frank remarked that if the demiculverin had not been moved from the position in which the pirates had placed it, and currents had not shifted the ship, the ball should land exactly on the spot where the sunken merchantman rested. "And that's where the treasure will be!"

"If your guess is right," Joe said, "we could get permission from the Coast Guard to fire one ball, locate the spot, and then hand over the cannon to Bowden—with our compliments!"

Frank grinned, but reminded his brother that whatever their plans, they must work fast. "Bowden is not going to let any beach grass grow under his feet!" he warned.

Driving directly to Pirates' Hill, they parked off the shore road as before and ran up the dune to rejoin Chet and Tony.

At the edge of it Joe stopped short. Grabbing Frank by the arm, he cried out, "Well, look over there! Bowden again! We can't lose him!"

At the site of the cannon, he and Sergeant Tilton were talking to Chet and Tony.

"Good-bye to our little plan," Joe said woefully.

"Maybe not," Frank remarked hopefully as they rushed forward.

Chet and Tony dashed up to meet the Hardys and whispered that after Frank and Joe had gone back to town the boys had continued digging. The two men had caught them off guard.

"You can see the cannon very plainly now," Tony said. "Chet and I thought we'd surprise you and dig out all the sand from the front of it."

Frank quickly related Bowden's visit to the house. Tony frowned. "Maybe that gossipy Sergeant Tilton told him we were here. They might even be in league!"

As the group reached the men, the Hardys received only a nod from Bowden, but the genial old sergeant began to talk excitedly. Today he was resplendent in the blue field uniform of a Northern officer of the Civil War. He explained that at Bowden's request he was preparing a charge similar to the one he used to test the mortar in the town square at Bayport.

In spite of Bowden's efforts to signal him to keep quiet, Sergeant Tilton continued, "An' I'm goin' to test the strength o' the barrel fer Mr Bowden. He wants to be sure it'll be safe fer him to fire off durin' that there Exposition in Floridy."

At once the Hardys were suspicious. "Are you sure you aren't planning to shoot a cannon ball off right now?" Joe asked.

The old gunner looked in disgust at the boy. "Of course not. That'd be against the law. I'd have to git permission from the Coast Guard."

"That's right," said Joe, eyeing Bowden to watch his reaction. But the man showed none.

As the boys watched Sergeant Tilton, he prepared the powder charge and fired the gun. A thunderous boom followed. As the smoke cleared, he rushed back to inspect the piece for the presence of any cracks.

"She stood up fine!" he exclaimed. "First rate!"

"Well, thanks, Sergeant," said Bowden. "I guess the cannon will do for the pageant. I'll see you later," he added as he walked away towards the road.

The old man began running his hands along the cannon and talking to himself. "Great piece o' work," he declared. He turned to Frank and Joe. "I'd like to tell you a bit about this."

"We'd like to hear it a little later," said Frank.

The Hardys were eager to try locating the old sunken merchantman. When their friends agreed to help, Frank asked Chet to drive to their boathouse in the convertible and pick up the aqua-lung diving gear. Tony offered the use of the *Napoli* from which to work.

When Chet reached the road where the Hardys' convertible was parked, Bowden was just driving away. As the car gathered speed Chet saw a piece of paper blow out of the window. Picking it up, he examined it curiously.

"Why, it's a stock certificate of the Copper Slope

Mining Company!" he said to himself. "It must be valuable. I'd better return it to Mr Bowden."

Then a thought struck him. "This was the tock Frank and Joe were talking about. It might be phony!"

At once Chet decided to leave the certificate at the Hardys' home for inspection later on. He got into the car and drove back to Bayport.

Out on the dunes, Frank was just saying to the old sergeant, "Tell us about this cannon."

Tilton beamed. "Firing a gun like this here one is a pretty risky thing."

He went on to explain that the demiculverin most likely had been used at some Spanish colonial fort before the pirates had captured it. The normal life of such a cannon was twelve hundred rounds. But in an outpost, where it was hard to get new weapons, a piece like this was always fired many rounds beyond that figure, increasing the danger of explosion with each burst.

"When cracks develop round the vent or in the bore," Tilton said, "you got to be mighty careful. The muzzle sometimes blows clean off 'em!"

"Look!" Joe cried. "It's chained to a boulder."

This convinced the Hardys that they had been right in their deductions. The cannon was placed so that a ball fired from it would strike one particular place in the ocean!

The boys took sights along the gun barrel and checked them with their compass. The barrel pointed due east. This would make it easy to estimate the approximate spot where the treasure should be. They chafed under the necessity of awaiting Chet's return.

"What are you fellows aimin' to do, now that you've got this mystery solved?" Tilton asked them.

"Look for another case, I guess," Joe replied. "Right now we're going for a swim." To himself he added, "And look for the buried treasure!"

"Hm," said Tilton. "I ain't been in the water fer nigh on thirty years."

He climbed off the gun emplacement just as Chet came hurrying across the sand. He was not carrying the diving gear.

"Something's up!" Joe declared.

Puffing, Chet halted in front of the others. "I've got big news. Chief Collig phoned your home, Frank and Joe. Latsky's been captured!"

"Honestly?" Frank exclaimed, hardly daring to believe it was true.

"Great!" Joe cried out. "How?"

"Latsky finally returned to the cabin. Seems he had money buried there and had run out of funds," Chet replied. "The police had no trouble nabbing him."

Joe grinned. "Latsky'll be back in his old cell for a long stretch."

After a brief discussion about him, Frank looked at Chet. "In all the excitement I guess you forgot our diving gear."

Chet laughed and told him it was in the car. The four boys said good-bye to Tilton and went to pick up the gear. On the way, Chet told the others about the stock certificate Bowden had dropped and that Mrs Hardy now had it.

"Swell work, Chet!" Frank thumped his friend on the back.

The diving equipment was carried to the beach. As

the boys waded out to the *Napoli*, Joe reviewed what they would do. Tony and Chet were to remain aboard the boat, while Frank and Joe did the diving.

"We'll work by dead reckoning on the first attempt," Joe told his pals. "Frank and I will go over the side at the estimated distance from shore."

"Let's get started," Tony urged.

"Hold on!" Frank said. "I think we're foolish to leave the cannon unguarded with Bowden loose. No telling what he may try to pull."

"What do you suggest?" Joe asked.

"That one of us go back and watch. If Bowden comes, our guard can signal and we'll get to the hill in a hurry."

"I'll do it," Chet offered. "But how can I signal you?"

Tony took a large, yellow bandanna and a clean white rag out of the boat's locker. He handed them to Chet. "Wigwag with these," he said.

"And be sure to hide behind a dune," Frank cautioned, "so that Bowden won't see you."

"Gee, I'm really going to be busy," said Chet, as he sloshed back through the water.

The others climbed into the motorboat and Tony started the engine. Frank and Joe gave directions to the site of the sunken treasure, using the church spire as a landmark and keeping on a course due east. Tony steered the *Napoli* carefully while Frank and Joe tried to estimate a distance of two thousand yards from shore.

"Stop!" Frank commanded presently. "Unless all our reckoning is wrong, the treasure ship must be directly below us."

There was silence for a few moments as the full

import of the boy's words struck them all. They might be about to make an intriguing find!

"Let's go down!" Joe urged his brother.

The Hardys donned their gear and climbed over the side.

Tony, watching Chet intently, suddenly cried out, "Wait, fellows! Chet is signalling!"

Back on Pirates' Hill their pal had seen Bowden sneaking up to the cannon. As he watched the man, terror struck his heart. Bowden was ramming a charge of powder into the ancient gun. Then he inserted a cannon ball into the muzzle!

All this time Chet was wigwagging. The boys on the water interpreted, *"Bowden here. Look out for—"*

The missile ready, Bowden ran to the back of the cannon and inserted a fuse into the vent hole. Chet's hands were shaking with fright. Bowden flicked on his lighter and held it to the fuse, then stepped back.

"Run!" Chet signalled.

Boom!

With a shuddering detonation the demiculverin sent the deadly ball directly towards the *Napoli!*

· 25 · *Divers' Reward*

WHAM! *Smack!*

The cannon ball hit the *Napoli* full force a second after the three boys had flung themselves away from it. Spray and debris flew in every direction.

The Hardys, only a few feet away, were knocked unconscious by the concussion. Tony, unhurt, was worried about his companions. He realized that in their diving equipment they would float and could breathe even if they were unconscious. However, he was afraid that his friends might not have survived the shock.

Catching up to Joe, he was just in time to see the boy move his arms. He was alive!

"Thank goodness!" Tony said to himself.

He told Joe a cannon ball had been fired at them and advised him to dive deep to escape a possible second shot. The boy nodded.

Tony went to find Frank. To his relief, he too had regained consciousness. Tony overtook him.

"Do you think Bowden meant to kill us?" Tony asked.

"It certainly looks that way."

Just then Joe surfaced and the three boys looked at the *Napoli*. One glance told them that it was doomed.

"Too bad," said Frank.

"Yes," Joe agreed. "Guess we'll have to swim to shore. Stick close to us, Tony."

The boys struck out towards the distant beach, but they had not swum fifty yards when they heard the roar of a motor launch.

"A Coast Guard boat!" Joe called out.

The launch circled once, then pulled in closer to pick them up. The young lieutenant in charge, who introduced himself as Ted Newgate, was glad to hear that the boys were all right. He glanced at the ruined *Napoli*.

"We heard two reports o a cannon and came to investigate," he said as the boys were hauled aboard. "What's going on here?"

"Someone on the hill tried to blow us out of the

water," Joe answered. "I want to get to shore as fast as possible and find him."

The powerful marine motor kicked up white foam as the boat headed towards land. Nearing Pirates' Hill, Frank gave a startled cry. "Joe, there's Dad!"

"Where?"

"Over there on the beach with Chief Collig and Chet."

Joe shaded his eyes. "And look who's handcuffed to Collig! Bowden!"

When the bow hit the sand, Frank and Joe hopped out and raced across the beach to greet their father, a handsome, strapping man in his early forties.

"Are you both all right?" he asked.

"We're okay, Dad, but no thanks to Bowden," Frank replied.

The police chief said, "You boys can thank your lucky stars you're still here to tell the story. The charge against Bowden will be assault and battery with intent to kill. And the Coast Guard will have something to say about his firing without permission."

Bowden looked completely beaten. The police chief explained that the man had stolen a cannon ball from the town square the night before, hoping to put it to use someday and locate the site of the sunken merchantman.

"When he spotted you fellows out there, Bowden saw a good chance to eliminate you from the race for the treasure."

Joe glared at the prisoner. "We didn't trust you from the start, but we didn't think you were a killer."

The police chief said Bowden had brought about his own arrest. "If the repercussion from that old cannon hadn't knocked him out, he would have got away before your dad and I showed up. He was armed, so Chet wouldn't have had a chance to stop him. Well, greed will catch up with a guy sooner or later. Bowden will have a long stretch in prison to think this over."

Frank asked his father how he happened to have come to Pirates' Hill. "Because I hoped Bowden was here and I wanted to have him arrested at once for selling fake stock certificates." Mr Hardy smiled broadly at his two sons. "You've helped me solve my own case of bringing a notorious gang of swindlers to justice. I've been tracking this fellow's friends all over the South. His real name is Layng. They've been counterfeiting legitimate types of stock, getting prospects through the mail and selling them phony certificates."

Chief Collig beamed. "I hear you fellows kept playing Bowden along like a hooked marlin!"

Joe inquired when Mr Hardy had arrived from Florida. "Only an hour ago," the detective said. "When your telegram arrived, I came up here in a jet police plane. Chet clinched matters by leaving the stock certificate he picked up when Bowden dropped it. The instant your mother handed it to me I recognized it as a counterfeit."

Hearing this, the prisoner winced, chagrined to think that he had given himself away by carelessly losing the certificate.

Collig started to walk towards the shore road. "We'd better get this man Bowden behind bars," he said.

The others followed. When they reached the police car, Chief Collig phoned headquarters to report he had a prisoner. In turn, the sergeant on duty reported that he was holding a suspect for the Hardy boys to identify.

"Follow me in your car," the chief told Frank and Joe, "and we'll find out who it is."

On their arrival at police headquarters, the brothers were first shown a black skin-diving suit and a yellow trimmed skull cap by the sergeant.

"Good grief!" Joe cried out. "The guy that nearly winged us wore gear like this. Where'd you get it, Sergeant?"

"From that man over there. His name is Guiness."

The Hardys turned to look. "The man who shot the rockets at us on the Fourth of July!" Frank exclaimed. "Say, Guiness," he said, walking over to him, "how did you know we were going to be there that night?"

"I didn't," the prisoner answered, "but my chance came right then and I took it."

Guiness admitted that he was in league with Latsky, whom he had met recently. But the prisoner denied knowing Bowden or anyone named Gorman.

"What about the paper with the name Smedick on it which the police found in your waste-basket?" Frank asked. "Didn't you know Smedick was Gorman?"

Guiness denied this, saying Latsky must have discovered Gorman's alias and dropped the paper on one of his visits to Guiness's room.

"Where is Gorman?" Frank shot at Bowden.

He did not answer, but this fact gave Frank a lead. As events flashed through his mind, an idea came to him.

"You had Gorman attacked at the back of the shack on the beach and you had him taken away in the boat he'd rented to get there. Later, you hid him in the boot of your car. We heard him moan."

Bowden's face went ashen. Frank's surmise had turned the trick. Bowden confessed that he had lied to the boys about Gorman's character. He had had him trailed and ambushed at the shack by henchmen. When the Hardys arrived unexpectedly, it had been necessary for the thugs to attack them too. Worried, they had taken the Hardys to the gully and dumped them. Then they had abandoned the car.

Coming back to the shack they had met Bowden and told the story. Later, Bowden had driven past the gully to check and received a real surprise.

"I had to rescue you because I wanted you to think I was on the level," Bowden said. "That moan you heard in my car was Gorman. I told you it had been made by the wind."

"What about him? Where is he?" Frank persisted.

"Gorman's in good shape," Bowden said. "You'll find him in the room next to mine at the motel, tied up. He's supposed to be sick and has an attendant. No one else goes in."

Chief Collig said he would send two men there at once to release Gorman and bring him to headquarters. While the others waited, more facts came out about the case.

During a prison term, Bowden had met Latsky who knew a lot about ancient cannon, including the story of the Battle of Bayport. Each man determined to find the treasure for himself after being released. It became a bitter race between the ex-convicts, with Gorman against both of them.

"First you had to locate the cutlass with the directions," said Frank.

"Yes," Bowden admitted. "Latsky tried to get the

old cutlasses from the Bayport Historical Society building but failed. Then I took them."

Joe snapped his fingers and said, "I see how it went. When you found none of them contained the parchment, you had Gil Fanning sell them for you. Latsky later purchased the five cutlasses only to find that none of them contained the parchment."

"Yes," said Frank, "and you had Chet lured off to be questioned and slugged and put in the gully with Joe and me."

As he was talking, two officers walked in with Gorman and an eighteen-year-old youth.

Chet gazed in amazement. "That's the fellow who got me in trouble!" the stout boy shouted, doubling up his fists.

"Take it easy," Chief Collig advised. "I'll handle this."

The new prisoner was introduced as Gil Fanning, Gorman's attendant. He said he was a newcomer to Bayport. His parents had died and he was now living with his grandparents. He had needed money, so he had started working for Bowden.

"I—I didn't think I was doing anything wrong," Gil said. "Then first thing I knew, I was in so deep I couldn't get out. It'll kill the old folks when they find out."

Bowden admitted that the boy had been his dupe, and hoped that harsh punishment would not be meted out to him. The ex-convict at first would not reveal the names of his henchmen, but finally he did, and Chief Collig ordered their immediate arrest.

The Hardys turned to Gorman and asked if he felt all right. "Yes," he said, "and I'm glad you fellows uncovered the secret in the cutlass, instead of Latsky and the others."

He told them that the directions to the location of the cannon, according to the legend, had been hidden in the cutlass belonging to the pirates' captain. It had been lost ashore during a scuffle among the pirates themselves.

"Go on! Go on!" Joe urged as Gorman paused.

The former Navy man said he had learned about the treasure and the demiculverin from an ancient diary. "It was written by the wife of the merchantman's captain," he said. "She tried for years to locate the site of her husband's sunken ship."

Gorman said he was a direct descendant of the captain and had the diary in his possession. After an honourable discharge from the Navy he had decided to try finding the sunken treasure.

Joe smiled and asked a question of Bowden. "Was it Latsky who threatened you in the message we found on your door and sent us one?"

Bowden nodded. "He later knocked me out when I was talking to you fellows on the phone."

"And tell me, who was hiding under the tarpaulin in the boat when Halpen warned us away from the sting ray?"

"I was," Guiness replied. "I told Halpen to give you that phony story. And Latsky hired me to dive for the sunken treasure ship. When you boys showed up while I was at work, I thought you were hunting too. So I shot at you with a spear to scare you off."

When the questioning ended, the prisoners were led away and the others left. Mr Hardy invited Gorman to stay at their home until he had recovered completely from the manhandling he had received.

"Thank you. I accept," the young man said, smiling.

"And please forgive Joe and me for suspecting you," Frank spoke up.

"I will on one condition," Gorman replied with a grin. "That you four boys show me where that treasure is and let me share with you whatever the government will let us take."

The Hardys laughed and Joe said, "That won't be hard to take!"

"But first," said Frank, "from whatever we get, I suggest that we buy Tony a new and even better *Napoli*."

The others quickly agreed, then Joe said, "I guess this treasure hunt will be the most exciting adventure we've ever had."

But another was soon to come their way, which was to become known as *The Flickering Torch Mystery*.

Two days later the whole group, in skin-diving outfits, climbed over the side of the *Sleuth* and descended to a depth of thirty feet. There lay the ancient merchantman, its timbers rotted away, and moss and barnacles covering the metal parts.

Cautiously Gorman and the boys swam in and out, removing the debris. At last their search was rewarded. There, in the uncovered hold of the old vessel, lay a vast quantity of gold bullion. Through their masks, the divers beamed at one another triumphantly.

The Hardys and their friends had found the ancient treasure!